THE
COLLECTORS'
SOCIETY

HEATHER LYONS

THE PLEASANCE ASYLUM

T HE CEILING ABOVE ME is a mysterious map of cracks and chipped paint, nearly undecipherable in origins or destinations. Voids unsettle me, though, so night after night, as I stare up at it, tracing the moonbeams that flit in between hills and valleys, I assign them my own designations. There, that bump? It's Gibraltar. That chunk? The Himalayas. The deep groove near the Southeast corner of the room? The Great Wall of China. The smooth patch nearly dead center is the Pleasance Asylum, which is vastly amusing to me.

I shy away from the splattering of flakes in the Northwest quadrant, though. Those ones, whose ridges grow on nearly a daily basis, are far too easy to decipher. I made the mistake of telling Dr. Featheringstone this during a fit of delirium, and he's not forgotten it. In fact, he's asked me about them again, just now, and he's waiting patiently for my answer.

"They're flakes of paint," I tell him. "Created from age and lack of upkeep."

As he chuckles softly, the thick mustache that hides his lip twitches. "Always the literal one."

I keep my eyes on his face rather than in the area he's quizzing me about. It taunts me though, just over his left shoulder. "Why shouldn't I be? Word games are silly and are best left for children or the elderly who seek to hold onto their wit." The muscle inside my chest works in overtime as I tell him this. He's heard my ravings, and knows my struggles.

"And you are no longer a child?"

I lean back in the still, wooden chair, delighting in how its discomfort bites into my bones. "I hardly think a woman of twenty-five is a child, Doctor."

In direct opposition to his faint yet genuine smile, pudgy fingers stroke his bushy mustache downward. "Many ladies of your standing are long married with family."

He says many when he means *most*. I smooth the stubborn wrinkles on my gray skirt. "It's a little hard to meet prospective suitors in . . ." I glance around the room, eyes careful not to settle too long above his head. "A fine establishment such as yours."

Neither of us mention where I'd been before here, or what I'd seen and done and experienced.

Another chuckle rumbles out of him. "Too true, dear. But you will not be at the Pleasance much longer. What then?"

My fingers knot tightly together in my lap. "I imagine I will be sent to rusticate at our family's summer house near the seaside. Perhaps I will find a nice stableboy to court me, and by the ripe age of twenty-six, we will be living out our bliss amongst seashells, ponies, and hay."

Featheringstone sighs, his face transforming into a look I could sketch from memory; it's given so often to me when I offer up an answer he doesn't like. I call it Disappointed Featheringstone.

My eyes drift to the one window in the room. "I am still not positive my release is the wisest course of action."

"You've been here for over half a year," the doctor says. "Most people in your position would be clamoring to taste freedom."

A thin smile surfaces. That's the problem. I've had a taste of freedom, true freedom, and I'm loathe to accept anything other than such.

"You are in good health," he continues. "Your need for confinement is gone. Your nightmares have decreased significantly." His chair creaks beneath his significant girth as he leans forward. "It is time for you to resume your life, Alice. You cannot do that here at the asylum. You are, as you pointed out, twenty-five years old. You still have many years of experiences ahead of you."

I have many years of experiences behind me, too.

"Perhaps I ought to become a nurse," I muse, keeping the edge of my sarcasm soft enough to not wound. "What a story mine would be: patient to nurse, a grand example of life dedicated to the Pleasance."

"I think nursing school is a grand idea." His ruddy face alights. "There are several reputable ones in London you could attend."

It's my turn to give him a patented look, the one he affectionately calls Unamused Alice.

"Your father has sent word he will come to escort you home at the end of the week."

Unamused Alice transitions to Curmudgeonly Alice.

Featheringstone stands up, glancing up at my past before shuffling over to pat me on my shoulder. He is a nice man, whose intentions for his wards are sincere. It's for this I both appreciate and resent him. An old schoolmate of my father's, he was selected upon my return sorely for this purpose. Too many horror stories about hellish asylums and nefarious doctors rage about England, but my father knew his friend would treat me with kid gloves. While the Pleasance may be physically showing its age, it's amongst the most sought after when it comes to those in the upper class due to its gentle hand and discreet employees.

Sometimes I wish my father hadn't been so kind. It might have been easier had he thrown me into one of the hellholes, where I could have gotten lost amongst the insane.

MANDATORY STROLLS ARE REQUIRED of all patients at the Pleasance, as Dr. Featheringstone believes, "Fresh air is the tonic to many ails." At first, I was resistant to such outings, preferring to stay in my snug room with the door closed, but after several tours with the good doctor and a team of nurses and orderlies, I determined he perhaps had a point. There is a nice pond that is home to a family of ducks, a small grove of trees, and a handful of boring, quiet gardens that house no red roses after the good doctor had requested them removed. Worn dirt paths lined with benches connect the Pleasance's outdoor pleasures, and one can experience everything in as little as a half hour. We patients are never left to our own devices during these Fresh Air Hours, though. Nurses and orderlies mingle amongst the residents, setting up tables for games of checkers, chess, or croquet, although I naturally recuse myself from such frivolity.

Half a year in, and I am still a stranger to most of the folk here. That was by my choice; many of the residents did their best to welcome me into the fold, but I was determined to keep my distance out of early fear of spies.

There is nowhere you could go in which we could not find you, little bird.

"A letter, my lady."

My head snaps up sharply to find one of the orderlies standing over me, an envelope in his hand. I eye the object warily; outside of my parents, whom I requested not to write to me during my stay, no one else of my acquaintance knows I'm here. "There is no need to be so formal with me. We are at an asylum after all."

I think his name is Edward, but it could easily be Edwin, too. Or perhaps even Edmund. A mere incline of the head is given, but I highly doubt my bitterly voiced suggestion means anything to him. The staff here is the epitome of propriety.

I don't want what he has to offer. "Toss it into the fire."

His smile is patient and kind, one borne of tempered familiarity. "Dr. Featheringstone has already previewed its contents." The open flap is jiggled. "Would you like me to open it as well?"

I sigh and set my sketch pad on the bench next to me. The ducklings in the distance scatter across the pond, leaving me without subject to capture. "Go ahead and read it aloud."

A slim piece of paper is extracted. Through the afternoon's golden sunlight, I can determine less than a quarter of the sheet is filled with thin, spidery calligraphy. *"Dear madam,"* E reads, modulating his voice so it sounds very dignified, indeed. *"It is my great hope that I may come and speak to you tomorrow afternoon about a matter of great importance. Yours sincerely, Abraham Van Brunt."*

"That's it?" I ask once the paper is refolded.

"Yes, my lady."

What a curious letter. "I am unacquainted with an Abraham Van Brunt," I tell the orderly. And then, as I reclaim my sketch pad, "I suppose Dr. Featheringstone has already sent off a missive telling him not to bother coming round."

Naturally, he does not know whether or not the doctor did just such a thing. "Would you like the letter, my lady?"

I'm already turning back toward the pond. "No. Please burn it."

The crunch of twigs informs me of his retreat, allowing me to reclaim my solitude. The ducks long gone, I spend my time perfecting the tufts of grass and reeds growing at water's edge on today's landscape.

Alice.

I focus harder, my charcoal furiously scraping across the paper until I remember I don't want to do anything furiously. Not anymore, at least.

Alice.

I close my eyes, focusing on the red and orange kaleidoscopes that dance across my lids.

Alice?

The paper in my hand crumples as easily as my heart. I leave it behind on the bench when I make my way back inside, because I'm positive there was an H etched into it. And to think that Featheringstone is convinced I'm sane.

I haven't been sane in over six years.

AN OFFER OF EMPLOYMENT

"**T**RY TO KEEP AN open mind, hm?"

I'm sitting in Dr. Featheringstone's ode-to-wood office, my hands folded primly across my lap. "Do my parents know about this?"

The corners of his mustache twitch upward. "As you've pointed out numerous times in the past, you are not a child. There was no need to inform your father about this as he is not your legal guardian."

My smile is tight. "If that's the case, then I must insist you turn the gentleman away at the door. I simply do not have the inclination to entertain a visitor today."

The good doctor is undeterred. "Since arriving at the Pleasance, you have spent very little time conversing with anyone outside of myself and the staff."

I nod vigorously.

"But, Alice, none of us live in a vacuum. Mr. Van Brunt's visit could be an excellent chance for you to practice your conversation skills."

"Do you find my ability to converse lacking, Doctor?"

He chuckles softly, no doubt remembering how I wasn't chatty with anyone, himself included, for the first month of my stay. To be fair, it is difficult to carry on an invigorating discussion when one is shaking so hard from withdrawals they fear they might shatter into thousands of painful pieces before a single word can be uttered. Plus, there was the whole bit of how once I did open up, I raved liked a lunatic about things no normal person could imagine being true.

"Certainly not," he says to me. "But as I must stay at the Pleasance and you must go forth into the world, it will do you good to practice on somebody new."

"Then send in one of the orderlies. Or one of the nurses. I'll happily chat with a staff member."

One of his bushy, out-of-control eyebrows lifts high into his forehead.

"There are people out there who are quite content being solitary," I point out. "Who do not need to converse with anybody but themselves and their dogs."

He sets his pen down. "What about cats?"

Rigor mortis sets in ever so briefly at this question.

"You father said you were quite fond of cats growing up. There was one in particular that you favored. Dinah, was it not?"

"I'm—" I have to clear my throat. "Lately, I wonder if perhaps I'm more of a dog person after all."

The mustache hides nothing. I'm patently aware of how the corners of his mouth turn downward. "Nonetheless, I'm afraid I must insist you allow an audience with Mr. Van Brunt."

Irritable Alice emerges. "Do you know this gentleman?"

"I do. He and I go way back."

"As far as you and my father?"

"Not that far." The frown gives way to another soft chuckle. "But far enough. He would not come here to talk to you if he did not have something important to say."

"How do you know it's him?" I ask. "How do you know the missive was not forged?"

Concern fills his dark eyes.

I push my advantage. He must be wondering if I've gone mad again.

"What if it's one of the Courts? Or their assassins?"

Fingers tap against the felt mat guarding the top of the wooden desk as he studies me. Just as I feel victory is within my grasp, he says, "You will take the meeting. Hear Mr. Van Brunt out."

I slump back into the padded chair. I don't wear defeat well. "Fine."

EASILY ONE OF THE TALLEST men I've ever seen, Abraham Van Brunt has to stoop ever so slightly to fit through the doorway into Featheringstone's office. He's wearing a smart gray suit with a matching gray vest, a thin chain of gold looping from button to pocket, announcing a watch I want to snatch off his body and toss out the window.

A hand is proffered. "Hello, Ms. Reeve."

It's interesting he's referred to me by the name my family chose to register me under for privacy's sake. I take in his dark hair, equally dark beard, and piercing blue eyes as I leave his hand lonely in the space between us. "You are an American."

"Indeed I am." The hand withdrawn, he lowers himself into a nearby chair. "From New York, to be precise. My name is Abraham Van Brunt—"

"You're a far cry from home, sir."

The door opens, bringing with it one of the housekeepers and a tray loaded with a teapot and biscuits. "That I am." His voice is deep and soft, yet filled with a hint of thunder. "I'm not gone for too long, though. If all goes as planned, I'll be heading back tonight."

"Before you do, though, you thought you'd stop by an old friend's asylum and have a chat with one of the unstable ladies within?"

A smile touches his full lips. "Not just any woman. I specifically wanted to talk to you, Ms. Reeve."

You would think I'd learned my lesson about curiosity, but apparently I have yet to fully embrace the dangers associated with it. "Has Dr. Featheringstone been talking out of turn about me?"

He waits until the housekeeper closes the door behind her before selecting a cup. "Would you like some tea, Ms. Reeve?"

The words practically have to be ripped from me, but I agree to the drink.

"Let me reassure you that the good doctor has not betrayed your confidences—at least, not much."

I stir a doily-shaped slice of sugar into my cup, my eyes refusing to leave his face. "I feel quite confident that any mention of my person is gross abuse of patient-doctor confidentiality."

The flowered teacup comes to rest just before his lips. "Rest assured, he merely informed me there was a woman he'd met who spoke of Wonderland. After that, I . . ." His smile is surprisingly boyish. "Well. Let's just say that I am quite talented at rooting out mysteries. I'm afraid that I had to know exactly who was mentioning Wonderland and left no stone unturned until I did."

The blood in my veins runs cold at how easily he issues this statement. "This is a madhouse, sir. I assume many of the residents here have concocted fanciful lands with equally fanciful names to explain away their insanity."

He sips his tea, and it is his eyes this time that do not stray away. "But how many of them specifically mention Wonderland?"

I silently curse myself when the porcelain in my hands clink against one another.

"It's not often," he continues, "that one meets somebody who knows of, let alone has been to and back again, from such a place."

I let out a carefully nonchalant scoff. "Who is to say that person is me?"

His head tilts to the side as he sets his drink down on a nearby table. "Are you denying it?"

I force my cup to meet my lips, willing every muscle in my arm to stay steady. "I would argue any ravings uttered under the duress of narcotics is suspect, Mr. Van Brunt."

His curiosity toward my statement is obvious, but his manners do not allow him to pry. "Let me be frank with you, as I know our time is limited today. I am aware precious few people are able to find the way to Wonderland." A tight smile curves his full lips upward, but no teeth peek through. "You are something of an enigma, Ms. Reeve. One I'm most keen to talk in depth to."

My quick shot of laughter borders on hysteria. "Careful with what you say around here, Mr. Van Brunt. Or you too will be sitting alongside me here at the Pleasance."

This amuses him. "Sometimes," he murmurs, "I wonder if I ought to be, after all the things I've seen in my life."

"Are you claiming to have gone to Wonderland?"

"I'm afraid I haven't had that pleasure yet." He leans forward, his arms resting against his thighs. "But as I'm certain you have, I am here to offer you a job."

I blink, startled. Of all the things he has said today, this is the most astounding of all. "A *job*?"

His words are crisp and even. "It just so happens I am in need of someone who has been to Wonderland and lived to tell the tale." There's that tight smile of his once more. "It hasn't been the easiest of tasks to locate just such a person, to be honest. In fact . . ." His fingers lace together as they drape over his knees. "You are the sole candidate."

It's unbearably gauche, but my mouth drops open for the briefest of moments. But then I pull myself together, my spine lengthening as I assume a pose of perfect propriety. "I do not find this joke funny, sir. Furthermore, I cannot believe Dr. Featheringstone would have allowed you in if he knew you would taunt me with such things."

"This is no joke, Ms. Reeve. I am most sincere in my request."

He appears earnest, but then I am not the finest at judging character nowadays. Too many things are still uneven in my mind; too many suspicions or deeply seated feelings are scattered amongst memories better suited to watercolor paintings abandoned during rainstorms. "What exactly do you need with such a person?"

His vivid blue eyes pin me to where I sit. "I would think that was obvious. I would need you to go back to Wonderland."

A buzz fills my ears; a trickle of sweat slips down the back of my neck. "Absolutely not."

He's undeterred. "You have yet to hear the reasons why."

My fingers curl tightly around the carved wooden chair arms as I erect my defenses. "There is nothing you could say to tempt me to go back."

"Ah, so you do admit to having been to Wonderland."

"We are done here." I rise to my feet, my head held high.

He stays exactly where he is. "What if I told you that, if you do not go back, Wonderland may cease to exist?"

I pause midway across the room, hating that his words have even stopped me thus far. Rage mixes with desperation. Does this man know the truth? Is he mocking me? "Is this some kind of twisted fairy belief? That, if I choose not to believe in Wonderland, it and its magic will no longer breathe life?"

"Not at all." He reclaims his cup. "I meant what I said quite literally. If you do not go back, alongside a team from my organization, Wonderland's very existence could wink out like a candle in a windstorm."

Damn him. I backtrack to where the bloody man is sitting, sipping his tea like he hasn't just thrown a bomb at my feet. "And my presence will somehow stop that from happening?"

"Your knowledge of Wonderland will." One last sip precedes the cup finding its way back to the table, and Abraham Van Brunt is on his feet, towering over me. "I will be honest with you, Ms. Reeve. All of my organization's missions to Wonderland have failed so far. Nobody has been able to breech its borders, let alone find an entrance point."

Craning my neck allows me to see the anguished anger burning in his bright eyes.

"Time is running short, and there are no options left for me save one."

My laughter borders on a gasp. "You truly believe *I'm* your answer."

"I know you are."

"You know nothing, Mr. Van Brunt. You especially do not know that, should I return to Wonderland, my life is forfeit. Lives of those I . . ." My fingers twist into the starched brown skirt I'm wearing. "Many lives will be forfeited."

Ah. Now I have his attention. Deep Vs form in his forehead.

"I'm sorry, Mr. Van Brunt. I am not your answer, no matter how much you wish I might be otherwise. I will not risk—"

A hand shoots out and curls around my bicep, startling me into silence. "Whether or not that is the case, if you do not go back with my team, all of Wonderland could disappear. All of those you think you are protecting will be gone. If you truly want to save those you care about—"

I loathe how, even now, even after nearly half a year, my heart clenches at such thoughts. "How dare you lay your hands on me!"

"—you will hear me out."

"I've heard enough. Unhand me, Mr. Van Brunt!"

11

He lets go of my arm. "My apologies."

"We are done here."

He blocks my exit. "You've barely scratched at the surface of the truth, Ms. Reeve. I am asking you to accompany me to my organization's headquarters and allow us to present our case to you. Once we've done so, if you well and truly feel you are unable to join us on our mission, then I will bother you no more."

Six months. It's taken half a year for me to feel as if the ground under my feet is beginning to solidify, and now it's taken less than a half hour for it to turn to quicksand once more. "I am still a patient at the Pleasance—"

"That is not even a pebble in our shoes, Ms. Reeve."

Survival instincts kick in, alongside rationalizations. "You have just indicated you are going to New York."

"The trip, if you agree to take it, will take far less time than you imagine."

"We are in central England, sir. Just to get to the coast will take a few days."

He is unmoved. "You'd be surprised at what I'm capable of, when I have a mind toward it."

"Why do you care so much about saving Wonderland, especially as you've never been there?"

"Because," he tells me softly, a hand dipping into his pocket, "I know what it's like to have one's world extinguished."

It's enough to still my arguments.

A soft rap on the door brings forth Dr. Featheringstone. "Everything all right in here?"

Mr. Van Brunt takes a step back, widening the space between us. "Your Ms. Reeve is a stubborn one, Doctor."

Featheringstone chuckles. "What say you, Alice? Are you up for another adventure?"

"Madness," I whisper. "I must be dreaming right now. Either that, or you're all just as mad as I am."

"I assure you that you are awake, my dear," Featheringstone says.

Van Brunt slips out his pocket watch and glances at it. "Now or never, Ms. Reeve. Countless souls are relying upon you, as unaware as they may be of who their savior is."

I face my doctor, desperate to find some semblance of sanity in an insane asylum for women of means.

"I cannot make this choice for you." A gentle hand rests upon my shoulder. "But, if it were me, I would go."

Pitiful words of excuse fall from my lips, instinctive ones that shame me. "I'm . . . I'm not packed."

"No need," Mr. Van Brunt says. "Everything you could possibly need is waiting for you in New York."

"But—the journey—"

"As I said before, you will be surprised at just how quickly it will go."

"You are asking me to be selfish."

"Not at all." He towers over me. "I'm asking you to be strong and smart and brave, and to protect those who cannot protect themselves."

How can this be? After everything, how could this even be a possibility? "Are you certain that . . ." I swallow. "If I don't go, the people of Wonderland will be at risk?"

He shakes his head. "Ms. Reeve, there is a strong chance they could perish."

I've been so resilient these last few months, so good at not letting matters of responsibility and the heart drive me further into madness than they already have. He says he wants a smart woman; the smart move would be to walk out of this room and never see this man again.

But I cannot take the risk he is right. My hand extends in the space between us. "I suppose you have a new employee then, Mr. Van Brunt."

His grip is firm. "I promise you will not come to regret this decision."

A strange beep sounds in the room. Van Brunt pats his pocket and then sighs. "Dr. Featheringstone, I need a moment. Ms. Reeve, please excuse me. I will return momentarily."

Once he steps into the room just off of Dr. Featheringstone's office, the doctor rounds on me. "I know you are guarded by your experiences, but I must caution you to go into this situation with the most open of minds." He smiles kindly. "Much as you did with Wonderland."

Until this day, our talk of Wonderland has always been grounded in ravings and the need to explain them away even though I know the truth of my experiences. But now that he says this to me, a new determination shines from his eyes. He is not rationalizing away my belief in a magical land I fell down a rabbit hole and discovered; he's informing me he believes in it, too.

"Trust Mr. Van Brunt to have your best interests at heart," he continues. "He is a good man, a trustworthy one who bears many heavy weights upon his shoulders. He would not be here for you if he did not need you, dear."

"Tell me, Doctor." My voice is low and firm, as now that much shock has rocked me, I'm desperate to reclaim the control I've sought after for years. "How will you explain my absence to my family when they come round to collect me at the end of the week?"

He extracts a slim, folded piece of paper from his inner coat pocket. "I have already drafted a missive, informing your father that a sudden setback requires more time at the Pleasance."

I take the sheet from him and scan what he's written. It is simple enough and says what he claims—increased talk of Wonderland has left the doctor assured I must deal with key issues before I am to return to my family's care.

"How clever of you." I head over to his desk in order to sign my consent directly below his own signature. "While misleading, there isn't a lie to be found."

"I truly do believe this is the right course of action."

I refold the paper and hand it back to him. "All those times I spoke of Wonderland, did you know it was real?"

"There are many things in this world difficult to explain." Whiskers turn in as his lips purse. "I knew, when you came to me, that you were desperate to leave behind this piece of your past. I wanted to help you do that, to move forward with a healthy, well-adjusted life here in England. But, sometimes, we must deal with our problems head on in order to let them go."

"That is not a proper answer, Doctor."

"And yet, it is the best I can give you."

Mr. Van Brunt reenters the office, his lips a grim line between his dark mustache and beard. "I'm afraid that time runs short, Doctor. I've just gotten word that another attack has happened."

Dr. Featheringstone is stricken. "Do you know where?"

"Any loss is terrible, old friend, especially of this kind," Van Brunt says, "but I can assure you that you have had no contact with this place before."

A tear slips from one of Featheringstone's eyes anyway.

"What kind of attack?" I ask. "And how did you receive word of this? Was a letter delivered?"

"I will be glad to answer all of this for you," the man tells me, "but I am desperately needed back in New York. Will you accompany me, Ms. Reeve, so we might continue our discussion at a later time?"

Dammit. Curiosity has gotten the better of me again. I am a foolish, foolish woman when I nod my consent.

Van Brunt tugs a slim book bound in leather out of his coat pocket. "Are you prone to hysteria, Ms. Reeve?"

"I resided in Wonderland for the past six years. What do you think?"

A smile overtakes his mouth. "I think that you have more fortitude than you suspect, and for that, I ask you to dig deep and fully embrace that strength. Sometimes life is more extraordinary than we might first imagine, and today is going to test your limits of imagination and acceptance."

Alarm plucks at my belly. He says this to me, a former resident of a world that subsisted on the fantastical?

Dr. Featheringstone pats my cheek. "Stay true to yourself, Alice. Perhaps we shall see each other again someday, although, if I am to be honest, I will hope we will not."

Before I can utter another word, the doctor I've seen daily for six months leaves the room, shutting and locking the door behind him.

Van Brunt removes what appears to be a white writing instrument out of his pocket. "Are you ready for your next adventure, Ms. Reeve? Are you ready to once more slip through a looking glass?"

I'm startled. How does he know such a thing?

He does not wait for an answer. Instead, he takes his strange pen and scribbles into the book in his hand. The world as I know it shatters once more, because before us in the middle of the room appears a shimmering door.

Magic. *In England.*

The book snaps shut and is tucked back in his pocket, leaving only the pen out. He motions with it toward the door. "Shall we, Ms. Reeve?"

One would think I've learned my lesson, that I know better than to foolishly go forth into the unknown. These sorts of choices always have consequences. The last time I chose to do so, I lost myself for years. I lost my heart and my pride. I lost my family. I lost my sense of purpose.

I wonder what the cost I will be forced to pay this time will entail even as my hand grips the doorknob.

Silly Alice.

I open the door anyway.

DOORWAYS

DOORWAYS ARE SO VERY common, and used so frequently that most people are often blind to what they symbolize. A doorway can lead a person into new spaces, and can allow in loved ones, enemies, new acquaintances, or horrible things that we never dare to dream about. They can also remove us from that we've just left, or present us a firm wall of acceptance we may or may not wish to embrace. The doorway in front of me leads to another room, one whose countenance I have never seen in all my twenty-five years of life. Not in Wonderland, and certainly not in England.

I take a step back and peer round the side. Behind the open doorway is Dr. Featheringstone's office, with no signs of a glowing doorframe stretching from floor to near ceiling.

Van Brunt opens his mouth to say something, but I hold a hand up. "I am merely finding my bearings."

"Bearings," he murmurs, "are better than hysteria."

I turn toward him; he's smiling, even if just barely. "Did you think

I'd run, sir? Scream at the top of my lungs to the fellow inmates of bedlam that there is a magical door in the good doctor's office?" I shake my head. "Just yesterday, a fellow resident lamented how angels played cards on her bed as she tried to sleep. They were quite noisy, she claimed, and smelled strongly of cat urine. Sleep is apparently difficult when eyes water such as hers did."

"You didn't believe her?"

"I'm afraid I believe too much nowadays." And yet I step forward anyway, through the threshold and into the room beyond the door. Van Brunt follows, and before I know it, the door is shut and winks out of existence.

A thin man with black, rimmed glasses and greasy hair that shoots straight up from his head turns away from a wall covered with moving, colored photographs. He appraises me with sharp, small eyes before saying to Van Brunt, "The latest acquisition was successful then?"

The hairs on the back of my neck bristle until Van Brunt extracts a child-sized cane from inside his frock coat. "It was."

The lanky man nods. "I'll let the Librarian know right away."

He smells vaguely of cloves and has a bit of a Cockney accent. He's also wearing strange clothing: worn bluish trousers, a chartreuse sweater layered over a peculiar shirt with what looks to be an image of a dog on it, and dirty black boots with steel toes. But then, everything about this room is strange. The furniture is all sleek metal, the walls covered in machines and buttons and screens filled with pictures both moving and still. The floor below me shines brighter than any tile in the Pleasance.

"I suppose you are going to claim this is New York City," I say to Van Brunt.

He shrugs off his coat and passes it to the other man in the room. "I did tell you we'd have no problem reaching our destination. Ms. Reeve, let me introduce you to my assistant, Jack Dawkins."

The man briefly holds out his hand before quickly yanking it back. Then he laughs, a flush stealing up his neck. "I'm a bit rusty at this. I can't quite remember how to best introduce meself to a lady of high standing."

I force myself to not roll my eyes as I proffer my hand. He takes it and squeezes first strongly and then limply before nearly tripping backward on a chair set upon rollers. It goes skidding across the room, and if I'd thought this Jack Dawkins was blushing before, he's positively scarlet now.

At least he didn't prostrate himself like other silly men I'd once known.

"That's enough of that, Mr. Dawkins." Van Brunt is brusque. "Why don't you take the catalyst to the Librarian? Find Ms. Lennox on the way back and inform her I have Ms. Reeve in tow. We'll convene in the conference room in ten minutes to discuss today's unfortunate news."

Jack brandishes the cane. "God bless us, each and—"

"I said," Van Brunt stresses, "that's enough of that."

Dawkins nods and then swiftly exits the room through a door he first must punch buttons into in order to open it.

"You're holding up quite well."

I turn away from the wall of pictures. Van Brunt is tugging off his tie as he studies me. Does he expect me to turn to the hysteria he cautioned me against? Or perhaps weep openly over things so foreign that I can't help but suspect I've stepped into yet another Wonderland?

He's sure to be disappointed, as I am not that helpless, intimidated woman. "Does my lack of hysteria disappoint?"

"Not at all. I've studied quite a bit about you, Ms. Reeve. I know that, despite your experiences in Wonderland, you are a staunch realist."

If only he knew how painfully right he was about that.

The tie is tossed onto a nearby table so he can motion toward the doorway Dawkins so recently departed from. "You must have a dozen questions for me, but for now, I'm afraid you are set for a baptism by fire. We've got a situation on hand that requires immediate attention."

We enter a bright hallway with lights illuminating the ceiling and walls to various other rooms made of glass. *This is New York City?*

"I thought you brought me here to save Wonderland."

"Yes, of course," Van Brunt is saying. "Although, I'm hoping that, once you hear our plight, you'll want to help save millions of other souls, too."

A woman exits one of the glass rooms, her hair bright green and her ears filled with silver loops. "I'll have the report in the conference room in three minutes," she tells Van Brunt.

"Excellent. Are Finn and Victor back yet?"

The woman shakes her head. "I expect them any minute." Her pale eyes find me. "Is this her?"

New York, it appears, is a very rude place.

Van Brunt nods distractedly, and she murmurs, "Thank god." She looks me up and down. "Would you like me to get you some new clothes?"

Ah. Now she'll address me.

The green-haired woman is wearing the same type of bluish trousers Jack was sporting as well as a sleeveless tight, thin top. While my blouse and shirt aren't the height of fashion—and why would they be, as I've been lounging around the Pleasance for months—I'm certainly more properly attired than she is. "Do you find fault with what I'm wearing?"

"I got rid of my corset the moment I could." Hands riddled with at least a dozen rings span her waist. "I'm assuming that, even though you came from a sanitarium, you're still wearing yours."

"An asylum," I correct. And then, because I can't help myself, "For the insane."

If this fazes her, she does not let on.

"Tick-tock, Ms. Darling," Van Brunt says.

Ms. Darling lets out a ringing peal of a laugh. "Oh, Brom," she says as she sashays away, "you are really too much sometimes."

"Brom?" I ask once she's turned a corner.

He shrugs. "A nickname for Abraham."

As we head down the hall and around a bend, I ask, "You claim you are part of an organization. Does it have a name?"

"We are currently within the headquarters for the Collectors' Society."

"What is it you collect, sir? Children's canes? Or *catalysts*?"

He's impressed. "We collect catalysts amongst other things."

Why do I get the impression he's just collected me? "Unless I am mistaken, a catalyst is an item or event that is the cause of important events."

"Indeed it is."

We arrive at a door bearing a plaque that reads: *Conference Room*. He pushes it open and ushers me inside. While the wall facing the doorway is all glass, so is the wall facing outside—windows stretch from floor to ceiling, allowing me to view a skyline unlike anything I've ever seen.

I side skirt a large table occupying the bulk of the room, ignoring the chattering from the few people already seated until I reach the glass. I am apparently in a building that soars high into the sky, as what lies below is tiny. There are roads filled with fast-moving objects and other vehicles of sorts buzzing in the air nearby as they circle similar tall buildings. My hands press against the cool panes as I stare out, agog at what I'm seeing.

London is a busy, majestic city. The four Courts in Wonderland are massive, elaborate architectural masterpieces. And yet nothing I've seen before comes close to the sights before me.

I quietly clear my throat and embrace the fortitude that has served me well in the past. "I have seen photographs of New York City, Mr. Van Brunt. None resemble this."

The door opens and brings with it a freckled woman with an indistinguishable hair color. Is it blonde? Red? Brunette? Honestly, it's a combination of all three in a muddied mixture that can best be described as light. "They're still not back?" She lets out a dramatic sigh. "I thought for sure they would be."

Van Brunt acknowledges her with a quick nod before telling me, "I can assure you that this is New York City, Ms. Reeve. Your questions lead to *where* you are. Perhaps you are best served asking me *when*."

Surely, I've misheard him. "Are you indicating we've time traveled?"

"You've journeyed to Wonderland and returned to tell the tale. Are you so sure time travel does not exist, either?"

The freckled woman rounds the table. "Brom, I see you've done yet another poor job at bringing your latest charges up to speed." She sticks her hand out. "I'm Mary Lennox."

I take her hand; unlike Jack Dawkins' before, her grip is firm from start to finish. "I'm Alice Reeve."

Papers rustle. Somebody at the other end of the room sputters, "But . . . I thought her name was Liddell?"

"Don't be daft," somebody else mutters. "That's Carrollean, not text."

What in the bloody hell is Carrollean? And how in the world would they know my father's name, when all I've used since my return has been my mother's surname?

"Oh, believe me," Mary is saying, "I know exactly who you are. I'm pleased to finally make your acquaintance."

Unlike the woman in the hallway, Mary is wearing a dress, albeit a short one that barely grazes her knees. It's black with sleeves halfway down her arms, and her shoes have heels several inches tall decorated with leopard spots. She's British, though, her accent similar to mine, if not a bit dulled.

"I'd hoped to have more time to ease Ms. Reeve in," Van Brunt says, "but I received word of the attack."

"Has Wendy brought in the details yet?"

Van Brunt pulls a chair out for me just to the side of his at the head of the table. "She will be with us momentarily."

Mary sits directly across from where I am, depositing a satchel covered in flowers on the table. As she digs through it, she snaps, her words filled with heat, "We cannot allow this continue!"

"A fact I am well aware of, Ms. Lennox."

The person next to me, a man of indistinguishable age, pounds his fist against the table. "That makes the third Timeline in a year! We must find this madman before it's too late!"

"Believe me," Van Brunt says, "you will find there is none in this room or indeed in the Society more dedicated to just such a purpose, Mr. Holgrave."

"Every day I live in fear," the man cries. "I wonder if it will be my Timeline next. *My* family that—"

Van Brunt smoothly cuts him off. "I do not think there is a single soul within the Society who feels differently, least of all myself."

Holgrave slumps in his chair, chastised. "My apologies, old friend."

The woman with green hair—Wendy Darling, is it?—materializes in the doorway whilst carrying a slim, silver rectangle. "Sorry for the delay, but my fricking computer crashed again. We really need to upgrade the network, Brom."

"Do what you must, Ms. Darling."

As Wendy comes to the front of the table with her metal box, Mary taps her writing instrument against the table. "Part of the problem is it's becoming increasingly more difficult to identify catalysts, let alone targets. If only there was a pattern to track."

Wendy flips open the box she's carrying; a lid, attached, shows photographs while the bottom portion of the inside box resembles a typewriter.

Curiouser and curiouser.

Van Brunt scoots his chair to the side, making more room for Wendy's box. "Nobody ever said madmen are reasonable." An apologetic glance is thrown my way, as if I might take offense to his characterizations of the insane.

I give him a cool smile. "Have no fear about speaking ill of those who attack innocents, if this is indeed what we are discussing. But I would like to know more about what kind of madman you are referring to. Is it a Wonderlander?"

It's Mary who answers. "Tell me, do you read much?"

I ignore how the hairs on my arms bristle at her inappropriately timed question. "I do, but I am afraid that is a pleasure I have not had much time to indulge in over the past few years."

"But you did once, no?"

I keep my answers as impersonal as possible. "I believe most children enjoy stories."

"Yet, you are familiar with the basic tenants of most books, are you not? There is typically a villain, or at least somebody or something that thwarts the main character's journey or growth."

"I thought we were here to discuss an attack," I say. "Or to even, as per Mr. Van Brunt, bring me up to speed on whatever it is the Collectors' Society does. And yet, you wish to waste time discussing the finer parts of storybooks?"

Her eyes, filled with amusement and surprise, flick toward Brom.

I am sorely tempted to remind this woman that I am sitting here, and if she has any further comments concerning my character, they ought to be voiced to me and not Van Brunt. But Mary doggedly continues her book lecture before I am given a chance to follow through. "I promise that the two are related. The point I was trying to get at was that in books you are often led to know who the villain is early on. Unfortunately, we do not know the name or identity of the ultimate villain in this situation is yet. But I can almost guarantee it is not someone from your Timeline."

This is the third time the term *Timeline* has been used.

At the front of the room, Wendy says, "We're all set up. Should we wait for Finn and Victor?"

"No." Van Brunt rolls his chair to the side. "They will be able to catch up. Ms. Darling, I'll let you run the presentation."

The lights in the room dim and then disappear; behind me, dark shades are lowering across the windows. An image flashes on a screen behind the head of the table, one of a book. There is what appears to be a windmill on the cover, and a thin man mounted upon a horse.

"At approximately five-thirty a.m., Greenwich Mean Time, communication with the Timeline associated with *Don Quixote* was severed." Wendy points what I can best describe as a small black clicker in her hand toward the picture; the screen changes from the image of book to a listing of facts. What magic is this? "As many of you know, *Don Quixote* has been one of the strongest, oldest Timelines in existence, so naturally, we were alarmed at the lack of contact."

I stare up at the screen. It says:

```
Nickname: Don Quixote
Official title: The Ingenious Gentleman Don
Quixote of La Mancha
Author: Miguel de Cervantes
Timeline origin: 1605, with modifications
in 1615
Designation: 1605CER-DQ
First contact: 15 June 1951
Current liaison(s): Mateo Serrano / 23
February 2011
Catalyst: Unknown
Status: DELETED
```

"Repeated attempts were made to edit," Wendy continues, "but all failed. An emergency signal was triggered, but no response followed."

Questions tickle the tip of my tongue, but I bite them back. For now, I will observe and glean what I can. After all, isn't that a lesson the Caterpillar taught me well?

The picture on the wall changes again. A colored photograph of a serious man with matching dark hair and eyes stares down from above. In his hands is a book that bears the title from the previous pictures.

"Last contact with Serrano was approximately two-and-a-half weeks ago during a routine check-in. Here is his last communique."

The picture changes once more. Instead of a still photograph, the man on the wall moves. He leans back, but quickly glances to the side. "This is Mateo Serrano from 1605CER-DQ." His words, although in English, are weighed down by a thick accent. "Attempts to locate the local catalyst have been so far unsuccessful. My team is still researching, though. Thanks to the Librarian's notes, we have narrowed down several locations. If all goes as planned, we ought to be able to retrieve it shortly." Something in the background beeps, drawing his attention briefly away once more. "Spain is in the midst of the beginnings of a civil war, so that may slow us down a bit. Keep your fingers crossed for us. Serrano over and out."

The picture stops moving, but I am on unsteady legs. The ground below me is now one I cannot begin to predict.

The lights in the room flare bright; the shades protecting the windows pull upward. There are sober faces in the room, sad ones, too.

"After the prerequisite attempts at both editing and establishing communication were deemed impossible," Wendy says, "we had no other choice than to accept that Timeline 1605CER-DQ has been deleted."

The door opens, and the sound is an explosion in the hush. Several people startle; others quickly wipe their faces as two tall men enter the room.

"It's about time you two showed up," Van Brunt says.

A NEWSPAPER

"OUR APOLOGIES." A HAT is tugged off the head of one of the
men, tossed onto the table before he runs a hand through his
dark yet impeccably styled hair. He is tall and thin and quite
good looking. "We'd have been here sooner, but unfortunately ran into
a bit of trouble during transition just prior to editing."

Wendy's immediately alarmed. "What kind of trouble?"

As the now hatless man sits down, his companion quietly rounds
the table and chooses himself a seat, too. I'm struck by how tired he
looks, as if he could fall asleep at any second. Dark, purplish smudges
color the skin beneath his eyes and his hair, shortish and golden brown,
has probably seen better days.

These must be the aforementioned duo of Victor and Finn.

"My pen glitched," the first man is saying. He's also British, and his
accent is even softer than Mary's. It's then I notice there is a small streak
of dried blood across the white of his collar. He's dressed in a sharp suit
with a long coat and smart tie, and it saddens me that the contrast of

sophistication and horror no longer shocks me. "It took some finesse to get it in proper working order again."

When Van Brunt asks, "Were you successful?" in the same mild voice he's used throughout the entirety of the day, I can't help but wonder what in his past has made him so guarded with his emotions.

"Yes. We ran into the A.D. upon arrival, so the catalyst is with the Librarian right now or will be shortly."

I discreetly crane my neck so I can glance down the length of the table at the man whose quiet words were just spoken. For appearing so tired, his tone is firm and steady. He's American. It's quite a mix they have here, isn't it?

"Good." Van Brunt leans back in his chair. "Ms. Darling, you may continue."

But before she can, the well-dressed man exclaims, "I'll be damned! You found her after all."

All eyes rotate back toward me. Tiny hairs stiffen on the back of my neck, but I resist the impulse to do anything other than coolly meet his curious gaze.

Mary sighs deeply, muttering something beneath her breath. He isn't paying attention to her, though. He's still staring at me like I'm the most fascinating, shiny object in the room.

It makes me want to slap the impertinence right out of him.

"You do go by Alice, right?"

I loathe that he knows my name but I don't know his.

"You look a bit different from what I expected." A hand thoughtfully strokes his smooth chin. "Not nearly as blonde as you're made out to be. And much older too, aren't you?"

Mary's latest sigh could probably be heard outside the walls, it's so loud. "Tact," she mutters. "Try using it for once in your life."

As for me, I say evenly, "Do I disappoint?"

He blinks once, twice at my quiet words before laughing. For a moment I'm sucked back into the past, during a time the Hatter and I stood on a table in the garden, soaked to the bone as we laughed and screamed maniacally up into the void. Stripped naked and covered in melting paint and frosting, the others carved deep grooves in the mud around us as they ran laps, chortling until they were hoarse.

"Do you hear that, Alice?" The Hatter's arms were thrown wide,

his head tilting so far back that his hat had disappeared behind us. "Do you feel it?"

I had, unfortunately. All too well.

A tiny spasm twitches underneath my left eye as I contemplate if I ought to climb upon this table and charge him. But no—I've left that all behind. My blade is elsewhere, too far out of reach.

The man he walked in with says, "Victor, listen to Mary for once, will you?"

Which must means he's Finn.

"Sorry, it's just, how fascinating is it how she looks nothing like how she's portrayed?" Victor leans against the table, his head cocked to the side, as his eyes run up and down the visible length of me.

The urge to bring him down to size is strong, but stronger still is a memory of sitting upon a mushroom while being reminded that those whose words are stingier are those who survive. So I ask lightly, "Exactly who is portraying me?"

His eyes go wide; before he breaks Van Brunt says, "Enough. As 1605CER-DQ has just been deleted, I'm afraid the opportunity to fully debrief Ms. Reeve has not yet arisen. Let her be until I can talk in private with her."

That wipes the mirth right off this Victor's face. His whisper is strangled. "1605CERT-DQ is gone? Nobody told us. When did this happen?"

"We are in the midst of hearing the details just now," Mary snaps.

Bleakness fills Victor's once-amused eyes.

Van Brunt turns to the woman standing next to him. "Ms. Darling? Please continue."

Wendy clears her throat. "We've been scanning various databases to see if anyone has claimed responsibility, but, like with the last two deletions, all is quiet. My department isn't giving up hope, though. There might still be some clues we've yet to uncover."

Mary's incensed. "It's maddening that whoever this is isn't behaving properly."

"And how should a proper villain act?" One of Van Brunt's dark eyebrows arches upward. "Should he announce himself to the world with a soliloquy? Perhaps write a note about his intentions?" What in definition is a smile appears anything but. "Come now, Ms. Lennox.

You of all people should know about the injustices of stereotypes. Unfortunately, this is no story with an easily guessed-at plot we're reading. We have no ability to flip to the last page in order to assure ourselves of certainty."

Splotches grow on Mary's cheeks. Farther down the table, Victor calls out, "I think what Mary was saying was—"

Van Brunt holds a hand up. "I know exactly what she was saying. I was merely reminding Ms. Lennox that this particular story is not as familiar as those we hold close to our hearts. We cannot simply expect that whomever is doing this will offer up an announcement that could easily bring about their apprehension. If that had been the case, we would have done so before."

Mollified (or perhaps mortified), Victor nods once before slumping back into his seat. The woman next to him leans over and says, "Dr. Frankenstein? Can I talk to you after the meeting?"

It's interesting that he winces when he hears the name. She immediately apologizes, her cheeks ruddy and splotched.

"What can be said is that the current pattern of attacks has a deletion at approximately every three to four months," Wendy is saying. "And that the last three targets have been substantial Timelines."

"Any common denominators between them?" someone on the other side of the table asks.

"Other than popularity?" Wendy shakes her head. "None that I can see yet. One was French, one was British, and another was Russian."

"All European," Holgrave murmurs.

"And yet, the one before that was American," Wendy argues.

Van Brunt extracts a small white and silver rectangle out of his pocket. "Nonetheless, I want your department scouring the Internet once more to see if a pattern does exist, Ms. Darling." He taps on the box of metal and glass. "Perhaps there are hints found in forums or the like. As for the rest of you, Mr. Dawkins will send out assignments within the hour."

The box that held the moving pictures snaps shut and is tucked into Wendy's arms. The rest of the audience rises when she does, and there is much murmuring as they file toward the exit. The object in Van Brunt's hands beeps, but he tucks it into a pocket. He turns to me, just a hint of an apologetic smile on his rugged face. "This must be much to take in all at once."

Unfortunately, it is. But before the first question I have passes my lips, he calls out, "Finn? A moment?"

Mary touches my elbow, and I start. I didn't even see her round the table.

"I need to go debrief with Victor, but I'll catch up with you in a little bit. Okay?"

She says this like we're old friends, ones who have reunited after years of life lived out between us. My spine stiffens, even though I know she means well.

Her fingers curl around my forearm and squeeze gently before she gifts me with a smile. Across the room, Victor shouts her name. "We need to go! I'm starving. The food was shite there!"

Once she's gone, she's replaced with the man who came in with Victor in the middle of the meeting. For a moment, the breath in my chest stills as I take him in.

He's beautiful. Handsome is probably a more dignified term, but the golden-brown hair, light blue-gray eyes, and tanned skin really do come across as more beautiful than anything else. He's tired, yes, but that does nothing to detract from his allure.

My fingernails curl inward into my palm, digging deep. I pull air in through my nose and then slowly out through my barely parted lips. But this small action, which normally focuses me, leaves me even more confused because rather than gifting me clarity, I just got a whole noseful of his scent. It's a bit warm, a bit minty, with hints of sweat and soap.

Oh, bloody hell. I do not need this.

Just as the door shuts behind Victor and Mary, Van Brunt asks, "Is there anything I need to know about?"

The man runs his fingers through his short hair; itty bitty chunks stand on end in unorganized, careless ways. "You mean, why are we so late?"

I'm now the awkward third stool leg. I take a discreet step back, pretending my focus is on the vista beyond the wide glass windows.

Van Brunt coughs. Says carefully, "I'm not accustomed to you being anything less than prompt."

Finn shrugs. "Shit happens, unfortunately. I wish we could predict how every mission goes, but you know we can't."

"Did the pen truly malfunction?"

I'm surprised by the distrust in Van Brunt's voice—and that he would say such things in my presence.

"Yeah, it did," Finn says. He's annoyed, I think. "It fell out of his pocket during our exit. Let's just say that pens and cars don't go well together." Out of the corner of my eye, I watch his head tilt toward me, like he knows I'm listening.

Van Brunt grunts. "Ensure that he gets it fixed. I don't want it used until we can ascertain it is in working order. Where was yours?"

"Wendy has been working on it, remember?"

Outside the window, birds swoop by. And for a moment, the crazed yet beautiful face flashes in the pane before me, sour judgment darkening its eyes.

I did the right thing. I did the right thing.

I did the right thing.

I did.

Don't do this. We will find a way.

I resist the childish urge to cover my ears with my hands.

"Ms. Reeve?"

I blink before turning around. Both men are regarding me as if I've done something crazy. And the sad thing is, I very well might have.

A cold sweat settles at the base of my hairline. Like they had for the first month and a half back in England, my fingers twitch so strongly I'm forced to lace them together. "My apologies. Did you ask something?"

The corners of Van Brunt's mouth tug downward, and Finn's eyes widen ever so slightly. Son of a jabberwocky. I *did* do something crazy, didn't I? But then Van Brunt says smoothly, "I would like to introduce you to one of your colleagues here at the Society, as you'll be working together. Ms. Reeve, this is Huckleberry Finn. Finn, this is Alice Reeve."

My knuckles turn white as my fingers tighten around one another. I force a polite smile on my face. "It is a pleasure to meet you, sir."

I'm unsurprised yet unnerved when he sticks his hand out. My fingers reluctantly disentangle from other another so I can proffer mine as well. When our skin touches, I realize my palm is damp.

Frabjous.

Thankfully, the connection lasts only a few seconds. I wait for him to discreetly wipe his hand across his pants, but he doesn't. There's a genuine yet surprised interest in his eyes as his lips gently curve upward. "The pleasure is all mine."

The sensation of his skin pressed against mine continues to linger.

Something trills in Van Brunt's pocket. He sighs deeply and extracts the small white and silver rectangle from before. "I've got to take this. Finn, will you stay with Ms. Reeve?"

When Finn nods, Van Brunt brings the box up to his ear. "Please tell me you have some good news."

As Finn doesn't answer, I open my mouth to offer something—anything, but Van Brunt turns on his heels and stalks out of the room. I nearly jump when the door slams shut, and then once more when an unseen Van Brunt bellows angrily in the distance, "That is not acceptable!"

"Are you okay?"

Discomfort crawls along my limbs as I stare up at the man who just asked me this question. He's got a good nose and full lips. I hate that I notice these things. My heels dig in and I clamor for control. *Little details*, the Caterpillar used to tell me, *make all the difference. Focus on them when everything else is wild.* "Huckleberry is an interesting name. A bit unconventional, no?"

That knocks the smile right off his face. "Yeah, I guess it is."

How puzzling. "It is a family name?"

He lets out an annoyed puff that smacks strongly of bitter humor. "I tend to go by Finn."

My hands lace together once more, the knots tighter than ever. I focus on the blue and red plaid of his shirt, and on how his sleeves are rolled up to just below his elbows. While I have seen many a man in a shirt, I've never quite seen one like this. And his pants. Goodness, do they fit him well. "Tell me, Mr. Finn—"

"Just Finn," he corrects. "It's more like a first name than anything else nowadays. Besides, I'm not as into as the whole formality bit as Brom is. Actually—nobody is. It's just one of his quirks."

"Mr. Van Brunt indicated earlier that we are in New York City."

Faint lines appear in his forehead. "That's correct."

"But he said I ought to be focused more on the when rather than the where. Would you perhaps clarify his statement?"

Finn's eyelids shut briefly as he shakes his head, but then roll toward the ceiling once open. And I'm a bit more certain I should not have left Dr. Featheringstone's office today—or even gotten out of bed for that matter.

"What has Brom told you so far?"

I'm annoyed everyone seems to have this same reaction. "He claimed I am required to help save Wonderland. But before he could tell me more, a situation arose that required his attention."

Finn bites his lip as he glances toward the door. A sigh heaves out of him. "This is going to be a lot to take in, so you may want to sit down."

"I'd prefer to stand, thank you."

He scans the room once more before holding up a finger. I watch as he crosses the room to where a black waste bin sits by the door. A newspaper is extracted and then shaken before he returns to where I am. "I'm not always the best at explaining things," Finn says. "Mary says I'm a bit like a bull in a china shop. But if you want to know today's date, it'll be on this."

I take the paper from him and stare down at it. *The New York Times*, it reads across the top. Just below that, in smaller letters, reads a date that cannot be. I shake my head and blink rapidly before holding the paper up to eye level. Once more, my stomach drops as I take in the date Finn claims to be this day's.

It's approximately one hundred and forty years later than the date I woke up on.

I carefully fold the newspaper, painfully aware of how strongly my hands are trembling. I clear my throat, but it doesn't help how raspy my voice is when I speak. "I see." And then, after another cough, "How curious it is that Van Brunt can produce a time-traveling doorway."

A warm hand cups the back of my elbow and leads me the scant distance it takes to reach a chair. "You should sit down. Let me get you some water."

Yes, because drinking water makes it all the better.

As he strides across the room toward a small side desk, my attention reverts to the windows before me. Tall glass buildings reflecting hazy sunlight stare back, taunting me in their alien construction. Memories of Wonderland's architecture surface, and while I'd marveled at how radically different the intricate gold-adorned buildings in the Courts looked compared to England's, they now seem positively antiquated compared to what I'm seeing right now.

A glass of so-called calming water is set on the table. "Are you okay?"

It's the second time he's asked me this question in less than a quarter of an hour. Hysterical laughter bubbles up my throat in response, but I swallow it back as he drops into the chair next to me. There's concern in those blue-gray eyes of his, concern that has no right to be there.

He doesn't know me. He doesn't know my experiences. If he did, the concern would go running into the distance.

I haven't been okay in nearly a year.

I sip the water slowly. It's icy cold, allowing me to trace its path down into my stomach. "I am fine, thank you."

Finn leans back into the chair. "Are you a reader?"

I slide the glass back onto the table. "I feel as if my day is looping, because Mary asked the same of me less than an hour prior. It leaves me to assume I've been brought to the future to discuss literature rather than save Wonderland."

He lifts a hand to scratch his forehead. "Actually, as weird as it may seem, you are here to do both."

It's enough to give me pause, and for the door to open and bring with it Van Brunt. "My apologies." No doubt taking in what must surely be my pale countenance, he asks Finn, "What all have you told her?"

Finn rises from his seat. "Not much. We'd only just begun." He taps on the newspaper lying between us. "But I'll leave it to you to finish the rest." He turns to me, and once more I spy concern shining out from his eyes. "If you need anything, I'm in 1510."

Van Brunt lowers himself into the chair so recently vacated. "The Librarian awaits your field paperwork, Finn. I'd hate to think of what she'll be like if it isn't filed within the hour."

How interesting it is that this man's name is familiar to Van Brunt's lips. Along with Victor's, they are the only one so far to be so.

Finn slides the newspaper underneath his arm. "I'm on my way to do it right now." When he makes his way to the door, I steal another glance just in time to watch him throw the paper away.

"Well now," Van Brunt says. "It's time for those explanations, isn't it?"

THE COLLECTORS' SOCIETY

THERE ARE MOMENTS IN one's life that always leave a person wondering if they're dreaming. I've had plenty of those moments— years of them, actually. In Wonderland, the amazing became mundane, and yet, the entire time I was there, I often speculated if I was in fact in England, asleep in my childhood bed. That perhaps I was riddled with fever, even close to my final sleep because I no longer questioned the extraordinary I lived through. Day after day, year after year, my existence devolved into one dream state after another until it was all I knew, all that I hoped for. All that I expected. When I was forced to leave it behind, and after I practically bargained my soul to do so, the promise of quiet, mundane events held me together when the urge to shatter into mindless grief and insanity proved nearly irresistible. For weeks, I was willingly restrained in a special coat that kept me from tearing my hair out, and lived in a room with soft walls that refused to allow self-harm. I howled, I raved, I frothed at the mouth. I tried to bite nurses who came too close, and I threatened to unleash an army against them more than once if they dared touch me.

I plotted how I could go back. Prayed I could find an answer, that perhaps now I had the clarity to find what I could not then. And then I despaired when I accepted I couldn't, shouldn't, and wouldn't.

Slowly, but surely, I acclimated to my new existence. My days morphed into the regulated and predictable. People who surrounded me became reliable and steady. I was in an asylum, yes, but hope sprung that I could put that foot in front of the other and move on whether it was my wish or not.

And now, here I am, a hundred and forty years in the future, with a man who possesses more secrets than any person I ever met in Wonderland, and I'm fearful I am once more trapped within a vicious cycle of unrealistic dreams.

He wants to send me back. Is it even possible? And if it is, could I even allow it?

"The Collectors' Society," Van Brunt says as he leans back in his chair, "has been in existence for really only a very short time—approximately a century, give or take." Strong fingers tap on the table beside us. "There are multiple ways to label people, as you may well know. In the literate world, we can simplify this in that there are readers and non-readers. Within the readers category, we can further label people by how passionate they are with the books they choose. Some people escape into the stories they read. Some read for purpose or information. Some read out of resentment or necessity. But let us, in this moment, focus on those who find books to be an escape or an extension of their imagination. These readers see, within their mind's eye, the characters and settings in the pages below their fingers. They feel the emotions woven between the words. They live through every heartache, every embrace, every terror. Books, to these people, become tangible, living things. The characters they read become genuine souls." A half smile curves his lips. "People like this are often accused of living within their fantasies. They're said to have their noses stuck in books. But the reality is that some of these people actually *do* escape into books."

My fingers streak through the condensation on the glass. "Are you inferring that . . ." I don't even know how to properly verbalize what I think he's telling me, it's so ludicrous.

"I'm not inferring anything. I'm telling you there are people who have the natural ability to lose themselves in a book."

"You are surely speaking of imagination."

The corners of his lips tick upward as he slowly shakes his head. "Not at all. There are people who literally enter books." Another hand is held up. "Let me clarify that. They are people who enter the worlds associated with books. We call them Timelines."

There's that word again: *Timeline*.

"To make a long story short . . ." He pauses, his mouth twitching at the inadvertent pun. "Every time a book is published and embraced by a large population, a Timeline is created—or at least made visible to the rest of us. Timelines are worlds filled with people who are living out their lives just like you or me. There are countless worlds in existence right now, and more being created every year. Our scope of the universe is not as small as we once imagined, Ms. Reeve."

For a long moment, nothing more is said between us as his words sink into me. What he's saying is madness. "You're telling me that . . . authors . . . actually breathe life to their characters?"

"While that point is debatable, the rest are not. There are countless worlds associated with books, Ms. Reeve." His voice, his words, are gentle but insistent. "I know this is a lot to take in, but—"

"Are you saying that authors are *gods*?"

At first, Van Brunt is startled by my question. And then he laughs, albeit quietly, briefly. "No. But there is something to be said about the power of stories. While not all in the Society possess the ability to naturally escape into Timelines, we have found technological ways around this roadblock."

I fly up, my feet clambering for solid ground. Water sloshes out of my glass as it skids across the table. "This is insanity." The chair I've abandoned skitters behind me on its rolling feet. "Until this moment, I would have said I'd become something of an expert in insanity, but this exceeds anything ever experienced in Wonderland."

He also rises until he towers over me. "Ms. Reeve—"

Confusion swirls throughout my mind so strongly I fear that this is yet another dream, and that I am back in my bed in the tulgey woods.

His large hand is surprisingly gentle on my shoulder. "How about we take a tour of the Institute, and we can continue our discussion as you get a feel for our work—or even table it until a later time, one in which you feel more ready to hear the truths we toil beneath."

A beep sounds once more in his pocket. Van Brunt sighs and tugs the small rectangle back out of his pocket. As he stares down at it, I choose to do so this time, too.

The glass on the front of the box glows with words: **Wendy Darling / V's pen unusable, will have to build a new one.**

Van Brunt angles the box toward me. "It's called a cell phone. In the Twenty-First Century, people are able to easily communicate with anyone they wish with small devices such as these. It allows you to send messages or speak to and listen in return to others."

I watch in uneasy silence as he taps on the front of the cell phone. Words magically appear: **Estimated completion?**

Just a few seconds pass before new words materialize. **1-2 weeks, tops.**

My voice is hoarse. "Is somebody communicating with you right now?"

He nods. "Ms. Darling. She's down in the tech lab." And then, no doubt after he sees the confusion on my face, he adds a bit more clarification. "The Collectors' Society is housed in a multi-purpose building we refer to as the Institute. It includes office spaces such as these,"—he gestures around the room before motioning me toward the door—"laboratories, an extensive library, common rooms, a gym, a restaurant, storage, and living quarters for members. One such laboratory is for the building of machines and devices. Ms. Darling is the head of our technology department, and she—"

These are facts. I like facts. Facts are solid. One can hold onto a fact when everything else is soft and muddled. And yet, right now, as the bigger picture both expands and contracts around me, I could not care less about whether or not Wendy Darling builds machines that apparently allow people to communicate across vast distances. There's only one thing I need to know.

"Am I from a story?"

His mouth snaps shut as he tucks the cell phone back into his pocket. I've stopped short of the door, my feet weighed down by invisible lead. I'm undeterred, though. If I'm going to sink once more into madness, I might as well get as many answers as I can before doing so. "We came through time and a magical door from the Pleasance to here. Am I from a story?"

For a moment, I wonder if he's going to ignore my question. But then he says quietly, firmly, "Yes."

I'm reminded of a time that I stood before the Courts, a bloody sword in my hand and my existence on the line, and I no longer knew if there were shins below knees or feet attached to ankles. But, damn if I didn't ensure my voice was steady when I addressed them. "Are you?"

He turns to fully face me. "Yes."

A breath is pulled in through my nose, out through my mouth. "What about the rest of the Society?"

"Some, but not all. We are an eclectic mix here."

"Are we real?"

Deep lines of confusion groove his forehead. "Pardon?"

"You claim we are from stories. Made up . . ." I swallow hard. "In somebody else's imagination. Are we real? Am I?"

Understanding fills the blue of his eyes, and something more. Something like . . . sympathy. "Do you feel real?"

I do not want sympathy, though. So, I tell him the truth. I tell him, "Not always." Not anymore.

A hand goes to the small of my back; I flinch at the light pressure. But Van Brunt has his way, because we finally exit the conference room. "Let us take that tour, Ms. Reeve."

Over the next half hour, Van Brunt takes me from floor to floor, showing me labs and offices and introducing me to people whose names I fear I will never remember. Everyone is polite, although some more voraciously friendly than others. There's a sense of recognition on their behalves upon introduction that I do not share, and my unease grows exponentially.

They know me. I do not know them.

To be fair, my focus isn't on any of these people and spaces, anyway. I'm too focused on what Van Brunt told me about before. This isn't the first existential crisis I've suffered through. One might even say this is old hat for me. It's just . . . this time feels differently.

Van Brunt is mid-way through the physical history of the building when I cut him off once more. "What book am I from?"

I give him credit that he does not look surprised in the least I've asked this. "There are two, actually, which combine to create a singular Timeline. The first is *Alice's Adventures in Wonderland*, and the second is *Through the Looking-Glass, and What Alice Found There*."

My mouth goes dry. "Who . . ." I desperately try to smash down the panic rising in my chest. Anxiety such as this, the Caterpillar used to tell me, was an ugly, pointless emotion. "Who is the author?"

Van Brunt steers us toward a staircase. "His real name is Charles Dodgson, but he wrote under the pseudonym Lewis Carroll."

The way he says this is all so matter of fact, like it is commonplace to be discussing the name of a stranger who supposedly created you out of the vastness of their imagination.

I'm a cruel woman, because my next question is spiteful. "What book are you from?"

There's no pause. "*The Sketch Book of Geoffrey Crayon, Gent.* by a man named Washington Irving."

"You are not Geoffrey Crayon."

A ghost of a smile touches his full lips. "No. I am not."

Midway up the stairs, my feet refuse to move farther. "Explain this to me. Explain how I can be from a book, that somebody made me up, and yet . . ." I pound a fist on my chest. "My heart beats. I feel pain. Pleasure. Love. Hate. I sleep. Eat. Grow. Age." But before he can say anything, I blurt out, "I'm real. I'm a person. I have memories—I've lived, Van Brunt. *Lived.* Are you telling me that my actions, my life . . . everything I've ever said or done is due to the words written down of some man who couldn't decide upon a name?"

My words ring throughout the stairwell and rattle the nearby windows, but Van Brunt acts if we're discussing the weather. "Not everything, Ms. Reeve."

I'm finding it difficult to find air to pull into my lungs, because I'm clawing for my breath. "This is absurd. It cannot be true. It cannot."

"All over the world," he says calmly, like I haven't been the first to rave to him about such existential fears, "there are people who believe in a higher power, one who created them, one who influences their actions and lives. Sometimes, when it all gets to be a bit much, I remind myself of this. Really, there is no difference in our existences and theirs. Ours just happen to be chronicled in enduring books."

"But—"

"Let us go to the library and find a cup of tea, Ms. Reeve." He gingerly offers me an arm. "It's not far now, just the next floor."

I am in the midst of a panic attack that would infuriate the Caterpillar if he were here, and Van Brunt wants to have tea. Laughter burbles out of me until I'm close to doubling over, but I take his arm anyway.

THE LIBRARY

"THIS," VAN BRUNT TELLS me, "is the heart of the Collectors' Society."

I wander through the mazes before me, grateful for the distraction. The splendid library Van Brunt brings me to spans two entire floors of the building we're in. Books line the walls and ornately carved wooden shelves are scattered throughout the room without rhyme or reason. Twisting, dark wooden staircases pepper the library like thin funnel clouds, while tables and upholstered, overstuffed chairs jut out between bookshelves. Stained-glass lamps litter the room alongside glass cases filled with various objects.

I lean in to examine the one closest to me. To my surprise, it's a threadbare carpetbag.

"Please don't touch the glass," Van Brunt says, and I'm startled back a few steps. "The attached alarms are deafening."

A glance around the glass case shows no wires, no bells. "Why is it protected?"

"It's a catalyst." He motions to a nearby pair of chairs. "Let me order us some refreshments." The cell phone is extracted once more just before he sits. "Do you have a preference? Chamomile? Darjeeling? Earl Grey?"

I wonder what he would think if I told him that I prefer a special blend that the Hatter makes. "Black tea, please."

I circle the chairs and rest my arms against the green velvet back of one facing Van Brunt.

After a moment of tapping on the phone, he leans back in the chair. "Some sandwiches will be brought up, too. Now. You had a question for me in the hallway. You wanted to know how you could be real. The answer is . . . I have no idea."

It isn't what I expected to hear.

"Nobody knows how Timelines are created, Ms. Reeve—except that they first start once a book has been published and embraced by readers. Or at least, that's when we first become aware of them. Time moves differently in each Timeline, so it's nearly impossible to pinpoint a true moment of birth. Is it magic?" He shakes his head. "I cannot say. This world we are in right now, though, holds no true magic. Not like some of the Timelines do." A wry smile curves one side of his mouth. "Such as yours, for example. Wonderland appears to be filled with much magic and mystery."

I lick my lips. "England does not."

"England in your Timeline does, though. It allowed you to move between what you thought was one world to another, but in reality are connected."

"And your original one? Does it have magic?"

"Debatable." And then, "You inquired about your actions, whether or not they are dictated by some intangible author. This is a much more complex question to answer. For the time period in which your origin story is told . . . we are not sure if the author fully dictates the moments of life captured on a page or somehow senses them and writes them down. Is there a higher being dictating these histories to authors? I'm not sure if we'll ever have such an answer. What we do know is that the span of a book is set and cannot be changed. Once published and embraced, though . . ." He shrugs lightly. "Life does as life does."

So many questions clamor for escape, but I need to control the burgeoning anxiety crawling through my veins. *One question at a time*, was one of the Caterpillar's favorite lectures. *Ask too many and articulation and comprehension will dwindle.* In the time it takes to come round the chair and sit, two deep breaths and two slow exhales are savored. I choose to systematically start at the top and work my way down. "What is the purpose of the Collectors' Society?"

He's surprised, I think, at the sudden change of direction, but his answer is just as smooth as the rest. "While we have many goals, the umbrella under which we work is the preservation and protection of Timelines. In that vein, we also promote establishing diplomatic ties between Timelines."

"How many Timelines are there?"

Another light shrug. "That is a question I often ask myself in the dead of night, Ms. Reeve."

"Are you the head of this Society?"

This one amuses him. "Currently, yes. But I have not always been so."

"How did you learn about such things?"

"Much in the same way as you did," he says evenly. "I was recruited by my predecessor and have spent the subsequent years working in various positions within the organization."

It can't be helped; a sly smile emerges. "Are you my predecessor?"

A bit of genuine laughter rumbles out of him. "Ms. Reeve, my reasons for recruiting you were honestly given. Have no fear—I have not targeted you as the heir to my position."

"How many people work for the Society?"

"It varies, but right now, there are . . ." He rubs his chin. "I'm almost ashamed to admit I do know the exact number offhand. We have at least one liaison within each Timeline we have made contact with. Over the years, some have retired and others have taken their places. Here at the Institute, there are approximately fifty full-time employees that reside within our dwelling at any one time."

A ding rings nearby, and a set of doors slide open. Dawkins appears, pushing a rolling cart rattling with clinking teacups, a teapot, and plates full of food. "Thought you'd want to know that somebody without credentials tried to access the back elevator," he tells Van Brunt.

From the little I know of him, I'd have placed a wager on very little evoking anything other than mild interest out of Van Brunt, but this bit of information has a thunderous expression darkening his face. "When was this? Why wasn't I notified? Did the alarms fail?"

Dawkins stops the cart a few feet away from where we're sitting. "Just about a half hour ago. Alarms were only triggered on the main floor. Wendy's already on the warpath and Finn's looking into the rest."

Van Brunt yanks his communication device out once more. "Who was it? Did you catch them on the security footage?"

Dawkins pulls the lid off the teapot and stares down into the liquid for a brief moment. "Well, that's the funny thing. The footage shows nothing at all. But Wendy swears the system indicates an unauthorized card was swiped."

A grunt escapes Van Brunt as he taps more fervently on the phone in his hands. "Could it be a glitch?"

"You know Wendy." Dawkins replaces the lid and pours a cup of tea. "She's insistent it's not, but unless it's a ghost, it's got to be, right?" A nervous titter follows before he passes me the cup. "Do you like sugar? Honey? Milk? I wasn't sure, and your story didn't really tell me, just said you drank tea, or at least, you know, were around tea, or helped yourself to some . . ." His face flames scarlet.

I'm positive mine turns ashen. "You've read whatever . . ." I force the word out. "*Book* I'm in?"

"Well, no, not really—not read it, per se, but more like scanned it when we prepped for your arrival. It's just, I couldn't help myself, see? I needed to know what the famous Alice was all about and—"

Fingers still flying across the surface, Van Brunt doesn't even look up when he addresses the young man. "That's enough, Mr. Dawkins. There is no need for further playacting. Ms. Reeve will know your character in due time, and will undoubtedly find games such as these as tiring as the rest of us."

An impish smile surfaces on the formerly stammering, awkward man in front of me. "Got to keep my game sharp and all, boss man."

My words are tart. "Are you from a book?"

He staggers back a step, a hand covering his heart. "You don't know of me?"

"Contrary to what you believe," Van Brunt mutters, "not everybody is as enamored with your legend as you are."

The naughty smile turns crooked. "Au contraire, boss man. Plenty of people find me irresistible."

Van Brunt is unimpressed, though. "Fellow thieves, perhaps. It's a good thing you were recruited when you were, Mr. Dawkins. I shudder to think what might have happened had you not been given a proper education and a legitimate reason to utilize your unique set of skills."

"The Society was lucky I agreed to come." Dawkins' grin spreads wide as he runs a hand through his hair. "I could have said no, and then where would you be?"

Van Brunt sets the phone down just long enough for a pair of chimes to sound from it. "The simple truth is we would be here all the same, and you would have lived the rest of your days out in a penal colony, stealing food and fighting for survival."

Dawkins' laugh is high-pitched and more than a little bit wicked. "And now I steal catalysts for you. One could argue I'm still fighting for survival, though. Right, boss man?"

"That'll do, Mr. Dawkins. Go see if you can find anything out of the ordinary in the sector indicated."

Dawkins salutes Van Brunt. To me, he offers a flourished bow. "Until next time, sweet Alice." When he leaves, his swagger is hampered by the slightest bowing of his gangly legs.

"A bit of advice, Ms. Reeve. Do not leave valuables on your person that can be easily accessed, at least in Mr. Dawkins' presence." He leans forward to pour himself a cup of tea. "He does so love a good challenge."

I watch as he slowly sips his tea. "You chose a thief to be your assistant?"

"Believe it or not, Mr. Dawkins' unique skill sets make him invaluable to our goals more often than not." He selects a small biscuit from the table. "Are you hungry, Ms. Reeve? I imagine you should be, as all you've had today is tea and treats. I can have the kitchen send up a more substantial meal for you, if you like. Dinner still isn't for a few more hours now."

I ignore the question, as the thought of eating right now is about as pleasurable as pulling nails off my toes. "Interesting how this is called the Collectors' Society," I murmur over the rim of my cup, "and not the Thieves' Society, as you apparently steal catalysts."

"Theft is such a nasty connotation, with nefarious undertones. While we," his lips twitch, "collect objects from Timelines, it is done so with the very best of intentions."

I turn toward the carpetbag encased nearby. "What was the intention behind this collection?"

"The same as any catalyst acquired," he tells me. "Preservation."

The threadbare carpetbag was obviously well-loved. "Does it hold a particular significance?"

Van Brunt discreetly brushes crumbs off his beard. "Ms. Reeve, one would think that, as tied to literature as we all are, we would have a handbook for our members. But, alas, none of us are as talented as those who first told our stories. I apologize that you will not get all your answers at once, but I hope you will stay with us long enough to learn what we know. But for now, I will tell you what I can. For some reason that is still yet unknown to us, each Timeline outside of the original has a singular object that represents its existence." He motions toward the carpetbag. "For example, this bag is the catalyst for a particular series of books that combine to form a singular Timeline we refer to as 1934/88TRA-MP."

"Explain the designations."

He's pleased by my question. "The numbers refer to the year or years of publication. The first three letters represent the author's surname; the last reference the title. For this particular catalyst, the Timeline associated with it has a series of books published between 1934 and 1988. While the titles vary, they all contain the name of the lead character Mary Poppins. MP." His smile is small yet indulgent. "The author's name was P.L. Travers. Thus, we have 1934/88TRA-MP."

I mull this over as I nibble on a biscuit. "You say these catalysts represent existence. What would happen if this bag was to be destroyed?"

His eyes shift away from me to focus on something in the distance. "Then the Timeline would be deleted, and all of the individuals living in it would be erased as if they were never there in the first place."

Chills sprout up and down my arms. Not lost, but *erased*. "What about the book? Is it deleted, too?"

Something I can't quite identify haunts his eyes. "No. The book remains. But it becomes only a book. Today we learned a Timeline associated with a very famous story was deleted. Somebody found its catalyst before we could and destroyed it."

My cup clatters onto the saucer in my lap. "Why would somebody do that?"

"We don't know," he says roughly. "I wish we did. Unfortunately, this is a recent development over the past decade. Somebody outside of the Collectors' Society has been targeting popular, famous Timelines and has been destroying catalysts."

"And yet you collect them."

His smile is wan. "We do. And then we store them here at our head-quarters, so that nobody can erase the lives of so many innocent people."

I place my plate back onto the cart Dawkins left. "You think this person might do the same to my Timeline. To Wonderland."

"It seems logical. Your story is immensely popular. Unfortunately, we have yet to be able to track down a catalyst associated with your Timeline, Ms. Reeve. Furthermore, we've sent a number of people into your world, only to have them fail to even find a way into Wonderland." The wan smile turns grim. "There are Timelines such as this that make catalyst acquisitions nearly impossible. You see, each of these worlds has its own set of rules, even more so when there is magic involved, so there is no consistency. For some reason, none of those in my employ are able to go into Wonderland."

I am numb once more, wondering if I ought to open myself up and reveal secrets I'd hoped to hide.

After a few moments of pained silence, Van Brunt says, "Some catalysts are easier to identify than others. Each is an item within the story that bears significant meaning and refuses to yield to time and age as others do. They—"

I throw caution to the wind. "Even if you send somebody in, it won't do any good. They'll never want to leave. It's the food and drink. If you have any while there, once you're past puberty, you become ad-dicted. Sending in your teams would be pointless."

He doesn't even let a beat go by. "And yet, you managed to escape. Did you go on a fast?"

A hint of bitter laughter ghosts out of me. "In a way, yes." My fin-gers curl into my skirt's fabric. "I also bartered for a potion of sorts from someone I knew that allowed me a small window of clarity." I twist the cotton until my fingers burn. "I say clarity, but it was really just a lesser degree of madness, because even then, I nearly stayed. I wanted to, you see. I ached to. Every muscle, every joint, every bit of skin and bones physically hurt when I forced myself out."

A thumb runs across his beard as he takes this in. "Yet you still left."

I wonder if he understands what I have just told him. "Yes."

I had to.

DOLLS AND BOXES

NEW QUESTIONS SURFACE, BUT for my recently acquired sanity, I place them on hold. I need to allow ones so freshly answered to breathe.

Van Brunt must sense this, because he uses his little communication box to summon Mary. She joins us in the library minutes later. "I swear, Brom, if you don't get the A.D. under control, I'm going to box his ears."

A heavy sigh escapes the large man. "Ms. Reeve, I must apologize for once more leaving you, but I must go address new security issues. Will you be all right with Ms. Lennox?"

Mary smoothly says, "Perhaps I ought to box *your* ears."

Amusement glimmers in his bright blue eyes. "Yes. Perhaps you ought to."

He's about thirty feet away when I call out, "Who is the Librarian?"

"Tomorrow, Ms. Reeve. You shall meet her tomorrow."

I turn back to find Mary picking through the remaining sandwiches. "I imagine that you feel as if your brain is melting right out of your head." She nibbles at a cucumber and cream cheese square. "At least, that's how it felt on my first day here. Bloody hell, this is awful." She tosses the sandwich down.

One of the best lessons I took away from Wonderland was that of not allowing others to see my weaknesses. I tell Mary, "This isn't my first pony ride."

For a moment, she stares at me as if I've stripped naked, but then a hearty laugh emerges. "I suppose for you something like this would be old hat, wouldn't it?"

Another ill-advised, involuntary bristle roils my skin. "Yes, I suppose so."

The humor fades away until all that's left is thoughtfulness. "I meant no insult."

I force myself to swallow back my carefully cultivated distrust of the unknown. "It's me who ought to be apologizing. You're right. This has been a long day, filled with many things that have . . ." I offer her a white flag smile. "Left my brain feeling as if it's melting out of my head."

"Brom is brilliant," she says, "but even he has difficulty explaining what most of us can barely wrap our minds around on a daily basis. It's a lot to take in, even for those who have lived with the reality for years now."

"Are you from a story?"

My question doesn't offend her. "It's called *A Secret Garden*." She leads me to the sliding set of doors she emerged earlier from. "A children's book, much like yours, although written a bit later." A small puff of annoyed laughter whistles between her lips. "Did Brom tell of your stories?"

I watch as she presses a small button on the wall. A children's book? How much of my life has been chronicled? "Not much," I admit. "But he did allude to multiple volumes."

"It was probably for the best. These sorts of things are best left for the Librarian anyway."

A ding sounds before the ornately decorated doors slide open. I'm embarrassed to find I've taken a step backward.

Mary's hearty laughter once more emerges as she takes a step into

the small room beyond. "This is an elevator. It's used for transporta-
tion."

I must look as angry as I feel, because she adds more contritely,
"Don't be embarrassed. I had the same reaction. It felt as if it were wiz-
ardly. Come on—let's go visit your apartment so you can have a bit of
time to rest. It's on the fifteenth floor, so unless you want to hike all the
way up, I advise you to step inside with me."

Once I'm inside, she presses a button labeled 15 on a golden panel riddled with numerals. The doors slide shut and the ground below
me lurches; I instinctively grab a bar circling the room. "You've been
assigned 1508," she is saying. "We're neighbors, you know. I'm right
across the hall."

The numbered buttons alight and count upward at a steady pace.

I feel her eyes taking me in. "Brom likes teams to be on the same
floor. I suppose for some people it makes sense, but sometimes it feels
like you can't quite get a proper breath without having your partner
breathing down your neck."

"Are we to be paired up as partners?" I ask as the lit-up numbers
switch from nine to ten.

"God, no. Sorry. Victor's my partner. You'll be working with
Finn—but as teams occasionally double up, and Victor and I tend to
find ourselves with Finn due to the obvious, I'm sure we'll be going on
plenty of assignments together."

I'm to work with Finn? That beautiful man? And what, exactly, is
the obvious?

"Victor was actually filling in for you today. Since Finn's last partner retired, he's been teamed up with various people. I was out with
just him last week, and for as many years as we've worked together,
you'd think it wouldn't have been weird, but it was." She scratches the
base of her neck as she turns toward me. "I just realized how that must
have sounded. It's not that it was weird working with him, per se. He's
excellent at what he does, and obviously is very easy on the eyes." A sly
smile curves her mouth. "But I've been teamed with Victor for the last
five years, and I guess there's a shorthand that develops between people
who work so closely together, you know?"

I do know, unfortunately. And I'm not keen on replicating such a
shorthand.

I refocus on the changing numbers. "I find it interesting that Van Brunt brought me in to supposedly save Wonderland, yet everyone assumes I'm here to stay."

She shrugs. "It's because everyone ends up staying."

The elevator slows once more. This time, when the doors slide open, Mary steps out into a richly decorated hallway. "This is our floor. Luckily, it's one of the quieter ones, especially our wing. Between Victor and his studies and Finn hardly ever being here, we've got it good."

The walls are dark green; the carpet below our feet is an unrecognizable pattern style. Mary turns to the right and heads down the hallway. "All of the living quarters have been modernized while retaining their historic flare." She looks back over her shoulder at me. "You'll be able to fully decorate your place however you see fit. I think most of us tend to favor what we know. It's like a museum in here."

Mary stops in front of a wooden door with a brass plaque bearing the numbers 1508 affixed to the front. A set of keys is extracted from her floral satchel. "Do you want to do the honors? It's the blue one—I put some nail polish on it so you'd always know which is home."

I take the keys from her. They're small, much smaller than I'm used to. And the doorknob is just that—a doorknob.

"Like I said, my place is across the hall." She points in the direction we just came in. "Victor's is that way." Her thumb hooks in the opposite direction, past my door. And then she motions to the door just before the turn. "There's Finn's."

A loud bang sounds nearby, followed by a string of indecipherable curses. Mary shouts out, "What did you blow up now?"

Something crashes, and a new set of angry words is unleashed. The door across the hall, midway between mine and Finn's, wrenches open. A dirty and disgruntled appearing Victor practically falls out. "Christ, Mary. I just can't get the solution right!"

She crosses the carpet and licks her thumb. "You couldn't wait for me, could you? And here I was just telling Alice that you were quiet as a dormouse." A bit of dirt close to his mouth is smudged away. "Now you've gone and made me look the liar."

Victor's dark eyes, shrewd and thoughtful, flick toward me as he stands statue still whilst Mary cleans another spot on his face with a licked-upon finger. "Are dormice truly quiet?"

It's a soft jab, but his message is crystal clear. "The one that I knew was more caustic than quiet."

"Yes," he murmurs. "It was, wasn't it?"

Mary swats his shoulder. "She'll think you a boor if you keep this up."

When his eyes turn back to his partner, they soften. "I *am* a boor. You just choose to ignore it." But then he sticks out a hand. "We haven't officially met yet. I'm Victor . . ." He pauses briefly. Clears his throat meaningfully before he says, almost as if he's resigned, "Uh, Victor Frankenstein. I'm one of the Society's resident doctors."

His handshake is brief and firm, and yet he appears unsettled, like he's waiting for a particular reaction. "What are you a doctor of?"

I must not give him what he expects, because Victor's muscles loosen in visible relief. "Officially?" He leans back against the wall closest to his partially opened door. "I specialized in general surgery, but many of the team here use me as their GP, too. You're free to do so as well, if you like."

My fingers curl so tightly around the keys that I can feel their imprint in my skin. "GP?"

"General practitioner, otherwise known as an all-around doctor." The grin that materializes can best be described as lazy. "They had those in your Timeline, correct?"

I take in the man before me, from his bare feet and frayed hems of his worn, blue pants to the thin, oil-streaked short-sleeved white shirt and the dark, twisted markings ringing both of his biceps. He's good looking, there's no doubt about it. Handsome, even. But the difference between him and the man I talked with earlier is that this one carries himself as if he knows his attractiveness is evident.

He's a peacock. And, thankfully, there isn't one ounce of attraction toward him to worry about.

"Yes," I tell him. "We had doctors in both England and Wonderland. Is it an uncommon occurrence?"

Victor's eyes light up. "No, no, doctors or their ilk are fairly common pretty much everywhere. I was just curious—oh, hell. I'd love to know more about the ones in Wonderland. Did they use magic in their practice? Or were they more akin to those in your England? I—"

"Are you forgetting that this is Alice's first day?" Mary pats his face. "Or that, just this morning, she was blissfully unaware of the Society or Timelines or nosy doctors who want to grill her when I'm sure she wants nothing more than to sit down and catch her breath?"

He has grace enough to appear sheepishly admonished. A hand rakes through his dark hair, leaving it askew. "Of course. Sorry, Alice. Maybe we can chat about this later."

"Perhaps," I allow.

"Did you hear about the security malfunction?" Mary asks.

Victor's startled. "What security malfunction? As soon as we finished eating, I popped up here for a nap and then got straight to work."

Mary crosses the hallway to stand next to me. "Wendy insists her system registered an unauthorized passkey attempt at the back elevator, but a review of the footage shows nobody there."

"What about the alarms?" Victor asks. "I heard nothing."

"Neither did I. Apparently, only the first floor suffered."

He scratches his forehead, his dark eyebrows veeing. "Did Brom shit a brick?"

"Brom," Mary says wryly, "wasn't informed of the incident until well after Finn investigated."

"That was probably wise." Victor shoves his door open wider. "After what happened last time, I'm surprised Finn told him at all. I sure as hell wouldn't."

"Finn didn't. The A.D. did, the little punk."

Victor glowers. "Fan-fucking-tastic. Tonight, they'll be cleaning up all the bricks that both Brom and Finn have shit, won't they?" He ends up shutting the door rather than going farther inside. "I ought to go downstairs and see what's going on. I'll let you know what I hear."

And then he comes over and presses a quick kiss against Mary's cheek. A hand briefly skirts across my shoulder. "See you around, Alice."

Once he's gone, I slide the blue key into the keyhole and turn the ordinary knob.

The flat I've been assigned is, well, extremely girlish. I'm talking *little* girlish—to the point its femininity is sickening. The walls are pastel pink, the floors hardwood and peppered with floral rugs. All of the art hanging on the walls is also floral and romantic, and porcelain dolls are found on nearly every surface.

Mary shuts the door behind us. "Don't mind Victor. Despite his lack of tact, he's got a good heart. And he's quite good at what he does."

My fingers trail across the shining, polished arm of a chair. Even the print on the furniture fabrics is floral. "You mean stealing catalysts?"

I can't tell if she's insulted or amused. "Well, that too, but he's a damn fine doctor. God forbid something goes wrong on an assignment, he's quite handy to have around."

I pick up one of the heavily embroidered pillows on a velvet couch. It's hideous. "Have things gone horribly awry on theses assignments before?"

The pillow says in cursive lettering centered above a tiara: *All Girls Are Princesses.*

"Not everybody appreciates having their belongings stolen," Mary is saying, "even if it's done under the noblest of circumstances."

How true that is. "Some thieves in Wonderland often found themselves without heads." I toss the pillow back onto the cushions. "At least, those who were caught."

She drops her purse down onto a small table. "The Queen of Hearts, right?" She pretends to shudder. "How macabre." And then, more cheerfully, "The housekeepers came in earlier today, so everything is clean." An arm sweeps in an arc before her, toward a hallway. "There are two bedrooms, one-and-a-half bathrooms, a good-sized kitchen—not that you'll need it much. Most of us tend to eat in the restaurant on the second floor during dinnertime. Which is six-thirty p.m. sharp, in case you're wondering." She smiles. "The chef here at the Society is divine. Communal dining, as weird as it sounds, seems to give us all a chance to catch up, especially if we've been gone on assignments or liaisons are in town."

We wander into a kitchen that looks drastically unlike any I've ever seen before. Everything gleams, all sleek metals and white-marble counters, and it makes me think back to my last kitchen and of the smoking stove that was left better unused. "How long do catalyst retrievals typically take?"

She lifts a silver lever and water pours from the faucet. "It depends, really. Some go incredibly fast. Others can take days, weeks. Very rarely, they can take months." The water is turned off before Mary turns toward an icebox. "They stocked the fridge with some basics. And I believe there's some tea in one of the cupboards." Her smile is wistful. "No matter how many years I am out of my Timeline, or work for the Society, the English in me refuses to let go of tea."

I want to talk about the Society; Mary wants to talk about tea. "How long have you worked here?"

"I'm one of the newer recruits, so . . . Officially ten years. Goodness. Has it really been that long?"

Which must mean there's precious little turnover.

Minutes later, I've toured the entire flat. Mary points out a stack of magazines on a dining table. While there are what she calls basics in the closet in my new bedroom, I'm encouraged to sift through the periodicals and select a new wardrobe to be ordered. Furniture can also be selected, if I do so choose to change what's already here. "After Sara retired," she tells me, "her apartment was left pretty much alone so there'd be a furnished place for the next recruit—barring it was a female, of course. But obviously not everybody has Sara's," Mary pretends to gag, "personal style preferences. Feel free to change what you want. If you desire the walls painted, just let Brom know and he'll have a team in here to change things for you." She picks up a small porcelain doll off of a vanity and grimaces. "I never got why she loved these so much. Or, for that matter, didn't take them when she left."

That doll, and all the others littering the apartment, will definitely be the first things to go. "Is the hope that I'll take this Sara's place?"

"Haven't you already?"

"Why did she . . ." I think back to the peculiar word Mary used, the one that indicated she must have been Finn's old partner. "Retire?"

"Sara is an incredibly sweet girl, the sort that always has a kind word for everyone that she meets. But . . ." she trails off meaningfully.

I'm blunt. "But sweet doesn't always cut it, not when lives are on the line."

She's pleased I've caught her drift. "No, it doesn't."

The room we're standing in is soft. A soft decor, as I've learned, does not represent a soft personality, though. Sometimes, it can be the delicate lure into insidiousness.

"The Society must not view me as sweet, do they?" I keep my words light, but I'm most keen to see how she responds. "Or is it they just see me as the only in they have to Wonderland?"

"If it's any consolation," she says matter-of-factly, "they don't see me as sweet, either."

Ah. She chooses to ignore my second question. "Why Mary," I ask, "were you not a good girl in your book?"

"I was a wretched bitch when I was younger," she says cheerfully. "And I can still be so as an adult. My filter is close to none. But, let us not be fully defined by what some people scribbled down centuries before, right? Books don't tell every detail, nor can they fully represent us as living, breathing individuals."

She doesn't sound the least bit bitter about her representation, and I respect her for that. "Do you know my story well?"

"I think everyone knows your story well."

"How was I portrayed?"

Her shrewd eyes study for me a long moment, but I do not cower under their weight. "Does it really matter? Would it change how you see yourself or your experiences? It's not as if you could go back and alter those words or memories, you know."

I tell her the truth, one I'd heard enough times that I've committed it to memory. "Knowledge is always one of the fiercest of advantages, and can be the difference between failure and achievement of purposes."

A slim finger taps against her lips as she considers this. And then, finally, plainly, "You pursued the truth, no matter how absurd it may have been."

I can live with that.

A knock sounds on the door, and for a moment, neither of us do anything. But then Mary says, "Aren't you going to answer that?"

Right. Of course. It's now my door, after all.

When I turn the knob and open it, I find the beautiful man I'd talked to hours before, his hands stuffed into his pockets. His hair is just a bit wet, his shirt and pants different from earlier. I'm given a smile that very nearly knocks the wind right out of my chest. "I wasn't sure if you were here or not."

I'm thrown by this reaction, unnerved that it could even be possible. "And yet you knocked anyway."

I watch how his lower lip is tugged between his teeth for the briefest of moments, like he's surprised I've said this. Goodness, he's got a beautiful mouth. "I'm reckless like that. I wanted to see how you were doing, especially after talking to Brom."

If I'm not mistaken, there's genuine curiosity and concern in his blue-gray eyes.

"Finn!" Mary calls out from inside the apartment. "Come in and see all the crap Sara left behind."

When he doesn't move, it takes me a few seconds to realize he's waiting for my permission to enter, not hers. And that leaves my stomach lurching, even if by just a tiny bit.

I step to the side. "Please, come in."

When he passes me, I get a faint whiff of his delicious scent. It's now tempered with a hint of stronger soap, and if I thought he'd smelled wonderful before, it's nothing like now.

They want me to work with this man? Oh, God. My determination to keep promises so freshly made to myself quadruples.

All work and no play makes Alice a good girl. Do you want to be a good girl, Alice?

I trail Finn into the sitting room. Mary has the couch filled with porcelain dolls in dresses. "I don't think I've scratched the surface on Sara's collection." Her hands fall to her hips. "For all I know, we'll hear poor Alice screaming in the middle of the night when she trips over one on her way to the kitchen. Or, god forbid, open a cupboard and have it fall out without warning. Christ, just thinking about these things popping up out of nowhere has given me the heebie jeebies. I may have to sleep with the light on tonight."

Finn peers down at the offending toys. "And to think you grew up in a place that was most likely haunted."

The sound that comes from Mary is almost audible sunshine. "Not by dolls, it wasn't."

"Maybe Alice likes dolls?"

I start at Finn's use of my name. But then, under the weight of both sets of eyes, I say smoothly, "I'm afraid I'm not much into such things."

"Of course you're not. You're an adult," Mary says. "Finn, call the A.D. and have him send some boxes up so we can pack away these nightmares-in-waiting." She reaches out and squeezes my arm. "And anything else you want gone. I'll be happy to help, unless you'd prefer to purge solo?"

When Finn tugs out what I think is a cell phone, I ask instead, "Who or what is the A.D.?"

"Oh, sorry. Brom's assistant—Jack Dawkins? People have called him the Artful Dodger because of his pickpocketing skills. I'd never say it to his face, as his ego is massive, but he's probably the best thief around. Every so often, one of us has to break into his apartment just to reclaim items he's nicked from fellow members. Just be warned—he likes booby traps, so there is that. And he's a bit of a skeevy perv, so you'll want to watch for that, too."

"Boxes are on their way up," Finn tells us.

Mary picks up one of the dolls and shakes it before him. "Why didn't Sara take these hideous things?"

"I'm positive she took a few." He takes it from her and stares down at the white face with heavily rouged cheeks. Something passes over his own face, fleeting emotions I can't quite decode.

"Seriously, though," Mary is saying. "I don't get why Sara never quite grew up."

Finn's sigh is filled with irritation. "We're not doing this again, especially as Sara's not here to defend herself."

Mary's a dog with a bone, though. "You've always had too many excuses for her. She—"

"Was adequate at her job," he says. "Not to mention, a genuinely nice person." And it's like he's daring her to say something further, because his eyes harden as he tosses the doll back onto the couch.

This makes Mary laugh. "See?" She nudges my shoulder. "I told you people think I'm a bitch."

I'm not touching that one. "Could we possibly deliver them to her? Perhaps she'd like them now." I glance around the flat. "Perhaps she'd like a lot of these things." All of them, if I'm being honest with myself.

Several seconds of silence pass by before Finn answers me. "Sara's dead."

I feel like a fool with her foot in her mouth, even though there was no way for me to know ahead of time. "I'm sorry to hear this. I'd thought she merely retired?"

"What he means is, technically, if you look at the time period she returned to and the one we currently inhabit, yes, Sara has been dead for quite some time now." Mary plops down in one of the velvet Queen Anne chairs and crosses her legs. "Around a hundred years, give or take."

I stare down at the dolls, loathing that confusion has been my constant state of mind for nearly the entirety of the day. "I thought you all could time travel?"

Thankfully, this doesn't amuse her. "We can edit into Timelines at different periods of time—although typically, it's only for member recruiting. It's Society policy to stick to the present as we don't like to mess around with possibly altering events and setting off the Butterfly Effect. Time moves differently in different Timelines, though."

Frustration over so many unfamiliar phrases and words being uttered is a bitter taste in my mouth. Butterfly Effect? "But surely, if she is a member of the Society, and these were hers in the first place, you could just pop in and give them to her. That couldn't possibly change the future, would it?"

"The thing is," Mary says, "some people, when they retire from the Society, are still active. They become liaisons or just members that occasionally interact with the Society. Then there are the rare people who, once they leave, choose to have nothing more to do with us. Sara was like that. She asked to be placed back into her Timeline at the exact moment she once left, and then basically washed her hands of us. We were too much for her."

"It's not fair to judge her for choosing a path that's different from ours." Finn's voice is low but firm.

Mary's mouth opens, but the look Finn gives her then has her lips snapping shut and her skin paling and then flushing considerably. Thankfully, another knock sounds at the door. Before I can move, Finn tells us he'll get it.

Once he's gone, Mary leans forward and whispers, "They were tight." She holds out two fingers twisted together. "Like, *super* tight. God forbid anybody have a negative thing to say about Princess Sara." She rolls her eyes. "I wouldn't be surprised to find out they once had a thing, you know? Although I hope not. God, I can't imagine. She probably laid there like one of her dolls."

Does she mean an attachment? "I take it you two weren't *tight*."

"Fuck, no. She was incredibly annoying. Always had to be little Miss Sunshine. Sorry, I'm being bitchy again. And on your first day, too. Normally I hide such thing for at least a week or so before letting this side show."

She's smiling, though. As bizarre as it may sound, I actually appreciate her honesty. And as I don't know this Sara, and it appears I never will, her words really have little bearing on me.

"Well, well," somebody drawls. "We meet again. I knew you couldn't stay away from me."

I turn around to find Jack Dawkins pushing a small cart with thick, brown sheets that look to be some kind of paper, a crooked grin on his rubbery face. He's winking seductively at me.

Finn comes up from behind and smacks him on the back of his head. "Nobody finds that shit charming."

Dawkins laughs. "Plenty of ladies find me irresistible."

"Blind and deaf ones, perhaps," Mary muses. "Or ones with head trauma that have left them with lowered IQs."

Dawkins ignores this. "Although things have soured between us, I would truly appreciate you not messing with my game. Just because we didn't find our happy ending doesn't mean Alice and I won't."

A little bit of vomit surges up my throat, alongside an urge to find a sword and show him exactly what I think of that.

Finn picks up one of the large sheets and expands it until it forms a square. "Thanks for the boxes." When Dawkins doesn't move, he adds, "Leave the cart. We might need it to send things down into the basement."

Dawkins rubs the back of his head. "I can stay an' help."

Mary stands up. "You can go through the boxes afterward. Get moving."

Van Brunt's assistant places his hands over his heart, wincing. "You wound me, Mary. After all we've been through, how can you treat me like this?" To me, he says mournfully, "Love is so fleeting. Ours won't be, will it?"

"The day you genuinely fall in love will be the signal of the End of Days," Mary mutters.

I watch Finn rip strips off a roll and use them to seal the flaps of the box shut. "Jack? Just one more thing before you leave." He straightens up. "If you ever go running your mouth to Brom again like you did this afternoon, especially before you have any facts to back up your claims, I'm going to have to kick your ass."

This makes Dawkins laugh. But it also has him finally on his way.

Mary grabs one of the folded boxes and sets about opening it. "Just to clarify, the A.D. and I never had a thing." She shudders.

"But . . . the chemistry between you two was undeniable. I could have sworn . . .?"

Both heads jerk up in surprise. I hide my smile by dipping my head while I claim one of the newly constructed boxes.

We spend the next hour packing up the bulk of Sara's things. While I appreciate the gesture behind not originally leaving the flat empty for me, it feels far too awkward to live amongst this Sara's things. All of her dolls, all of her flowery wall art and embroidered pillows, all of her little porcelain figurines are put into boxes. During this time, I listen more than talk as Finn and Mary chat about a variety of subjects both related to Society matters and not. Despite their prior disagreements over the flat's previous inhabitant, there's an ease between the two that I envy in a way.

Mary leaves to go help Victor with one of his experiments. I know I ought to ignore him, or keep him at arm's length, but there's something about Huckleberry Finn that idiotically, impossibly draws me in like a moth to a flame.

So I talk to him.

I like his voice. It's got just a hint of a rasp and is warm and alluring. I like how he talks with his hands, too, and how he's all too aware of such actions and tries to combat them by stuffing them far too often into his pockets. I like how his eyes are so expressive and yet guarded all at once. I like that when he moves, it's done with confidence.

He tells me about the building, and of many of the people who live here. I ask about views beyond my window, and he's patient with his explanations.

My knees weaken when he asks if there's anything he can get for me, because he's been in my shoes. It shakes me, these sudden, inconvenient feelings. I don't want nor need them. Thankfully, though, Mary reappears with Victor in tow. They've brought wine, beer, cheese, and crackers, and we all sit down in my emptied living room and share the treats. They ask me questions, but I always manage to divert them back toward things I wish to know about them.

When memories creep up upon me, ones of ease I've shared with others, I force them back. There's no use in reliving these memories, no point in wondering *what if* or *what once was* no matter how desperately I wish things differently. For now, I need to focus on the people before me, the ones I'm supposedly to work with. I need to take in every little detail I can, because what I told Mary earlier is all too valid.

Knowledge is always one of the fiercest of advantages a lady can have.

ALARMS

WAKE UP TO sirens.

I'm out of bed, disoriented and stumbling toward the closet in this new, unfamiliar bedroom. The ear-blistering wail seems to be coming from both inside and outside my apartment, leaving my bones rattling as I fumble for a sweater or robe to wrap around myself.

Beyond the main door to the apartment, I find a shirtless Victor, his arm around a tiny satin-robed Mary. He's shouting into one of those hand-held phones. The moment they notice me, though, Mary disentangles herself and comes over to where I am.

I raise my voice to lift above the din. "What's happening?"

Before she can answer, Finn's door wrenches open. He stumbles out, hopping on one foot as he yanks a shoe on. I try not to stare at how his shirt is not pulled all the way down, or how the last few buttons of his well-fitting trousers are undone, too, but I fail miserably.

One would think surreptitiously staring at him for hours as he helped pack up dolls would have been enough, but it appears I've yet to learn my lesson about beautiful men. And it's patently ridiculous, because I don't know him, he doesn't know me, and chances are I'll be leaving once we find the catalyst for my Timeline anyway.

Suddenly, the building goes silent, leaving Victor's last few words echoing down the hallway. There are a few other people in their pajamas or robes, milling about outside their doors.

Victor passes his phone over to Mary, who tucks it into one of her pockets. "Couldn't hear a bloody thing anyway. What's going on?"

Finn finally tugs his shirt down, covering what appears to be a well-defined chest. Frabjous. I'm still staring, aren't I? What in the world is the matter with me? "An attempt to open a window on the second floor, just off the fire escape."

I tighten my sweater around me, my hands crisscrossing beneath my chin. "Do the windows here not open?"

It's almost as if he's just now realizing I'm standing outside my door, because Finn's eyes widen for the teeniest moment as they flick from the top of my head to my bare toes. "Um, yeah, of course they do." His voice is adorably husky, like he'd also been rattled straight out of sleep. "We have to enter a code into the system, so security measures can be set into place, though."

"What he means," Victor says, "is that little invisible laser beams are shot out across open windows, and if tripped, an alarm such as this sounds. I wonder if somebody simply forgot to enter their code."

Yet another thing I feel ignorant about. Laser beams?

"Wendy says it was tripped from outside," Finn is saying. "You guys ought to go back to bed. I'll go down and meet up with Brom, see what's going on."

His slightly raised voice carries down the hallway, and it's enough to send the remaining curious stragglers back into their flats.

For a moment, Victor says nothing. But then he holds out a fist—and just when I think there might be posturing or fighting, Finn holds his out and knocks it against Victor's. "Update in morning?"

"Of course."

Mary yawns as she rubs at her wild hair. "G'night, then." But she pauses before she turns back toward her door. "Oh, and Finn?"

"Yeah?"

"Finish buttoning up your pants. Your blue boxer briefs are distracting me." She nudges the man next to her. "See? I keep telling you boxer briefs are the way to go. Look at how yummy they can be."

A slight, charming blush steals across Finn's cheeks as he turns around to do so. Victor rolls his eyes, though. "Come on, then. We can discuss an overhaul of my undergarments behind closed doors. Good-night, Alice. Finn, we'll talk in a few hours."

And now I'm blatantly staring as I watch Victor follow Mary into her flat. Well, now. Partners, indeed.

"You should get some rest, too," Finn is saying. "You must be tired, what with all that's gone on today."

He's the one who appears tired. "We're to work together, correct?"

He shoves his hands into his pockets and rocks back on his heels. "That's the plan."

"Is it a plan you support?"

I've thrown him a bit off, which is nice, considering how he managed to throw me a little off over the course of a singular day. "Of course. I wouldn't have agreed to it if I didn't."

"Nobody asked whether I agreed or not."

And now I've thrown him a bit more, because his eyes widen. "Um—"

"I'm not airing complaints. I'm merely stating facts. That said, if I'm to be your partner, I ought to go with you to investigate whatever is going on."

"You don't have to. It's late, and—"

"I need to put something on that's more conducive to interacting with people. Do you mind waiting for me, since I still don't have the best lay of the land?"

I'm pleased when he doesn't argue further. "As long as it's quick." He's smiling, though. It's small and it's bemused, but it's a smile all the same.

I push open my door. "You can wait inside."

"Are you sure? Because I can—"

"You spent the better part of the afternoon and evening inside my flat. How is this any different?"

"It's three-thirty in the morning," he says, but his feet cross my threshold.

I shut the door behind him. He's got manners. My knees register that with yet another ridiculous, inappropriate weakening. "Victor is inside of Mary's flat at just such a time."

The chuckle I'm given is warm and delightful. "That's different."

I flip on a lamp in the sitting room and tell him to make himself comfortable.

Inside my closet, I flip through the foreign clothing that hangs there. Are these Sara's? I have no idea, and didn't think to ask earlier. I'm uncomfortable with the idea of wearing her castoffs, alongside living amongst her things and working with her partner, but I figure the clock is ticking. So I grab a pale-green dress that barely grazes my knees and throw it on, and then rummage around until I find a sensible pair of boots.

I twist my hair up into a bun and head back out to find Finn sitting on the edge of the couch. "Shall we?"

Minutes later, we're on the second floor and inside an office just off the kitchen for the Institute's restaurant. Wendy, Brom, Dawkins, and a few men and women I've yet to formally meet are already inside, talking and peering at a large window. Lights flash beyond the pane.

"Tardy twice in the same day?" Wendy mutters to Finn. She's got pens sticking out of the green hair piled high on her head as she clicks away on the metal box from earlier in the day. "Who are you and what have you done with the Finn I know? For a moment, I worried you slept through the noise."

Before he can answer, I say stiffly, "It was my fault. I asked him to wait for me."

Wendy looks up in surprise, but my presence doesn't faze Brom one iota. He acknowledges me with a nod of the head before returning to a conversation with another man.

"You texted me," Finn's saying to Wendy. "And I texted in return. So, obviously I did not sleep through the alarm."

She grunts, her focus returning on the box in front of her. There are words on it, much like the phones they're carrying. Finn leans into me and says quietly, "It's called a computer. Specifically, a laptop."

"Was I so obvious?"

He shrugs, smiling that charming small smile of his again, and I remind myself there are more important things to focus upon than smiles and delicious-smelling men. "Maybe just a little."

I take my eyes off of him and angle them toward a flashing light. "Perhaps I need paper, so I can keep track of all of this."

One of the women, dressed in a man's suit, presses a finger against her ear. "There are scratches alongside the window frame, sir."

Van Brunt frowns as he strokes his neat beard. "Have photos sent directly to my phone."

"Dammit!" A fist smashes down against the wooden desk Wendy's sitting at. "Camera 2-04 was disabled!"

Van Brunt's eyebrows lift high. "And pray, how did one of your cameras become disabled, Ms. Darling?"

She briefly looks up from her computer, rage flashing in her eyes. "I'm working on it."

Van Brunt turns to Finn. "One might say that's more bold than coincidence. What have you found out?"

"Franklin Blake reported that the man and woman seen lurking around the Institute last week were, in fact, present earlier today." Dawkins comes over and hands Finn a folder while my new partner is speaking. "They were tracked seven blocks away before they entered a shop. They stayed there for approximately two-and-a-half hours before they exited into a taxi. From there, they were tracked to a warehouse in Queens."

Van Brunt rocks on the heels of his immaculately polished shoes, his arms behind his back. "What is the nature of the warehouse?"

Finn flips through the folder before extracting several sheets of paper. I'm surprised when he passes them to me rather than Van Brunt. "Officially, restaurant supplies, although it's been raided by the police twice in the last five years for drug distribution."

"And the shop they went to?"

"Ex Libris. It's a secondhand bookstore owned by a F.K. Jenkins."

I glance down at the papers I've been handed. On top, there is a pair of colored photographs featuring a man with slicked-back blonde hair, a closely cropped beard, and large black-rimmed rings forming holes in his earlobes. The woman is almost sickishly pale and reed thin. Wild dark hair dipped snow white at the ends curl down toward her waist. Another sheet logs dates, times, and locations, and several others that feature noted physical details on the duo.

Van Brunt moves closer to the window. "Have you spoken with

Jenkins?"

"I went to the Ex Libris bookstore at approximately 9:47 this evening to do so." Another colored photograph is extracted and passed over to me. "Police records show Jenkins is sixty-two, was born in a small town in Nebraska, and has been arrested four times. Twice for disorderly conduct, once for petty theft at the age of eighteen, and once for failing to pay for parking tickets."

The corners of Van Brunt's mouth tick upward. "How many tickets?"

"Twenty-four. The arrest was two years ago, and he was released within an hour. He no longer has a car nor a driver's license."

I stare down at the photo. F.K. Jenkins is an immensely rotund man with a sour face. Even at the angle he was captured within, his head turned off to the side, there is little doubt that he possesses eyes both sharp and calculating.

Van Brunt runs a finger along the edge of the window. A face appears beyond the glass and illuminated by a beam of light, mouthing: *photos sent.* Van Brunt nods and turns back toward Finn. "Anything else of note?"

"The shop is four-story and cluttered. Stacks of books fill nearly every available surface. It's obvious there isn't much turnover, and many of the items for sale are in poor condition and priced accordingly. When I went to the second floor, which is also filled with books, there was a locked door marked *no admittance*; downstairs there was an out-of-order bathroom, a small office behind the sales desk, a door leading to the alley behind the building, and another locked door. From what I can tell, Jenkins resides on the third floor. I'm unclear about the purpose of the fourth floor, though. Building schematics have it officially listed as an attic."

"Any books of note?"

Wendy's fingers still over her computer as her head snaps up. Everyone else in the room goes silent as they turn to face Finn and Brom.

Finn says, "All were present."

I shift through the paperwork Finn has handed to me find a listing of book titles. At the top of the list is *The Ingenious Gentleman Don Quixote of La Mancha*, the book whose Timeline was deleted recently. Other titles that quickly catch my eye are: *The Three Musketeers, Ham-*

let, and *Anna Karenina.*

"Are you saying you think this F.K. Jenkins is the culprit?" one of the men nearby is asking.

"All theories are subject to verification, Mr. Fleming." Van Brunt crosses his arms. "Finn, I want the identities of the other two as soon as possible."

"Aha!" Wendy thrusts a fist into the air; the multitude of bracelets lining her arm clatter. "They think they were so clever, disabling 2-04, did they? Too bad that Camera 3-06 and the one from the street light across the way were in fine working condition. I've got a visual on the perpetrators." She grins. "As an added bonus, I've got a little something-something to show you from earlier today, too, thanks to that asshat in the next building's shoddy security system." A hand is lifted up so she can blow on her nails whilst swinging them back and forth. "I guess we have a purpose for his rabid conspiracy theory paranoia after all."

Everyone closes in on Wendy and her computer, but it isn't until Finn places a warm hand against the small of my back that I join in the small semi-circle. The touch is brief, and I'm dismayed that the skin beneath my dress tingles long after his hand moves away.

It makes me nauseous to think that such a feat is even a possibility.

Upon her computer, a grainy black-and-white moving photograph (*video,* Finn quietly lets me know) flips back and forth between views. There is a man dressed in dark colors, his head covered by a distinctive hat that has a long bill in the front that leaves his features in shadows. He's got a belt of sorts around his waist, filled with what appears to be tools. One is extracted; it's a small box he slides up to the side of the window. Buttons are punched as he squats down on his haunches.

"That little bugger," Wendy marvels viciously. "He thinks he can hack my system."

Suddenly, the man leaps to his feet, startled. The box is shoved into the belt and he flips over the railing with a competence I haven't seen in months.

Wendy taps at the letters on her computer. "Here's the earlier attempt."

This time, there are two people in the video—both in dark garb and similar in height. The faces are obscured due to the distance of the camera angle. A small rectangle is extracted and pressed against something I cannot see. Within seconds, the people startle and flee the scene.

If the people gathered round wanted pictorial proof they'd caught F.K. Jenkins in the midst of treachery, they've come away sorely disappointed. None of the figures presented remotely mirror what the photograph in my hands shows.

A snort escapes Wendy. "What a bunch of fucking imbeciles."

"I want security beefed up," is Van Brunt's immediate response.

Her face flushes red with indigence. "Did you not just watch what I did? There's no way those freaks are getting through my system."

"Pride cometh before the fall, Ms. Darling. And no system is infallible. No harm can come from attempting to better our defenses. I'll expect an update at our afternoon briefing later today."

She sighs, but grudgingly offers a salute.

Soft chatter resumes in the room as Van Brunt heads back over to the window. I ask Finn, "How many people know about the Society?"

"Thousands," he admits, "but most of those numbers are liaisons— or contacts—within Timelines. Here in New York, though? Pretty much only the people in this building."

"You are a secret society, then."

One corner of his mouth lifts up. "*We're* a secret society, yes."

"Why hide the truth?"

"Not everyone is like you. Not everyone can easily accept that there are worlds outside of their own, or different peoples, or even magic."

"Who says I've easily accepted this all?"

He accepts the papers back and stuff them into the folder. "You did, for the most part."

I lift an eyebrow. "I most certainly do not remember us having such a conversation."

"Ah," he says, "but we did. Upstairs, in the hallway. When you insisted on coming with me."

For a moment, I wonder if my memory is muddled once more, like it was for so many weeks at the Pleasance, and I'm left uneasy. "I'm positive I did not say such a thing."

"Your actions told me," he says as we head toward the elevator, and I'm right back in Wonderland, sitting beneath a red-and-white mushroom.

"You're sloppy, you're loud, and you talk too much."

Sometimes, I wondered why I willingly came back time and time again for such abuse.

The Caterpillar dragged his hookah over to the pillows we were lounging on. The sun was hot that day, the air heavy and acrid with each smoke ring he blew. I was never offered a puff on these visits—not that I ever would have taken one, but sometimes I wondered what it would take for just such a gesture.

"What's wrong with talking?"

His beady eyes narrowed as he grunted. I had to wait nearly a full minute before he answered. "It's hard to hear others when your own words overwhelm your thoughts."

"How am I to get answers to my questions, if I do not ask?"

A perfect smoke-shaped jabberwocky floated away from us, its jaws snapping. "The most truthful answers are found through observation. Words allow lies." One of his little silk slippers dangled from a foot as he huffed in irritation. "For example, I can say that I am the White King."

I'd laughed. "Don't be silly. You don't look a thing like him. For one, you're a caterpillar. Secondly, you're much older than he is. And thirdly—"

More forcefully, "I am the White King, Alice."

I was annoyed, but more so weary of the constant riddles. "Of course you aren't."

He blew a perfect representation of the White King's face. "I've said I am, so I must be."

"Fine. Two can play this game. I'm the Caterpillar," I announced.

"You are a child," was his retort, "who will never achieve her goals if she doesn't grow up."

"I'm eighteen!"

He merely puffed away on his hookah.

"Even in Wonderland, those who are eighteen are adults."

He continued to smoke in silence; his beady eyes, once narrowed, glazed over before eventually closing.

"I don't have to listen to you, you know."

He blew a smoke Alice in a little dress, running in circles.

But I continued to sit with him for the rest of the afternoon, even though no more words were said by either of us. I was continuously a failure in his eyes, the worst of his pupils who just couldn't seem to learn her lessons.

THE LIBRARIAN

"**S**O, YOU'RE THE FAMOUS Alice from Wonderland."

The only word that could aptly describe the woman sitting in the chair across from me is sumptuous. Long, dark hair, pale-blue eyes rimmed with black fringe, and perfectly molded lips are only a few of the features that have me feeling as if I'm the plainest, homeliest girl to ever be born.

"I am Alice," I say carefully.

She smiles and leans back in the rich leather chair, crossing her legs as she takes me in. "You're a bit different than expected." Her accent is soft and one I can't immediately place. Indian, perhaps?

"So I keep hearing."

"I'm the Librarian." No name is offered—only a title. It's a small yet familiar comfort, even though the feel of her eyes upon me is distinctly uncomfortable.

We're sitting in a large office at the west end of the library, sharing breakfast. I've got my tea, she's got strong coffee, and together we've picked at plates of fruit and toast in tangible silence for the better part of three minutes.

"How are you liking the Institute so far?"

I run a thin line of jam across a dry piece of toast. "I've been here too little to form an adequate opinion."

She chuckles. "Across Timelines, all people tend to form opinions nearly instantly. It's only later, after observation and experience, do they decide whether or not their initial feelings were spot-on."

I gingerly set my knife down on the edge of my plate. "I find it best to withhold judgment until I do have those experiences."

Her slim fingers curl around a white cup bearing black words that I am only partially able to make out. Elegant script says: *In paginis mundūs*. "That is a noble sentiment you hold, yet I wonder," she muses, "if it can actually be put into practice." Her meaning isn't lost on me. An impression has already been made of the famous Alice sitting before her, and I have yet to figure out if it is favorable or not.

"I've asked for you to join me this morning so we can have a chat." She slowly sips her coffee before continuing. "I'm sure Brom has mentioned me to you."

Amongst others.

"The Collectors' Society is somewhat like a living organism. Its members act as functioning body parts. If we were to argue that Brom is the brain, I would then follow as the heart."

My interactions with hearts have not always been favorable in the past. "What would I be?"

Her smile would do the Cheshire-Cat proud. "That is a most excellent question."

I must lose my mind, because I continue on when I ought not to care one iota which ridiculous body part I'd be in this bizarre analogy. "I am told I am Huckleberry Finn's partner. If we continue with this analogy, what would he be?"

A strawberry is dipped into clotted cream. "You're *told?*"

My frustration rises, but I do not give into temptation to let her know I've had enough word games for an entire lifetime.

"It was my impression you already stepped willingly into that role."

I nearly burn my tongue, the tea she's poured me is still so hot. "The question stands."

"One might argue that Finn is the right-handed fist." She's completely serious as she tells me this, no lingering hints of amusement present to suggest a game.

Interesting.

"Each member of the Society plays an important function," she says after savoring the sweetened strawberry. "Even when there are times when one might feel as if they are a missing limb."

The back of my hand covers a carefully constructed yawn, although images of people already met fly through my mind. Is she trying to tell me something? Or, is she trying to warn me?

"Joining the Society," she continues, "is not something to be taken lightly."

I allow a bite of toast before answering. "I do not believe I've officially joined your little club. I'm here for a singular goal, am I not?"

Her laughter is soft yet darkly charming. "Then why is it, just hours ago when you could have been sleeping or plotting your way back to the asylum we found you within, you insisted on throwing yourself immediately into Society matters?" Her head tilts to the side. "Come now. You know as well as I, had you truly wished to stay in your England and live the boring, reclusive life you feared you'd been resigned to, you would not have followed Brom through his door. To stay in your Timeline, on the path you were . . . it never would have lasted. Sooner or later, you would have chased yet another adventure."

In my lap, my fingers curl inward until nails bite skin.

"You sought excitement as a child multiple times. And then, when you were grown, when you should have been out in polite society, you chose to go back to Wonderland." She gently shakes her head. "No, Alice. It has always been your intent to be *more than*. That is why you are here, with fellow members and their intentions, and it is those which bind us together."

"What is your intent?"

My question pleases her. "Those that concern you best are my efforts to ensure the safety of Timelines."

So. She's going to play her cards close to the vest, too. "And yet, you are a librarian. Or rather, *the* Librarian."

She reaches over to her nearby desk and picks up a pair of worn, red books with gold trim. One is held aloft for me to see—in the middle of the cover is a golden illustration of a girl clutching a pig. A quick twist of the book shows me the spine; words in matching gold read: ALICE'S ADVENTURES IN WONDERLAND.

I forget how to breathe. My body forgets how to pump blood through my veins.

The second book is help up for my inspection. Another golden picture is on the cover, one of a stern queen. The spine reads: THROUGH THE LOOKING GLASS.

Curling my fingers into fists barely keeps me from snatching them out of her hands.

The Librarian sets the second book down in her lap so she can reclaim the first. The cover is opened, a few pages are sifted through. "The girl in these pages liked to ask questions. She was constantly trying to figure out how the world she was in worked."

Although I'm positive my face is drained of all color, there is no doubt my cheeks match the red of those books.

"Some members, upon learning the Society's secrets, become fixated on the pages that chronicle bits of their lives. Some even become obsessed." She flips the book to show me an illustration of a girl looking up at a cat in a tree. "Obsession is rarely a good thing. Wouldn't you agree?"

Goose pimples break out along my arms. There's a smile on the cat, one that isn't entirely docile in nature.

"I'd like to think that, being familiar with the repercussions of obsessions, you would want to shy away from such things. Let's just say that some books are best left upon shelves, with pages filled with mysteries rather than the known."

"And yet," I say, voice embarrassingly hoarse, "I do know what those pages contain, don't I? So they can't be too much of a mystery."

She closes the book and sets it on the table next to her mug. "Living through something and reading another person's opinions and views of your choices and existence are two very different things. There are lenses looked through, colored perceptions taken into account. Very little good has ever come of any member of the Society reading such things."

"But they do read each other's."

A dainty shrug displaces a chunk of her lustrous hair. "When necessary."

"Have you read your stories?"

She folds her napkin and sets it on the table. "Who says I'm from a story?"

When I don't answer, the Librarian stands up. She's so tiny that I wonder if the top of her head would come to my chin. "I'm off to go get a case ready for the catalyst you and Finn retrieve. I will see you two when you come back."

I'm on my feet as well. Sure enough, I tower over her. "The one from Wonderland?"

"Goodness, no." One of her hands briefly curls around my shoulder. "You're not ready for that one yet. Oh, and Alice? A word of advice."

"Yes?"

"You're going to have to decide whether or not he's worth your trust. That decision is going to have far-reaching consequences."

My eyes narrow. "Trust who? Van Brunt?"

But she exits the room, leaving me with far more questions now than I arrived with, and still far fewer answers than I'm comfortable with.

"ARE YOU NERVOUS AROUND weapons?"

I conceal the unwanted smile forming by purposely turning away so I may examine more closely one of the large paintings hanging in the hallway leading to Van Brunt's office. "Are you asking if I occasionally find myself besieged by the vapors when I'm in the presence of strong men wielding weapons only masculine hands might possess?"

That charming blush I first saw in the early hours of this morning steals across Finn's cheeks once more. He rubs at his hair, his head ducking as he chuckles ruefully. "Vapors . . . As in fainting? Shit, put it that way and my question sounds sexist, doesn't it? I haven't heard that word in forever."

"Sexist?"

"Gender discrimination."

Hmm. "Are modern-day ladies much prone to vapors?"

"None that I know."

"And from your story—or rather, your Timeline?"

"Maybe," he admits, and there's a cautiousness to him I haven't seen before. "But I think a lot of so-called fainting spells were really just excellent examples of acting."

"Then yes," I tell him coolly, although I am secretly amused. "That does sound rather sexist."

He starts. "I didn't mean—"

"I've never fainted before. Have you? Perhaps men in this modern day and age are now the vapor-prone."

"I faint all the time."

It's my turn to start. His face is serious, his eyes earnest as he says this to me. A quick glance of his body, from the thick boots on his feet to the plaid shirt with sleeves rolled up over strong arms, leaves me doubtful, though. "Truly?"

"Sorry, no." An impish smile curves his mouth, one that has me inappropriately itching to touch my fingers to his lips. "I can't think of a time I've ever fainted."

Van Brunt has summoned Finn to his office to discuss matters, whatever they may be. Luckily, once I left the library, I intercepted my new partner on the way to do so, only to nearly tear my hair out when he suggested, when questioned as to why I wasn't also informed about the meeting, that I ought to take at least a few days to acclimate to my new surroundings.

"I don't need a few days," I told him.

He was not dissuaded. "Most people tend to—"

"I am not most people."

We had a stand-off, and it was then it became somewhat obvious this man before me was used to getting his way.

I told him, "Don't treat me gently, Finn. My looks are deceiving. I will not break, no matter how many times I am thrown to the ground."

And then he said, slowly, carefully, "You were found in an asylum for the insane."

I'd rather wanted to punch him right then, beautiful face and all.

He backpedaled, his apology sincere as he attempted to explain he meant it'd been obvious I was at the Pleasance for a reason, a healing reason, and that it was certainly understandable if I wanted to take my time with everything that's been thrown at me. While his flustered, flurry of words grudgingly charmed me, they also made me want to prove him wrong. Because, I am quite used to getting my way, too.

So now we are wandering down a long corridor toward Van Brunt's office, and it's obvious Finn's doing his best to try to engage me when I can tell he'd rather me go back upstairs, or at least go find Mary and do something patently idiotic and wasteful of my time, like redecorate his former partner's flat.

Sexist, indeed.

"How convenient," I tell him now. "I've never fainted, either. And I most certainly wouldn't do so simply by being around some weapons."

Something in him hardens and softens all at once. "Violence isn't pretty, Alice."

"No," I admit. "It isn't, is it?"

He studies me for a long moment, his blue-gray eyes narrowing significantly. It's almost as if he's trying to peel back my defenses and ferret out all of my secrets. Too bad for this Huckleberry Finn I have no intention of letting him or any other person inside this building to do so. I've worked too hard to place my past behind me—or at least wrestle it into compartments I can deal with.

"Perhaps the question I should have asked is: Are you familiar with any weapons?"

I offer him a falsely sweet yet coquettish smile. "Yes."

I wait for him to ask which ones, but he surprises me by simply saying, "Good."

Minutes later, we are inside of Van Brunt's large office. There are paintings lining the walls, ones of large, unsmiling individuals who all hold in their hands a large bronzed plaque bearing a darkened logo. It's circular, almost clock-like in nature and yet similar to a compass, propped upon the open pages of a book. The same Latin words from the Librarian's cup, now expanded, ring the shape: *In paginis mundūs invenimus. In verbis vitam invenimus.* A quick scan of the room finds the oft-painted plaque hanging prominently above Van Brunt's massive desk.

My Latin has always been abysmal, much to the disappointment of my learned father, and for the first time in a long time, I wish I'd listened more closely to his urgings.

"How did you find the Librarian this morning, Ms. Reeve?"

I tear my eyes away from the plaque, its words now firmly rooted in my mind. "Smug."

Finn coughs into a fist, but Van Brunt is oddly unsurprised by this assessment.

I can't help but stir the pot. "We discussed books and body parts and their functionality. It was a most invigorating discussion. I wonder, though, who the breasts of the organization are? Or perhaps the testicles? Personally, I would love to know who the arse is. Is that person the fool of the group?"

Whatever Finn has just murmured under his breath may not have been clear, but it makes the corners of my mouth lift all the same.

It's Van Brunt's turn to cough. "Good. Excellent."

Something beeps, but the man behind the desk chooses to ignore it. "I'd hoped to ease you into our work, Ms. Reeve, but something has come up, leaving me little other choice than to send the two of you on a quick retrieval mission. Upon reflection, it will be an excellent opportunity for you to see how assignments go."

The cracking of knuckles has me glaring at Finn. He sounds bored when he asks, "Timeline?"

A good five seconds pass before Van Brunt says, "1814AUS-MP."

"You've got to be shitting me."

I'm startled enough to lose a few centimeters between me and my chair at this explosion.

"Finn," Van Brunt says, "I know this isn't ideal—"

The man next to me is out of his seat, his hands flat on his boss' desk. "Is she here at the Institute?"

"I spoke with Mrs. Knightley via communique this morning." Without breaking eye contact, Van Brunt straightens a stack of papers on his desk.

Finn doesn't back down, though. "Send Victor and Mary instead. There is no fucking way I'm going, not after what happened last time."

"Language," Van Brunt says mildly.

"I don't have time for her pointless games. Just because she's a Janeite doesn't mean she gets free rein over Society members."

"There is something to be said about fostering good relations amongst the various blocs, Finn."

"Oh, is that how we're putting it? *Good relations?*" Finn's face darkens.

"Victor's pen is still out of order, and Ms. Lennox's is misplaced, unfortunately."

Finn's triumphant, though. "Are you forgetting my pen isn't in functioning order right now?"

"That is true, but I am told that Ms. Reeve's is. She simply needs to register it prior to your departure in a few hours."

Finn curses under his breath. "Why now? Is she bored? Not enough balls or locals to keep her occupied? What the fuck is wrong with some people?"

"The Janeites are terrified that one of their stories might be next, especially after the loss of 1847BRO-JE. They feel as if—"

"First of all, Timeline 1847BRO-JE isn't part of the Janeite League. It's Brontë, not Austen. Secondly, its deletion happened two years prior. The latest attack was for a Timeline much older than either of these."

I'm fascinated by the discomfort Finn's trying to carefully hide behind anger. Why would a right-hand fist even question the motives behind a catalyst retrieval? And what games are he referring to?

"Nonetheless, you know that the Janeites are one of the strongest coalition blocs, and I do not fancy another go around with them when it would take you one, two days tops to retrieve the catalyst."

Finn snaps, "Two days?" at the same Van Brunt says, "And that is the end of it."

Apparently, my partner doesn't know what that means, because he follows up Van Brunt's threat with, "This is a gross misuse of Society time. This isn't fucking high school!"

I notice Van Brunt does not argue. Instead, he says, "Mr. Dawkins will send you the relevant details of the catalyst shortly. From what I can tell, it will be an easy retrieval, as the family in possession has a member on the Janeite council."

"The catch?"

Van Brunt clears his throat. "You're to have dinner with the family and stay the night, as several members of the Janeites want to meet with you in the morning to discuss some concerns."

"A Timeline was deleted yesterday." Finn's voice is low and firm. "We've had two break-ins, and there are still suspects to be identified. And you are asking me to take time away from what's important so I can go speed dating and then listen to a bunch of busy-bodies talk about things that don't concern them?"

"The preservation of Timelines concerns us all, Finn."

"Send the A.D. He'll be more than happy to play her games."

"You were specifically requested, Finn." Van Brunt sighs. "Be pleased it is an easy retrieval."

Finn won't let it go, though. "If it's so easy, one of the Janeites could bring it in. Just why in the hell haven't they already, anyway? Why do we cater to this bloc, Brom?"

"Finn. Enough."

I can't help myself any longer. "What exactly is speed dating?"

Finn won't meet my eyes, he's so angry. So I try again. "Who are the Janeites?"

It's Van Brunt who answers. "They are our liaisons from Timelines associated with an influential late Eighteenth-early-Nineteenth Century author by the name of Jane Austen."

"Timelines can form leagues? Or blocs, as you call them?"

"Some do, especially if they have a similar author in common." Van Brunt taps his fingers against his desk. "Mary will help you select the proper wardrobe, Ms. Reeve. I'm afraid that, even though the people you are going to go meet are fully aware of Timelines and are associated with the Society, they still cling to decorum. You will be expected to be dressed appropriately."

Minutes later, once we're back in the hallway, I ask Finn, "Shall I pack some weapons?"

Some of the heat leaves his eyes. "What?"

"You'd asked me earlier if I was familiar with weapons. I was inquiring if I ought to track some down to take with us. It sounds as if you might need defending."

For a moment, I wonder if rage will once more overtake him. But then he laughs. It's soft, almost a mere puff of breath, but a fraction of the tension eases from his body. "I'm afraid it would be like shooting fish in a barrel. There would be no sport in it for you at all."

Unwelcome warmth spreads throughout me at his voiced confidence in an ability he has yet to witness so far. "Will there be swooning? Shall I prepare myself to witness the vapors in full effect?"

"No swooning." His lips twitch. "And no vapors. They're a sturdy bunch, but they're gentry, so there is that."

"Are you gentry, Huckleberry Finn?"

He blinks at my use of his first name, an uneasiness once more tightening his shoulders. "No."

I have to jog to catch up with his sudden long strides. He doesn't look at me when he says, "I'd prefer you not use that name."

It's a beautiful name, I think. A unique one. And it saddens me to hear he does not favor it.

We've just reached the elevator when he says, "I apologize for snapping. It's just, I haven't gone by Huck in a very long time, and I'd prefer not to restart anytime soon."

The doors slide open and we step inside. "Van Brunt introduced you as such."

"Brom," he murmurs, "is a sentimentalist."

"Why the change?" ·

He's quiet for a long moment before answering. "Most people know that name. It would stand out like a sore thumb."

Interesting. "What name do you give them instead?"

Not a single muscle on his face ticks, not a knuckle whitens when he tells me flatly, "Legally, my name now is Finn Van Brunt."

I don't know why, but that bit of news has my mouth falling open.

"And before you ask, yes. Brom is my adopted father."

I stupidly say, "He doesn't look old enough to be a guardian."

"Apparently, the Van Brunts age well. He's in his mid-fifties, by the way."

I don't know how to keep my mouth shut, because I compound my rudeness by asking, "And your mother? Is she here in the Society, too?"

He won't meet my eyes. "Dead."

Frabjous. I keep wedging that foot of mine deeper into my mouth.

"A lot of people at the Institute don't go by their original names. It's not like I'm the odd duck around here."

"Would people recognize my name?"

His head tilts just enough so that our eyes finally meet. "Not if you keep going by Reeve, they won't."

He's shared something with me, so I decide to share something with him. "For years, surnames were irrelevant. They're not common in Wonderland at all."

It's enough to pique his interest. "You were just Alice there?"

I lie and tell him yes.

A PLAYBOOK

"WE DID NOT KNOW you would be bringing a guest with you."

Finn gives the distinguished man before us a neat bow. "I apologize if there's been any miscommunication. May I present my partner, Ms. Alice Reeve."

The women all curtsey, the men bow. I've enough manners left in me to return the favor.

Shortly after meeting with Van Brunt, I found myself in a whirl-wind that left my head spinning. Proper clothing had to be located for both Finn and myself in a vast closet organized by time periods. Wendy requested an hour of my time to go over the little machines she made for me.

"Pens," she intoned as I discreetly glanced about her white yet messy laboratory, "are tailored specifically for their user. It's a way to safeguard people from illegally moving between Timelines."

"Does that happen often?"

"Believe it or not, it happens more than you think it would. While most of us personally need the pens, there are those who can slip through Timelines naturally. The grass is always greener on the other side, right?"

It was wrong of me, but that made me glance at her brightly colored hair.

"Stick out your finger."

I did as asked, and regretted it seconds later after she poked me with a sharp needle. Finn, who was across the room talking with the A.D., looked up at the sound of my gasp of surprise.

I wanted to kick myself. That was going to be the last bit of weakness I was going to let them see. And honestly, a prick? I've borne wounds much, much worse.

"The pens are coded with their user's DNA," Wendy explained. "Thus, the need for blood."

I called out to Finn, "You could have warned me about this."

He shrugged, mouthing: *I'm sorry.*

My finger was held over a small glass vial and then milked until I nearly kicked her from beneath the table we were at.

"I'll get to work on getting the coding completed." She turned away to put the vial in a large white and black machine. "You probably ought to go get ready to leave."

"Are partners able to use one another's pens?"

It was enough to bring Wendy's attention back around. "Huh?"

"If something were to happen on one of these missions, would the pens work for other members present?"

"No." Wendy was already back at work doing whatever it was with my blood. "Nobody but you."

Shortly afterward, I stood in a quiet room alongside Brom and Finn, the newly, mysteriously coded pen in my hand. "Promise me it doesn't write with blood."

Van Brunt surprised me by laughing. I stared at him then, at that formal, serious man, and wondered how it was he became a young father to a man such as Finn.

"No," Finn quickly assured me. "It doesn't have any ink in it at all."

I didn't feel like telling them I'd seen too many letters written in blood.

I was passed two slim books: one that said *Mansfield Park* on the cover and another that had pictures of the Institute in it. I was told to put the Society book in my traveling bag but to keep out the other. Finn stepped behind me, his heat immediately mingling with mine.

I was a statue, flooded by far too many memories and sensations.

"It's easier if I help you through it the first few times," he was saying while I fought against things better left in the past. "Intent is key when we're editing into a Timeline."

There was that word again. *Intent.*

His arms looped around me, his hands curving around mine so that he and I both held the book in one pair of hands and the pen in the others. Despite my best efforts, I lost my breath when his thumb slid past mine to wrangle the book open.

I hated that this happened. Hated that, after all I've been through, my body allowed such foolishness. He doesn't deserve it. I don't even know him.

"First, you find a page that mentions the place you want to go. For example, we're heading to an estate in England called Mansfield Park. Here is a scene that is just beyond an outward door. That'll be a good place for us to go, especially since they're expecting us."

A shudder fought its way out of me at the touch of his breath against my cheek.

"There is a button on the side of the pen. It's very small, and not visible." The thumb on his right hand shifted one of my fingers to a spot in the middle of the pen and gently pressed against my skin. "There won't be a sound. Wendy's got this latest model of pen nearly impossible to distinguish from others. It's all by memory. Do you think you can remember this spot?"

When I nodded, it was done confidently, not jerkily like I feared it might be.

"Like I said, editing is all about intent. You—"

"Are these magic?"

He told me, "I don't know how they work, to be honest. None of us do."

"Not even Wendy?"

"Not even her. She was taught by another member who is now

dead."

I also hated that confusion got the better of me. "But, she *makes* these."

"Sometimes," he told me, "you can have something, hold it in your hands or feel it in your bones, and still never understand the working mechanisms behind it."

Isn't that the brutal truth.

I was glad when he turned back toward the matter at hand. "Editing is subjective, and everybody does it a little differently, but I find that the simplest lines are the most effective. My intent right now is for us to arrive at the front doors of Mansfield Park on a specific date, although that is not always necessary during editing. So, I—*we*—will write, *'Arrive at front doors of Mansfield Park, 15 July 1821 at six o'clock in the evening.'*"

"I thought it was not desirable to time travel?"

His chuckle is soft. "It's not. Some of the Janeites were contacted concerning membership over the last decade, but most refused to become active participants due to obligations at home. But they insisted on keeping in touch, so even though their lines have continued on for centuries, it feels as if we're always reaching into the past when it comes to their Timelines. Not to mention, time moves differently in their Timelines."

"Make sure you give Mrs. Bertram my letter."

My head snapped up, nearly colliding into Finn's nose. For several foolish minutes, I'd forgotten Van Brunt was still in the room with us.

Once Finn reassured his father he wouldn't forget, he asked me, "Are you ready?"

I was, surprisingly so. Together, we wrote his sentence—and although he assured me no ink was to be used, glowing, golden words appeared on the page anyway, warming our hands until they buzzed. And then, in a burst of golden light, a door.

And now here we are, standing in front of what appears to be a rather large family whilst dressed in clothes considered to be vintage even by my standards, and curious eyes practically trace each step I take.

Introductions are made. We are surrounded by a horde of Bertrams and a lone Price who can't seem to take her eyes off of Finn. "It is good of you to come," one of the gentlemen says to my partner. He's a clergyman in possession of what appears to be a gentle countenance. "After Fanny got back from her meeting, we were all most eager to get matters dealt with as swiftly as possible."

None of Finn's earlier anger is at all visible when he tells them it is our pleasure, and I'm grudgingly impressed by it. Experience has shown me that people who can't control their emotions are not valuable allies in battle.

The woman standing next to the clergyman takes a step forward. "I have brought the volume requested. I thought it best to get it out of the way so the rest of the evening may not be spoiled."

I'm the one to take the book from her. *Lovers' Vows*, it says on front. It's a playbook. There is nothing remarkable about it at all—just worn pages and words like any other well-read book.

"It is hard to believe that this is a catalyst." Fanny Bertram's voice is soft as she stares down at the object in my hands. "It's hard to believe, if this were to be destroyed, so would we all."

"What my sister is saying is that it is much consolation to know that we will no longer have anything to fear, at least when it comes to this," another of the ladies says. I root around in the names so freshly given to find Susan Price. But it turns out she isn't talking to me—no, her attention is still squarely on Finn. And she's smiling a bit shyly, a demure blush stealing across her porcelain cheeks.

He nods politely, but doesn't say anything in return. Doesn't even look her directly in the face, which is blatantly rude of him and radically unlike the man I've known for the last two days. The poor girl blushes even harder as the conversation progresses, Finn chooses to ignore her even more, and it occurs to me that this, here—this woman and her blushing—very well may be the product of whatever speed dating may be. Eventually, she sidles up to him and refuses to leave for the remainder of our talk. It's only when he spies children peeking around a corner is he able to shake her off.

Finn wanders over to where they are and extracts several objects out of his pockets. He's brought them toys. Simple wooden ones that fit their time, but at the sight of the gifts, the children could not be more delighted. And I am reluctantly enchanted as I watch him squat down before them and explain how they work. One of the children, a little girl with brown ringlets, throws her arms around him and he allows it. There are cultured adults here and he's spending his time instead making children happy.

Finn Van Brunt has manners. He's kind to children.

I hate the tingling that spreads in the pit of my belly.

Once we're upstairs, and I'm tucking the playbook in my bag I've brought, I attempt to dispel the warm feelings brought on by watching his generosity by teasing him. "One of the women down there seems to be quite taken with you. Have you two had a romantic entanglement in the past?"

He shuts my bedroom door, which is surprising as decorum insists unmarried men and ladies behind closed doors is a firm no-no. "One of the Janeites has made it her mission to make as many matches as she can because apparently she has nothing better to do. A Mrs. Emma Knightley. We met a year ago, and she was horrified and then delighted I'm single. That poor girl has probably been told I'm her perfect match." Another attractive flush steals up his neck as he perches on the edge of my bed, picking at a loose thread on the waistcoat he's borrowed from the Society's archives.

I come to sit next to him. "I shudder to think what might happen once this Mrs. Knightley finds I'm unwed."

"Oh, there's no doubt about it. You'd be her latest obsession. I'm sure she's got a long list of 'quality husbands' just waiting to be passed out."

I laugh, and in turn, he smiles. There is an easiness between us that shouldn't be there. One that hasn't been earned yet. One I can't afford to allow. One I don't even know if I *want* to allow.

An hour later, we are all seated at a vast table in a room lit by dozens of candles. Finn and I are separated by nearly the entire length of the table—he, to sit in between Fanny and her infatuated sister Susan, I to sit in between the clergyman and his baronet brother. As the men next to me ask inane, polite questions, I spend more of my time absorbing the distinct discomfort that's plaguing Finn. All of the amusement we shared in my room is lost, all of the joy he showed the children vanished without a trace, and in its place is annoyance he is clearly desperate to contain. Thankfully, he's never rude to Susan, but the one time she touches him, he jerks away as if her fingers are filled with fire.

Honestly, I'm enthralled. I've only known him a short time, but so far, Finn Van Brunt has struck me as a confident man who can hold his own. So to see him so grossly uncomfortable leaves me wondering what the story here is.

I refocus on the men sitting by me. "Do you mind me inquiring if either of you knows a Mrs. Knightley?"

Both of the men surrounding me set their spoons down on their plates. The clergyman says, "If you are speaking of the Mrs. Knightley I think you are, a Mrs. Emma Knightley, she is a member of the Janeite council alongside Fanny."

"She's a bloody nuisance, it what she is," the baronet mutters. His wife, seated farther on down the table, shoots a glance weighed heavily in disapproval. He, in turn, scowls even harder.

"I would have thought that you might know Mrs. Knightley," the clergyman says. "Being that you are part of the Collectors' Society and all."

There is no good answer to that that would be pleasant conversation, so I merely lift a full spoonful of soup to my mouth.

"Mrs. Knightley is a busy body," the baronet says loudly, clearly goading his wife. "Nothing pleases her more than the blasted act of matchmaking."

Susan Price gasps and blushes. Finn goes stock still. So I was right. Speed dating has something to do with matchmaking.

"She is charming nearly to a fault," the clergyman argues.

The baronet scowls but says nothing further.

At the end of dinner, the men are to retire to a separate room, with none so much relieved to do so than Finn. The ladies present invite me to join them in a card game, but the truth is, all I can think about is a soft bed and good sleep, especially considering I'd had very little sleep the night before. I think they're disappointed in me leaving, but I'm realistic enough to know when I'd be poor company. I relent and allow Finn to escort me as far as the stairs, and when I stumble up the first few steps, he's right there to catch me.

It's an unbearably sweet gesture that has me fumbling to reinsert an arm's distance. I jerk away from his touch more strongly than I ought to.

"Are you feeling okay?"

My eyes widen in confusion.

"I ask because you're flushed."

Well, now I am.

"If you don't feel good, we should leave." He's on the step below me, and I still have to look up at him. "You can be in your own bed tonight and then sleep in as long as you like in the morning."

Too many complicated emotions ping throughout my chest. There's that concern again, and the easiness that ought not be there yet. I met this man two days ago. He's a stranger. An attractive stranger, a kind one, but one all the same.

Besides, the bed he's talking about doesn't feel like mine. It feels like Sara's, and I am a momentary interloper who is wearing her clothes, surrounded by her things, and working with her partner. My bed, my real bed, the one that holds the most meaning to me, is elsewhere.

Sadness threatens to crush me.

Somebody calls out Finn's name, to let him know a card game is about to begin. And yet, rather than going like he ought, he waits for my answer. Part of me wants to tell this man yes, but all-too-familiar yet necessary defenses go up once more. "Don't we have a meeting in the morning to attend?"

"Screw the meeting."

His quiet vehemence makes me smile. "I'm going to need a modern-day vocabulary primer, aren't I?"

There. He's smiling once more. It's not as wide as I've seen, but it's a start.

It takes me several minutes to make it to my room in Mansfield Park, and once I do, I'm met with a surprise. A man I've never met is in my chamber, one whose photograph I examined early this morning. He's of average height, with a neat blond beard and large holes rimmed in metal in his ears. He's dressed entirely in black and wearing a tool belt, a black hat with a long bill covering what is undoubtedly slicked-back hair. But more importantly, he's holding a book in his hands. A certain playbook.

Specifically, a catalyst.

We stare at each other for what feels like forever but in reality must be just a few seconds. And then he growls, "Fuck me."

I shut and lock the door behind me, my eyes never leaving him. "I'd rather not."

A soft, menacing giggle floats between us. "Be a good gel and step aside. I don't want to have to hurt you, but if you force my hand, I won't have a choice."

"Funny," I tell him calmly. "I was about to say something similar. Only I wish you'd set the playbook down first."

The bastard slides the book into the band of his pants. And then, out of the tool belt, he slips out a pair of switchblades. Once he flips them open, he performs a bizarre, grandstanding performance of swirling them around, all the while grinning like an egotistical fool.

I have no time for such uselessness.

Confusion reigns in the room, because I dart toward the fireplace at the same moment he charges me. A poker is claimed just as one of the blades grazes the skin of my arm.

Muslin has been torn. A dress has been destroyed.

"This," I tell him flatly, "was not my dress to ruin."

His eyes widen as another malicious laugh escapes him. I happily wipe it straight off his face when the poker whips out and strikes him squarely across the arm he appears to favor. No howl sounds, though, just a grunt as he stumbles back.

It's my turn to rip the dress, straight down from the hip right before he charges me once more. I let loose a roundhouse kick to his throat that sends him sprawling. Granted, it's only momentarily, but it's enough for me to jab the poker smartly into ribs once, twice. Blood is drawn.

I show him my teeth.

The blades in his hands sweep in swishing arcs as we begin our dance. Clang after clang, strike after strike, slash after poke, I eventually make headway and angle the would-be thief away from the door. He catches me off guard once, sweeping me with a leg until I fall onto my bottom, but I've always been quick on my feet.

When I knock off his hat, I tell him, "You're boring me."

"See," he volleys back in what sounds vaguely like the bastard child of French and Cockney accents, "I was just thinkin' what a delight you are."

A kick sends one of his blades skittering out of his hand. "Polite gentlemen introduce themselves to ladies they find delightful."

A vase nearby shatters; a table overturns in our dance. Part of me revels in this, as I've been removed from such pastimes for far too long. And I'm inordinately pleased when a simple yet solid kick planted against his ribs leaves him winded and wincing.

I spin as he stumbles back, gaining traction to slam the length of the poker across his nose just as he catches my shoulder with his blade. Blood spurts as he curses, and I use his momentary distraction to snatch the book right out of his pants.

He howls, "Bitch!" from between blackened yet bloody teeth when I shove the catalyst down the front of my dress.

Another well-placed kick sends him right where I want him, flat on his arse and without his second blade. "And here I was thinking I was delightful."

He wheezes, his eyes nearly bulging in fury. "I'll enjoy slitting your throat."

It's time to put this sorry fellow out of his misery. The dance is over. I punch him squarely in the face. Thankfully, his head crashes hard enough against the dresser behind to leave him finally languishing in unconsciousness. The mirror above falls and shatters in a deafening din. A bowl topples over, spilling water everywhere. Never one to trust one knock on the head to be enough, I straddle him and haul his newly bleeding skull back before slamming it as hard as I can into the dresser. Bits of wood splinter in his wake.

His body slumps to the ground like a wet noodle.

Amateur.

A quick dig through his pockets leaves me empty handed, but when I reclaim his fallen switchblades, I find what I'm looking for. Carved neatly into each blade is the following: *S Todd.*

I lean down and pet his damp hair. "Perhaps you'll have better luck next time, Mr. Todd."

Shouting fills the hallway, and pounding sounds on the door. I stand up and smooth what is left of my tattered dress. "Be a good boy and stay where you are."

But before I can open the door, it crashes open, halfway ripped off its hinges. Finn is right there, a gun in one of his hands, as the rest of the men and women of Mansfield Park huddle behind him, terrified.

"Alice! Are you—" He shoves the gun in a holster hidden beneath his coat I hadn't noticed earlier. "Jesus! You're bleeding!"

I glance down at my arms. Thin lines beading with red crisscross through destroyed muslin. I've seen worse, much worse, so these don't even register as noteworthy. "It's nothing. We ought to be more concerned with this fellow." I hook a thumb behind me. "I caught him trying to remove the catalyst."

Someone behind us screams. Scratch that—two or three somebodies scream. Well, wasn't Finn mistaken? The vapors have arrived after all.

But Finn isn't looking at our sleeping thief or even the hysterical women behind him. His attention is still on me, his worried eyes running up and down my ruined dress. There's shock there, but hints of that genuine concern, too. "Are you all right?"

"I'm fine. Honestly, Finn. If you only—"

He reaches out and gently tilts my head. "Did that asshole hit you in the face?!"

I try not to melt at his touch. *Stranger*, I tell myself. *Stranger. Finn Van Brunt is a stranger. You're not allowed to feel this way.* "Bruises heal. Just have a look at our guest, would you?"

It's reluctant, but he does as I ask. And then his eyes widen before they narrow as they take in my latest dance partner. I pass over one of the blades. "S. Todd. Sound familiar at all?"

He takes a deep breath before tugging me away from the body. "Is he alone?"

"I'm afraid I didn't have a chance to ask him that one yet. I'm sure we can pour some water on his head and wake him up, though."

Finn turns to our hosts—correction, host, as only the baronet is still present. He beckons us to the hallway with a trembling hand. "A word, please?"

Before he says whatever it is he wants to, Finn tells him, "I'm afraid we won't be able to stay tonight. It's best we get back to the Institute with the catalyst right away."

The baronet pales. "Edmund took the ladies away, thought it not best to see . . ." He wipes a hand across his face. "I didn't . . . I knew Fanny said, but I didn't truly believe . . ."

He isn't the only one. I suppose I hadn't believed it all, either. I mean, I'd heard what they'd said, saw photographs and videos and what not, but it'd been an intangible threat.

The bruises on my hands now tell me differently.

"Will you be taking the fiend with you?"

But before either of us can answer the baronet, the sound of glass shattering fills the room behind us. Finn and I race back in to find one of the windows broken and no body left upon the floor. Somewhere outside, somebody yelps in terror.

"Bloody hell," I murmur. "And I was positive he was out for at least a good two hours." Am I losing my touch?

The baronet is off and running, shouting for men to begin a search outside as he heads down the hallway. But Finn and I know it's done in vain, because when we reach the window, an all-too-familiar light flashes in the dark, illuminating a doorway for two figures to run through before winking away just seconds later.

Finn slams his fist down against the blood-stained dresser. "Well, if that isn't the fucking worst news possible. Whoever these people are, they're capable of editing."

I peer out of the demolished window. Men with lanterns swarm the courtyard. "Wasn't that assumed, considering you all claimed the villains were going into Timelines and getting hold of catalysts before you could?"

"We knew they were getting into Timelines, but this is now proof they're editing." He's furious. "What if they've somehow gotten ahold of one of our pens?"

"Wendy claimed they're coded specifically to each person assigned one."

"Exactly!"

I retrieve the other switchblade from the floor. "And to think your father insisted this would be an easy assignment for me to start out on."

Finn stares intently at me for a long moment. "You really kicked his ass, didn't you?"

I shrug.

"*'Oh, I'm familiar with weapons, Finn.'* Ladies and gentlemen," he sweeps a hand out, "may I present Alice, the master of understatement."

Unwelcome amusement fights to be released. "Your falsetto is terrible."

He steps into my space, our bodies just mere inches apart as he examines me further. "You need to see Victor, just in case some of those need stitches."

"I told you before, I do not break easily. Tonight was nothing. It was a mere skirmish."

He lifts up my hand, his attention fixated on my now-darkening knuckles. "Still."

I'm unnerved by this gentle touch. Furious with myself for even letting it register within me. "We ought to go. Our presence here, and that of the catalyst, can only be a dangerous temptation to our guests."

He lets go of my hand, and although it's what I needed him to do, it isn't lost on me that it felt sublimely good to have concern and attention from just such a man.

The guilt within me is corrosive.

THE MUSEUM

THE BASEMENT OF THE Society's Institute looks much like what a normal basement looks like: there are plain walls, old bits of furniture and boxes, and dark corners filled with items once loved and now forgotten. It feels vast, though, as Finn leads me through what can barely be referred to as a path.

When we arrived in New York, nobody was there to greet us, which made sense as we weren't expected until well after brunch. It was the dead of night, and other than security guards stationed on each floor, the building felt like it had fallen into a tremulous stasis.

Honestly, all I'd wanted to do was sleep, but no amount of arguing swayed Finn from his insistences I visit Victor first. The poor doctor was rumpled when he answered his door, sleep clinging to his eyes and muscles. A yawn preceded, "You're early," but once a few good blinks passed, he became alert.

"What in the bloody hell happened?" he'd barked at Finn while practically shoving me into his home office. "I thought this was one of

Emma's set-ups, not a fight!" He leaned closer to one of my arms. "And an ugly one, too. Christ, Alice. You need stitches."

A meaningful look passed between Finn and myself.

"I really don't," I began to say, but Finn told Victor he better get at it.

After that, my partner didn't say much, which troubled me. As I perched on a leather exam table, he hovered nearby with arms crossed, his bottom lip tugged between his teeth. At various points, I could have sworn he was angry, but other times an unfamiliar sting accompanied what I could only describe as disappointment.

But as he wasn't talking much, it was up to me to fill Victor in about the night's events, and of the would-be thief. Once my tale is done, the doctor whistled. "I'll admit to not seeing that one coming."

"You mean that somebody would be willing to steal something from beneath your noses?"

He shook his head, and I winced as he tugged the needle and thread through my skin. *"Our* noses, and yes. Not to mention I would have never guessed that the Demon Barber of Fleet Street was the one trying to break into the Institute. Bloody hell. Finn, this isn't good. Not good at all."

The Demon Barber of Fleet Street . . . Well, if that isn't a dramatic name, then I don't know what is.

"So, you know of this man?" I pressed. "This S. Todd?"

Out of the corner of my eye, I watched the muscles in Finn's body tense even more so than just a minute before. Victor leaned in closer to examine his handiwork. "Sweeney Todd is his name, and he's an infamous serial killer who, if I'm not mistaken, was apprehended by the police. Tended to cut his victims across their necks with straight razors." A quick slash across his neck with a finger preceded a glanced to his friend. "Was Lovett there?"

A slight shrug was all Finn allowed outside of, "Somebody went through the door with the bastard. They were in the shadows, though—and the door they went through was dark, too."

"Who is Lovett?" I asked.

"She goes by Mrs. Lovett and was his henchman. Or lover." Victor's voice echoed in the room. "The stories say she'd cook Todd's victims into pies. She might be dead, though. Some stories have him poisoning her. I guess even villains have trouble sticking together, eh?"

I could honestly admit I had absolutely nothing to say in return to that, which was all right, as the rest of my stitches were sewn in moody silence. It gave me an opportunity to think about the puzzle pieces I'd been handed over the last few days. Todd and Lovett have been seen around the Institute on several occasions. Timelines are disappearing, catalysts are being destroyed. Todd tried to steal the catalyst from 1814AUS-MP right out from underneath us, in the guest bedroom I was to stay in and not in the family library. And that left a question a question most unwelcome, because . . . how did he know where it was? Normally, the family kept the catalyst in their library, but Todd wasn't searching there.

He was searching in *my* room.

The obvious answer is simple, but a conclusion I'm reluctant to embrace. And, as I weave through bits of furniture and dusty boxes, I'm not too sure whether or not Finn, his father, or any other member of the Society is willing to hear it, even if it's what they suspect, too. Could somebody in this building have tipped Todd off?

Afterward, Finn had wanted to bring the catalyst to the Librarian by himself, claiming I needed to rest, but I insisted on tagging along. "This is growing wearisome," I'd told him.

When his eyebrows formed a V, I added, "You telling me to stay behind. Do you not think me capable?"

Finn surprised me by directing us to a small alcove, out of the way of a group of people walking down the hall. "God, no. That's not it at all, especially as you proved you're more than capable in a fight. It's just . . . you were hurt. I mean, you just got six rows of stitches. Nobody would blame you for wanting to crash."

I really need that vocabulary primer. "And nobody could blame me for wishing to see where the Librarian keeps all the catalysts, either."

He ran a hand through his short hair, staring at me so intently my toes curled within my boots.

I wished he wasn't so beautiful. I wished he didn't look at me, our acquaintance so new still, with that slight shine of caring in his eyes. I wished he wasn't so kind.

"I told you. I'm not fragile. I've faced worse, and here I am, standing with you now, all in one piece. All I ask is that, if we are to truly be partners, you don't shut me out."

That frustrated him. "I'm not trying to shut you out."

"And yet, every time something comes up, you tell me to stay behind. Did you do that with Sara?"

My question wasn't met with favor, that's for sure.

"Mary says Sara was too nice," I continued. "That some people aren't cut out for this work because their temperaments don't allow it."

Anger flashed in his blue-gray eyes. "Mary should keep her mouth shut."

"I'm not always so nice, Finn. And I'm not one to sit by, idling twiddling my thumbs while strong men go out and fix all the problems. So, whether or not you mind, I'm going with you to drop off the catalyst. You might as well stop trying to urge me to stay behind from now on, too, because it'll only leave you frustrated when I tell you to bugger off."

That was a quarter of an hour ago. I ask him now, as I trace a path in the dust covering an old piano, "Have you spoken to your father yet?"

"No. I figured we'd do this first, and then we can go talk to him."

Good man. He's learning quickly.

"I would think a basement is an obvious place for thieves to look for hidden treasures."

I catch his profile in the dim light from overhead. "None of the catalysts are on this level. Just hang on a sec, and you'll see where we're really going."

A minute later, he's shoving aside a dust-covered bookshelf against the far wall to reveal an elevator door. A small door roughly at eye level is flipped open to reveal a glass screen and a slot. He pulls a white card out of his pocket and runs it through the slot. Once a red light flashes, he leans in. Green crisscrossing lights scan across his face, zeroing in on his eye, before a disembodied voice says, "Welcome, Finn Van Brunt. You may proceed."

The elevator door slides open as he closes the small door. "Ladies first."

I step into the mirrored elevator; he follows, making sure he slides the bookcase into place with a hidden lever on the backside. Another button is pushed, and the elevator door shuts just as peppy music fills the space.

I lift my eyebrows up, and he shrugs. "The Librarian likes her Muzak. What can I say?"

The compartment lurches and then moves downward. Finn takes a deep breath and says, "I'm sorry."

"For?"

"For not being there with you when Todd attacked."

I'm a bit stunned at the heat in his voice, and of the anger in his words. "Well," I say carefully, "it's not as if you knew he was waiting or anything."

He sighs, the fingers of one hand curling momentarily into a fist by his side. "Still. What's the point of a partner, if they're not there to protect you?"

"If I'm not mistaken, I held my own quite adeptly."

His disappointment last night suddenly makes sense. He wasn't disappointed in me—he was upset at *himself.*

It's such a bittersweet, familiar sentiment that my heart clenches.

"If this is really Sweeney Todd, he's a brutal killer. Nobody should have to go up against him alone."

"And here I was thinking he was a barber," I murmur. "A demonic one, no less. How ghastly. Do you know this scoundrel?"

"In the sense that he was a character in books and movies, yes. But the Society rarely interacts with Timelines associated with villains."

"Meaning?"

He looks away from me, but in the mirrors surrounding us, I see the hardness in his face. "Meaning, when there are only so many of us to go around, collecting catalysts from Timelines whose claim to fame comes from horror isn't exactly at the top of the list."

"There are innocents in those Timelines, ones whose actions have nothing to do with a character in a book. Can you really tell me that every person's existence in Todd's Timeline is less worthy of life or protection than any other?"

He isn't amused, though. "Aren't you the little philosopher?"

"There are villains in my Timeline." It's my turn to look away. "Ones whose deeds are often unspeakable. I cannot imagine that any other Timeline is different. Along with good, there is always evil. It's just the way it is."

The elevator slows to a stop, but the doors do not open. Finn flips open another panel, one I hadn't noticed before, and presses his left thumb against the glass. "Identity verified, Finn Van Brunt. Enter code for entry."

Numbers fill the screen, from zero to nine. He types in an eleven-digit code, and the same disembodied voice announces, "Code verified," seconds before the doors finally slide open.

"We'll have to get you inputted into the system," Finn says as we step out into a wood-paneled hallway.

"Will it require my firstborn?"

It annoys me how much I like his laugh, even as soft and brief as it is right now. "Oh, most definitely."

The hallway we're in has no doors and is lined in crystal sconces. It stretches quite a distance before offering two directions; Finn leads us to the left. One more turn has us in front of the only door so far. Once more, Finn flips open a panel and presses his index finger against a circular button with a concave center. The disembodied voice announces, "Hold still, please."

When Finn retracts his finger, I notice a drop of blood welling upon the pad. "Blood is required?"

"It's nothing. A pinprick." He sucks briefly on his finger as the voice tells us, "Identify verified. Clearance has been approved, Finn Van Brunt."

A click sounds, and then the door slides open to reveal the largest room I've ever seen. Two sets of mosaicked steps lead down to a room whose chandelier-adorned ceiling soars above us. Row upon row upon row of brightly lit glass cases stacked upon one another stretch as far as the eye can see.

"This," he tells me, "is the Museum."

The same strangely bland yet peppy music from the elevator continues to play in this room, although I can find no direct source of its origins.

"There you two are. I was wondering how long it would take for you to come. I'm having trouble pinpointing your arrivals and departures, aren't I, Alice?"

I hate that I start when the Librarian's words echo around us. She's standing at the bottom of the stairs, just to the right, so that had she not spoken, I would not have easily spotted her.

Finn trots down the steps. "Alice had to see Victor first."

She peers up at me, her eyes running the length from my head to my feet. "I'm glad to see there is no lasting injury, little bird."

I'm halfway down the steps when my feet freeze. "What did you just say?"

Her head cocks to the side, her face carefully neutral as her dark hair falls to her waist.

The brightly colored ground below my feet feels soft and unsteady. In between blinks, the Librarian both smiles widely and remains impassive as she looks up at me.

I'm about to ask her to repeat what she's said, but Finn has reached where she's standing and is kissing both her cheeks in a familiar gesture that inappropriately bothers me. "Do you have a case ready?"

"Of course." She returns the kisses, her hands on his shoulders. "Come along, Alice. There's no time to dawdle. You have a long night ahead of you, so you'll want to rest up as much as you can."

I trail the pair down several rows before hooking right into one and then another right and then left. The Librarian comes to a darkened box halfway up a row of five, accessible by a small, rolling ladder already present. A small button is pressed near a glass handle, and a light I cannot pinpoint the source of flares to life. She pulls out a small black card and runs it through a nearly invisible slot just to the side of the handle.

"Each catalyst is stored in a temperature-controlled environment," she says as Finn hands her the playbook. "Although that might be a tad overkill, considering it takes active intent to destroy a catalyst. Left on their own, they are nearly immortal."

"Then why not leave them on their own?"

The playbook is set upon a bookstand inside the box, opened to the title page. "Because there are always those whose intent is to destroy." The door is shut, and the white card is once more inserted into the slot. "Isn't that right, Alice?"

There is nowhere you could go in which I cannot find you, little bird. Nobody is safe if I don't want them to be. Not little birds, not diamonds, not grinning cats, not even kings.

I swallow, hating how the echo of these words are just as strongly felt today as the day I first heard them. "Is your intent pure, then?"

She chuckles as she descends the ladder. "Is anyone's intention ever one hundred percent pure?"

With no hesitation, I tell her, "Yes."

"Tell me, Alice. Has your intent always been pure?"

My nails dig once more into my palms. "I think it depends on the situation."

"What about when you left Wonderland? Was it then?"

Long seconds tick by as a standoff forms between us. I know I ought to hold my tongue, but I snap, "You don't know the first thing about what you're talking about."

Because it was pure, dammit.

It was.

It had to be. Even though I had no choice.

There's that smile of hers again, the one that is off-putting. "No creature is completely selfless. Not even those whose hearts are more gold than tin."

Finn clears his throat. "We ought to leave you to your work and go fill out the report."

The Librarian pats his cheek. "Try to remember it comes from the best of places, will you?"

Finn rolls his eyes, but doesn't say anything in return.

The Librarian leads us back through the maze of catalysts until we reach the steps. "Alice, do not take offense that the documentation has been sent to Finn. You have no knowledge of technology yet."

The hairs on the back of my neck bristle, but then she reaches over and pats my cheek, too.

"I told you not to take offense." And with that, she turns around and disappears back into the rows of catalysts.

When we're back in the elevator, heading to the basement, I ask Finn, "How did she know we were back early?"

He's quiet for a long moment, like he's weighing what to tell me. Finally, he offers, "She just did."

I wait patiently, but he doesn't add anything. So I'm forced to ask, "Is she always like that?"

"Like what?"

"Creepy."

For a moment, he simply stares at me, like he can't believe I said such a thing. But I've been around plenty of creepy beings in my time, and so far, the Librarian stands right up with them.

"Does my honesty bother you? I thought partners were supposed to be honest with one another. Isn't that a basic tenant of a successful business relationship? Because even in Wonderland, we typically tried to be honest with those we were allied with."

He scoffs. *"Typically tried?* What the hell does that mean?"

I don't tell him that, more often than not, it seemed deceit and subterfuge were necessary. Instead, I say, "My point stands, Huckleberry Finn."

Something in the man before me shuts down, like the off switch to a machine. "I asked you not to call me that."

The elevator door slides open. He holds his arm out and waits until I exit first.

He does not say anything further.

WHAT THE LIBRARIAN WAS undoubtedly referencing with her eerie warning to Finn was Van Brunt's volcanic explosion once my partner and I debrief him on the night's events and the identity of the would-be thief. This leaves her ever creepier in my opinion, no matter what disappointment Finn may have in me for believing such.

In other news, I find Van Brunt's lack of decorum comforting in a way. I'm mesmerized by this side to the normally unflappable man. Finn, for his part, sits in stony silence as his father paces back and forth whilst lecturing us. Eventually, he says flatly, "I get it. I fucked up."

That steals the wind right out of Van Brunt's sails.

My response is immediate. "You most certainly did not."

Finn won't look at me, though. His attention shifts to a small ink drawing hanging near the bronze plaque above Van Brunt's desk. It's of a boy and a man on a raft with a pole. Even more disappointment fills Finn's eyes before he angles his head toward the windows.

Van Brunt finds his chair and offers in a much calmer voice, "I want Todd found. If he is, in fact, the culprit behind the mass deletions over the last couple years, we cannot leave him loose upon the streets."

"Isn't it obvious he is the culprit?" I ask. "He is the same man in Wendy's video."

Van Brunt muses, "Although I don't know his story too well, if I recall correctly, Todd rarely acted solo. He had a partner, even if it was a tenuous connection that ended in murder. The truth is, I'm surprised to hear he was alone in your room, Ms. Reeve."

I feign casualness when I say, "It's curious that he appeared to know exactly where the catalyst was, wasn't it?"

Finn stands up and heads over toward the window he'd just been staring at. Van Brunt says, his eyes on his son rather than me, "Yes, it is, isn't it?" And then the recently seated head of the Society is also on his feet. He reaches out and gently grabs his son's arm. "I apologize for the fool's errand."

For a moment, I wonder if Finn will tell his father off. But he remains silent.

Van Brunt continues, "I thought to placate the Janeites and humor what I saw as harmless, but after you left, your brother and I had a chat."

I perk up. Brother?

"Katrina would have raked me across the coals for such stupidity, that is for certain. In her place, your brother did so quite admirably."

Finn briefly glances over his shoulder at me. He tells his father, "We should focus on finding this S. Todd."

Van Brunt does the only thing he really can do by nodding before reclaiming his chair, his face impassive as ever. "It appears, Ms. Reeve, you have hidden talents that our research did not unearth. It's impressive you were able to best a known killer."

I allow a modest shrug, but do not clarify further.

Van Brunt steeples his fingers as he leans back in his chair. "What were your impressions of him?"

As his son doesn't turn around from his post at the window or answer, I assume he's talking to me, as I'm the one who had the most face time with the fiend. "Overly confident, when he clearly did not have the skill to back up his claims." My nails click against the wooden arm of my chair. "He also has poor hygiene. His teeth were blackened in places. Interestingly enough, though, he didn't smell rancid."

"Sweeney Todd has allegedly butchered hundreds of people. As distasteful as it sounds, one might believe his confidence in his ability to kill is well earned."

I repress a shudder. "And yet, we are in possession of both of his knives, and I would bet every last cent of mine that he's sporting a wicked concussion alongside a broken nose and some cracked ribs today. Had I not followed into the hallway, we most certainly would be in possession of his body, too."

Before another word is said, Finn stalks across the room and out of the door. He does not slam it, though, but my body jerks with the click just as surely as if he had.

Van Brunt sighs quietly once his son is gone. "Do you ever hold yourself to unreasonable ideals, Ms. Reeve?"

"Doesn't everybody?"

"No," he muses. "I don't think they do." His bright blue eyes zero in on me. "Sometimes our pasts are chains we cannot let go of, even if the key is in our hands. They define us in ways we resent, and yet they are somewhat precious, too. Because, logically, we understand that our pasts have made us who we are, even if we want nothing more to close our eyes to them."

I shift in my chair, unsure of what to say. Finn Van Brunt holds himself to unreasonable ideals?

"Did you know that I was the villain in my particular story?"

And now I have even fewer words at my disposal.

"Maybe not so much a villain, but an anti-villain." He scoffs quietly. "Whatever that means."

For a moment, I can't help but wonder if I am sleeping, because there is no way the man sitting before me could be anything less than honorable.

"I think of this label often, Ms. Reeve. Not a day goes by in which I don't reflect upon the documented follies of my youth, of how abhorrently irresponsible and petty I was in my actions and behavior. I look back on that man and do not recognize him. I suppose these are chains that most do not find themselves shackled with. They grow up without their names attached to deeds and actions that enjoy longevity due to the compulsive resilience of beloved stories. They are allowed the luxury of maturing, of evolving as all people do rather than being forced into a tight box of expectations."

I'm well aware and more than a bit ashamed my eyes widen in surprise.

"Most of the people here in the Society bear scars from the stigmas surrounding them," he continues. "It is a natural inclination, I think, for many to act out against such injustices while ironically holding them close to the vest. To hold themselves at a much higher standard, to prove that they are more than just words in a book written by a person they've never met. I hope you can remember that in the coming weeks and months, Ms. Reeve. Each of us here has a story, but it's not necessarily the one people think they know."

I think to myself, I'd like to know Huck Finn's story. But until then, I have another mystery to solve. "What do the words on the plaque behind you mean?"

Van Brunt twists in his chair. "*In paginis mundūs invenimus. In verbis vitam invenimus*. In pages, we find worlds. In words, we find life."

How fitting.

When I exit the office minutes later, Finn is nowhere to be seen. The A.D. is, though. He's leaning against a wall, arms and legs crossed like he has precious few cares in the world. "Just the beauteous woman I've been hunting high and low for."

I wonder if he'd still feel that way after a well-placed knee to the groin.

If my face appears as surly as I feel, he pays no heed. "Wendy wants you in the lab. It's time for a little crash course in technology, luv. You've been skipping protocol left and right. Instead of going around and beating the crap out of people, you ought to be spending your time acclimating to the Twenty-First Century."

I tell him sweetly, "Call me luv again and you'll have to go get yourself a nice piece of meat for the bruised eye you'll be sporting."

He pretends to swoon, an arm across his forehead. "Be still me heart." And then, with a rubbery grin, "Do you talk this dirty to all your beaus?"

I'm halfway down the hall when he catches up with me. "You're no fun, little Miss Alice."

It's my turn to playact, a hand pressed against my heart. "That wounds me deeply." And then I smack his hand as it brushes up against my pocket. He yelps, but thankfully there are a few more feet between us now.

"Steal from me, and I'll do more than gift you with a black eye. Keep your hands to yourself. Understand?"

"No fun at all," he mutters sadly once we're upon the elevator.

THE 21ST CENTURY

F OR MUCH OF THE rest of the next few days, I am Wendy's captive
pupil as she drags out machine after machine in an effort to, and I
quote, "better prepare for situations that might arise during assignments." I neglect to inform her that I handled myself quite well with
only a fireplace poker, but that is neither here nor there. I'm given a laptop computer, a cell phone of my own for what she calls *everyday use*,
a secondary cell phone for *emergencies*, a tablet for *research*, an email
for *internal communication*, something called login codes for *Internet
access*, and two white key cards to access various doors within the Institute. She goes over each item at a rapid speed, and more than once, I fear
the tools of the Twenty-First Century will get the better of me.

Automatons and machinery have officially taken over the world.

"Keep your phone on you at all times," she says. "In addition to
letting other members call or text you, it also has a GPS that will prove
handy if we need to track you. I've had to work around satellites and
towers to ensure that, even in different Timelines that bear different

technology, you'll still be able to track your partner if needed."

Goodness knows what GPS is.

"I've had your phone pre-programmed alphabetically with all current Society members' numbers." She slides her finger across the screen and presses random buttons that don't actually exist. "Don't worry about having to memorize any."

Thank goodness for that, because I'm wondering how I'm going to remember any of the rest of the things she's just taught me.

Hours are spent programming me into the Institute's security system. My iris is scanned into a computer, my fingerprints and multiple vials of my blood collected, and my voice is recorded. I'm given codes to memorize. And then I'm sent to Victor for a physical (during which I give up more blood) before finally ending up on the tenth floor with a stoic man named Kip who smacks strongly of Viking heritage.

"I'm told you can fight."

I glance around the spacious room we're in. There are mats on the floors and weapons of all shapes, sizes, and kinds lining the walls. "I can hold my own," I tell him. Did Finn tell him this? Or Van Brunt?

Speaking of . . . I haven't seen much of my partner over the last few days. At night, I'll listen for sounds of life in the flat next to me, but they're few and far between, and then when I realize what I'm doing, I berate myself for hours for my continued stupidity.

One would think I'd be pleased with the distance. It's a desire I ought to embrace. And yet, when Finn and I do talk, the ease I felt with him for those first few days comes flaring back into existence. It's maddening, because it shouldn't exist.

How could it?

"Toxicity is such a nasty thing to possess, isn't it?"

"What do you prefer?"

Grateful for a distraction, I muse, as I lean in to examine a battle axe that is much more pitiful than the one I'm familiar with, how that's a more tasteful question than: *How do you like to kill or maim people?* "I suppose swords and daggers, but it's been my experience that most objects can become weapons when necessary."

"What about guns?"

I lightly touch the silver head of a mace, desperate to block out the memory of a rather large one used by a certain Lion to bludgeon heads like they were grapes. "I've never used them. Do Society members run around with maces often?"

He does not smile, and frankly, I wonder if he even knows how to. "Maces can be handy." He pulls out a tablet much like the one Wendy assigned me hours before and taps on it. "A schedule for shooting lessons will be sent to you before the night is over."

A tiny, blackened spot of dried blood on a quarterstaff catches my eye. "Is it optional?"

He doesn't even bother looking up at me as he taps away. "Society policy states that active members be trained in a variety of weapons for a variety of different situations. People gravitate toward what they like best, obviously, but it's good to have choices."

I do my best to ignore the pang that plagues me when I consider what has served me best in the past.

"Do most of the Society's assignments require weapons?"

He's blunt. "No. But some do, and it's always better to be prepared than be caught unable to protect yourself."

My eyes gravitate back to that speck of blood. What a quaint collection of weapons. "Do you go on these assignments?"

"No. Members are also required to come in for sparring practice three times a week when they are in residence," he continues. "You'll also be expected to work out in the gym for a minimum of an hour a day. We have treadmills, if running's your thing, but there's also an indoor track you can use, too. You'll scan in your hours with one of your key cards, so we can keep track of your progress."

Gyms. GPS. Tablets. DNA. Retinal scanning. Speed dating. Key cards.

The Queen of Hearts needn't have worried about taking my head, as it's obvious it'll explode right off of my body without her having to lift one of her pudgy fingers.

"Are you from a book?"

I'm finally given his attention as he tucks the tablet away. "No. I'll be your personal trainer, and I'm also a licensed nutritionist in case we need to fine tune your diet to maximize potential."

Is this truly an Institute? Perhaps it's more along the lines of a prison?

Kip pulls out a folder and flips through it before slipping out a few sheets of paper. "You have homework tonight. I want you to list your favorite weapons so we can find the right match for you on assignments. I know you said you like swords, but those are a bit harder to hide in public spaces. You may want to consider daggers or even sais."

I'm considering crumpling the sheets he passes me and depositing them into the nearest waste bin. Homework, indeed.

"Any questions?"

None for his ears, that's for sure.

When I'm at the door, he calls out, "Oh, and you might want to ease up on biscuits and dessert at mealtime." He smacks his bottom meaningfully.

I am unable to resist the urge to snatch a throwing star off a nearby wall. It is sent sailing, barely nicking the cartilage of his ear.

He leaps about a foot into the air, his hand going to his hardly bleeding ear. "Shit! What was that for?"

I tell him, tapping on my own behind, "You ease up on the biscuits and dessert."

For a moment, he simply stares at me. But then he says stupidly, "You missed."

I smirk when I leave, because I most certainly did not miss.

☽ I'm supposed to find Mary to go over modern-day clothing and the like, as she's disappointed I've yet to order anything from the catalogues left, but instead I find myself a nice bench in an empty corridor and tug out the phone Wendy gave me. If I have to go through one more lesson, one more lecture, one more reason to acclimate myself to the Twenty-First Century, I might very well go ballistic and that would do none of us any good. And then, because I am clearly a fool, I spend the next few minutes searching for the list of numbers she claimed were pre-programmed in, and then another few minutes trying to remember how to actually use the one I want.

I barely know him, and yet, I want to hear his voice. I'm craving that connection, that ease I thought, hoped even, that I'd never experience again.

Loud, unfamiliar ringing fills my ears; I'm left wincing. When Finn answers, he says, "Look at who's finally using her phone."

"Do people not greet one another in this day and age?"

He's silent for several seconds. "Hello, Alice."

A smile fights its way out of me. "Hello, Finn."

"I'm not one for phones, to be honest," he tells me. "I've always been better at face time."

And what a face it is.

I've done a lot of things in my life. I've faced plenty of daunting situations that required nerves of steel. So, it's frustrating I'm forced to muster courage to say the following. "It has occurred to me that I've spent nearly a week in New York City and have yet to actually exit a building—not counting our ill-fated trip to England. And even then, I was outside for mere minutes."

I fear I've stunned him, because he doesn't respond. So I plow forth with, "I'm used to enjoying a bit of fresh air every day."

Continued, lingering silence follows. I add, more resolutely, "I'm told that there are many things I ought to see here in the Twenty-First Century, but so far, outside of this building, I'm not even positive they exist."

"You're not a prisoner here, you know. You're free to walk out the door any time you wish."

Oh, Lord. He's taken it the wrong way.

"I'm assuming you'd want to come back because of room and board," he continues, "but nobody has a gun to your head saying you have to."

Bloody, insufferable man. Now he's simply teasing me.

I drop the phone at the same time I drop my head into my hands. I scramble to pick it up, but when I do, I shake it with both fists wrapped around the small machine.

A faint voice says, "Alice? You still there?"

I lift the phone back up to my ear. "Yes, sorry. I dropped this blasted thing. Why does it have to be so tiny?"

"Where are you right now?"

"Tenth floor, avoiding more technology lessons and lectures. Furthermore, I just had some nitwit assign me homework and tell me to lay off the desserts because I apparently have a fat arse or something. I have to tell you, Finn, I'm displeased at the lack of decorum and manners that this century has brought about."

For a tense moment, I wonder if he's going to chastise me again for maligning yet another colleague. But then he says, "Kip, right?"

"The very one," I mutter.

"He's an asshole. And he tells that shit to everybody, so . . . I know it's hard, but don't take it personally. It's meaningless. He might as well be telling you that the sky is green and grass is red."

The thing is, though, I've seen both of those things before. "Have you been informed your arse is fat?"

"Actually," Finn says solemnly, "I have. On multiple occasions."

I laugh then, genuinely laugh until my cheeks hurt from smiling so much. "Perhaps you oughtn't be called the Collectors' Society, then. Perhaps it should be the Fat Arse Brigade instead."

"*We* are the Collectors' Society," he corrects, "and speak for yourself. My ass is just fine, thank you very much."

It is, actually. I've had many an inappropriate peek at it in the last couple days.

I get up off the bench and wander over to a window. The sky is gray and peppered with heavy clouds, but rain isn't a bother to me. Not anymore, at least. "I can just leave, any time I like?"

"You'll need door cards and ID to get back in, but yes." And then, more gently, "I'm sorry if you felt like you'd been trapped here. Had I know . . ."

"Don't be silly. Not trapped. Just . . . confused." In so many more ways than one.

"I get it," he tells me. "Believe me. I've been where you are before."

I press a hand against the pane. It is cool to the touch, and my fingers leave behind impressions in the condensation from my body heat. "I got those cards you were mentioning during yet another one of Wendy's attempts to drain my brain of any functionality." He chuckles then, soft yet rich, the sound curling around me even though it's coming from a tiny machine held to my ear. "But I suppose that means I'm a proper member now, even though I haven't been through any initiation rites. I'm sorely disappointed in that, too, Finn. One would think a secretive group such as yourselves would at least have some mystical ceremony to solidify new members. You ought to speak to your father about that."

"What kind of initiation would you like? Black robes, candles, chalices, that kind of thing?"

My smile grows larger at his amusement. "Maybe. Solemn vows, rites of passage. Perhaps choral music in the background. Gregorian chant would be nice."

"My fraternity in college did that sort of shit. It was . . ." He search-es for the proper word. "Comical, actually. They took themselves so seriously, like it was a great honor for anybody to join, and for what? Keggers, mostly."

I bite my lip to keep from laughing. "What, pray tell, is a kegger?"

"College parties during which people get drunk off their asses and do stupid things."

Some things never change. "My father works at a university, you know. Oxford."

"Does he?" He sounds surprised at my admission.

I think I'm surprised by it, too. "Did he do so in my book?"

Finn clears his throat. "No. At least . . . No. But, the real, um . . . the person who it's said Lewis Carroll based your story off of? Her father worked at a university, too."

My mouth goes dry. "There's a real Alice?"

"That came out wrong. *You're* the real Alice," he says firmly. "The one on the pages was a representation of *you.*"

"But there's a woman out there, who looks like me? Has—had my life? My father? Was her name Alice, too?"

"She's been dead for a long time, but—"

"What was her surname?"

It takes him a good few seconds before he says, "Liddell."

My legs give out from beneath me, and I drop to the ground before the window. That's my last name. *My* real last name, not the one I've used for privacy since coming back from Wonderland.

My name.

Mine.

Isn't it?

"If it's any consolation," he continues, his soft voice laced with a bitter rue, "it's said I'm based off some guy that Mark Twain knew, too. That's who wrote my books, by the way."

I root around for my voice. "But . . ."

"I wish I could give you all the answers, but I don't know how it works. I really don't. That name was never in your story, nor was your father. But the Librarian tells me that it's the *intent* that matters. Maybe Carroll somehow instinctively knew of your history. Maybe his intent, when it came to that book, was to have a girl named Alice Liddell whose father worked at a university."

There's that word again. *Intent.* "But how could there be another one? Another Alice Liddell?"

"Some scientists insist that there are always doppelgängers out there in the world. Maybe it's like that for Timelines, too. Maybe each Timeline has somebody who is similar to another somewhere else. I don't know, though."

"With the same *name?* Same *family?* Same face?"

"You and she look nothing alike. I can promise you that."

I close my eyes, dragging my knees up to my chest. Son of a jabberwocky, am I about to have a panic attack? I can't remember the last. No, that's a lie. I can, and it's a day I'd really rather never recall for the rest of my life.

"I know this is a lot to take in—"

My sigh is bitter as I drop my head to my raised knees. "That's putting it mildly."

"But maybe *this* is your initiation. Have you considered that? Because it's one we all go through. Nobody has an easy time grasping this, Alice. Nobody. There are no robes, no candles, no vows . . . There's just an identity crisis. If you can make it through to the other side, you're in."

I mutter, "It's a bloody shoddy initiation."

A touch to my shoulder startles my head up. And there he is, squatting down in front of me, his phone to his ear. "I know."

Something inside me quakes, wants to break free, but I refuse to allow it. I allow a shuddery breath and then force my body to comply with my wishes. "Aren't you the quiet one? Do you normally like sneak upon unsuspecting ladies?"

He shrugs as he tucks his phone back into a pocket. "You don't need the phone anymore."

My face flames as I yank the blasted machine away. "Right. Of course."

"So." He fully sits down, scooting against the wall next to me so that our bodies are just an inch or so apart. "About your request . . ."

"I had a request?"

"You wanted me to show you around New York, right?"

Bloody hell, do I feel like a tomato right now. "I wasn't—"

"I'd be happy to."

My head tilts to face him, but the truth is, it feels as if we're been spinning rather than sitting.

"Can we start small, though? I have somewhere I have to go in a few hours, but a walk would be good. Maybe coffee? We can do the more touristy stuff later."

Could my skin warm any further? Of course he has plans. Why wouldn't he? Just because I'm his partner doesn't mean he owes me anything. "I don't want to inconvenience you—"

"Besides. For all of us who weren't born in the Twenty-First Century, the true initiation is a coffee shop, you know. There's one about six blocks over that's good. It's always crowded, but their espressos are worth the wait. It's like liquid crack." At the look on my face, he quickly clarifies, "It's addictive."

"I don't drink coffee."

His eyebrows lift up.

"I'm English, remember?"

Oh, those beautiful lips of his curve upward again. "Plenty of English drink coffee."

"I prefer tea."

"Luckily for you, they have tea at coffee shops. And hot chocolate, if that's what you like."

I glance down at the dress I'd found in Sara's closet. It's white and loose and barely grazes my knees, with crocheted lace trimming the hem.

As if he knows what I'm wondering, he assures me, "You look fine. Very boho. It's a good look for you."

"Boho?"

I'm annoyed at how much I like the quirk of his mouth. "Bohemian. Do they not say that in England? Are bohemians coffee drinkers, maybe? A rare breed?"

I give in and allow myself to giggle. A small weight lifts off my shoulders, even if momentarily.

READING BOOKS

WHEN A LOUD HORN beeps, Finn grabs my arm and tugs me back up onto the pavement. "Careful!"

My hair flutters in my face as a bright-yellow vehicle with the word *Taxi* on it zooms by. "Do you ever get used to this?"

"Actually," Finn says, "yeah. You do."

The Twenty-First Century is chaotic, loud, and terrifying, to be honest. According to Finn, people travel in cars on the road and planes in the sky and, from what I can tell, they're all in constant motion. He's been good about pointing things out to me, and not talking down as he explains how things work in this modern day and age, but panic steadily rises in my chest anyway. I have questions about all that he's already said and more, but I'm afraid it'll be too much if I let them out. He assures me that, over the coming weeks (and months and years, if I choose to stick around), I'll get to know this city and century like the back of my hand. While that, too, is a terrifying prospect, I choose in this moment to focus on the mystery next to me, to narrow down my focus onto something, and someone, I can handle.

"How long have you been here?" And then, realizing my question smacks more strongly of accusation than curiosity, I clarify, "In New York, with Van Brunt."

Finn's hands stuff into his pockets as he angles us toward a street corner with colored lights on it. "I was recruited when I was fifteen, so that makes it thirteen years now."

He's just a few years older than me.

We stop alongside the crowd. Does the light have something to do with movement? "When I came here, Brom got me the best tutors money could buy, put me into high school, and then paid for college. He wouldn't let me officially work for the Society until I graduated, although I did work on numerous missions prior to that." His smile is a bit naughty. "Unofficially, of course."

I watch a couple nearby laugh over something on one of their phones. Goodness, does anyone go anywhere without theirs? "During that time, he adopted you?"

"He and his wife, yes."

But the flat yet anguished look on Finn's face books no room for further questioning on that subject, no matter how much they burn inside me. Is Brom married? What name had he mentioned? Katrina? In that vein, hadn't Finn mentioned his mother was dead? And oh bloody hell, how could I have forgotten the mention of a brother?

"Victor came here even younger." He stares off into the distance. "I think he was like three or four. And Mary came when she was a teen, too. The A.D. was also young. A lot of members come as kids."

"Like a sweatshop," I say with mock solemnity.

His laugh is a puff of surprise. "Or a child army."

"Are they your siblings, then? Has Van Brunt adopted the lot of you?"

"Victor, yes," he admits. "But not the others."

Aha! And also, really? "Victor's last name is . . ." I search around in my memory for the distinctive surname. "Frankenstein. Correct?"

Finn rocks back on his heels, like he's unsure if he's telling secrets that are better left to others. But then he says, "It's his birth name. Legally, he's now Victor Van Brunt."

"Would people recognize his name, like they would yours?"

A small, glowing man appears in the black box across the street at the same time the light above turns green. The crowd surges forward. *Green means go.* "Worse. Way worse."

"But he goes by Frankenstein at the Institute."

A pair of young women strolling near us whisper furtively to one another, their eyes hot upon us. Have I spoken too loudly?

Luckily, Finn blocks their stares with his body. "It's complicated. Honestly? I'm surprised he told you that name at all. It's an extremely touchy subject."

I'm glad when the women turn down a different street than us. "Some woman was the first to say it. At that first meeting."

I wait for the man next to me to explain the discrepancy between Frankenstein and Van Brunt, but he doesn't. So I say, instead, "I should have liked to have continued my education. Like I told you, my father was a learned man."

"Didn't Wonderland have schools of higher learning?"

He sounds genuinely curious. "You all don't know much about Wonderland, do you?"

"No," he admits. "There are those Timelines that are still mysteries to us thanks to the fantastical elements of their stories."

"Is there no magic in your original Timeline?"

He pulls in a deep breath. "None." And then, more gently, "I'm fascinated by those that do, though. And even though I go in, knowing it will happen, I'm still amazed by what I see."

I'm quiet for a long moment. "There are many amazing things in Wonderland."

His head briefly tilts toward me before we reach another intersection.

My fingers curl inward, nails digging into my palm. "To answer your question, yes, there are schools of higher learning in Wonderland. But I never attended any." My smile is tight. "I suppose you must think me uneducated or ignorant, having spent so much of my formative years running mad amongst Wonderlanders."

"Not at all. And I'd be the last person who could judge such things."

There's bitterness there, and hints of intriguing resentment. But this, too, is made clear to be a closed subject, so I prompt, "You said the Society recruited you when you were fifteen? Why then? Why not when you were younger, like Victor?"

Silence settles between us on the busy street for several seconds. "That was shortly after the last official book I was in ended. Nobody can leave a Timeline until that happens."

It's weird how much I enjoy these tiny morsels of information he's reluctantly doling out to me. "How many books were you a subject of?"

The question embarrasses him, because his tan cheeks color ever so slightly. "Four. Although . . ." He sighs, running a hand through his sandy hair. "I'm told there were more, but they were unfinished. So, I guess they don't count, thank God."

It's a sobering thought. "And I was in two."

He motions toward a shop several doors down, nodding. Suddenly, a woman wearing sky-high shoes falls to the ground a few feet away, knocked down by a man paying more attention on his phone than on the sights before him. Finn is immediately there to help her up when the man refuses to give her a single glance, and gently holds onto her until he's assured she's okay. And then, once that's done, he obtains her a cab and pays the driver to take her wherever it is she's going.

She lowers her window as the cab pulls away. She's as enchanted with this man as I apparently am.

"Sorry," he tells me.

"What are you sorry for now?"

"We were in the middle of a conversation, and I—"

He needs to stop this. I won't ever be able to resist him if he doesn't. I promptly cut him off and ask, "Have you ever read your books?"

"One," he admits. "The first one. After Brom explained the truth to me, I went to the Librarian, curious. She cautioned me about reading them, though—as I'm sure she cautioned you. It sat on my dresser for months before I touched it."

"That must have been . . ." I search for the right word. "Unnerving to read about people you know in such a way."

He opens a glass front door for me, and a blast of strong aromas tantalizes my nose. So this is a coffee shop. It's crowded and loud, just like he cautioned, and filled with people drinking and talking and playing on their phones or computers. Some people are dressed elegantly, some in barely anything at all.

I am enraptured by what I see.

"I wish now that I hadn't, to be honest," Finn says in a low voice once the door closes behind us. "What made it worse was being around other people who'd read those books, too. Other kids in school. Adults I knew. Miniseries or movies shown on TV or in classroom. References made in passing that were like little jabs coming out of nowhere. Lots of talk around Banned Books Week. People thinking they knew me—" He shakes his head. "They don't know shit. Authors can only allow readers to learn so much about their characters. As much as they try to build someone three dimensionally on a page, words are still limited and subject to imagination and interpretation."

He leads us over to one of the few unoccupied tables, in the back by a large window. The woman at the next table looks up at Finn, her eyes widening in appreciation before she spots me.

I ask him, "I take it your stories are popular?"

A hard breath is blown out. "I guess you could say that." He's contemplative. "Nothing like yours, though."

I swallow my unease. "Reading them, though . . . Was that as unnerving as having to listen to people talking about them?"

"It was a complete mindfuck. What would you like to drink?"

I blink up at him, startled by how easily he switched subjects. "A hot cocoa, please."

One of his impish grins graces his handsome face. "Not tea? But, you're English!"

"What can I say? I'm a contradiction."

"Your words, not mine." He leans down, a palm planted on the table, another on the back of my chair. "It's hot as hell outside, or didn't you notice?"

It's suddenly hot in here, too. But I tell him primly, "Aren't you going to be drinking something hot, too? Or is coffee served cold nowadays?"

He leans in closer, leaving me wondering if I'd only imagined the cool air. "Yes, coffee is served cold. It's called . . ." He lowers his voice to a mere whisper. "Wait for it. *Iced coffee.*"

I shove him away. Prat.

That's not entirely fair, though, because right now? This teasing? It feels good. It feels . . . hopeful.

"Your wish is my command, though. If the lady wants hot cocoa, she will have hot cocoa." He wanders back to the front of the shop to stand in a line fifteen people deep. I watch as he tugs his phone out of his pocket and stares down at it just like nearly every other person in the shop. Like a sheep, I pull the one Wendy gave me and wrestle with it until I find what she called the search function in the browser.

Curiosity burns like wildfire through my veins.

I type slowly: *Huckleberry Finn.*

A million and a half responses come back. In addition to . . . What did Wendy call them? Links? In addition to plenty of those, none of which I select, there are also illustrations of a young, mischievous, yet dirty boy wearing a ragged hat and holding a gun. The same child that was in the drawing in Van Brunt's office.

This is my partner? This *child?*

I can't help but glance back and forth, between the beautiful man I've just recently come to know and the pictures. My attention is quickly drawn to the person at the front of the line digging through their wallet, though. The elderly fellow is dirty, his hair bedraggled and his clothes in poor condition; it's obvious they don't have enough money to pay for their drink. People behind him are furious, saying disrespectful things, but Finn steps out of line so he can go up to the front and give the flustered man several bills from his own wallet.

A buzzing fills my ears, a sickening drop lands in the bottom of my stomach. My heart hammers hard, like I'm betraying his confidence by staring at such secrets, so I go back and change the wording at the top. One much more acceptably selfish.

Sixteen million hits come back for *Alice in Wonderland,* leaving me confident I very well may lose the contents of my stomach all over this coffee shop.

There are images here, too, of girls and women all with blonde hair and blue dresses, some dressed modestly, some dressed so scantily that I'm blushing once more. There are rabbits and pocket watches and cats with grins and men with silly, tall hats. There are tea parties and rageful women with crowns.

My hands shake so hard I drop the phone once more.

A man at a nearby table reaches down and claims it for me. "You okay?"

I take it from him. "Fine. Thank you."

He has a twangy accent I can't place. "Want me to go get you some water?"

There's the *trusty water will save you when you're upset* bit again. A smudge of hysterical laughter climbs up my throat. "No, thank you."

"You're white as a sheet. Should I go get your boyfriend?"

A fist reaches inside my chest and tries to squeeze what's already been wrung dry. But then I realize he means Finn. Of course. Finn. The man I came in with. The one who now has his phone pressed up against his ear and his back facing me.

"No. I'm fine. Thank you for your concern, though."

He's dubious, but the man finally leaves me alone and goes back to his computer.

I stuff my phone back into a handbag I'd found in Sara's room and spend the rest of my wait people watching. Truth be told, it makes me homesick. And when I catch a fleeting flash of pale skin and dark hair outside of my window, the homesickness trebles until I fear all the joints in my body might disappear.

"I will keep searching. I won't give up. There's always a loophole."

But there wasn't. And there isn't.

Black hair fades to golden brown as Finn returns to the table. "Careful," he tells me as he sets a paper cup down. "It's hot."

I blink a few times, praying my eyes have stayed dry. And then I pull the drink toward me, grateful for the distraction. "It wouldn't be called hot cocoa if it wasn't hot, would it? It would be warm cocoa, or perhaps lukewarm cocoa, or even room temperature cocoa."

He mutters, "Smartass," before sipping his own drink.

"You were telling me about reading your own story." And telling me his secrets.

A sigh precedes his cup finding its way back to the table. "I think the best advice I can give you concerning that is to not give into temptation and read yours. That's what this is about, right?" He bites his lower lip, and my fingers have to curl around the cup in order to not reach out and gently tug it loose. "You're naturally curious. You want to see what some man wrote about you well over a century ago, but don't do it. I wish now that I hadn't read mine. And I really wish I hadn't said anything to you earlier, either. It's pointless. It means nothing."

"Were they unflattering? Is that what soured you on them?"

"No—well, yeah, in a way. Our stories are told from somebody else's perspective, so that colors how you come out. But that wasn't what got to me. I think it was just . . ." He blows out a soft breath. "It's an existential thing, I guess. Knowing that my life *could* have come about thanks to some man I don't know, and that all of my problems did, too, is a hell of a lot to swallow."

A small, dirty boy, in threadbare clothes and a straw hat—with a gun, no less. My curiosity nearly blazes, it's so strong.

"Do you resent this Mark Twain, then?"

"Actually," he says softly, "I do."

The look in his eyes is so intense I'm forced to glance down at my drink. "Have you read my stories?"

I hear, rather than see, his sigh. "Brom asked a few of us to read up on you before tracking you down."

"So you'll read others, but resent your own."

"I try not to read up on coworkers, no. At least, fully read their books. I'll skim instead. But you weren't easy to find. We couldn't just edit a Timeline and locate you. You disappeared into Wonderland again several years after the end of your second story. We needed clues. None of our trips to England found any traces of your presence." He takes another sip. "Truth be told, we almost gave up. It wasn't until Brom's friend sent him a message about some woman mentioning Wonderland."

"Dr. Featheringstone."

He nods as he takes another drink.

"Did you go to England looking for me?"

"I did," he says. "Twice."

I tug on my long braid. "When I first came to the Society, Victor said—"

"Christ. Do not put stock in whatever Victor had to say. If you haven't already noticed, he loves to talk out of his ass." I'm given a smile, though. "He's English, for the record."

Does everyone find this man as ridiculously charming as I do? "Victor said," I continue, "that I did not look the way I should have. Do you feel that way, too? Especially as I apparently don't look like the other one?"

"Alice—"

My eyes hover somewhere over his shoulder, focusing indirectly on a man with orange hair standing straight up. "I suppose it shouldn't matter. But I'm curious. Are there pictures in my story?"

I know there must be. When I searched for my name, little drawn images of a blonde girl in a blue dress popped up.

Another sigh fills the space between us. "Of course you were different. The books have you as a child. You're an adult now. It would have been weird had there not been differences."

My fingers drum against the table. "It bothers me, knowing you all have an idea about my past and I'm blind to yours."

"Only your childhood," he corrects. "And only the part that the author chose to talk about. It's not like I had a play-by-play of every second of your life. And there are your later years in Wonderland that none of us know about."

Thank goodness. Cocoa burns my tongue when I finally take a sip, but I refuse to flinch or ease up on my gulps. "Do you ever wish you were back in your Timeline?"

There is no hesitation. "No. I'm where I belong. This place . . ." He gestures around the coffee shop. "This is who I am. This is where my family is. When I think about the stories I'm from, they no longer seem real to me. The years I've spent here do."

It's nearly identical to what his father said.

I envy him, this feeling of belonging and rightness. Because, as alien and fresh as this all feels, my history weighs down nearly every breath I take. I didn't belong in Wonderland. I didn't fit in in England. I don't know if I'll ever feel at home in New York.

"Do you ever wish you could go back to yours?"

I hide behind my cup, sipping the stinging chocolate as I try to piece my answer together. *Yes, God, yes* is there. *I can't* is equally strong. *I'm confused* and *Even if I wanted to, I shouldn't* are right there as well. I eventually tell him, "Until Van Brunt found me, I never planned on going back to Wonderland."

His blue-gray eyes study me in the amber light coming from a pendant fixture overhead. "Do you mind if I ask why you left?"

"There is no room for misinterpretation. There is nothing unclear about the meaning. Your head, or your departure. Are you really so selfish you would put yourself above Wonderland?"

I clear my throat. Focus on ensuring my words remain steady. "I found myself not wanting to allow madness to dictate my life." My smile is thin. Brittle. "There was no future for me there." No matter what I had hoped or believed.

"And at the Pleasance?"

"Are you asking if I felt I had a future in an asylum?" I love that his grin is sheepish, so I take pity on him. "As bizarre as it sounds, there was more of one for me there than where I'd been."

"Do you miss it, though?"

"The asylum? Not really. It wasn't as bad as you might think, though. My brain wasn't drilled into, so there is that."

"You know that's not what I meant."

I lift an eyebrow. "Do you?"

There's no hesitation. "No."

INTENT

OVER THE COURSE OF the next fortnight, I am immersed in all things Society and Twenty-First Century. I learn what televisions are, which wars have occurred, how man has flown into space and to the moon. I discover how music has changed and of how women's and civil rights have advanced. I'm finally coerced into choosing a new wardrobe (Mary can be relentless until she gets her way) but am relieved to find out the items previously hanging in my closet were not Sara's.

"Oh, those," Mary said one morning. "They were things I picked up before you arrived. God, you would have hated Sara's clothes. She looked like a prissy bridesmaid all the time."

She's disappointed in the choices I make, though. Whereas Finn made bohemian sound like a good thing, Mary makes it sound like I'm playacting as an urchin on the streets.

I spend countless additional hours with Wendy, going over all her gadgets until she's certain I am comfortable with them. Comfortable is her word, though, because they actually leave me vexed more often than not. She sets me up with videos on my computer to help fill in the blanks about history and modern-day culture, and I will admit to watching them long into the wee hours of night, fascinated by what I see.

More hours are spent with Kip, training. I purposely ignored his request for weapon preferences for a solid week before I relented and told him I'd go with daggers—but only because they're small and can be strapped easily to my legs under skirts. I'm forced to endure gun instruction and target practice, and it's there I come to realize I am, in fact, not naturally talented with all weaponry. I am a terrible shot.

Finn isn't, though. Finn's accuracy is frightening, and so is how coolly he is able to point his gun at a great distance and fire once, only for it to find the exact spot he wanted. He's also brilliant at swords and archery, even more so during sparring matches. I surreptitiously watch him during our shared practices, and hate that his talent makes him even more compelling.

Mary, on the other hand, is awful with weaponry. Kip berates her on a daily basis, but rather than breaking down in the face of his disapproval like I think many men or women would, she revels in it. Taunts him at how lousy an instructor he is, and gleefully breaks bō staffs and arrows at alarming rates. She admitted to me how she'd learned the fine art of poisoning from Victor, and I wasn't sure if I ought to be impressed or horrified by such a revelation.

"Not all poisons kill," was her response. "Many merely incapacitate."

Victor, like his adoptive brother, can more than hold his own when it comes to fighting. He's much stronger than he looks, and I'll admit to not wanting to get in between the two during sparring practice. I like watching them interact, though. There's a subtle bond between the two men I didn't notice during my first few days—and while there are plenty of insults and arguments, there is also deep respect and loyalty.

At the end of my second week, Victor and Mary are sent off on a retrieval assignment after Wendy proclaims his pen rehabilitated. I learn that, at any point, only three teams can go out on missions, leaving the rest behind to research identifying catalysts or whatever else it is they do in their off time. Grounded locally, Finn follows through on his offer to show me around New York City. After communal dinners, he takes me out exploring, sometimes until the sun rises slowly back over the horizon. We sneak out to Central Park on more than one occasion and walk in comfortable silence or minutes filled with words and questions for one another. He borrows one of the Institute's cars and takes me outside of the city to a place called the Hamptons. With my toes buried beneath sand, salty air licking my face, and a man finding seashells for me, long-lost snatches of pure, unadulterated wonder and joy burble to the surface.

Slowly, slowly, I get to know him through these outings.

Finn's smart. He's funny, he's honest, he can be maddeningly sarcastic, and sometimes, he bears too much weight on his shoulders. I've learned that the Society views him as Van Brunt's second in command, so he's constantly inundated with questions and problems that no one else outside of his father gets asked. He takes it all in stride, though, and listens without impatience and strives to do what's best for all he knows. Including me, even when instinct kicks in and I try my damnedest to keep him at arm's length.

Impossibly, I'm weakening toward his charms.

I've finally allowed myself to admit a truth that I thought never could be. I'm utterly attracted to him. He's honorable and kind and, on a superficial note, he's gorgeous—terribly, painfully sexy in a way that leaves me wishing I'd been assigned a different partner. Not that I'd ever act out on this pathetically burgeoning yet undoubtedly one-sided attraction, but I've dreamed about him more than once (which I insisted to myself later on could at least be viewed as hopeful progress, no matter how shameful it may be). Fantasized when I ought to have been focusing in on more important things.

Like where the bloody hell Sweeney Todd went to.

Since our run-in, the weasel has vanished. No sighting of him or the woman he was initially photographed with has surfaced on security cameras Wendy has running day in and out. No further break-in attempts have occurred, no alarms set off unexpectedly.

It doesn't sit well with me. Not when there are lives at stake, and catalysts he could be destroying.

I'm thinking about this after our breakfast plates are removed one morning two weeks after I first arrived. "We ought to go to the bookstore, the one Todd disappeared into for hours. Remember? We could talk to the owner there. See if he knows anything about our barber friend."

Finn sets down his coffee cup, now emptied. He's amused. "I was wondering how long it would take you to finally say this."

Somehow, that stings. "Meaning?"

He shrugs an infuriatingly charismatic yet annoying shrug that leaves me assuming he doesn't want to tell me what he means.

I stare at him for a long moment before frustration rips through me. Perhaps I've been the blind one. Perhaps I've let myself be dazzled by something that I had no right to let myself feel. Finally, a fault of his to cling to.

Defenses rise up out of freshly tilled ground. "Was this a test, then? See how long it takes poor, befuddled Alice before she screws her head on just right?"

I might as well have slapped him, Finn's so taken aback by my quiet vehemence. "What?"

I refuse to allow myself to be taken in by the hurt that flashes in his eyes. My napkin is thrown on the table and I storm out, purposely choosing to ignore the curious stares of fellow diners.

Right before I reach the stairs, Finn grabs my hand. "What just happened?"

The skin beneath his fingers tingles. Too many memories fight to surface. I'm not ready for this. I'm not. "Let go of me."

He does so with alacrity. "Talk to me. What's going on?"

"My leaving changes nothing. How could it?"

"Nonetheless, I will always hope it will."

I need to push him away. I can't do this—I . . . I can't believe I even momentarily entertained the notion of letting someone so close again. "I do not appreciate you testing me."

His eyes widen in surprise. "What are you talking about?"

I've had more than enough games to last three lifetimes. "You're wondering how long it would take me to finally come to a conclusion."

Somehow, my icy statement relieves him. "All I meant was that I'd been wondering when you'd be ready."

Never, I vow. I'll never allow myself to be ready for vulnerability again. But I won't allow him to know that. Instead, I play naive. "Ready for what?"

"Anything. Your first night here, there was a break-in. Your second, you were attacked. It's okay to ease into—"

My defenses double. "I've been watching movies and learning to turn on computers like a mindless puppet while some fiend is undoubtedly collecting catalysts. Situations like this do not call for easing, no matter how alluring it may sound." My words ring through the empty stairwell. "I told you before, I am not fragile. I will not break. I do not need to ease into anything. I'm—"

"Stop. Just stop." He runs a hand through his hair as he slumps back against the wall. "I know you're not fragile. But you're also not a superhero, so—"

"What in the bloody hell is a superhero?"

"Somebody with magical powers. All I'm saying is, we've thrown a lot at you. *A lot.* Probably more than we do anyone else." I open my mouth to argue, but he keeps going. "Actually, I can verify that one. Nobody since I've been here has ever had so much of the Society's secrets and histories thrown at them so quickly. We like to ease members into their roles. People tend to freak out over the existential shit. They'll be fine, think they're fine, and it'll hit them out of the blue. They freak out. Retrievals have been ruined. We just thought—"

I'm livid. Is this what he's thought of me all along? *We?* Has there been an official discussion concerning the newest recruit? Behind closed doors, perhaps, while I'm off in a child's classroom, learning how to dial a damn phone?

He grabs my arms. Forces me to look at him. Says quietly, calmly, "I need you to tell me what's going on right now, Alice. Because I've gotta admit, I don't have a clue."

I can't.

I can't.

I say, hating how cold my voice is, "I was told that if I didn't come along, Wonderland might disappear. And yet, nothing has been said about going back since that first day."

"We don't go into magical Timelines without preparation. And the Librarian is still researching what the catalyst might be."

He fights me with logic. It makes me want to break down in maniacal laughter. Wouldn't the Caterpillar approve of this man? "How is it we can find a playbook at some fancy house yet can't figure out one for Wonderland?"

"We will figure it out. We'll go. It's only a matter of when. Never an if."

My hands shake. I'm confused. I want to lash out again, force him and his kindness away. Because if we are to go back to Wonderland, and he as my partner . . .

What if I can't keep him safe? What if—

My heart sinks. Ice fills my veins. Vivid images of *what ifs* spring forth. Too much blood has been spilled over the last few years, too many lives lost. Too many dreams crushed beneath the feet of reality.

I barely know this man, but something inside tells me if he were to die because of my inability to follow the peace accords, I would never be able to forgive myself. But then, I also don't think I can live with myself if something were to happen to all the people I left behind if I get caught once I cross into Wonderland's borders.

A thumb brushes across my cheek. I flinch back, but Finn's still here. "What are you not telling me?"

Everything, I think.

"Why won't you talk to me?"

"Maybe you and I come from different time periods. I come from a time in which people didn't offer up intimate details freely. In my time—"

"We don't."

I blink in surprise.

"My original Timeline's dates were similar to yours. I've just been here longer than you, that's all."

I think back to the dirty, young boy in ragged clothes I saw on my phone that day in the coffee shop. Since then, I've refused to search for anyone else, myself included. I know nothing other than what they've all told me, which is not much at all, to be honest.

Not much at all. It's easier that way, especially when it comes time to walk away.

"What are you so afraid of?"

I tell him quietly, "Not a damn thing." I'm pleased that my words don't wobble.

Liar, liar, liar.

"Do you think I'm going to use whatever you tell me against you?"

Knowledge is the sharpest of weapons.

"How are we supposed to work together if you don't trust me?"

I have begun to trust him, which is the problem. I'm terrified to trust him, which is an even bigger problem. Trust is an intimacy I cannot bear to risk again. "Do you trust me?"

"Yes," he says without hesitation.

"You shouldn't."

A pair of Wendy's tech team walks by. Finn steers me to a small room just off the stairway filled with brooms, mops, and cleaning supplies. Once he shuts the door, he asks, "Why shouldn't I trust you?"

"This is a delightful place for a meeting."

He sighs. "Why shouldn't I trust you, Alice?"

My back is literally and figuratively up against a wall. "Trust can be . . . fragile. Fleeting. Changing. It can be used against a person."

"Do you plan on using my trust against me?"

I'm chewing on glass when I say, "Trust is not any easy thing for me."

"News flash," he says softly. "It isn't easy for most of us."

"You can't possibly trust *me*. You don't even know me."

"Your choice, not mine."

I'm stunned.

He takes a deep breath. Puts several feet between us as he leans up against the opposite wall. "Every time we're together, you're constantly asking me questions about myself and my history. But whenever I ask one in return, you clam up. Switch subjects. I know nothing about you outside of the books from your childhood and that your father works at a university."

"That's not true!"

He doesn't say anything. He doesn't have to, because he's telling the truth. I do hide my past from him, from all of them. We've spent hours and hours together, many just the two of us, and in that time I've slowly picked away at the shell he hides behind.

He has let me. And in return I've only continued to fortify my shield.

His frustration is nearly tangible. For long seconds, the standoff between us in unbearable, and I fear that I've crossed a line I may never be able to erase.

But then he says, "Let's go to Ex Libris."

Just like that.

We take a cab to the bookstore, and while we're stuck in mind-numb-ing traffic, he says nothing. Asks nothing. Doesn't even look at me. He spends his time doing whatever it is he does on his phone. I choose to follow suit and scan a file he's sent me rather than stick my foot any farther into my mouth.

F.K. Jenkins has owned the business for years after inheriting it from a spinster aunt. From what the Society can tell, he makes very little profit except for the rare first edition book that's found by eagle-eyed hunters on the search for buried treasure. Such surprise sales, often found within dusty, long-forgotten shelves, seem to fund his existence alongside the remnants of a trust from the aforementioned aunt. There are several notes indicating Jenkins has tried his hand at writing, too, but none of his books ever made it past slush piles. A copy of a form rejection from five years prior stares up at me when the car slows down at a light. Impersonal and short, it simply tells him that his work isn't what the publisher is looking for.

According to the notes, Ex Libris has been under surveillance ever since Todd and his lady friend were first tracked there weeks before. A camera was surreptitiously placed on a building across the way to face the front door, but so far, there has been no indication that Todd has returned. Jenkins himself seems to rarely leave the vicinity, and when he does, it's to shuffle down to a nearby local grocery store for supplies. Most of his food is delivered, though—twice a week, two boxes each time. A look at past orders shows he never varies in his requests.

What is it about this particular bookstore that drew Todd and his cohort?

I think about this as we slowly make our way through what Finn calls gridlock. Todd searching out books would not be a surprise, especially if he's using them to edit into Timelines or to search for catalysts. The real question is, though—why Ex Libris? Is it because it's local to where he lives, convenient for his needs? Or is it the opposite—does he travel across the city to an unfamiliar location, one that makes it all the harder to track him to his home base?

I read his story a few days back, during the dead of night while everyone else slept. I found a scanned copy of it online, as it'd fallen into public domain over the years. The thing is, Sweeney Todd died at the end of *A String of Pearls*. Victor had thought he'd merely been apprehended, but the story insists he was hanged for his crimes. And that troubles me, because Finn insisted that whatever happens in a story cannot be altered—Timelines, yes, but not the period of time described in the books themselves.

Sweeney Todd died hundreds of years ago. How is it he is running around New York City?

The silence is stifling. I clear my throat and ask, "Did you ever read the Penny Dreadful called *A String of Pearls?*"

I feel the driver's eyes settle on me via the rearview mirror.

Finn shifts in his seat as he angles his body toward me, his eyebrows lifting in question over the dark plastic frames of his mirrored sunglasses.

"I did. The villain in it died." I cock my head to the side, as if it has a noose around it and hold a fist aloft as if I'm holding the rope. A smile I hope might surface on his face never does. "Are ghosts real?"

"As far as I know," my partner says, "I don't think so—at least around here."

The driver coughs, but it suspiciously sounds like he's muttering, *"Cray-zee."*

I open up the texting function Wendy forced me to learn. I type out slowly: **If he died, how could he be here?**

When Finn leans over to read my message, I get that faint whiff of soap and man and mint and it makes my head fuzzy. He takes my phone and types in: **I don't know.**

It said something about him passing. Referenced his body as a swinging corpse.

It isn't until the cab drops us off a block away from the bookstore, and the bill has been paid, when Finn says, "Books can be subjective."

I'm glad we're back on common ground, that we have something more positive to focus on. "Meaning?"

"What if he didn't die?"

I'm flabbergasted. "I'm pretty sure that a swinging corpse means death, Finn."

"Brom and I aren't so sure that he's dead."

Scratch that. I'm flat-out agog. "You said that events in books can't change. His book, Todd's book . . . it says he's dead. If that's the case, then—"

"I read it."

I blink in surprise.

"Of course I read it. That asshole attacked you and tried to steal a catalyst. I read every last word I could get my hands on about Sweeney Todd."

His vehemence roots me to the spot I stand.

"Brom read it, too," he continues. "As did Victor. We—"

"Victor read it? You've all been talking about Todd without me?"

"Well, we three read *A String of Pearls*. And then I read pretty much everything else there is about that son of a bitch. Afterward, we discussed it. You weren't the only one wondering how in the hell he knew where it was. Or who he really might be."

I wish I could see his eyes behind those glasses of his.

"The blades you found suggest it's Sweeney Todd—but S. Todd could also refer to somebody else, possibly even somebody local that has stumbled upon Timelines. Wendy has been searching all the S. Todds in the area, but there are a lot to sift through. Even then, if it is *the* Sweeney Todd, if his story is somehow wrong, that he didn't die, he could be using an alias like many of the rest of us. Nothing we'd read or found answered whether or not it was him—and if so, *how*. Chances are, though, it's somebody else."

He had been thinking about this. A lot.

Finn turns away from me. "Let's go see Jenkins."

EX LIBRIS

T HE SMELL OF STAGNANT dust and paper is immediately over-
whelming. Row after row of cluttered, labeled shelves crowd the
store, many with yellowing pages sticking out into aisles to brush
against those who lose their way in the maze.

Something crashes deep within the store; a loud curse is bellowed.
When I round a bend, from *Mystery* to *Historical Romance*, I find an
older, rotund man limping toward us, clutching an intricately carved
cane topped with an even more intricately carved ivory wolf head.

"Goddamn books never stay stacked when you want them to." His
voice is guttural, no doubt in thanks to the cigarettes that the stench
wafting off of him insists he must smoke in droves. There's a hint of a
lisp, too. No—that's wrong. Not a lisp, but more like a slur. "Can I help
you find something?"

The left corner of F.K. Jenkins' mouth droops a bit as he says this,
but his eyes are just as shrewd as they were in the photograph I viewed
weeks before.

Finn's arm suddenly drapes across my waist and tugs me closer. I'm too surprised to do anything other than allow it. "Any chance you happen to have a first edition of *Strange Case of Dr. Jekyll and Mr. Hyde?* We've been on the hunt for a decent copy of that one forever. My father collects first editions, and that's one of the few that's slipped through the cracks."

Jenkins grunts as he stops before us. "Stevenson was a hack. Don't know why your pop would want that steaming pile of shit in his collection."

Finn's fingers tighten around my waist, curling in the soft fabric of my dress when he lets out a charming, albeit bemused, chuckle. "He's a sentimentalist, and the book reminds him of his childhood."

I'd say Jenkins' head tilts to the side, but there is no distinction between neck and head. "You've been here before."

"She's also a reader." Finn nudges me. "Thank God, she's not into first editions, though. Don't think my bank account could handle too many of those sorts."

Jenkins turns his attention to me, his small, calculating eyes lingering far too long on my bosom as they sweep my person. "Romance, right? Erotica, most likely."

The way he said that was so derisive, so belittling. My hand itches to knock that petty judgment right out of him.

"I'll bet you're one of those who like lady porn. I don't carry that here. What kind of self-respecting writer comes up with that shit?"

Finn must sense my anger, because his grip on me tightens significantly. "So, do you?"

I feel dirty when Jenkins eventually tears his eyes off of me. "Huh?"

My partner is less friendly when he addresses the book seller now. "Do you have the edition?"

"No Stevenson first editions that I can think of. Especially that one. Always thought it stupid. You're free to look around, though." We are dismissed when he abruptly limps away.

I'd already made up my mind to let Jenkins know what I thought of his misogynistic tirade when Finn leans in. My breath stills in confusion as one of his hand drifts up to my face to brush stray hairs away from my cheek. And then I'm a statue when his lips close in on the soft skin just to the side of my ear. Is he . . . Is he going to kiss me? After me basically telling him I will never trust him?

I can't even—I can't even *think*—

Soft words brush my skin. "1886STE-JH was deleted. Cameras everywhere."

Anticipation sinks to the bottom of my stomach. He's playacting for Jenkins' benefit. But then, right when I think he'll let go, he does kiss me—gently, those full lips of his on my skin just long enough to leave my knees and thoughts soft and yet electrified.

Callooh, callay, indeed.

"None of that in here!"

I startle, my head whipping around to find the source of the voice, but Jenkins is nowhere to be seen. But when Finn pulls away, I realize he was testing the shop owner to see just how carefully he's watching us. Discreet glances around pinpoint cameras in every corner of the store, and others overlooking dark aisles. The message is clear. We cannot discuss with one another anything related to why we're here.

But oh, God. That moment there, where he kissed me . . . It was not good. Well, all right. It *was*, but it can't be again.

For the next hour, we wander the store on the pretense of first edition hunting rather than serial killer tracking. Nothing discriminating is said, nothing nefarious hinted at. All of Finn's conversations with me revolve around books, and more than once I am left wondering if he is still playacting or if there is any sincerity in his genuine fondness for particular stories.

On the second floor, as Finn and I head into different rows, I stumble across a section marked *Children*. And there, sitting atop a stack of books in the middle of the aisle, is a book that says *Alice's Adventures in Wonderland*.

Don't do it, I think to myself. *Don't pick it up. No good can come of this*.

And yet I pick it up with trembling hands anyway. And I stare at it until I'm surprised the cover doesn't catch fire.

"You look a bit like her, don't you?"

It's not Finn, though. It's Jenkins, tapping his cane against the peeling wood of a shelf.

I set the book back upon the stack. For someone with a limp, he certainly managed to sneak upon me. "Pardon?"

"The book. Alice." The cane juts in my direction. "You look like her."

I allow my eyes to drift back to the illustration on the front. A girl is there, her hand raised as cards rain down upon her. I smile a bit indulgently as I humor him. "You think?"

He grunts. "Carroll was a fucking pervert and probably a druggie. Should have been castrated, to be honest. How he is still celebrated is beyond me. People are goddamn morons for continuing to support that asinine book. What kind of message does it send kids? Being a nosy, defiant brat is acceptable, as long as you're pretty? It's a fucking shame."

Finn reappears at the other end of the aisle, brows furrowed.

"For a bookstore owner, it doesn't sound as if you like books very much." I'm frigid when I address Jenkins. "So far, I've yet to hear about any you approve of."

His lips thin, leaving him comically bulbous.

I turn to one of the shelves and extract a book with a bear on the cover just as Finn reaches where I'm standing. "Is this one acceptable? Was it, too, written by a perverted druggie? Or maybe just a hack? I suppose it's okay to sell such wretched books as long as a profit is earned. Money trumps morality, right?"

Those narrow, sharp eyes hone in on me. "What the fuck did you just say?"

I'm merciless, but he deserves nothing less. "As you're the one making comparisons between me and a little girl, perhaps *you're* the pervert who requires castration."

It's a miracle the shop does not explode.

"Get out of my goddamn store or I'll call the cops." Spittle flies out from his lips as he shouts these words to me.

Finn takes a step forward, his tall frame filling the space between me and Jenkins. His fingers curl inward, the muscles of his back tighten. "Don't," he says in a low, even voice that sends a shiver down my spine, "ever speak to her like that again."

Jenkins slams his cane against the stack of books topped by mine, sending them scattering. But neither Finn nor I flinch, nor do we move from where we're standing. "Shouldn't be a problem when that goddamn bitch gets the hell out of my store!"

My grip tightens on the book in my hand. If I let it go, at just the right angle, I could hit his windpipe just so. Or his testicles, which might be a better target considering his apparent predilection toward blonde girls.

But Finn's right there, extracting the book from my grip. And then his fingers lace through mine, squeezing before I can snatch yet another one. "We're done here anyway."

We most certainly are not bloody done here. How dare this disgusting man speak to me in such a way.

Another squeeze is offered, one that lets me know Finn's just as livid as I am, but it's also a reminder that we have to play our cards right. Fine. I'll allow him this, but if Jenkins says one more thing to set me off . . .

"Don't let the door hit you on the ass on your way out!" Jenkins bellows from behind.

Halfway down the stairs, as steam pours out of my ears, I see it. There. Behind the desk, only visible at this height, from this angle of the steep stairs. Sitting on a stack of old newspapers is an open switchblade nearly identical to the pair back at the Institute. Same black horn, same gleaming silver accents.

Gotcha.

Once we're outside, Finn lets go of my hand as if it's on fire. Without another word, he strides away, back toward where our cab deposited us hours before.

I'm stunned. Is he really so angry with me? But then I'm pushing through the crowd, rushing to catch up. It isn't until a block later do I find him just standing by a gated, abandoned shop, his head angled against the graffitied brick and concrete.

I lean next to him, staring up at the same dilapidated metal fire escape. "You want to know something about me?" My fingers dig into the gauzy fabric of my dress. "I have a temper that can get me into trouble."

"Is that one of your secrets? Because if it is, it's a terrible one. I knew that pretty much from Day One."

"You should have let me hit him. Just once, at least."

His head rolls to face mine. "So he could have you charged with assault?"

My grunt is unladylike. But, goodness, is that ease between us back with a vengeance.

"Truth be told," he's saying, "this couldn't have worked out better in our favor."

My eyebrows shoot up. "How so?"

"He thinks he's run us off. Thinks you're nothing more than some bitchy woman who reads smut and has a ridiculous boyfriend not willing to back you up in an argument."

I'm the ridiculous one, because I say, "But you did."

"My first inclination was to beat the shit out of him, and then force him to apologize to you. The fact that I didn't?" He stuffs his hands into his pockets. "Assholes like him see that as a weakness. He's probably gloating over how he told us off, how he got the best of us."

I shift against the wall, so I'm now leaning on my shoulder as I full face him. "I saw a switchblade—"

"Behind the desk. I saw it, too. Upstairs, there was also a brand-new copy of a graphic comic book starring none other than a certain murderous barber shoved in between books on birdwatching."

I straighten. "Do you have it?"

"No. A camera was trained right onto that aisle, so I pretended to flip through one of the nature guides. I saw the title, though. It was clearly about Todd. Interesting coincidence, right?"

"There is no such thing as coincidence," the Caterpillar used to tell me. *"Only truth."*

"Is it normal to have so many cameras in a bookshop?"

He shakes his head. "For a used bookshop, it's suspicious, right?"

Why did you kiss me? is on the tip of my tongue. What I actually say is, "We'll need to disable the cameras when we sneak in next."

A small grin curves his mouth. "Listen to you and your Twenty-First-Century talk. *Disable the cameras.* Wendy would weep in joy if she could hear you now."

Like an addict, I want to keep up the banter between us, so I ask, "What's her story, anyway? She's obsessed with all her gadgets."

When his lower lip sucks in between his teeth, I'm spellbound. "You ought to ask her that."

"Is it a secret?"

He rubs his chin alongside his shoulder. "No. Of course not. It's just, some people in the Society are touchy when it comes to their origins. Wendy is one of them."

"Is her story bad?"

"She's not from a story, and that's the problem."

I'm confused.

"A Timeline, yes. But she was never a character in a book. Her great-great-great grandmother was." He kicks at a plastic cup on the ground. "Her name is actually Gwendolyn, and I'm told that, growing up, everyone called her Gwen."

"Why the change?"

"To make a long story short, she's been obsessed with her family history for as long as she can remember."

"Which is?"

I can't tell if he's amused or mildly disgusted when he says, "There was this . . . guy, for lack of a better word, who used to show up and take the women in her family to a magical island for like an extended vacation. Wendy's family died when she was five, though, and I guess because she moved into an orphanage, he never came for her."

"So she was recruited instead?"

He shakes his head. "Not like a lot of us, no. 1911BAR-PW's catalyst was a family heirloom of hers, and she busted the team that was sent in to collect it. Somehow, she weaseled the truth out of them and then insisted on coming back to New York. She was young then, maybe ten? Already great with technology, thanks to one of the nuns at the orphanage she lived at."

"So, if she's Gwendolyn, how'd she become Wendy?"

"Wendy was her great-great-great grandmother's name."

"Why is she resentful about not being from a book? Personally, I find it appalling there are storybooks out there that spill my secrets."

He shrugs. "You'd have to ask her about that one."

"Van Brunt didn't adopt her?"

"No. She didn't want to be adopted. Said Peter would never find her if her name was different—even though she technically bears her father's surname, not her mother's. She even insisted everyone call her Darling. It's kind of weird, to be honest. But it makes her happy, so we do."

"Who is Peter?"

"The guy who—"

Right. I finish up for him. "Kidnaps the ladies of her family."

Goose pimples explode up and down my arms when he laughs quietly at this. "Well, if you put it *that* way . . ."

A smile of my own eases across my face. Why is Finn Van Brunt so difficult to resist?

I take a deep breath and say something I told myself I wasn't going to let myself do again. I tell him, "I want to trust you."

He takes it the wrong way, though. "But you don't."

"But I want to." I take a step closer, my heart upon my sleeve. "And I want you to trust me."

He squints into the fading sunlight. Straightens from his position against the wall. There's a vulnerability there that he hasn't let me see before, one that tugs at strings I'd thought I'd clipped.

"Besides," I murmur, "aren't you all telling me that it's the intent that counts?"

GIRL TIME

A DOOR SLAMS, ONLY to be followed by a string of curse words and stomping feet.

"God, these walls are thin. Popcorn?"

I stare at Mary as she passes over a bright-red bowl filled with white, popped kernels fresh from the microwave. "I thought Finn was out tonight."

"Finn doesn't slam doors or typically shout like a drunk sailor. That's Victor." She grabs a handful of the treat she's fixed us. "Door slamming is par for the course when he knows he's in the doghouse."

Mary and Victor arrived ahead of schedule, just hours after Finn and I returned from our visit to the Ex Libris Bookstore. Since then, she's declared the next pair of days *girl time* and has instructed our male counterparts to stay away unless they're prepared to binge watch what she calls rom-coms, go dancing at something called eighties clubs, and imbibe in terrifying sounding concoctions that go by *frou-frou* drinks.

This announcement came as we all stood outside our respective flat doors in the hallway, each ready to either head inside or leave. Congregations like this are becoming increasingly common, leaving me feeling as if our living arrangements are more akin to boarding school than anything else. "Alice needs to know that there's more to life than work. You're doing a piss-poor job of that, Finn."

Not that he needed my help, but I tried to defend my partner. "He—"

Mary wasn't listening, though. She'd already wheeled around to Victor, snapping, "It'll be the perfect time for you to think about your actions."

The poor doctor looked like a startled yet mournful puppy dog. "But—"

She was already back to Finn, a hint of a sneer twisting her lips. "Don't you have somewhere to be already?"

Finn, for his part, looked utterly bored and unwilling to engage in her verbal sparring match.

"Mary," Victor protested, "this is between us. Finn hasn't done anything, and you know it. You don't need to—"

She took hold of my doorknob. "Like he's innocent." And then, before another thing could be said, she flung herself through my door, slamming it so hard behind her that the ground beneath our feet trembled.

Um . . .

"What the hell happened this time?" Finn asked his brother.

Victor kicked at the rug below our feet. "Nothing. She's blowing things out of proportion."

"Nothing?" My partner was incredulous. "Mary doesn't lose her shit like that over *nothing.*"

"She bloody well did this time, okay? And I don't want to talk about it. Stop breathing down my neck already!" Victor then turned around and flung himself through his door, slamming it twice as hard as Mary.

I asked the only other person remaining in the hallway, "Do I even want to know?"

From inside my flat, Mary bellowed my name.

Finn rolled his eyes. "Either Victor flirted with another woman, failed to live up to some expectation she didn't explain to him, or he did something he'd promised Mary he wasn't going to do."

"Like what?"

His eyes had flitted toward his brother's door. I waited for an explanation, but none came. Instead, Finn said, "Get used to the drama. Those two . . ." He shook his head. "It's just always like this. It's like high school, only worse. You think after all the years they've been together, all this would stop. Just try to keep your head down and not get stuck in the middle."

"Apparently," I said dryly, "I'll be squarely in between, in the midst of *girl time*." I'd paused. "Whatever that is."

Said with utter seriousness, "Good luck with that."

He was dressed nicely, a pressed shirt and well-fitting jeans, with a pair of thick leather and metal cuffs ringing each wrist. "Are you going out?"

My question made him uneasy, suddenly so. "Yeah."

And then I was uneasy, because uneasiness was an unfamiliar feeling between us. "Oh. Yes. Of course. I'm keeping you, naturally."

"No—not keeping, it's just . . ." He ran his fingers through his golden-brown hair. "I promised I'd be there at nine, and it's already eight thirty, and . . ."

And I was fixated on his mouth, remembering how it felt pressed even for the tiniest of moments against my cheek. My face flamed. I nodded like a Rocking-horse-fly gone wild. "Of course. Right. Nobody likes being late. I mean, some, yes, but not you. Naturally. Right?"

I needed to crawl under a rock. Or at least walk away with my head held high.

"Yeah, no. I . . ." He glanced over my shoulder, a hand cupping the back of his neck. "Um, so I should . . ." A hand wove between us. "Get going. So I'm not late or anything."

Good God, did he look handsome just then. And good God, did I sound like a mimsy nincompoop.

"ALICE!"

My back hit the flat door. "Have a good night then. I'm going to just . . ." I tapped the wood. "Go have girl time, whatever that is."

I'd been reduced to regurgitating gibberish.

"ALICE!"

When he walked away, I wondered where the blazes all of that had just come from. And now I'm going on the second night of girl time with Mary, watching some movie about people meeting on the top of a building, and she's throwing popcorn at the screen and yelling about the perceived idiocy of the couple.

I've come to like her immensely, but she's been a bear all day. Perhaps I'm not cut out for *girl time* after all.

The moment my eyes drift shut, she grabs the remote control and turns the movie off. "That's it. Let's go out."

A quick glance at a nearby clock shows it's almost eleven o'clock in the evening. "Now?"

She claps her hands. "Now. I know the perfect place. Go get changed—no, not in those sack dresses you favor, but in something sexy."

"I'm really rather tired, and—"

"And, you're not in an insane asylum any longer. Let's go out. You're single. I'm . . ." She swallows hard. "Why shouldn't we have fun?"

"Sleep is fun," I assure her.

"I'm closing in on thirty!"

Girl time, I'm also learning, can be emotionally exhausting and more than a bit confusing.

She's pacing, her bare feet slapping against the wood floor. "I'm almost thirty years old, and Victor can't put a bloody ring on my finger!"

Now I feel like an idiot, because I really should have known this would have cycled back to Victor. I knew they were romantically attached, but had no idea marriage was on the table. "Perhaps you two ought to talk. It's obvious—"

"Talk?" she scoffs. "No. He's had his chance to talk. All I hear is how it would be unfair to saddle me with his, and I quote, 'obscenely heavy baggage.' How he loves me too much to even risk it. I mean, shit, Alice. How much can a lady take before she simply lets go?"

I scratch my head, unsure as what to do. When I was younger, my sister and I weren't particularly close and all of my playmates tended to be boys. After my first pair of go arounds in Wonderland, I was ostracized by many for my fanciful tales. And then, in my subsequent years in Wonderland, I was too wrapped up in all of my own personal drama to cultivate the kind of relationships that I think Mary is seeking from me.

My confidants were few. My secret holder was singular. And these are not the sort of conversations we ever indulged in. Plus, as I've discovered, a lady can take a whole lot before she must let go.

"Baggage?"

Mary points at me. "How much do you know about Victor?"

Is she sincere in her request? I'm not so sure until she prompts me with an impatient wave of her hand. So I recite, "He's a doctor, was adopted by Van Brunt when he was young, has a surname that is recognizable." I shrug. "That's it, to be honest."

She nods grimly. "Exactly."

I sigh and settle back onto the couch. "Mary, I really don't understand where you're going with this."

"His original name. Frankenstein. This is what I'm talking about! It's always about that bloody name." She tugs at her hair and lets out a tiny, muted scream. "Like I judge him on it. Like any of us judge him. He thinks we do, you know. You don't, do you?"

"I can safely say I don't, as I have no clue what you're talking about."

She sinks onto the couch next to me as I pour us both cups of tea. "I know. I'm sorry. Victor's biological father was a mad scientist." She spins a finger around her ear. "A total crazy person." A wince follows this. "Sorry."

I shrug. I'm not offended.

"He . . ." She glances toward the hallway that leads to my front door. When she speaks, her voice is hushed. "His father cut up dead people and sewed them together so he could bring them back to life. Made a murderous monster, one that wanted to kill him in return."

I choke on the sip of tea I've just taken. Mary smacks me on the back until I stop coughing.

"The book that tells his story is one of the most famous horror stories ever told. There are countless movies, books, television shows that feature the monster and even his father."

I don't even know what to say, I'm so horrified.

"Victor isn't in the book, by the way. Not even referenced, because he's one of those *in-betweener-slash-intent* events the Librarian always prattles on about. He was," her voice lowers even further, "the product of a night of comfort with a lady of the night before Frankenstein Senior's eventual death. The Society found him as a toddler and brought him back. Brom raised him since then, so it's not even like he knew his biological father. But he believes everyone is just waiting for him to follow his father's footsteps." She sighs, fingers lacing tightly across her knees. "The thing is, it's like Victor's waiting to go bonkers. Like he thinks it's inevitable he's inherited his father's inclination toward corpse mutilation. That's stupid, right?"

I search for my voice, but I'll admit to still being fixated on the whole monster creation bit.

"Sometimes," she murmurs, "I wonder what things would have been like if I'd ever given into my impulses with Dickon. How it might be so much easier."

My brain feels tired from all of this already. "Who is Dickon?"

"A guy." Sadness fills her eyes. "A friend. Or was a friend, anyway." She picks lint off her tiny black shorts. "My uncle thought he wasn't suitable."

"Why not?"

"Money." Her smile is grim. "It doesn't matter anyway, does it? He married some local girl, I left and joined the Society. Sometimes love isn't enough."

"No, it really isn't." And that's pure honesty if I've ever said it.

She stands back up. "Let's go out. Have some fun."

Nearly an hour later, as the clock ticks toward midnight, Mary's winsome smile has us bypassing a red velvet rope outside of what she calls, "One of New York's best hidden treasures." Inside, the air is heavy with sweat and the smell of alcohol, and loud music pulses so strongly that each beat supersedes that of the muscle in my chest. People are crammed into the dark space, their bodies pressed up against each other just so they can hear what the others are saying.

Is this a rave? Because, sleep definitely sounds more fun than a rave right now.

Mary rejected all the dresses in my closet ("God, you need to get over the Victorian vibe. I sure as hell did."), so I'm wearing one of hers that is so scandalously short, it's a miracle I can even walk without flashing my bare bum. Every few feet we cover in the club, some new man or woman comes up to me and asks rather seductively if I want a drink.

"You want a drink," Mary yells into my ear. I'm steered toward a long, gleaming bar crowded with people flirting. I fight back a yawn, especially when Mary flicks my shoulder. "None of that!"

A *frou-frou* drink is . . . well, I honestly don't know what's in it. It reminds me of something the Dormouse would favor, all sickeningly sweet and almost syrupy, but the ones Mary ordered us, complete with paper umbrellas and what appears to be weird, rubbery cherries, makes her happy, so I don't argue.

As she sucks hers down at an alarming rate, a well-dressed man sidles up to me. Over the course of the next minute, he tries his best to catch my eye.

I'm flattered, to be honest. I must be more tired than I thought.

When I finally offer him a cool smile, he asks, "You come here often?"

I nearly gag on my most recent sip. "Sorry, no."

The man chuckles at the expression on my face. "Let me get you something better." A hand is lifted, and the bartender sways back toward us. "Two of your best whiskeys." He looks me up and down. "Neat."

The moment I set the curved *frou-frou* drink down, Mary slides it toward her. She leans over me, her chin settling on my shoulder. "This is Alice! Alice is new to New York. I'm Mary."

Subtlety is not her strong forte.

The man leans against the counter and grins at me. From what I can tell in the dim light, he's quite handsome, with curly brown hair laced with silver threads and a cleft chin. "Welcome to New York, Alice. I'm Gabriel Lygari, but my friends call me Gabe."

"We are not friends."

He laughs, delighted at my flatly stated observation. "I'd like to be." And then he sticks his hand out. I fight against the impulse to walk away and stick mine out in return. He's got a gold ring with a flat, mottled blue stone on his pinky, and his grip is firm.

This man oozes sexual charm.

Mary whispers in my ear, "He's hot. How much you want to bet he's well hung, too?"

I guess I'm not the only one noticing his allure. And speaking of noticing, her whispering isn't as quiet as she must think, because the man standing next to us coughs into his hand, his eyes twinkling.

"You a New Yorker?" Mary asks Gabe from over my shoulder.

"For now." He nearly blinds us with gleaming white teeth.

Mary murmurs, "Well, then," before reclaiming her (my?) drink. But, thankfully, the bartender shouts out the arrival of two whiskeys. Gabe claims them before sliding one of the small glasses toward me. And then, leaning in close, his drink aloft, he says, "May you have the hindsight to know where you've been, the foresight to know where you are going, and the insight to know when you have gone too far."

Our glasses clink. The amber liquid burns in my throat, but tastes infinitely better than Mary's *frou-frou* drink. "What is that from?"

Whiskey swirls in the glass dangling from his fingers. "It's a traditional Irish blessing. But it seemed fitting for a British girl named Alice experiencing a new place for the first time."

My heart trips inside my chest. "Why is that?"

"Don't tell me you never get Alice jokes." Gabe chuckles and leans in even farther. My head swims with warm male cologne. "Growing up, a friend's sister was named Alice. We always teased her about the whole Wonderland thing. You know, falling down rabbit holes, going to new places, getting into trouble by sticking her nose into places she doesn't belong, stuff like that. All the subsequent Alices I've ever met are adventurous sorts."

Frabjous. I go to a modern bar and meet somebody who knows about my book within minutes.

An arm is slung over my shoulder. "Alice is all about new places and experiences."

Alice, I think sourly, is nearly all about telling Mary that her breath smells like a carafe of spoiled wine.

The twinkles in Gabe's eyes expand. "Is that so?"

"We should dance." Mary slams the remains of my *frou-frou* drink down on the bar top. "Gabe, do you have any friends here?"

"Actually," he says, "I do. They're at a table upstairs. It was my turn to buy a round."

"And yet, you have no round of drinks."

Gabe smiles at my sly reflection. "Went to a bar, met a beautiful lady . . ." His head ducks in false shyness. "I think they'll understand."

Mary, though, isn't listening. "Excellent." She tugs down her equally short dress and shimmies. "Let's go make friends, shall we?"

When she pushes her way into the crowd, Gabe leans in close so he can tell me, "Don't worry. I won't let anybody take advantage of her."

Is he referring to my colleague's rapidly accelerating inebriated state? "Don't worry," I reassure him in return. "Neither will I."

Gabe tugs me through the crowd so we can catch up to a directionless Mary. When his fingers touch mine, I have to fight the impulse to recoil. It's not that it's a horrible feeling, or that his hand is hairy or sweaty or anything out of the ordinary, but . . . it's just a hand. Just a palm and fingers and smooth skin that belong to a handsome man and nothing more.

And that realization leaves me more relieved than I can say.

The music pulses stronger, the volume turns louder. Bodies around us press up against one another as they slide and shiver and sway. Mixed within the strong wafts of sweat also lie the faint musky hints of sex.

Memories bombard me as we push through the throngs. Dark, underground raves filled with barely clothed people high on hookah and the Hatter's infamous juice. Frenetic music. Flashing, glittering lights. Hands on my hips, lips against my neck and then lower still. Heat flooding me so strongly I actually exploded in the middle of the crush and no one else knew it, they were all so engrossed in their own delirium.

Somebody knocks into me, jarring me back into reality. It's a woman with long red hair and a nose that looks like it was glued on. She glares at me before looping her arms around the man she's with.

"You okay?"

I blink. Gabe comes back into focus as the redheaded woman fades. I offer what I hope to be a flirty smile. "Are *you* okay?"

He laughs, and I soak the sound up.

Gabe finally overtakes Mary so he can lead her up to the second floor of the club. Tables scatter around another crowded dance floor, but what has my attention is a bar just off the stairs.

"Are the drinks up here terrible?"

The man still holding my hand is confused at first, but when I nod my head toward the gleaming bar, he laughs once more. "Busted. I was with a friend, standing next to one of the railings, and I saw this gorgeous blonde woman come in, so . . ."

He doesn't blush, but I get the impression he wishes he could, simply to up his charm factor.

"Your penance for lying is another whiskey," I tell him.

Another burst of laughter escapes him. "I like your style."

Fresh drinks in all our hands, Gabe leads us over to a table filled with three other men and an ethereal woman who practically glows, she's so delicate and pale. They all stand as soon as we arrive, and before I know it, Mary has planted herself in one of their laps under the guise that there simply aren't enough chairs.

Perhaps I'm old-fashioned, but I can't help but wonder about Victor. I know she's hurting, but this?

As she leans over to grab her drink, I discreetly duck my head toward the man she's with. "Treat my friend improperly, and you will be a eunuch before sunrise."

She nearly falls off his lap at the strength of his flinch.

Three—or is it four?—additional whiskeys later, I'm on the dance floor with Gabe. He's a good dancer, but he talks too much. I tune him out and tune in the music, letting my body learn the beats. My head swims from the alcohol. Things blur. More memories bombard me, and for the first time in months, I feel . . . normal.

Well, Wonderlandian normal, at least.

We're hip to hip, and my arms are above my head and his hands are dangerously close to my breasts. I can feel his interest in me growing, we're pressed so closely together.

And then a flash of white-tipped black hair floats across my field of vision.

I'm blinking, trying to focus even as Gabe's mouth lowers until his lips curve around my earlobe. Tiny darts of heat pluck at me, tempting me back under the lull of alcohol, but no.

There.

Pale woman. Wild, dark curly hair dipped in white snow. The one in the photograph with Todd.

I search for Mary. She's still on what's-his-name's lap, appearing as if she's telling a story. So far, he's kept his hands to himself. And she has, too.

I startle out of Gabe's arms. "I—" But I don't finish it. I simply leave him on the dance floor as I push my way through the gyrating crowd. Where did she go? I hear my name behind me, brushes of fingertips as I keep moving, but I don't stop.

I need to find her. Find her, find Todd.

I break out of the dance floor, but there's no fresh air to clear my mind. Just more people mingling with their drinks. Where did she go?

Flash of white and black to my right, alongside glowing skulls against a dark backdrop. Toward a set of a different set of stairs. I'm halfway there when I hear my name again, colored with shock.

But it's not Mary. It's not Gabe.

It's Finn.

This time, I halt. He's at a table near the railings overlooking the first floor, a beer in his hand and a confused look on his face. There is a woman next to him, a stunning brunette who is sitting so close they're practically in each other's laps. "Alice?"

My heart thuds. My face flames. And then I see Victor is at the table, too, eyes closed as his head rests on another woman's shoulder. She's got an arm around him as she chats with the woman with Finn.

Bloody. Hell. And to think I was just feeling sorry for the wanker!

My partner stands up just as Gabe catches up with me. Before Finn can say anything, Gabe grabs my arm. "Hey. What happened back there?"

I glance toward the stairs. There is no woman with two-tone hair there. I dart toward the railing, just to the side of Victor (and miraculously do not punch him in the head), and lean over to scan the area.

She's not there. Did I imagine her?

My head swims. I jump when a hand closes over my shoulder. "Alice?"

It's Gabe. Finn is just a few feet away, and he looks . . . is that anger? Guilt? Confusion? I can't tell. Everything blurs. Even still, I tell Gabe, "Sorry. I thought . . ." But I don't finish that. How can I?

"What are you doing here?"

I turn to Finn, hating that I can't pinpoint his emotions right now. Everything is too fuzzy. He's with someone. A woman. Of course he is. It's not . . . We're partners. Why does this bother me? We're partners. Adults, free to do whatever we wish. *We're partners.* "Having a good time," I tell him. And then I look down at his lady friend and say, "Which is what it appears you're doing."

I guess I'm not too fuzzy to be that not-so-nice Alice I warned him about.

"I thought you were with Mary? Doing girl time or—" Finn looks me up and down, his eyes widening at the dress of Mary's I'm wearing.

Gabe wraps a protective arm around me. "Let's go get another drink, huh?"

I'm tired of logic. I'm tired of feeling. I'm tired of holding it all in. "Yes. God, yes."

"No," Finn interjects. He's now closing in on where I'm standing. "Are you drunk? Who the hell is this, Alice?"

"What's going on?" the woman he's with asks. She's got one of those sultry voices that always annoy me when she repeats his question. "Who is this, Finn?"

But before he can tell her anything, Victor's name is screeched so loudly my ears ring amidst already blisteringly strong music.

"YOU SON OF A BITCH!" Our mutual friend flies out of nowhere. "I CANNOT BELIEVE YOU!"

Victor creaks an eye open just as she descends upon the Van Brunt brothers' table. His words slur right out of him. "Hallllloooooo, Mary. Didja see Alice? I think she's wearin' your slutty dress."

Mary slaps him, knocking his head off of the woman's shoulder, but it bounces down upon her rather amble bosom. The woman shouts, startled, and Victor's eyes finally open wide. All of a sudden, chairs are scraping, people are squealing and yelling, and I've got my arms around Mary as I haul her backward.

Victor's stumbling to his feet, calling her name, and Finn's suddenly putting his body between all of us. "Okay. Hold on a minute. Mary—"

"DON'T YOU MAKE EXCUSES FOR HIM!"

The woman with my partner grabs his arm. "Finn, what is going on?" She gives us a look that even I can read correctly right now.

I'm tempted to tell her who I am. What I can do.

And just that thought is a slap in my face. I ask Gabe, "Can you help me get Mary home?"

"No!" Victor's crying. "Mary, I swear, just . . . Let's talk this out, let's . . ."

Her fury knows no bounds. "YOU AND I ARE DONE." And then, for good measure, she screeches, "AGAIN!"

Finn shoves an arm out, holding his brother at bay. "Alice, wait. I'll get us a cab, and—"

I turn my back on him. Ask Gabe, "Can you?"

He glances briefly at Finn before showing me those blindingly white teeth of his. "Absolutely."

DRAMA ISLAND

MARY RAGES FOR THE rest of the night.

After we left the club, Gabe tried to accompany us in the cab he flagged down for us, but I wouldn't let him. Mary was already ranting and less drunk than I previously thought she might be. I thanked him for his assistance, allowed him to press his lips against the corner of my mouth (and blessedly felt nothing), and then bid him farewell.

He protested. "I want to see you again."

I patted his cheek and slipped into the waiting cab.

Mary didn't want to go back to the Institute, though. Instead, she ordered the driver to take us downtown to a hotel. "I'll break all his things," she vowed. "Every last bloody fucking thing he owns."

I believed her.

Her phone chirped and rang repeatedly, which only left her even more infuriated. I eventually took it from her to hide in my purse when she threatened to yank every last one of Victor's pubic hairs out if he dared to call her again. As for my own, I only managed a quick text to

Van Brunt, apprising him that Mary and I were to stay in a hotel nearby for the night before I had to hide mine from her, too.

The hotel we're in is ultra-modern, with clean lines and precious few extraneous items to add flavor. I decided upon a two-bed room, just to keep an eye on her. She didn't cry, though, nor did she follow through on any of her threats to destroy things. She yelled, she rationalized, she threatened, and finally lost her voice. And now she's sleeping and I'm staring down at the three texts on my own phone, alongside notifications of several missed calls.

Answer your door. I just want to make sure you guys are okay.

And then, a half hour later: **Where are you? Security footage shows you didn't come home.**

Finally, just two minutes ago: **I don't know what the hell happened last night, but I really would like to know you and Mary are okay. Where are you?**

As I sip the tea recently delivered via room service, I remember I'd left my phone on silent and never took it out of my purse. I type: **We're fine. At a hotel, letting Mary sleep it off.**

His answer is nearly instantaneous. **What hotel?** And then, before I can type a word, my phone rings.

I quickly step out onto the patio to answer it.

"What hotel?" he asks once more.

"You really need to work on your greetings," I tell my partner. "I know this modern day and age is much more casual about manners, but I'd like to think we can still greet one another properly on the phone."

"You disappeared last—"

I talk right over him. "I'll start. Good morning, Finn."

"Night, with that *guy*—"

"Which is typically followed up by: How are you?"

"And you never came home! And then you wouldn't answer your phone—"

"You'd ask me how I am doing, and I would tell you that I'd had precious little rest over the course of the last five hours."

"And, what was I to think?" He's still going. "For all I knew, that asshole kidnapped you two and—"

"Oh, for God's sake. Kidnapping? Finn, I'm twenty-five years old, not five. And I'm quite capable of staving off would-be attackers."

"Fine. Abducted. Is that better?"

I'm shocked by the level of anger in his voice. "Am I the only one who remembers you could have pinpointed my location at any point? Don't our phones have some kind of . . ." I search for Wendy's description. "GSP that allows partners find one another?"

"GPS, and yes, they do. But we typically only turn on the function during an assignment. I didn't think I'd need to activate yours on a Friday night in New York when I thought you'd be watching movies with Mary back in your apartment!"

I set my teacup down on the glass table. The view from the hotel room is a busy one, of bustling streets and honking cars. "I wasn't aware that I was required to inform you of my every move, Finn. Did I miss that in all of the lectures I suffered through? Was there a rule that claims partners must inform one another of their locations at all times? Because if that's the case, you've failed miserably at that the entire time I've known you." I'm teasing, though.

He's not when he bites out, "What hotel?"

"Didn't your father tell you? I texted him on the cab ride over."

"Why in the hell did you tell *him?*"

I have to admit, I'm taken aback by his incredulousness. "As you were busy, it seemed the logical choice? But no matter. I'll have Mary home later on today, when she wakes up. She's terribly hurt, Finn. And I'll be honest, I don't think it would behoove anyone to have her around Victor or his things right now."

"Just tell me the name of the hotel already."

"I don't actually remember." I'm exasperated. "Mary chose it, and I was more focused on ensuring she didn't smash apart the lobby. Besides, there's something more important for us to discuss."

I can practically feel his frustration through the phone against my ear. "What could possibly be more important than—"

"I saw Todd's companion last night. At the club."

A full four seconds tick by in silence. "What?"

"You had me look at some photographs of Todd and some woman, remember? Back when they were attempting to break into the Institute. I saw her last night at the club. Wild dark hair, with snow-white ends? Painfully thin. I wonder if she knows food is necessary for survival."

"What?"

I hold the phone away from my ear. Am I using it correctly? I tell him more loudly, "I saw the woman—"

"No, I got that. You *saw* her? When? What was she doing? Was Todd there?"

Through the window, I watch Mary roll onto her side and curl into a tight ball. "No Todd, and it really was only a flash, but I'm positive it was her. She wasn't really doing anything. I tried to follow her, but that's when I ran into you." And then I think to myself, because I am a bit petty: *and your lady friend.*

"Why didn't you tell me?!"

"I'm telling you now."

He says, clearly between gritted teeth, "Why didn't you tell me *then?"*

"Well, see, Mary discovered her paramour's head upon some other woman's bosom, and she took offense to it—quite loudly, I may add."

"We're partners."

"A fact I am well aware of, Finn."

He sighs. "What hotel are you at?"

"I don't—"

"It's not rocket science. Go back inside and look at the pads of paper they leave you. Or the pens. Or the sign on the back of the door. Or on the phone. Or on a thousand other places in the room!"

"I told you I'd bring Mary back later—"

"Alice! For the love of God, please just do this one thing, okay? Can we stop arguing long enough for you to just tell me what hotel you're at?"

I eventually do, and the next thing I know, he's telling me he's on his way.

I meet Finn in the lobby twenty minutes later after leaving Mary a note. I don't think she'll wake up (it's only been a few hours since I managed to get her into bed anyway), but I worried she would immediately charge the Institute and carry through on several of her threats.

When Finn arrives, I'm surprised to find him in the exact same outfit he was in at the club. The only difference is he looks exhausted, and it reminds me of the day we first met. A day not so long ago, just a couple months now, and somehow, it feels like forever and a week ago.

Have I really only known this man for such a short time?

I fight back the surge of sentimentality. Assume my game face. Prepare to inform him it was pointless to come all this way when we would have arrived before the day's end when he strides right up to me and folds me in his arms.

I lose all of those words and more.

Goodness, does it feel good to be hugged by Finn Van Brunt. His arms are warm and strong, and his head resting against mine is enough to elicit a sigh of relief I didn't even know I was holding in. But, as comforting as it may be, it's the tingles that are weakening my knees. Every inch of skin he's touching has suddenly decided to catch fire.

I murmur, "What is this for?"

A hand comes to cup the back of my head. "I was worried, okay?"

He was worried.

Part of me insists that I push him away, that I just walk away right now. I'm feeling things I vowed I would never allow myself to feel again. Never even thought was possible to feel. Last night, with Gabe . . . it was wonderful, because there wasn't a spark with him. There was nothing there. Nothing that would hold me to him, no unbreakable strings that would connect our hearts. Men like Gabe are safe. Men like Gabe are all I promised myself I would ever allow again. Men like Gabe cannot demolish me.

Men like Huckleberry Finn are not like Gabe.

When we disentangle, I'm left exposed in a way that rocks me to my core.

"Mary's still asleep?"

I nod. "It's for the best. What about Victor?"

"Also asleep."

We head over to some unoccupied couches in the lobby. "What was he thinking?"

When we sit, there isn't much space between our legs. "I know you probably won't believe it, but Victor wasn't doing anything with Pippa last night. He was drunk, and ended up falling asleep on her shoulder. She's been a friend of ours for a long time."

I think of how Mary sat in Gabe's friend's lap, and of how I didn't see one bit of meaningful flirting happening outside of that action.

"Victor and Mary . . ." Finn blows out a hard breath. "It's like they're permanently stuck on Drama Island."

An eyebrow quirks up. "Drama Island?"

"A stupid reality show. I tried to warn you. This is par for the course. They fight, they make up, they fight some more. Honestly, I've always seen it as incredibly unhealthy, but there's genuine love between them, so it's difficult, you know?"

I do know. "Sometimes," I say slowly, testing the waters between us, "love is not enough, though. Not when everything else is wrong. Sometimes you must move on, even when it hurts to do so."

He scratches the back of his neck, head tilted in just a way to let me know he's wondering if that's merely an opinion I've just offered up or an experience. But letting him know this, even as guarded as it comes across, is oddly liberating and crushing all at once.

I tug at my hair, wishing I had a brush. "What are we going to do about Todd's lady?"

"You're sure it was her?"

I nod, but he looks unsure, and it's not hard to guess why.

"Being drunk is . . ." I grip my knees as I stare straight forward. "It is a little like what life was like the first year or so in Wonderland. Things may have begun to blur and loosen, my inhibitions lowered, but one could argue in states like that, I'm a high-functioning lunatic."

He doesn't laugh, not like I thought he would. Instead he sighs. Shifts on the couch next to me. "Who was the guy?"

My heart stutters. How—

"The guy you were with last night."

Is he truly interested? Oh. *Oh.* Is that . . . *jealousy?* "I suppose I could ask: who was the woman?"

There's no pause. "Avery Lincoln. We went to both high school and the same college together. Outside of the Society, she's one of my closest friends. In case you're wondering, Pippa Kaliszewski was someone we hung out with in our college years, who happened to be in town for a few days and wanted to catch up with everyone."

When I don't say anything, he adds, "Although Victor went to university in England, he hung out with us during all his breaks."

"That's something he needs to tell Mary."

A quiet sigh of frustration escapes him. "She knows Pippa—or at least, she's met her. Pippa and Victor had a weekend fling, years before he and Mary got together, and I guess it's always bothered her."

And this Avery Lincoln?

But I don't ask that, even though curiosity corrodes the insides of my chest. Instead, I say, "I think we ought to go back to Ex Libris. See what's behind some of those locked doors. Maybe even find a certain lady or blade-loving man."

He nods. "I'll get Wendy on some ways for us to disable Jenkins' security systems."

And then, I realize something. He'd asked me a question, and I made him tell me something about himself instead. It's a bad habit of mine when it comes to this man.

I clear my throat. Dig my fingers a little harder into my knee. "Gabe. His name was Gabe Lygari. He's just some guy I met who happens to be a good dancer. I doubt I'll ever see him again."

"You like to dance?"

I find myself smiling. "I was at a dance club, after all."

He says, so softly that all the air in the room disappears, "I wish I'd known."

THE WALL

FINN, FOR WHAT IT'S worth, looks twice as beautiful tonight in his all-black clothing. Despite the sweltering heat of summer days transitioning to fall, he's wearing a fitted long-sleeved shirt that clings to all of his well-defined muscles and a pair of track pants that have me forcing myself to avert my eyes every time he turns away because ogling one's partner's arse isn't seemly at all.

I'm also in black, in a similar garb. I've got my hair tied back into a neat, low bun and am sporting a matching headset with an earpiece, tiny microphone, and clear shield that covers one eye.

"Checking communication systems," Wendy's voice in my ear says at the same time a flickering image of her appears in the shield. "ALR, do you copy?"

"I'm disappointed in the lack of fanciful code names," I tell her in return. "All the spy movies I've watched have them."

"ALR's systems are a go." Her voice is crystal clear. "FVB, do you copy?"

Finn adjusts the matching headset he's wearing. "Affirmative."

We're on the roof of a building less than a block away from Ex Libris. After going over building schematics, it was determined our best course of entry was from a window located on the east side of the fourth floor. But as Jenkins' security system turns out to be more advanced than we previously thought, there wasn't an angle from below we could successfully reach the building from.

So we're coming from above. Once I told Van Brunt I'd seen Todd's cohort, no time was wasted. We're to hit the only location we've been able to pin them on and keep our fingers crossed we can find something. Personally, I'm hoping to find *them*.

"FVB's systems are a go," Wendy's saying. "VVB, do you copy?"

Victor's voice, just as clear as Wendy's, answers, "Affirmative."

"VVB's systems are a go. JD, do you copy?"

The A.D.'s response is immediate. "Affirmative."

Well, bloody hell. I'm the only one not technically affirmative.

"JD's systems are a go," Wendy intones, eyes locked on a screen just off to her side. "JD, what is your location?"

"Ground floor of the dry cleaners next door. Readings show the system originates in the basement, so I'll be en route."

Finn slips a pair of sleek black guns into equally black holsters strapped to his chest before tugging on his dark knit hat. I've got no guns, though. I've brought with me a set of blades Kip had fashioned just for me. I'm fumbling with the blade sheaths strapped to my thighs, though, and before I know it, my partner's hands circle my upper thigh so he can adjust one to fit more snugly.

I forget to breathe until his hands leave my body. And then I mentally kick myself for swooning, because obviously this is neither the time nor the place for such trivialness.

"Did you ever break into somewhere before?" Finn asks me.

I'm mesmerized by his grin. "That's debatable."

He chuckles quietly. "Are you nervous?"

Not about the mission, I'm not. I shake my head. He passes me a knit hat and asks, "VVB, status?"

His brother wastes no time answering. "In position."

According to the plan, Victor is to be on point across from Ex Libris with a sniper rifle, just in case things don't go the way we hope. Who knew doctors were such gifted shots?

"I thought this would be simple." I tug the hat over my hair. "Sneak in, nose around, sneak out."

He brushes stray hairs that have slipped from my bun beneath the knit of the hat. "Better safe than sorry, especially when you're dealing with people with predilections toward sharp weaponry. Are you ready?"

I nod. As if the hair bit wasn't enough, Finn's hands settle on my shoulders. "Any last questions?"

I shake my head. We both tug on our gloves.

"AF is a go," Finn tells Wendy. "Radio silence to commence in three, two, one."

AF. Alice/Finn. Goddamn my knees for being useless body parts. Why is it always my knees to go first? Don't they know a lady needs to stand?

"Affirmative, FVB. JD, you have ten minutes. Countdown begins now."

The A.D.'s laugh fills our ears. And then Finn takes a deep breath and sprints at full speed toward the ledge. He goes flying right off the edge, his body poised five stories above the pavement, before he hits the gravel on the other side. A duck and roll steadies his landing before he gets up and turns around. I'm already following his lead, though.

When I sail between the buildings, exhilaration I'd thought I'd left behind in a former life slams back into my chest.

We sprint across the rooftops, flying as we close the gap between our starting point and Jenkins' bookstore. His cameras are too plentiful, especially on the ground floor, and our faces too recognizable. Our only hope of entry lies comes from above, and even then, Jenkins is inside the building.

Good thing Finn and I are both quiet when it counts.

"JD, three minutes," Wendy intones right as I roll a landing on yet another building.

He's exasperated. "On it!" Numbers and words flash across the shield. "His Wi-Fi is shite, WD1. The virus upload is crawling."

A map flashes across my shield. "Triangulating new signal," Wendy says. "Get it finished, JD."

We're two buildings away now, and there's a one-story drop. Finn warned me of this when we were in Van Brunt's meeting room. "It's gonna hurt if you hit the ground wrong, even snap your knee or ankle. You need to hit the right trajectory when you jump."

I briefly considered letting him know about some of my more lurid past exploits in the spirited sense of sharing more about myself, but figured this one might be fun to let him find out first hand. "I'll be okay," I assured the team.

Kip was present, and surprisingly offered up, "She's got good balance."

It was the highest praised I've received from him so far.

"Two minutes, JD," Wendy calls out.

He's unruffled. "At seventy-two percent."

The drop is a hundred feet away. Finn picks up traction, and I'm impressed by how he doesn't appear winded in the least. His moves are smooth and strong. He's talented, I realize as I watch him kick off into the groundless darkness. I mean, I knew he was. I'd watched him in training often enough. But seeing him in action right now?

I'm inappropriately aroused.

I'm also right behind him, my body flinging through the void. I hit the roof below hard, but counter it with a much more sophisticated roll than before. I match him move for more.

"One minute," Wendy says.

"Eight-eight percent," the A.D. returns.

The possibility that the building will explode in alarms only pushes me faster.

"You take unnecessary risks." The Caterpillar blew out an Alice in armor, her arm raised as a bodiless arm with a battle axe swings viciously above.

Whispered later, when the Caterpillar turned back to his hookah with closed eyes, "Without risks, we never really know if something's worth the trouble."

I'd smiled. We were taking a risk then and there.

"Thirty seconds."

Finn holds up a hand as he flies across the final rooftop, two fingers closing down into a swiped fist.

I nod, even though he can't see me.

"Twenty seconds."

My heart rate accelerates. Endorphins flood my bloodstream.

"Ten seconds."

My feet push me faster until I'm parallel with Finn. And then, as if our bodies were puppets being controlled by the same master, we both leap across the divide in perfect unison before latching onto twin bars at the top of the fire escape. The entire metal structure shudders, but thankfully doesn't groan.

A split second before my body slams into the brick wall, I swing my legs up into an arc, flipping across the bar. And then Finn and I wait for the wail of alarms.

None come.

He tugs out a circular glass cutter and suctions it onto the window. As he gets to work, I peer into the pane, searching for signs of life.

"T-minus two minutes before system reactivated," the A.D. says. "I have a loop going, but it won't hold."

Finn swings what I first believe to be a blade in the cutter but then determine is a miniature laser in an arc. The glass silently melts until he can pop the piece out. I'm standing above him, spraying a can of lubricant along the top and sides of the wooden frame. The circle removed, I pass Finn the can so he can spray the latch before twisting it.

"Thirty seconds, AF."

Finn slides the window up and holds out an arm. Ladies first.

I'm in, and he's right on my heels, sliding the window shut and latching it with a full second to spare.

"Security system back in place," the A.D. tells us. "AF, you have sixty minutes before exit reboot. Cameras on fourth floor are currently on a new loop."

We've entered a cluttered, dark attic, but it's apparent within the first few glances that it's not a forgotten one. There are several beds in various states of use, alongside a dresser and armoire. Clothes litter the floor around one of the beds, and a quick peek shows both feminine and masculine stylings. Of note, there is a familiar skull-covered tunic.

I nudge the pile and give Finn a thumb's up.

A thump sounds, but it's not in the room. Somebody bellows—and by somebody, I mean Jenkins—followed shortly by hysterical laughter and a slew of cuss words telling him what he can go do with himself.

We immediately get to work. Finn and I split up, with him searching one end of the attic, me the other. Books are everywhere—dusty ones, open ones, forgotten and well-loved ones. Piles of newspapers litter corners and chairs, many as recent as this past week.

All have been opened to the Entertainment sections; more specifically, to book reviews.

I snap pictures of all with the special shield attached to my headset and send them back to the Institute. Van Brunt and Wendy are ready to go over all data we send back.

A quick, quiet snap of fingers lifts my eyes to Finn. He's standing over a disintegrating cardboard box tilted to its side. Switchblades spills out.

I leave the newspapers alone and head over to where he's standing. And then the muscle in my chest stills, because each and every single blade—and there are dozens and dozens of them—are scratched with a familiar name. *S. Todd.*

My God.

Another few minutes of searching brings about new blades scattered throughout the room. Some are rusty, some gleaming, some covered in blood, some pristine. Some are open, many are closed. All are of the barbershop variety.

A faded photograph sticks out from beneath one of the graying, poorly covered mattresses. It's of a pair of adolescents with heads leaning against one another, their fresh faces smiling. It's Todd and his mysterious lady.

I think back to the man I'd encountered at Mansfield Park. He was a far cry from his teens . . . Mid-forties, I estimate, although to be fair, I'm terrible at guessing ages. Wonderlanders age differently than those I knew in England, so somebody there who looked forty could be two hundred, and somebody who looked two hundred could be twenty.

In any case, the years in between this photo and now have hardened these two.

I scan the photo and send it to Wendy before shoving it back under the mattress. Finn motions me over to a dilapidated desk with a large, yellowing curtain hung behind it. He pushes it aside to reveal, taped from floor to ceiling, hundreds of newspaper clippings, photographs, and torn pages from books. As I stare at the sight before us, my heart sinks, ices over, and then melts in fury.

Circled in red, with a slash straight through is, is an illustration of a man on a horse in front of a windmill. A date is scrawled in the same crimson ink, a date that I know well.

It's the date I joined the Collectors' Society.

I'm frantic as I search through the photographs. Some have question marks, some have red circles and slashes, some are untouched. Some have dates, some curse words, some are yellowed with age. There's no rhyme or reason to their postings, except for one thing. They're all about books. There's a slash through *The Three Musketeers*. Through *Strange Case of Dr. Jekyll and Mr. Hyde*. Through *Jane Eyre*.

There are circles around books I now know are about people whose lives mean something to me.

Finn drops a hand on my shoulder. Forces me to look at him. He mouths: *Focus. Take pictures.*

I let my furor force me into compliance. Together, we capture the entire wall, but as soon as I give him a thumb's up, something crashes again. Something much closer than before.

We both freeze.

Footsteps clomp up an unseen set of stairs. A woman shrieks, "You're both fucking idiots! You can both go to hell!"

A quick glance at the small running countdown in the corner of my eye shield shows we have twenty minutes before the A.D. resets the security system. Finn sweeps the curtain closed and quickly leads me toward the armoire. We have nowhere else to go, nowhere else that would allow us cover. The doors protest loudly when I wrench it open; they're not completely attached. The space is tiny, packed tight with clothes and items upon the floor I'd rather not think about. Finn's tugged my bottle of lubricant out of the belt around my waist and is spritzing it on the hinges a split second before I yank them shut and back into place, enveloping us in darkness.

A different door creaks and then slams. "ASSHOLES!"

Make that muted, cramped darkness cut by slivers of light from the broken doors. The armoire we're in is minute, with barely enough room for the two of us outside of the (surprisingly clean smelling) garments squished onto a bar. I feel a hand on top of my head gently pushing downward, and then another hand on my back urging forward. We duck under the shirts and dresses and squeeze up against the back wall, our bodies smooshed together like sardines in a can. My hands have nowhere to go except settle on his hard chest; his fall on my hips.

"Hello?"

Neither of us move. Breathe. My heart decides to run another caucus race; his does, too, just not for the same reason.

I am a foolish, foolish girl. I should not even think of such things right now. Or, hell, care—we could be caught. We've just broken into a heavily alarmed residence after circumventing the existing system and we could get caught and I'm thinking about how bloody attracted I am to this man.

For God's sake. *Priorities*, Alice.

"Today's been a bitch of a day."

Finn's breath, all minty and tantalizing, whispers against my ear. "She's on the phone."

That silly muscle in my chest now decides it must win the race. I need to get out of this closet, out of such close proximity to this man.

"Get the fuck out!"

When an involuntary jerk spasms through me, my nose crashes into Finn's. Both of us hiss in pain, but miraculously manage to keep it to just that. She's not talking to us, though, because the next shout has her saying, "I say, let's burn them all. Fuck, I need some E or something. Got any? I'm desperate for a hit. I'll take coke, too."

It's my turn to put my mouth up against his ear. "Sorry."

I feel, rather than see, his slight intake of breath.

I don't know how long this still nameless woman talks on the phone. It feels like forever, with each second warmer in the small closet than the last. I'm pressed up against the wall, so is Finn. The only thing that separates us is the width of my hands on his chest.

It's torture, plain and simple.

She's not talking about anything we'd care to know. Her words tell us nothing but her love of drugs. I lose interest in her lengthy complaints and find myself focusing instead on the man I'm pressed up against. His heart is thumping just as hard as mine. I focus on my breathing, but every time I pull a drag in, all I smell is Finn: clean soap and man and a hint of mint and spice. Sweat trickles down the back on my neck, and my knees ache from the weird angle we're forced into. And yet, the woman keeps talking.

I lean my head back and stare into the gray darkness above. Finn shifts, his head ducking awkwardly beneath the low ceiling, but the brush of his body against mine scorches already overheated skin.

It's my turn to shift when the ache in my shoulder turns unbearable. Another tiny intake of breath on his behalf sends my pulse skittering once more. Underneath my fingers, the beat in his chest drums harder.

I remind myself: *He's my partner*.

I put on repeat in my head: *Love—lust—has only ever brought you heartache*.

Another crash sounds beyond the armoire doors. I tell myself: *Nothing but trouble can come from feeling this way*.

When Finn shifts again, his fingers tightening around my waist, I'm resolute: *Get your head on straight, Alice*.

The longer the woman bemoans her ails (lack of drugs and a stupid paramour, from the little I can tell), the stronger the heartbeat underneath my hands resonates within my ears. And I'm left wondering if this Timeline is addictive, too, because everything is turning upside down in this warm dungeon we've found ourselves in.

My head drops back down until our noses are mere inches apart. He'd been staring at the door, but the moment he notices I've moved, his eyes find mine in the graying darkness. I can't match their color, but it doesn't matter. In my mind, I see them: clear blue-gray and oh-so-beautifully expressive.

The nerves that run between my brain and hands cease functioning, because my fingers curl into the softness of his dark shirt. Another sharp intake of breath fills the space between us, and I'm no longer overheating.

I've burst straight into flames.

It would be so easy in this moment to close my eyes. Just pretend that nothing is happening, that his touch does nothing to me. I've closed my heart off before. It was difficult, but I did it. I walked away from the only person who consumed my everything for years and still does in many ways, and I did it with one foot in front of the other. What I said was true. Love isn't always enough. Sometimes, a person must let go and mean it.

Any second, we could be discovered. And yet . . . when his head lowers toward mine, I keep my eyes wide open.

We share the same air for many seconds as the woman outside the door lowers her voice to where her words are barely distinguishable. Those I do catch continue to be meaningless, just snatches of irreverent talk that tells us nothing about the wall of book pages. Our lips are precariously close; all it would take would be the most minute of shifts for skin to touch skin. And then my name falls out between us, a barely voiced set of syllables that hold so much more than simple identification.

My fingers tighten in his shirt. Tug ever so gently, when there really isn't space to lead him into. He reaches up and gently slides the screen from my headset back and then does the same to his. I know nobody can see us; an active transmission has to be triggered by the user. Even still, a thrill shoots through me at his purposeful action.

Something else crashes in the next room; maniacal giggles follow. But none of that matters any longer, because the moment she yells out, "Holy shit, I think I cut my toe," my lips meet Finn's.

Live wires explode throughout my body. Logical thought disappears like a magician's trick.

Hands curl tighter around my waist, pulling me into him. My own drift higher until they loop around his neck. His mouth is soft and hard and warm and addictive, and when his tongue touches the seam that holds the last of my restraints in, I lose the battle.

It was a good fight, but this is better.

Our tongues trace one another, and I'm tasting mint and Finn and it's just as drugging as anything in Wonderland. The situation is less than ideal, risky as all hell, even, but stupidly, none of that matters. His body leans farther into mine, pressing me up against a wall I'd already been trapped against, and yet he isn't close enough. I want—no, *need*— him closer. He instinctively must sense this from me, because the next thing I know, our legs overlap in the tiny space and he's erased the separation. I'm aching and desperate and we kiss until we consume all the air in the closet and then continue to do so long after dizziness sets in.

This isn't my first kiss, nor even my hundredth. I am no inexperienced girl. And yet, as my knees go weak and my heart beats in a wild symphony and my nerve endings become painfully aware of every inch of his body pressed up against mine, I marvel at how it all feels so new.

Time blurs together until it's meaningless, until the closet and clothes disappear around us. Everything in this moment is touch and sensation, and I'm drunk on it. Finn whispers, just barely, my name again, his mouth traveling down the length of my chin to the sensitive skin just below my ear, and it sounds like a benediction coming from him.

"ROSEMARY, GET THE FUCK DOWN HERE!"

We startle apart at the male voice. It's Jenkins. Reality slaps us both straight across the face, but at least now we have a name. *Rosemary.*

"GO FUCK YOURSELF!"

Feet clomp on stairs and another rip of a creak fills the room. "What crawled up your ass and died today? Are you on the rag?"

I know that voice. My fingers curl tighter into Finn's shirt. I whisper, right up against his ear, "That's Todd."

He's breathing heavily when he nods his confirmation. A small sound beeps in our ears, letting us know our window for escape has passed. Have twenty minutes truly passed so quickly? He slides both our eye screens back into place right as Wendy's voice says, "AF, do you copy?"

"This is bullshit!" she yells. "He thinks I'm his fucking sex slave or something!" Pounding sounds against the floor. "GO TAKE AN ACID BATH, YOU SICK FUCKING PERVERT!"

Apparently, I'm not the only one who sees the bookstore owner as such.

Finn presses a button on his earpiece, alerting the team to the fact that we are in no position to orally copy.

Something is kicked and sent skittering across the room. It bounces against the armoire, sending Finn's hand to his holster.

"Until we get what we want, you are his fucking slave and everything else if that's what it takes," Todd growls. "Which means you need to get your ass downstairs and deal with the matter at hand."

Her voice lowers. "We don't need him."

"Do you not remember that some bitch from the Society showed up? Took what was ours?"

My fingers tighten on Finn's shoulders, but not in a good way. Wendy says, "JD, I'm sending a new virus packet to recode the system."

"You should have taken the damn shot last night, Rose," Todd's saying. "If you had, we wouldn't be in this mess right now."

The A.D. says, "Copy that, WD1."

"You think I didn't want to?" Rosemary's voice raises significantly. "I had a bead on her. I was ready to go!"

"VVB, do you have a visual on AF?" Wendy asks.

I suck in a breath. Another object in the room crashes to the floor, and I have to grab Finn to stop him from throwing the doors wide open. It isn't my first assassination attempt, after all. It isn't even my second, or, hell, my third. This Rosemary better step up her game if she wants to compete with the big girls.

Okay. Just the thought of her going up against the Queen of Hearts and her wicked battle ax brings an inappropriate grin to my face.

Finn touches my face. His brows are furrowed, and it takes me a moment to realize he's wondering what's got me mimicking the Cheshire-Cat. I shake my head and wave my hand. *Later.*

"Negative, WD1," Victor is saying. "Current view is Jenkins."

"You'll have another chance," Todd tells Rosemary. "Little Alice from Wonderland can't be too charmed, can she? We'll blitz her world next, and then she won't think too highly of herself any longer. I'm just waiting for the go ahead."

He knows who I am. *They* know who I am. And they've threatened those and what I love.

I have to yank Finn's arm back once more. He's shaking in anger, and in the dim, filtered light from the poorly hung doors, I can see cold determination fill his eyes. I want to reassure him that I've faced worse than these two, that, after all I've been through, I am still standing. I am still breathing. But I can't do that right now, not with two murderers arguing just feet away from where we're hiding.

They're mine now, though. They just don't know it yet.

I press a kiss against the corner of his mouth. Whisper, "Hold your ground." Just as I pull back, green letters race across my field of vision, telling me that an extraction will be executed within fifteen minutes if we do not make it outside on our own.

My partner leans forward and whispers softly in my ear, "Get ready."

I'm always ready, unfortunately.

Jenkins bellows once more, demanding that the "two shitheads get downstairs right now." I expect them to refuse, or at least Rosemary to do so, but a door creaks and footsteps and voices recede.

We give silence sixty seconds before we pry open the armoire doors. The moment we're out, Finn grabs my face. He mouths: *Are you okay?*

Warmth spreads in my belly. I nod, and then he tugs me forward for a tiny hug.

I melt.

When he pulls away, all the parts of me that had been touching him protest. I never learn.

Just before we dart toward the window, a door creaks open. And there, her mouth and eyes wide in shock, is Rosemary.

My daggers are out immediately. So are both of Finn's handguns, and they're trained right on her. God, he's alluring when he's serious like this.

"What. The. FUCK?" she screeches. "HOW DID YOU TWO GET IN HERE?!"

I let one of my blades fly, but she's quicker (and far more limber) than I gave her credit for. Her body nearly folds backward as she skids to the ground, and then she rolls over and snatches a bō staff hidden along the baseboards I hadn't noticed before.

"Move another inch," Finn says, cold as ice, "and I'll blow your head off."

She moves. Of course she moves. He shoots and strikes her shoulder just like he'd meant to. And yet, she doesn't even falter. Doesn't flinch, doesn't cry, doesn't do anything except continue to scream at us. Is she even human? I don't have time to investigate, because feet are slapping up the stairs. Todd has come to join the party.

"Gunshots heard," the A.D. is saying. "VVB, status on Jenkins?"

As Todd whips out a pair of his switchblades, spinning them in an overly dramatic circle that has me rolling my eyes, another gunshot explodes through the building. Only this one isn't from Finn, because glass shatters and a roar from a floor below nearly shakes everyone to their feet.

"Bleeding," Victor replies grimly.

Todd charges Finn; my partner fires yet another bullet. Society protocol dictates we disable suspects in consideration for future questioning, but I can't help but notice Finn's mark is perilously close to the barber's heart. Another roar fills the attic, but just as shockingly as with Rosemary, Todd does not go down.

I do, though. Right when Rosemary slams her staff across my belly while I wasn't paying attention to her. I roll to the side as Finn fires again. He's clipped Todd's right shoulder. And then I throw my dagger out as Rosemary swings once more.

I connect with her leg. It's her turn to finally scream. They're a loud bunch, aren't they? And extremely high on drugs, from the looks of it. Both fiends' eyes are glazed and crazed.

It's not a good combination. No wonder Finn's shot didn't slow her down.

Another shot sounds below. Todd, bleeding and deranged, throws himself right at Finn. But my partner doesn't even bat an eye—he headbutts the barber before kicking him backward. "Did you delete those Timelines?" he rages when Todd sprawls before him. "Did you personally destroy the catalysts marked on your fucking target wall?"

Todd's laughter is terrifying.

"You bitch!" Rosemary is hissing, tearing my attention back to my assailant. She yanks out my dagger and throws it to the ground as she surges to her feet.

Wrong move. I immediately counter her, sweeping her fresh legs out from beneath her. And then I'm straddling her scrawny body, slamming her head into the hard wooden floor. She howls, kicking, but I'm stronger than I look.

A hand shoves my chin up; fingers try to close in around my throat. I'm undeterred, even though spots float before my eyes. She'll have to squeeze harder if she wants me out. When her scrambling turns frantic, I manage to tug over my blade.

As much as I want to shove it right into her windpipe, I flip it over and slam the butt against her temple. I need information. "What do you know of Wonderland?" She howls, and I repeat the action, harder than before. "How did you know of the catalyst in Mansfield Park?"

She spits on me. I spit right back.

A fresh surge of adrenaline has her finally shoving me off. Behind us, Todd is crashing into the armoire we hid in. Finn's right there on top of him, throwing a pair of punches to the chin before kicking him so hard the barber slumps to the ground. "Did you murder all those people for fun? How did you know about the catalysts?"

Blood spurts from Todd's nose and lips, but, outside of his maniacal laughter, says nothing.

Where are Finn's guns?

I don't have time to look, though. Rosemary tries to take me down again, the bō staff reclaimed. She may be fast, she may be flexible, but I'm better. I let go of a roundhouse kick, sending her sprawling. And then I grab her shirt, hauling her up. "How do you know of the Society?"

She's demonic with her laughter, and for a moment, I could swear she was a Wonderlander.

"AF, situation compromised," Wendy is saying in our ears. "Security system override unnecessary. Extraction in T-minus three minutes."

"I'll kill you," she snarls.

How cliché of her. I slam her down, bringing my elbow down on her temple. Blood trickles from a split lip as her eyes roll back. "Better people than you have tried."

Finn clicks the button on his ear right as one of Todd's blades make contact with his leg. My heart swells over how he doesn't flinch. Not once. "Copy."

But, like a robot, Rosemary is miraculously back on her feet. So is Todd. Both are bleeding far worse than either Finn or I, but it's not a good sign that they can fight so easily through the pain.

It took me a good two years to learn how to do so.

Finn throws another punch at Todd's battered face as Rosemary rams my stomach with her surprisingly hard head. But, somehow, Finn's there to catch me before I fall.

"Two minutes to extraction, AF," Wendy says.

Finn kicks Todd squarely in the chest, sending him flying back a good five feet. It's my turn to throw a punch, and when Rosemary goes down, she doesn't get up so easily.

Finn and I sprint toward the window. He kicks out the pane and shoves me out first. "Climb to the roof," he says just seconds before Todd yanks him back into the room.

I scramble to get to him, but my partner yells, "GO!"

Against my better judgment, I'm up the few metal stairs that it takes to get to the roof. A helicopter comes swinging into view, and for a moment, I'm immobile because Mary's in the pilot's seat. The A.D. is next to her, dark glasses obscuring his eyes.

A ladder drops. I hesitate, especially when I hear the sound of yet another gun shot.

"ALR, get on the helicopter. Departure in T-minus forty-five seconds."

Panic laces through me. I won't leave without Finn. I won't. I fumble for my blades, but both are in the attic.

"ALR," Wendy says more forcefully. "Get your scrawny ass onto the helicopter right now."

Another gun shot, followed by a scream and then a crash. Sirens blare in the distance. I'm halfway to the ledge.

"ALR, get on the helicopter right now." It's a furious Van Brunt.

I'm about to tell them what they can all do with themselves when a hand appears at the junction of room and stairs. And then, a second later, Finn appears.

My heart clutches again. He's bloody, but he's here.

I climb the ladder.

WE NEED TO TALK

"HOW ARE YOU FEELING?"

Finn glances up from his laptop, clearly startled to find me leaning against the doorframe to his bedroom. He's spread out across his bed, propped up on elbows and shirtless, and sinful thoughts fill my mind.

I know how it feels to be kissed by this man now.

I really should have just stayed away and left well enough alone. A thousand rationalizations peppered my thoughts once we got back to the Institute the night before, ones that made sense. *It was the heat of the moment. Stakes were raised. Our adrenaline was already spiked. I shouldn't be feeling this way. It was a momentary lapse in reasoning. We're partners, nothing more.*

But other thoughts made sleep difficult. Was he hurt worse than I thought? We'd both visited Victor to have our wounds looked at before sitting in on an hour-long meeting during which Van Brunt and the Librarian had us relating every last detail of our time in Ex Libris' attic.

We were given morphine shots (under Van Brunt's orders—both of us protested but were overruled), and over the course of the hour, it became apparent the drug made Finn more than a bit loopy to the point he started to slur his words together and doze at the table.

It was then I demanded we table further discussions until the next day.

His brother and father eventually dragged him upstairs to his flat to sleep it off. I'd trailed along (under Mary's watchful eyes), but morphine and the like are akin to alcohol to me. Things blur, but I'm more than capable of functioning under such duress. But I laid awake, reliving the night's events.

I kissed him. He kissed me. Guilt tore holes within my chest. Worse yet, Todd and Rosemary know who I am and plan to target Wonderland next.

I'd rolled over on my side and stared out of the window. The moon was fat and round and bright, reminding me of far too many nights I used to stare at it and wonder what the next morning would bring. And there I was, wondering that infernal question once more, as I tried to make sense of the evening's events.

Hairline fissures grew in the shields I'd carefully built around me over the last six months.

After I got dressed this morning, I couldn't help myself. I told myself it was because I wanted to see how he was doing, but the fact was, I simply wanted to see *him*. So, I knocked on his door and he'd called out for me to come in. Now here I am, in his bedroom and his flat for the first time, wondering if I'd hit my head too hard hours before, because I'm surrendering to the attraction between us, aren't I?

He closes the laptop and gifts me with a smile Mary once noted to be a panty-dropping grin. It's an apt description. "Sorry. I thought you were Victor. If I'd known it was you, I would have gone and answered."

The muscle in my chest thumps to a stronger rhythm. I cross my arms, hating that I can't seem to control these reactions. Too bad I wasn't paired with a cruel, stupid man. "It's fine. I'm a big girl who knows how to open doors by herself. It's terribly scandalous, but what can one do? A lady doesn't always have a man around to open doors, after all."

"Those with manservants do."

My laugh is a burst of surprised air. "Alas, I no longer have those in employ."

He rolls off his bed and slowly wanders over to where I'm standing. Golden sunlight spills through the slated blinds on the windows, leaving strands of his honeyed hair glinting. I'm struck once more by just how beautiful he truly is.

I clear my throat. Lick my lips. Ask again, "How are you feeling?"

His eyes settle on my mouth, of that I'm sure. "Good as new."

"No pain?"

He shakes his head. "You?"

"None. I'm not the one who got stitches this time, remember?"

He glances down at his leg. He'd objected last night, but Victor had insisted. Honestly, I'd sided with the doctor.

"What were you doing?"

"The Librarian had some questions, so I was amending our report."

The rhythm in my chest changes, becomes more forcefully strong. "It couldn't have waited until later? You need your rest."

He lifts an arm and plants a palm on the wall just above and to the left of my head. Our bodies are inches away from one another—not as close as they were in that closet, but with such a lack of space that the heat from his body meets mine and the delicious smell of this man fills my senses. "I slept for eight hours, which is longer than I have in probably five years."

It's bloody annoying how my cheeks flush. Even more so annoying is how ridiculous I feel for even coming in here. "Your body needs to heal."

"My body is fine."

Is it ever.

I'm ready to take the necessary, wise step backward, when a hand comes out to curl around my arm. "Wait." I watch his chest rise and fall with a measured breath. "I'm glad you stopped by. We need to talk about what happened."

We need to talk . . .

Perhaps I'm being dramatic, but the words *we need to talk* feel dire in just about any Timeline. And shameful, too, when shame shouldn't be an issue. "Honestly, Finn. There isn't much to discuss."

His head tilts, and for such an intelligent man, there's a bit of confusion in his eyes.

"Things like this happen." Ignoring the lump forming in my throat, I shrug.

"Not to me, they don't."

I'm genuinely surprised. "I assumed that you and Sara . . ."

He shakes his head. "What? Why would you—?" But before I can answer, he rolls his eyes and swears softly under his breath. "Mary, right? She doesn't know what the hell she's talking about. Sara and I weren't like that."

The adage about assumptions Mary told me about recently rings loud and true in my head. I do feel a bit like an arse right now. A delighted one, but an arse all the same.

"The entire time she worked at the Society, she had a boyfriend in her Timeline," he adds. "But more importantly, there was no attraction between us. So, no, Alice. Things like this do not just happen—at least to me."

The windows are open, but the room seems to lose a bit of its oxygen. "They do with Mary and Victor. Or at least, they did."

"We're not talking about them. We're talking about us."

Us.

Two letters combine to make a tiny word whose connotation is massive. There is an us here. He and I, we're partners. We are also part of the Society and have a shared sense of being misunderstood characters in beloved books. But when he says this word, when these two letters combine to make a single syllable from his mouth, it feels more than that. It feels both broader, more significant. And yet smaller and exclusive all at once.

Us is a heady, dangerous word.

He lets go of my arm, only to trail his fingers across my shoulder. I shudder at this soft touch, tremble at the look in his eyes. "Do these things happen to you?"

I wish I could offer him the same answer as he gave me. I wish I could say *no, this is unique*, because it is . . . And yet it would be a lie, too. But before I can say anything, he tells me, "Don't answer that. It doesn't matter, anyway."

My voice is husky, like I have no control over it any longer. "It doesn't?"

He touches my face, tilts my chin upward. And then he shakes his head again. "The only thing that matters right now is if what happened last night between us in that armoire meant something to you."

My defenses are peeled back and I'm left vulnerable in his wake. Part of me insists I'm to tell him no—no is the safest answer. There would be awkwardness for a bit of time, true, but we could get over it. We would move on. Eventually, if I chose to stay on with the Society, it would become a long-lost memory that rarely revisits its owners. We could laugh about it in the future, scoff over how we let ourselves go during the most inopportune, inappropriate time ever.

But the thing is, it did mean something to me.

I am attracted to him. Desperately so. I've tried not to be—heaven knows how attraction in the past has led me to ruin, but it's here all the same. And kissing him did me no favors, because it only fanned the embers until a flame was ignited.

I tell myself: *This time could be different.*

I rationalize: *It's not like my past can be changed.*

I fear: *I lost everything before.*

And yet . . . I hope.

This attraction . . . it's different. There are obstacles, yes, but they are nothing like those I stumbled across before.

He waits patiently for my answer, as if we're not expected downstairs to finish the meeting he fell asleep in, or that our absence would be noted. He waits with one arm planted on the wall next to me and the other cupping my cheek.

No is the safest answer.

I tell him, "Yes."

His head ducks farther, tilts toward mine. My entire senses are filled with all things Huckleberry Finn Van Brunt, and I swear all my joints have taken to trembling and my insides to aching need. "Good." The word is whispered hot and lovely across my mouth, and then uttered once more, more meaningfully.

I throw caution out the window and to the wind. I disentangle my arms and wrap them around his neck just as his mouth finds mine. And oh, oh, if I'd thought those stolen moments we shared in the armoire were scorching, they are nothing to the wildfire lacing my bloodstream right now. His hand curves around the back of my head, tugging me closer, and I am nothing but willingness to indulge this whim.

His tongue strokes mine, mine strokes his. Sensations I believed dormant, ones I've wished away, come roaring back to gloriously colored life. Something in me clenches in desperate need, even more so when I feel his own desire pressing hard against my leg.

I marvel over how he feels this undeniable chemistry between us, too.

I'm tired of fighting it. I can't live in the past. So, with one hand firmly keeping his head in place, I use the other to shove him backward, back toward the bed he so recently vacated.

If this surprises Finn, he doesn't show it. His arms wrap around me, holding me close until I'm no longer the one leading. He's now dragging me to where I want to go. His mouth doesn't even break contact with mine when he somehow locates his laptop and gently tosses it onto a nearby nightstand.

I push him down onto the bed, and it's then we finally separate. He scoots back, his glazed, beautiful eyes looking up at me with such heat, such wanting, that I'm surprised my undergarments don't catch fire and melt right off my body. I climb up onto the bed and straddle him, my thighs outside his. For a long moment, we simply stare at one another, our breaths mingling in uneven, hard bursts.

Now would be the moment I climb off this bed. Now would be the time I end this. Now would be the smart move.

He leans up on his arms, his mouth closing in on mine, but I place a finger against those enticing lips of his. Blue-gray eyes widen, yet no words come out of his mouth.

My lips drop to his ear; I gently bite, then tug on the lobe. His groan tells me everything I need to know.

He lays below me, his heart pounding so hard I can see its beat through his tanned skin. I trace the thin trail of darkening hair from just below his navel to the rim of low-rising shorts first with my finger and then with my mouth. Soap clings to his skin; he must have showered recently.

I want my mouth all over him. And I would like his to do the same to me.

Finn says my name softly, like it's a prayer, or a plea. I lean up and place my finger across his soft lips once more. His tongue peeks out and touches my skin briefly before he sucks the digit in, and I swear I very nearly come right here and now, it's so erotic.

I fight to regain my hard-won control.

My mouth is the one to reconnect with his. My hands are the ones to pin his down, even if for the smallest sliver of time before I allow them to touch me. My body is the one to move first, to tempt the other until he's writhing underneath me, desperate for what we both so clearly want. And I revel in this control.

I don't know how long it takes before I finally relinquish my dress, but when I do, when it's finally tossed onto the floor nearby, I am rewarded by a barely voiced gasp. For a moment, I'm sucked back in time, into the tulgey woods, but when hands reach up to cup my breasts—Finn's hands—I force myself to remember where I am. And with who. And how these feelings are just as painfully, beautifully genuine.

Soon, he's lifting his hips so I can slide his shorts off. I take my time removing each subsequent piece of clothing, each languid removal just that bit more erotic in anticipation. We kiss, we suck, we touch, we stroke, we graze, we worship, we learn each other's bodies like they're maps we must memorize for future missions.

I am just about to lower myself over him when Finn whispers I must wait. Warring fear and aching need arise, but he leans up and kisses me slowly, reverently. "We need protection," he murmurs, and I'm sucked back in time once more until I realize this man doesn't mean guard contingencies or swords nearby.

I watch in fascination as he first digs through the drawer of a nightstand, and then through his wallet, no doubt searching for the modern-day protection Mary told me about one day when we went to a drugstore and she was purchasing several boxes. "I'm sorry," he says to me, half embarrassed, half amused, "It's not like I've ever had to find one of these here before . . ." He clears his throat, giving me a look so hot, so meaningful, my insides melt to liquid lust. "Obviously, I don't bring women I date back to the Institute. So . . ."

I rise up on the bed, up onto my knees. A sly question rests on the tip of my tongue, one that would inquire about where he does take those lucky women, but I realize I don't care. He's right. It doesn't matter. Nothing that has come before matters. What does is right now.

Finn finds what he's looking for, wedged behind credit cards and business cards. A small, silverish square is brandished before the wallet gets tossed to the side. I pluck it out of his fingers, and part of me is surprised that this man, usually so in control of every situation he's in, has been utterly willing to let me take control here. "Lay down," I tell him quietly, and he does so, no questions.

It isn't hard to figure out. Seconds later, I roll the small bit of rubber down over his hardened length. A low, rolling hiss emerges from his throat, one that I want to eat right up. For now, I kiss him, and it's like our mouths go to war with one another, and sweet victory is claimed by both. And then I'm finally straddling him again, lowering my body over his until we fit like completed puzzle pieces.

He says, he moans, "Oh, God. Alice."

I move. He does, too. Together, we move in exquisite unison until we're both dangling over a precipice neither of us can come back from. And then he surprises me by flipping us over, so that he's now leaning over my body, driving into me so masterfully that all thoughts and meanings fly free of my head, leaving behind only sensation.

When we explode together, right on key, I'm surprised the windows don't shatter.

Afterward, as we fight to catch our breaths, sweaty and tired, his arms wrapped around me and his mouth pressing gentle kissing against the base of my neck, I murmur, "I thought you wanted to talk."

His nose nudges a line toward my chin. "We did talk."

Tiny bubbles of incandescent happiness filter throughout my chest. "I could have sworn very little was said between us tonight."

He gently tugs me onto my back, so I'm staring up into those mesmerizing eyes of his. His kiss is slow, and yet fans those flames high within me once more. "Then you weren't listening closely enough."

LATER, AS FINN DOZES next to me, I send a quick message to his father, letting him know we're both tired from the night's events and will be more than happy to discuss the matters at hand with them later in the day. He's fine with it, claiming it's for the best as a number of non-residential Society members want to attend and are en route.

But it doesn't mean I don't think about what's happened.

The photo I found, the one stuck underneath one of the ancient, thin mattresses, showed the pair of catalyst thieves as teenagers. Fresh faced, clearly in love, happy even. But more importantly, they were wearing modern albeit dated clothing. T-shirts featuring band names the A.D. has mentioned to me before and jeans were most definitely not the clothing du jour in Victorian England.

There is no doubt in my mind that S. Todd is not the Sweeney Todd of *A String of Pearls*. And Rosemary is no Mrs. Lovett—and, as far as I can tell, no baker (or at least one who enjoys sampling her wares). While obviously trained in weapons, they are no longer the infamous duo of serial killers we feared they might have been. So that leaves the question: if they aren't the real Sweeney Todd and Mrs. Lovett, who exactly are they? Copycats? It wouldn't be the first time people have attempted to replicate fiends they have admired. These two reside in a bookstore, and have plenty of access to Sweeney Todd's story. There are movies. Plays. Musicals. Comic books just like the one Finn found on a second-floor shelf in Ex Libris.

How do they know who I am?

Jenkins hadn't. At least, I didn't get the impression he did. He compared me to the illustrations in the book, yes, but I'm certain that was done in a much more perverted fashion than a sly one. And yet, Todd and Rosemary are clearly in league with Jenkins, as tenuous of a connection as that may be. But exactly what connection is it? Does Jenkins know about the wall? Or is he merely a landlord, or a place for them to base their nefarious actions from? How do they get in and out without being seen? The Society has cameras trained on the front of the building, and there's been no sight of any of them leaving in days.

Questions upon questions pile up in my mind, and none will allow me sleep.

They know about Wonderland, I remind myself. They've marked it as a target, and I'll be damned before I let them follow through on their plot. And then I nearly laugh because, after all that has happened, I am going home after all. I just need to figure out how to inform Finn I'll be doing it alone.

When sunlight pours into his sparse bedroom, I try to focus on absorbing small details that I had yet been privy to. There's a singular painting in the room, of a river bank. On his dresser are a few framed photographs—from this distance, I can tell one is of Finn and Victor, another of an older, dark-skinned man, another of what I assume to be the Van Brunt family. There's a blonde woman with the two teenage boys, a beautiful one whose smile nearly spreads the width of her face.

I wish to look at it closer, but I'm reluctant to move away from his warm side.

While Finn is obviously a predominately tidy man, there is a small pile of clothes strewn in front of a partially opened closet. Books line the shelves of a bookcase, but none seem to be familiar titles. A stack of papers sits aligned neatly upon his nightstand, alongside his laptop so recently abandoned.

I realize that Finn Van Brunt values self-control just as rabidly as I do.

For long, quiet moments, I study him as he sleeps. His golden-brown lashes, the exact color of his hair, are obscenely long. I'm inordinately jealous of them. He doesn't snore, but every so often, there's a soft hiccup of air. A pair of freckles adorns his neck just below his chin, and another small dot sits right below one of his eyebrows. Across the bridge of his nose is a constellation of barely there kisses from the sun. His fingers curl into fists, like those of a little boy's during naptime.

I am enchanted.

Seeing him like this for the first time, really seeing him, leaves me shaken and confused and hopeful.

Later, when he wakes, our mouths find one another once more. No words, no questions, just soft kisses that build to something more.

I am more than enchanted.

I fear I am doing the impossible. I fear I am falling in love.

THE TRUTH

VICTOR HAS ASKED TO have a look at his brother's stitches be-fore we all convene, and it gives me the perfect opportunity to slip away and seek out the Librarian. She's in her office, and there are stacks and stacks of books surrounding her that serve as a fragile maze.

I knock upon her open door. "May I have a moment?"

She doesn't turn to look at me. "You're later than I thought you would be."

Aren't I always, according to this woman.

Despite her stiletto heels, she goes up onto her tiptoes so she can slide a book on top of a stack taller than herself. "You are wondering if I've identified the catalyst for 1865/71CAR-AWLG, hmm?"

Although her question unnerves me, I decide to go with the flow. "If that's the identification for my Timeline, then yes. I am."

The book placed, she smacks her hands together. "I have."

I wait, but she turns away to claim another book off her desk to stack. Finally, when it becomes blatantly obvious she isn't going to offer up the information unprompted, I ask, "What is it?"

"Shut the door, please."

Once I do so, she motions to a chair partially filled with books. "Shall we have some tea?"

I shift them around so I can squeeze into the green velvet seat. "If you don't mind, I'd rather—"

"He won't let you."

My fingers freeze on a book wedged against my spine. "Pardon?"

"Neither will," she hypothetically clarifies.

I toss the book onto the floor, annoyed. "I'm sorry. Who won't let me do what?"

She shimmies between several tottering stacks and comes round to sit behind her desk. "Don't be angry when you don't get your way. All things happen for a reason."

She could give the Caterpillar a run for his money, that's for certain.

"Now." The Librarian folds her hands in front of her. "You wanted to know what you ought to be on the outlook for. Are you sure you don't want some tea?" Her smile is impish. "You don't want to be dehydrated after this morning's activities, do you?"

My face flames. This woman really is too much. "What activities?"

She tsks. "Your inability to act demure has always been one of your downfalls." A red button is pushed on the turquoise old-fashioned phone on her desk. "Tea it is. Oolong will do. Now, where were we?"

Sticking noses where they do not belong, I think sourly. "You were about to tell me what the catalyst for my Timeline is."

"Ah, yes. Of course. I feel terribly annoyed with myself that it took so long to determine, but things have been a bit hectic lately. It's your crown, naturally."

It's also a swift strike to my belly.

"You'll have to tell him, you know. I know you think you don't, but you really should."

I've had more than enough of her creepiness. "Stop talking in riddles."

"How can I be talking in riddles," she says calmly, "when you know exactly what I mean?"

Fine. I'll play. "If any of the people here at the Institute have read my books, then they will know I was crowned as a child. My stories do take place when I was a child, correct?"

"Stories," she says, smiling patiently, "are subject to interpretation, author voice, and embellishments. Yes, the books associated with 1865/71CAR-AWLG cover two trips to Wonderland when you were a child. But they are whimsical and surprisingly loaded with mathematical secrets. One book even has you moving through the story via chess moves."

"Chess moves!"

She shrugs. "Authors take liberties. What can I say? They tell a story in the way that they like. Your author liked chess and math." The Librarian leans forward, her nails clicking against her shiny, lacquered desk. "There is a game that people talk about here called Telephone. One person whispers a secret into an ear, then that person whispers it into another ear, and then so on and so forth. By the end, elements of the original secret still remain, but many of the details have been altered due to interpretation. Authors do this, too."

"I thought the events in books *couldn't* be changed. Timelines, yes. But not the actual books."

"Yes," she says simply.

I'm even more annoyingly confused.

And she's amused. "No story is uninfluenced by the voice it's told in. Lewis Carroll had many delightful, absurd things to say about your time in Wonderland. Children for generations have come to view it as magical and whimsical. But you and I know it's not entirely like that, don't we?"

My lips thin as I give her a tight nod.

"Now, you've wondered if the members here knew you were crowned. Those who perused your story in our quest to find you did know that. However, it comes across in the story as a chess move. To them, it was part of a game, which you eventually won. You went back to England. That was that. The board reset for another game to be played. None of them actually know you are a true Wonderlandian queen."

Frabjous. Simply frabjous.

A knock on the door sounds. The Librarian calls out, "Come in!"

The A.D. is there, with a small golden tray filled with a tea pot and two cups.

"Give it to Alice, Jack. And then go tell Brom we'll be there within the half hour."

I expect the A.D. to make a snide comment, or at least a perverted one. But he merely nods, hands me the tray, and leaves without another word.

"What have you done to him?" I ask suspiciously.

Her laughter tinkles in the closed room. "Jack is a dear boy. Misguided, but dear. He and I have an understanding—much like you and I do."

"We," I stress, "understand nothing. You don't know me."

"Oh," she says lightly, "but I do. I'll let you pour. Hurry now, and don't spill. We'll want to go down and talk to everyone so you can begin the preparations to return to your Timeline. The clock is ticking."

As there is nowhere else to set the tray, I balance it on my thighs as I pour our cups.

"Now, about your crown. Any ideas where it might be at the moment?"

"You seem to know an extraordinarily large amount about my past." The tray wobbles, forcing my legs to spread a little wider to stabilize it. "So why don't *you* tell *me?*"

"I have no idea, to be honest." She takes the cup I offer. "Do you?"

Tea splashes out of my cup, given the force I use to shove sugar cubes in. "I gave it to a friend for safe keeping."

"Your affections for steadfast, honorable men are admirable."

I suck in a frustrated breath.

"I suppose it would be pointless for me to remind you to be careful and watch your head."

"Oh, ha ha. You're quite the comedienne, aren't you?"

"No," she says thoughtfully. "I'm a realist."

As am I, unfortunately.

Thankfully, she does not accompany me to the conference room. But as I make my way there, taking the long route via the back stairs, I can't help but wonder about what she's said—and of how certain she was that none new of my royal status. Granted, nobody had teased me of it, or even mentioned it, but it was assumed once many admitted to skimming my books that this was a well-known fact.

Suddenly, the trip to Wonderland feels all the more dangerous.

Oh, bloody hell. She was right. I'm going to have to tell them, aren't I?

Finn sits to my right at the long conference table and it's torture. There's no production of us being here together, no hint to the others that anything has shifted, but I feel it.

He does, too.

Underneath the table, for the teeniest of moments while Van Brunt is talking to the group, Finn's fingers find mine. Just brushes, really, our digits lacing in and out of each other without truly knotting, but I'm positive the electricity in my body these small motions generate is enough to power the entire building.

Wendy has brought in her laptop and is showing off the pictures we'd taken in Ex Libris' attic. Multiple laptops are open up and down the table, and worried, angry people are skimming through them, desperate to find their own stories or those from beloved friends and family. Finn has his laptop, too, and since it wasn't even a consideration for me to bring mine, I'm forced to share his while the discussion around us rages.

People are scared.

We go over in excruciating detail everything we saw and did last night—well, sans inappropriately timed kissing in an armoire. Questions are asked, some more than once. Finn and I, just as frustrated as the rest, do our best to answer each query patiently and thoroughly. I share my beliefs that Todd and Rosemary are not the real Sweeney Todd and Mrs. Lovett, but instead some kind of sycophant copycats. I point out details in the photograph that support my hypothesis.

Jenkins, though, remains a mystery to us all.

"The solution is easy," Mr. Holgrave says. I haven't seen him much since that first day, but here he is, and in full possession of all information. "We simply assassinate these fiends. If they're not alive, then there's no way they can continue collection catalysts."

A good deal of the crowd smooshed into the room nod their heads in agreement. Members flocked to the conference room to hear the details, and many are forced to stand due to a chair shortage. The A.D. has been wheeling them in from other offices, but even then, even in a large room such as this, there simply isn't enough space.

"The dead," the Librarian says from the doorway, "cannot answer questions, I'm afraid." And then her eyes find me, and she smiles indulgently, like we've been sharing girlish secrets.

She's maddening, that one.

"The Librarian is right," Van Brunt says. He's at the head of the table, looking like he hasn't slept a wink. "Right now, we need answers. We need to know how they're editing into Timelines. From Finn and Ms. Reeve's accounts they appear to have our technology. How is that? We need to also know if the collection of suspects are at two, three, or even more. Are there more—even sleeper cells to consider?" He shakes his head. "The best course is to capture them for interrogation. We can discuss more permanent solutions further on down the road."

Despite my past, I shiver at his coldly voice words.

"Our current needs are two-fold," Van Brunt continues. "FK Jenkins, S. Todd, and Rosemary are to be apprehended as quickly as possible. Current surveillance of the Ex Libris Bookshop shows no activity, which is worrisome. A team will be organized to hunt them down; I personally will head it. We will have movement on this front by the evening."

To be honest, I would find it fascinating to watch Van Brunt in action.

"There is also a dire need to obtain the catalyst for 1865/71CAR-AWLG. Comments made last night by Todd and Rosemary indicate that this is a top priority for them. We cannot afford to let them gain one more deletion. Within twenty-four hours, a team will enter 1865/71CAR-AWLG to retrieve the catalyst." Van Brunt turns to the Librarian, who has been hovering by the wall off to the side. "Has it been identified?"

She passes Wendy a small blue rectangle. "Yes."

Wendy flips open the rectangle and sticks it into the side of her laptop. After a moment, a new picture appears, one of a young, blonde girl in a blue and white dress sitting between two life-sized chess players. All three wear golden crowns. And for a moment, as I stare at this picture, I'm stunned, but then a sharp bark of a laugh escapes me.

This is how they see the Red and White Queens?

"What's wrong?" Finn asks me.

I don't even know how to start with this. How to let them know how bitterly wrong this illustration is, how . . . *innocent* it looks.

The Librarian spares me, though, because she angles a slim silver tube toward the screen on the wall. A red dot appears right in the center of the crown on top of the young girl's head. "The catalyst is the Queen of Diamond's crown."

The room falls silent. Every pair of eyes angles toward me, yet I refuse to meet any. I simply continue to stare at the illustration, agog at how such a momentous occasion could be pared down into a cartoon, and utterly livid that the Librarian dared to force my hand.

She had no right to tell them my secrets. None. Anger surges up in my throat.

A few people cough. Chairs shift. Outside of standing up and leaving, they're expecting something from me. I do my best to ensure my teeth aren't too gritted as I speak. "I know whom to contact about the crown, so at least that part won't be too much of a problem."

"You're a queen?"

This comes from Mary. She's sitting across the table, gaping at me as if I were a stranger. They are all like this, though. Judging me, when they have no clue about what I've been through, what I've seen, or what I've done.

"Yes."

The silence continues. Coming from my right, it's especially un-nerving. All it serves is to do is send my body into defensive mode.

Mary keeps on going. "Like, a *real* queen?"

My answer is cool. "Yes."

"Did you rule part of Wonderland?" Her eyes are wide as saucers.

"Yes."

"And you *left?*"

Once more, much more flatly, "Yes."

The woman I've come to consider a friend tears her gaze away from mine to stare upon the glowing illustration upon the wall. And then she looks back at me, and there's hurt in her eyes that don't belong there.

I don't owe her my past. I don't owe any of them my secrets. I didn't seek out the Collectors' Society. They sought *me*.

"You were found at an asylum," Victor says. He's at the far end of the table, as he and Mary are still on the outs.

"I was," I confirm. I can practically feel ice crystals peppering my skin, I'm so furious.

"But—"

My impulse is to stand up and walk out of the room, but too many years of formality are engrained in me. I sit perfectly still, practically daring him—or anyone—to follow that up. I haven't hidden that I was at an asylum, so for them to throw it back at me now?

I turn to look squarely at the Librarian, and it's like she knew I would, because she's already focused on me. She's smiling that damn smile that would make the Cheshire-Cat want to pat her on the back, it's so smug.

Van Brunt clears his throat. Says, "You said that it would be easy to get the catalyst. Do—"

"Not easy," I clarify, and, miraculously, the Librarian looks away first. "I said I know who has it, and that at least we wouldn't have to search for clues. There will be no part of a trip to Wonderland that will be easy. None."

Someone whose name I don't remember asks, "Why?"

"Because I left for a reason, and it was expected by all parties involved that I was not to come back. If I am caught doing so, my life is forfeit." The removal of this long-worn splinter is not an easy one. "Anybody with me would be held to the same fate. But that is only one of many concerns."

"How so?" another nameless person asks.

"The food and water in Wonderland are, for lack of a better word, addictive to those past puberty. They will lead a non-native Wonderlander to madness and an inability to leave. You will cease being able to determine the extraordinary from the ordinary. You will no longer utilize logic as you once have—if you try, it will be distorted. Madness is more than just the stereotypical person who laughs and eats plates. Madness is leaving behind your realities and inhibitions and embracing impossible ones."

Van Brunt must have never shared this tidbit with the rest, because now everyone is horrified. Good. They're learning.

"If I am to go back to Wonderland, I'll need to bring a supply of my own rations. Even the tiniest bit will alter a person."

"And yet," Finn says quietly, "you managed to leave."

I won't look at him when I say, "I paid a hefty price to do so."

"Is that why your life is forfeit?" Victor asks. "Because you managed to escape?"

"No." I take a deep breath. Force myself to stay the course, to remain calm. "I left because, had I not, I would have been the cause of countless deaths." My nails dig into my palms. It's a piss-poor summation, but there it is. "There are prophecies in Wonderland, as silly as that may sound. And it just so happened I was the subject of one." I finally stand up. "That said, it is best that I go alone. I refuse to risk any of you, either. Now, if you'll excuse me, I had better start preparing myself for the trip."

I'm halfway up the stairs when Finn catches up with me. "Wait. Where are you going?"

I'm mute, terrified I might break down. Too many nameless emotions—or emotions I can't let myself name—take hold.

For a moment, I think he's going to let me have it. Rip into me for secrets and *why didn't you tell mes* and *how could yous* and all of those other things people feel they have a right to demand of others. But he surprises me by lacing his fingers through mine and taking us to the nearest elevator. Once the doors slide shut, he presses the stop button and we hang, suspended in the shaft between floors.

He turns to face me. There isn't hurt there, nor anger. *He's concerned.*

I don't apologize for holding onto my past. And he doesn't ask me to. Instead, he says, "If you think you're going to Wonderland by yourself, you've sorely mistaken."

"Do you know what will happen if I get caught?" *Do you know what will happen if you get caught with me?* My voice is low and controlled, even though my insides quake at such imaginings. "If the Queen of Hearts is the one to find me, I will lose my head and it will be either impaled in front of her castle for all to see or sealed within a glass box for her to exhibit in her trophy room."

His eyes widen; his face pales.

"If it's the Red Queen, well, I'll probably keep my head upon immediate capture, but she'll crucify me and place me on display, to die slowly. Once I began to rot, she'll ensure all of my limbs are torn from my torso and fed to bandersnatches during arena games."

"Jesus." It's a whisper.

"And if I'm caught by the White Queen, she will personally drain me of all my blood and replace my insides with stuffing so I can join her doll room. If you thought Sara's were creepy, I assure you they are nothing compared to what she has collected."

He's horrified. Good.

"And those are merely what the Queens would do. Shall I tell you about some of the other monarchs? No? Then, I cannot ask that any of you join me on this retrieval. I cannot guarantee your safety, Finn. I refuse to take that risk."

He lifts a shaky hand to run through his hair. And then, "You don't have to ask. I'm coming."

"Did you not just hear what I had to say?" I jab him with a finger. "Did you not just hear what could be *your* fate?"

"I heard," he tells me. "Believe me, I heard. It doesn't make a difference, though."

The muscle in my chest spasms. These words of Finn's are resolute. Sincere. Filled with determination.

He steps closer, his hands settling possessively on my waist. I ask, "It doesn't?"

He shakes his head slowly. There is no fear in his eyes.

"It should."

A slow, rolling shrug that's indifferent rocks his shoulders. "Sorry to disappoint."

"I may not be able to protect you," I whisper.

"The nice thing about partners," he says just as softly, "is that two are always stronger than one."

"The book isn't how Wonderland really is. The people there, the animals, the sights . . . None are silly and cartoonish, Finn. Wonderland has its mysteries and beauty, but there's a lot of darkness there, too."

Another shrug. "There's darkness everywhere. Every day, in every Timeline, people are robbed. Belittled. Attacked. Raped. Abused. Murdered. But you can't let it dictate every move in your life. Sometimes, you have to take a chance. Sometimes, you have to step over the ledge and fall, even though you don't know what's underneath you."

I'm terrified. "I can't talk you out of this, can I?"

When he shakes his head this time, a hint of a smile emerges.

"Why?" bursts out of me.

His head ducks down, his lips just centimeters away from mine. All I smell is the warm, beautiful scent of man and soap and mint. Everything goes fuzzy yet laser sharp, and my heart is back in that caucus race.

Fingers wrap around my golden strands. He tells me, he whispers, he melts me with, "I finally found you."

My mouth finds his.

He lifts me up, and my legs wrap around his waist. My back is against the wall of the elevator, my hands in his hair. We kiss and touch and then, when the need within becomes too strong, join our bodies together here in a small box that is used to take our colleagues from one floor to another. We are never good with appropriate time and places, it seems.

Something in me clenches and sighs and fears and covets as we move together, and when we explode in unison, right on cue, I concede the truth.

After all that I've gone through, after all I've lost, I've finally found my true north star.

FISSURES AND SECRETS

I T'S NOT ONLY FINN who will accompany me to Wonderland. So will Mary and Victor. I vehemently argue against this need, but, much like their friend, they cannot be dissuaded. Van Brunt insists that, if Wonderland is as dangerous as I make it out to be, we need Victor's expertise for emergencies. Rationally, I know he's nearly as skilled as his brother at fighting, and chances are we will need his medical skills at some point, but I still wish he'd reconsider.

When I argue Mary's placement on the team, she takes my vehemence in stride. "I'm damn good at what I do," is all she'll really say, and as I've seen her at training fumble with just about every weapon there is, I can't imagine what it is. But I am overruled. The Collectors' Society is a team, I'm reminded. And the betterment of all trumps that of an individual. In many regards, I can respect that, as it's dictated my moves for years now.

We spend the rest of the day in Van Brunt's office going over details. The A.D. is having rations packed for us, alongside heavy bottles of water that will slow us down, but there is no other option. We cannot risk otherwise. Over and over, I remind everyone that there can be no slip-ups. No water drank, no food, no tea, no anything. No water from rivers, no rain on tongues.

I draw out a rough map that is not to scale. "Our entry point will be here." I tap my finger against a dot on the paper. "We'll need to first go to an ex-associate's house for supplies," I tap on a building a short distance away, "and then journey to confer with my Grand Advisor."

Mary peers over the map. "Where is he or she?"

I'm honest. "I don't know. Hopefully, my former associate will be able to point us in the direction."

"Is your advisor the one who has the catalyst?" Van Brunt asks.

I shake my head. "No. But he will be able to point us in the direction of the person that does."

"Will this person be reluctant to give the catalyst up?" Victor asks.

"No. The difficulty lies in a meeting that does not reach any of the Courts' ears."

"Maybe you ought to tell us about this prophecy," Victor murmurs. "Why would so many people's lives be forfeit with your presence?"

For many long seconds, I debate the wisdom behind a revelation. My natural inclination has me leaning toward avoiding the question, but recently sparked feelings of camaraderie damn me. And this is a small group, a group of people I've come to at least consider the option of trusting, so I find myself finally opening up. "Although Wonderland is much like England in the sense that it is a country, it has several sections that have been divided up and are ruled by kings and queens. Unlike England, however, these monarchs are not from dynastic lines but rather chosen by Wonderland itself to be rulers."

"You mean, like a democracy?" This is from Finn. "Where rulers are voted into office?"

My back aches, it's so stiff from sitting on the edge of my chair. "No. Wonderland—the land itself—chooses its monarchs. Nobody knows how it's done, or what the qualifiers are behind choices. If you are selected, a crown appears on your head. And it will be your crown until the day you die."

Victor snaps his fingers. "I remember a scene in your story that has a crown appearing!"

"There are currently four ruling Courts in Wonderland. The Hearts, The Reds, The Whites, and the Diamond. Normally, when monarchs are crowned, they are done so in pairs. Occasionally, a few days may lapse between a King and Queen being crowned, sometimes even as long as a month, but they typically begin their rule as a pair." I take a deep breath and let it out slowly. "For some reason, after I was crowned, no King materialized—not even during the years I had returned home as a child. Wonderlanders are a deeply superstitious lot, and this did not sit well with some despite everything I did for the country. History has always shown that there are pairs, so that there will be balance in a house. My Court, though, was seen as imbalanced. Even those who are insane fear imbalance in Wonderland."

Mary slams a hand down on the table. "Is this because you were a woman? Because there wasn't a man to help you?" Another pound sounds against the table, rattling the map. "What a lot of misogynistic pigs!"

This only endears her to me.

"Go on," Finn urges quietly, and when our eyes meet, all I see is support and compassion.

So I take another deep breath and once more let it out slowly. "Other ruling Courts were unsettled by this. While those living in my domain came to see me as fair over the years, and a champion to their causes, tradition is a difficult beast to slay. Dissension was fostered by some of the monarchs who found me an aberration. A non-native and a solo ruler?" My smile is bleak. "It was not to be borne. We squabbled for years, but in the end, it didn't matter. A prophecy was discovered, claiming if the ruling Courts in Wonderland were left at an odd number and the deck shuffled, apocalyptic disasters the like had never been seen before would befall the populations. War broke out numerous times, citizens were suffering. People were dying. Diseases never seen before were emerging, often eradicating entire villages." I lace my hands together in my lap so tightly the skin turns hot white. "Summits were held . . ."

I have to stop. The memories are still too raw.

I'm out of my chair and across the room, wishing I could open one of the windows. Outside, beyond the glass, life in New York City continues to move on, blissfully unaware of the atrocities of my past. And yet, in this room, it's weighing me down just as heavily as it always had, and I'm editing it for ears who I hope never hear the full truth.

I really am damned, aren't I?

"You are a selfish girl who thinks she can take whatever it is she wants without consequence."

I slapped her. Hard. "How dare you say such things when you are the one sending innocents to their deaths!"

"Your greed, your lust, will be the downfall of every last one of us, little bird," the White Queen sneered.

But the thing is, the more I thought about it, the more I reluctantly admitted she was right. All of the differences I had made, all of the advancements in health care, education, and women's rights meant nothing if I allowed the prophecy to consume us. I refused to tell her that, though. At least on that day, because we both knew her selfishness and greed could rival my own.

"I suppose in the end, all you need to know is that I willingly chose to leave." My voice cracks, and I hate myself for it. "Part of the summit accords has me promising not to return in lieu of the ultimate of punishments."

"Couldn't you abdicate?" Victor asks.

I do not turn away from the window. "I am the Queen of Diamonds, and I will be until the day I die. Hopefully then a new Queen and King will be selected, and the land will right itself in balance. Better yet, another Court might emerge in the Diamonds' ashes. Perhaps the Clubs or Black. Four Courts are needed. Eight monarchs."

"But you are here, Ms. Reeve," Van Brunt says. I'm startled by his quiet foray into the conversation. "You are still alive. Does that not affect Wonderland's balance?"

I shrug. "Some of the Grand Advisors to the thrones felt that six monarchs in three houses were better for the land than seven monarchs in four houses." A wry yet bitter smile twists my lips. "I tried to argue that six plus three equaled nine yet seven plus four equaled eleven. Broken down, eleven has two ones; added together, they make two, which is an even number. Nine could not be broken down. It would always be odd. My logic was abhorrent to them, though. It only proved my alien status."

Such logic is apparently abhorrent to those sitting with me now, as they all look at me as if I'm raving.

"If you were addicted, how did you leave?"

Finn's question is enough to finally draw me back to the table. "An exceedingly rare poison my advisor obtained for me." I allow a small, bittersweet smile. "A poison that granted me lucidity the likes I hadn't experienced for years."

This captures Mary's attention. "You allowed yourself to willingly be poisoned?"

I tell her gravely, "I would have done that and more to save the lives of my people. Besides—it allows me to not fall back into a trap in which my inhibitions are lowered and my emotions heightened to the point that violence means little to me." I pause. "Although, I must admit, I still feel those bits of madness every so often. It's why I'm handy in a fight."

"Then I guess it's a good thing," she says evenly, "you have a person good with potions and poisons joining you on your team, hmm? I would like to get my hands on this concoction—or any others we might encounter during our trip."

We spend hours late into the night laying down the foundation for our trip the next day. Victorian clothes are obtained, although they will need to be switched out for Wonderlandian styles shortly after our arrival. Bags are packed. We go over detail after detail of things the team needs to know about Wonderlandian society. Manners they will encounter, and expectations others will have of them.

And then I tell them the most important thing of all. "You are never to mention my name if we are captured or detained. You are to disavow any knowledge of me—or, if necessary, claim I've abducted you and coerced you into doing my bidding."

"But," Mary begins, but there are not buts.

We are given four days' rations. As it is, food will be tight and water doled out in small but regular intervals. None of us can carry any more than that, considering I cannot guarantee us horses or carriages to our various destinations.

It is well after one in the morning when the meeting dwindles to a close. Once Victor and Mary leave (separately while making a point to one another they weren't heading in the same direction), Van Brunt asks Finn to stay behind for a word, so I decide to head upstairs and try to get a few hours' sleep before we leave for my Timeline.

I'm going home.

I don't know how to feel about it, honestly. Numb is probably the best way to describe my state of being. It's extraordinary how I can go from such highs this morning to this current sense of static. But then memories bombard me: threats and joys and terrors and horrors and things so beautiful, so magical, that I wonder if these recollections could possibly be real.

My past is about to meet my present.

I take a shower, letting the water get so hot that visibility in the bathroom is difficult. Hot water beats down upon me until I slide down in the stall, my knees up to my chest as I loop my arms around them. It's hard to breathe. In, out. In, out. Just like the Caterpillar taught me: *If one doesn't breathe, how are they expected to do anything else?* In, out. It'll be okay. My lungs just need to expand, just need to find the proper amount of air. In, out. In, out. I can do this. I will do this.

I have to do this.

A fissure in my chest erupts. Anger sears my veins. I am a queen, the Queen of Diamonds. I am terrified, I am elated. I am strong, I am weak. I am powerful, I am helpless. I am the bird who soars. There are people who are depending on me. I may not be able to make a difference any longer in Wonderland, but come hell or high water, I will find my crown and protect them.

The fog dissipates. The water turns cold. The door to the shower opens, and the knobs are turned to the off position and he climbs in with me, him fully clothed in contrast to my shivering, blue skin, and we sit there together, his arms around me, until I can breathe again.

AT SIX O'CLOCK IN the morning, the Institute is wide awake and bustling with activity. Van Brunt has organized a team to track Todd, Rosemary, and Jenkins, and they're mobilizing at the same time we ready to leave. Ex Libris will be their first stop, but according to the A.D., nobody is in residence.

"I had meself a look around," he tells Van Brunt as he straps on a shoulder holster. "There's a tunnel out of the basement that allows them entrance and exit without detection. It leads to a store a block away. A block away! The bookshop looked like it'd been ransacked, by the way." To me and Finn, he said, "You two make a right mess, all right."

I ask, "The alarm system wasn't working?"

"Not any longer." He grins, his teeth crooked. "Don't worry, sweet Alice. When you all are done playing around in Wonderland, we'll have some new friends for you to come and visit with here at the Institute."

His blatant confidence is finally refreshing rather than annoying.

We're in the weapons room, picking out our pieces for our respective missions. I've warned my team to travel light—just the basics, as we can get weapons better suitable to Wonderland once I track down my ex-associate.

Van Brunt is slipping his own shoulder holster on, tightening the straps across his broad chest. "Is there anything else you need?"

Finn passes his father a sleek, black gun that looks a lot like one of his. "No."

The head of the Society's eyes flick over to where Victor is. The doctor is dressed smartly in his three-piece suit and long trench coat as he selects an antique-looking gun. "Does your brother have his medicine?"

What's this? Medicine? Medicine for what? Is Victor sick? I glance over to where he is. He looks healthy—thin, pale, but healthy.

"Yes," Finn is saying. "And Mary has a supply, just in case. I'm glad she agreed to go."

I'm not the only one with unspoken mysteries, it seems. The Society is filled with those who clutch their truths close their chests.

Van Brunt grunts, but there is a softness there I haven't seen before. A worry. He turns his head as he loads the chamber of his gun. "When you get back, I want you to take a few days and go see—"

"No." Finn picks up one of his guns. "We've already talked about this."

Van Brunt sighs. "I think you're making a mistake."

"That's your prerogative." Finn shrugs.

"He misses you."

Finn's unmoved, though. And I'm now burning with curiosity.

"Will you at least consider his request?"

"I've considered it," Finn says flatly. "And my answer is still no."

Victor wanders over to where they're standing. "Everything okay?"

"Fine," Finn bites out before going over to where Wendy, Mary, and the A.D. are discussing the schematics for the local mission.

"What was all of that about?" Victor asks his father.

I have no shame in continuing to listen as I sharpen my blades near-by.

Van Brunt tells him, "Tom contacted me this week."

Who's Tom?

"You need to back off that," Victor says. "There's too much water under that bridge."

"Jim would—"

Who's Jim?

"Jim would want Finn happy," Victor interrupts. "Bringing up bad blood isn't going to solve anything. Let him be. If and when Finn ever wants to address all the shite that went down, he will. And if he doesn't, that's his choice."

Van Brunt sighs heavily, one hand cupping the back of his neck. "I wish your mother was here."

"Me, too." It's a broken whisper, followed by quiet, steely anger. "Find those fuckers, Brom. If they were the ones to delete 1820IRV-SGC . . ."

"Then I will deal with them."

Van Brunt's coldly voiced words send a shiver down my spine.

"Promise me you'll wait for us." Victor grabs his father's arm. Van Brunt doesn't say anything, but the look on his face tells me he plans for no waiting.

"They were our family, too," Victor says hotly. "Our mother. Our grandfather. We deserve to be there when these arseholes are forced to pay for their sins. Don't you dare take this away from us."

"I expect you will take care of yourself," Van Brunt says in return. And then, "Ms. Reeve? A word?"

Knowing he's been effectively dismissed, Victor goes over to where his brother is.

I don't even pretend I haven't been caught sticking my nose in where it doesn't belong. "Yes?"

"Let us take a walk."

I follow Van Brunt to the door and then out into the hallway. "How much has Finn told you about our family?"

About as much as I've told him of mine, I think. "That you adopted

212

both Victor and him, and that his mother is dead."

"My sons," he tells me evenly, "are all I have left outside of my work with the Society. I ask you to remember that during your travels in Wonderland."

I bristle. "If you are so concerned with them, then you ought to have conceded to my wish to walk this path alone."

"Please do not misunderstand me, Ms. Reeve. My sons are incredibly skilled at what they do, and I have no doubt that they will be the perfect assets you will require in the catalyst acquisition. Society policy does not allow singular members to conduct retrievals, as there are too many factors and opportunities for things to go wrong. But the thing is, Ms. Reeve . . ." His lips purse together as we stroll down the nearly empty hallway. "It has come to my attention that you and Finn have become . . . How shall I put it? Close."

"That," I tell him smartly, "is none of your concern." Has Finn been talking to his father about me? About us?

"Perhaps not," he concedes, "but I'm concerned nonetheless after a discussion with the Librarian about it this morning."

Ah. Now I understand. That woman is a bloody menace.

"I am already troubled by the dissension between Victor and Ms. Lennox. While that is nothing new, both have assured me that they will not let it come between them during this assignment. However, feelings are not always rational, and there is always a chance for heightened senses to flare up at the most inopportune times."

My silence is stony.

"My younger son," he tells me quietly, "does not trust easily. The truth is, I'm surprised at how quickly he has given it to you. I do not believe he has ever trusted any of his former girlfriends."

Van Brunt has my full attention now.

"Finn's childhood was difficult in ways yours nor mine ever could be. Those who have read his story have idealized it, glorified it, criticized it, and dissected it, and yet still do not understand the scars that such a childhood leaves behind."

Gross discomfort creeps across my bones from discussing such things behind Finn's back. "I don't think any of what you're talking about is my business, especially as he is not here with us."

"I mention this simply because, until now, he has entered any assignment as most of the rest of us do—with a goal for acquisition and nothing more. I fear that today's assignment is different, however. That his and his brother's purposes are multi-fold."

"I tried to dissuade Finn," I snap. "I made it very clear what is at stake."

"I have no doubt that you did, Ms. Reeve. I just want you aware that, all of a sudden, the situation is painfully personal to them."

"Because of me?"

"For Finn, partially, yes." He strokes his neat beard. "And Victor, in response, will back his brother up because that is what they do for one another. The reverse is true, naturally—Finn is always keenly aware of Ms. Lennox's safety on any assignment. But I need you to be aware that your recent discovery of S. Todd and Rosemary's wall has left the boys in a situation that I fear might be overrun by heightened emotion. And I am asking you to be mindful of such over the next few days."

"Because of 1820IRV-SGC."

He does not chastise me for regurgitating clearly overheard information. "Exactly."

"Maybe you ought to explain to me the significance of this Timeline," I say quietly, "so I might be better prepared to understand any unexpected actions on their behalves."

"1820IRV-SGC is my original Timeline," he says flatly. "And it was deleted two years prior, right around Halloween." His eyes hold mine. "My wife Katrina, the boys' adopted mother, was there for a visit with her elderly father. Both boys were off on assignments when we got word that it'd been deleted."

The agony in Van Brunt's eyes is crushing.

"I'm sure it is not difficult to imagine how hard that was on us. As Society members, we were devastated yet another Timeline was gone—that millions of souls were winked out of existence as if they were nothing. As if they'd never breathed or laughed or had children or lived."

"I'm so sorry," I whisper, but my words are meaningless, nothing compared to such a thought.

"We are always devastated when a Timeline is deleted," he continues flatly, "but of course, this one was painfully personal to us. Their mother was gone. Their grandfather. We had no body to grieve over. She was here one day and gone forever the next, and I remain because I was here and not there. I . . . Perhaps I've indulged in their determination to find the culprits behind this. It's been two years, but now we have a lead. Suspects. Truth be told, Ms. Reeve, I am glad they are going on your assignment rather than mine. Vengeance and the acts done in its name are terrible burdens to bear when you are young, no matter what they make think otherwise."

Unfamiliar tears sting my eyes.

"Neither of my sons are good with sharing their emotions, I fear. They've let their anger build up within them, refusing to let it out for anyone to see other than perhaps me. We argued the night you and Finn returned from your raid of Ex Libris. Both immediately wanted to hunt down the suspects, but eventually came to accept that hastiness would get us nowhere."

"Finn was heavily drugged," I say, frowning. "He was falling asleep at the table during our debriefing. I find it difficult to imagine he argued much of anything with you that night."

"He roused long enough, once we were in his apartment, to voice his concerns. That said, obviously his drugged state did not allow his arguments to stand up quite as strongly as his brother's." Van Brunt's smile is in no way cheerful. "I feared that, once he emerged from his morphine haze, he might insist on being here with me like his brother initially had, but it appears you have done me a favor, Ms. Reeve."

"Some favor," I mutter. "I'll probably ended up getting us all killed."

"Finn has endured much loss in his life," Van Brunt says softly. "They both have. I cannot say it for certain, but I believe my son will not allow what you fear to happen simply because he will not be able to bear to lose one more person."

I think back to the discussion about Victor's medicine, and of how Van Brunt might be hinting at that, too.

"I mention all of this because . . ." We pause in our loop around the floor's corridor. "The Librarian mentioned something troubling to me. About your past in Wonderland."

My fingers curl inward. I refuse to allow anything that woman says about me illicit another response.

"I will not meddle in either of my grown sons' lives, Ms. Reeve. And yet—"

"And yet," I say primly, "you are right now. Whatever is or isn't between us is of none of your concern."

"I am merely asking you to take into consideration that there are many layers to this assignment. Ones that might not necessarily accompany others."

I'm not the only one uncomfortable right now. Van Brunt is just so as well, and it strikes me that this must be a difficult conversation for him to have. His sons are adults. Victor is over thirty, Finn is nearing so. But whether or not appropriate, their father's heart is in the right place.

Nostalgia bites at me. I left my parents in a constant state of confusion each time I entered Wonderland. I never gave them a chance to be close to me, or to meddle thusly.

I tell Van Brunt gently, "Noted."

He nods and we head back to the weapons room to reconvene with the others. The crowd has grown; many people have come to see us off and get their fill of information concerning today's manhunt. While Van Brunt addresses the mass of bodies, I can't help but steal glances at both Finn and Victor. Both are wearing impassive faces and yet there is a fire to their eyes I'd not noticed before. Was it because I never knew what to look for? That, because I didn't know their secrets, I chose to ignore anything I didn't want to see?

To them, this manhunt could produce the people who murdered their mother. And they will be going with me to Wonderland, instead.

Screws inside me loosen; my defensive shell cracks even further. I make a vow right here and now that I will not fail in Wonderland. I cannot allow this happen to me. I cannot allow this to ever happen to another Timeline again.

My attention settles on Finn again. He and his brother are standing in nearly identical poses, with their arms crossed defensively and feet slightly spread apart. Anger straightens their backs. This is personal to them. Very personal.

Victor is whispering something in Finn's ear, and the man I'm newly falling in love with issues a tight nod in response.

If the villains are not apprehended before we come back, I will do everything in my power to track them down.

THE LAND THAT TIME FORGOT

WE ALL HAVE PENS in our pockets, but Finn is the one to write our way to my Timeline. He didn't want to burden me with the pages within my books, and although I wanted to argue, I realized his gesture came from a good place. I would not be so willing to force his past upon him, either. So, he is the one to write a sentence, and when he does, golden light fills the room and a door appears.

I am the one to open it. To go through it first.

I've requested us to be taken the base of the craggy rocks behind my parents' holiday home on the Welsh Coast, on a date nearly two months after I left the Pleasance. There is a whistling breeze blowing across the fields, and the heavy scent of saltwater perfumes the air. Petals and crisped leaves dance about our feet, and, for a moment, the impulse to turn around and go see if my family is in residence nearly derails my purpose.

"It's beautiful here," Mary murmurs as she takes in the vista.

Victor adjusts the straps of his backpack over his beautifully tailored black coat. "Does it remind you of Misselthwaite at all?"

"Misselthwaite is in Yorkshire," she snaps. "This is nothing like Yorkshire."

"It's Wales," I tell them. Only Finn knew ahead of time that this was our destination. "What is Misselthwaite?"

"The manor I grew up in." Mary smooths imaginary wrinkles from her full Victorian skirt. "It's much to the north from here."

Refusing to show how stung he might be from Mary's hostility, Victor says, "I guess I always thought your story occurred in England, Alice. Not Wales. You're English, after all."

"I've entered Wonderland in England before," I admit. "From my parents' house in Oxford. But, the first and third times, it was here, in Wales, albeit from two different holes as the first collapsed and was sealed shortly after I returned. Does the book say differently?"

"It's suggested you're next to a river," Victor says. "Says you're laying next to a bank with your sister." He glances around. "There are no rivers here, are there?"

I shade my eyes with a hand as I turn toward the hills before us. "We were sitting on that slope over there," I point into the distance, "when I first saw the White Rabbit. I suppose a slope can be mistaken for a bank, no?" I give a small smile. "There is water nearby, but alas it is the ocean and not a mere river."

"Will we be falling down a rabbit hole?" Finn asks. He's mildly amused, though, and his small smirk tests my willpower because I want nothing more than to kiss it.

But alas, that will have to wait. "Yes. But we'll be using a different one than the first I traveled, considering that one is defunct. When I left Wonderland for the last time, I had this one built just for me. Nobody else is able to access it—or at least, that was what I was led to believe."

We trudge up the rugged yet green hill. Mary asks, "Who built it?"

"The White Rabbit. Despite his allegiance to the Heart Court, he owed me several debts."

"Why did you return as an adult?" Mary asks.

"Because," I say simply. "I am the Queen of Diamonds."

Minutes later, we're situated before a number of small holes and caves carved into the rocks. I count them carefully before finding the right one. It's marked by the Rabbit's footprint, in just such a place the average person would not notice.

"Are you all sure you want to tumble down this hole?"

Finn's hand presses against my lower back. "We're with you one hundred percent."

I lean into his touch, my eyes meeting him. It's utterly contradictory, but even though I wish he'd stay at home, safe from Wonderland's madness, I'm beyond glad he's here with me right now.

"All right then," I say. "Let's go to Wonderland."

I crouch down before the hole and sweep away branches, leaves, and rocks. There is a silvery spiderweb covering one corner, a small, fat, happy spider clutching onto its freshly wrapped prey.

"We must enter this hole," I tell it. "Would you mind moving to the side? My associates and I will do our best to not break your beautiful web."

"Alice, are you talking to spiders?" Mary asks, but then she—all of them—hear, in a soft yet firm voice, "Of course, Your Majesty."

One of its tiny legs comes to cross its abdomen; two others allow it to fall into the equivalent of a spider bow. "I have watched over this hole, just like you asked me to," it tells me. "No one has crossed through."

"I am most grateful for your service." I reach out and gently touch the top of its head. "You have done well."

"I will continue to watch over it until the day I die," it tells me. "It is the least I can do for the Queen of Diamonds."

I turn back to face my friends. "The drop will be sharp and will last less than five minutes. If it is possible, do not scream. You will land on your feet as long as you right yourself at the start of the fall. Try not to step on any of the spiders below. They are soldiers of mine and are only doing their duty."

Mary is still eyeing the spider suspiciously. "Do they bite?"

It chooses to answer her before I can. "Our bites are painful and deadly, and there are no cures."

Her eyes alight.

"Sound the alarm," I tell the spider. It plucks at its web, and a nearly inaudible peal rings forth. And then it picks up its lunch with its mouth before scurrying to the top of the rock.

I'm on my knees, crawling through the hole; Finn is right behind me, followed by Mary and then Victor in the rear. After scooching a few yards, I feel the lip of the tunnel.

I take a deep breath and then, before I can change my mind, I drop into the hole. It is wide enough for me to stretch my arms out and still have yards to go until they reach the sides. Sparkling spiders scurry up and down the walls, murmuring excitedly. The alarm triggered from above rings its way down the tunnel, from web to web, and by the time I finally reach the ground, the tiny soldiers have laid out soft padding to catch our falls.

Lights flare to life all around us. We are in a small chamber that is completely filled with small, glinting black bodies—thousands upon thousands of soldier spiders only three inches long apiece.

"Mother of God." Mary's whisper is a strangle—an awed one, but a strangle no less. Victor's mouth drops open. And as for Finn . . . my heart swells when he does not flinch one bit.

All around me, the spiders fall to their knees in reverent bows. "Your Majesty," they murmur in unison. "Long live the Queen of Diamonds."

"Dear soldiers," I tell them, "I commend you for your dedication and hard work. No queen is luckier than I to have such loyalty at her side. I fear my visit is not a pleasurable one, and I am aware I am breaking the accords set forth last year. I have returned as Wonderland is in danger, and I cannot stand back and do nothing."

A gasp carries throughout the chamber.

"I am here to ask for your help once more."

"Ask and you shall receive!" is cried over and over again.

"I ask that you continue to guard this tunnel so that when we return, we shall be able to leave safely."

Cheers rise up.

I crouch down. "My gratitude toward you all overflows."

A path opens up before us as the spiders scurry to opposite sides of the chamber. I rise up, hold my head up high, and lead my friends out of the arachnids' sanctuary.

Outside, the air is brisk. It's nighttime, and the moon is just a sliver in the sky. We're on the far side of a sleepy town of precariously fat yet tilting brick buildings best known for its treacle production, and most of the residents are undoubtedly snoozing in their beds. Even still, I flip the hood up on my cloak and motion for the rest to follow me. I weave through cobbled side streets lining crooked buildings, ensuring we go nowhere near the heart of the town. There will most likely be a constable on duty; a sleepy one much like his town, but a constable all the same. We stick to the smaller, less-traveled paths until we reach the front of a large, thatched building.

I press my hands against the gray, crumbling walls. The plaster throbs with a heartbeat. Good. I had feared things might have changed. I round the building until I find a small wooden door that I must crouch down so I may knock. A slat slides open, revealing a narrowed pink eye.

"Elsie, Lacie, and Tillie," I tell it.

"In what particular order?"

"Age first, then alphabetical, and then by temperament."

A grunt sounds before the slat slides shut. But then a rattle then a creak follows, and the door groans angrily as it swings open.

A spotted rabbit wearing a purple waist coat stands before us, a quarterstaff brandished in his left hand. "Welcome to the Land that Time Forgot."

I right myself after crawling in through the door, ensuring that I tug my hood down lower. The ceiling soars above us a good story or two high, but I still cannot risk being noticed.

I lower my voice. "Might you direct us to one of your hosts?"

The rabbit snaps to attention. "His Lordship, the most . . . um, grand—no, *illustrious* of Hares, the, uh, March Hare, is yonder." The quarterstaff juts toward the left. "His divine master of . . . of . . ." The rabbit hacks into a paw.

I try not to roll my eyes. "His given name will be enough, Rabbit."

Gratitude shines in his eyes. "The Dormouse is this way." The quarterstaff juts to the right. "But he is undoubtedly sleeping. He works hard, my lady. It's best to leave him be."

Try telling that to someone who doesn't know better. "And the Hatter?"

"The most generous, the most, um . . . virile, and, err, talented—no! Manly—"

I cut him off. "Is in which direction?"

His small shoulders slump. "I am not allowed to tell, my lady, under penalty of punishment."

The March Hare it is, then.

The rabbit swings open another series of doors, which open directly to a set of dark stairs. On our way down, I murmur, "It may be intense down here." I glance at the trio, a blush stealing up my cheeks. "Well, let's just say if you act prudish, you will be immediately singled out and forcibly ejected."

"Where are we?" Mary asks.

"A rave," I say, although in actuality, it's more lurid than that.

Once we reach the base of the stairs, I push open the heavy wooden doors and we crash immediately into a wall of throbbing music and throngs of writhing, sweaty bodies. The crowd is thick tonight, in various states of undress, and well on their way to delirium or ecstasy, depending on their evening's purposes.

Some things never change.

I push through the throng of people and animals of all shapes and sizes, toward a throne situated on the eastern side of the immense floor. Above us, firebugs and glowing nitnot flowers light up the roof, casting moving shadows down upon the dancers. We keep getting stopped to be offered Mindly pills, and I collect a handful to stash in my pockets; one never knows when a Mindly pill will come in handy. Behind me, I note Mary is doing the same as well as collecting bits of any and all other pills the revelers have to offer. Men and women tug at us as we pass by, beckoning us to join in the dance, and it's utterly tempting. I think back to the last time I danced, with a strange man I'd never met before, and of how I'd secretly wished it was Finn. And here we are, on a dance floor once more, and I'd love to feel his hands on my hips as we sway to the seductive, heavy beats in the air.

I'm about to throw caution to the wind when I spot him. There. Upon the white iron-wrought throne, sits a familiar face.

A line snakes around a gilded, raised platform, many holding cups of tea as they wait. The Hare is currently distracted by a woman straddling his lap, though, and appears to be in no hurry to see any of them.

I forgo the line and step directly onto the platform. Two ex-card soldiers peel off the wall, their spears ready. "Halt!" they cry in unison, and it's enough to bring about the Hare's attention.

His eyes go saucer wide. He blinks several times and then stands up so quickly the girl slides right off his lap and onto the floor with a loud thud.

"This is a Hare?" Mary asks. Her eyes travel from the tip of his matted hair to his boot-covered feet in derision. "But . . . he's a *man.*"

"Debatable," I murmur.

The Hare falls to his knees. "Your—"

"Get up already. I would ask you to take me where we may speak in private."

Trembling, he stands back up, snatching a nearby brown, long-eared hat. Two long, quick whistles slip out of his lips. The card soldiers immediately melt back up against the wall, allowing one to swing a curtain apart.

"This way," the Hare tells me.

When we follow him behind the curtain, the pulsing music dims significantly. He drops to the ground again, his nose pressing against the floor. I finally do roll my eyes, because really. The Hare is an absurd creature if there ever was one.

"Your Majesty," he moans. "Your Majesty."

"Is this guy for real?" Victor asks.

The Hare's head pops up as if he hadn't noticed my companions yet.

"Unfortunately," I tell Victor, "yes. Very." To the Hare, I say, "Where is the Hatter?"

His lower lip quivers. "Busy."

I'll just bet he his. "Let us unburden him them."

The Hair scuttles backward before leaping to his feet. "Your Majesty, if you just wait, I think it would be less—"

"I believe," Finn says in a low voice, stepping next to me, "The Queen of Diamonds told you to do something."

The Hare jumps about two feet off the ground when he takes Finn in, but he nods and twists his way down the darkening hallway before us.

We follow, but something pricks at my belly. It's the first time Finn has called me by my title—and I'm not sure how I feel about it. It isn't like I haven't heard that term enough. Goodness knows that for years, it was all I heard. I wasn't really Alice anymore. I was simply the Queen of Diamonds. But from him?

It lends a connection to Wonderland and my past that unnerves me.

The Hare stops before a door with a yawning knob. "Are you sure, my lady? Because I can take you to a much more comfortable room and have the Hatter come directly to you. We have a fresh jug of juice—"

He acts as if I haven't caught the Hatter in a compromising position before. "Open the door, Hare."

His Adam's apple bobs as he asks the knob to open. The door clicks and swings wide. The scent of incense flavored by arousal hits us like a storm passing by. There, on an immensely large bed covered in emerald velvet, is a very naked Hatter surrounded by at least a dozen naked men and women in various sexual acts. He's got his head thrown back as a woman suckles his throat and a man licks a line from his belly button to his obscenely large, erect penis.

"Good God." Mary's voice in unnaturally high. "Is this . . . is this an *orgy?"*

Victor is stunned. Finn is too, although after a split second, he's clearly fighting to hold back his laughter. "Clear the room, Hare," I tell the quivering mess standing next to us.

I step to the side and wait as the Hare goes around the room, ordering people out. There are tears and confusion—so many of Hatters paramours are high as kites, teetering on the point of insensibility. Hatter himself continues to lounge on his bed, languidly puffing away on a hookah pipe as people shuffle out of the room, clutching their clothes.

Finn leans back against the wall next to me, his arms crossed. "Is this normal?"

"For these two? Very, I'm afraid." I peek over at Mary; she's turned her back to the mess and appears to be lecturing Victor about keeping his eyes averted, too. "Is it wrong that I am delighted to find something that has finally rendered Mary prim and proper? And your brother, too?"

He finally laughs. It's quiet, yet I feel this warm, beautiful sound deep in my bones. "Sometimes, she can't help it. She grew up in a very prim and proper environment. As did you, if I remember correctly."

"Wonderland corrupted me. This is," I motion at the scene before us, "sadly, commonplace. Modesty isn't always one of the highest prized virtues around here."

When his eyebrows lift in amusement, my cheeks flare scarlet. "Not that I'm saying I personally don't appreciate modesty."

"Oh, of course."

I bite my lip to keep from giggling. "And you?"

Finn's head tilts to the side. "Are you asking me if I prize modesty?

Or if I grew up around this sort of stuff?"

I wave my hand toward the few stragglers that are being shoved out the door by the Hare.

"Let's just say I didn't grow up in the prim and proper environment you and Mary did."

"So orgies were common?"

"Morning, noon, and night," he says with a straight face. My heart significantly swells at his teasing. But as much as I want to throw my arms around his neck, I know we're here for a specific purpose. Once the door is shut, I tell the Hare, "Ensure it is locked so that no more revelers slip in."

"Who are these sweet treats you've brought me, Hare?" Hatter slurs. He's yet to get off the bed, and if he realizes all of his guests have gone, he doesn't show it.

I shove my hood off and pass the Hare my cloak. "You've never thought me sweet before. In fact, more than once you've accused me of becoming too serious for your tastes. Has my absence changed your opinion so much?"

The Hatter goes still, his hookah pipe halfway to his mouth.

The Hare drops to the ground, his nose once more touching the floor. The Hatter, on the other hand, crawls onto his knees on the bed, blinking repeatedly as he takes me in. Surprisingly, this does nothing to lessen his erection. Frabjous. "I see your drug use hasn't ceased. I'm rather disappointed in you."

"Is this—this cannot be. The Queen of Diamonds here, in my chambers?"

I clear my throat meaningfully.

This has him scrambling off of his bed so he can prostrate himself next to his compatriot. "Forgive me, my lady. Had I known you were to arrive, I would've ensured that—"

"That what? You weren't in the midst of an orgy?" I tsk. "It's getting old, catching you like this."

He grovels incoherently.

"Oh, for goodness' sake. Stand up already. I don't have time for your incessantly bothersome games."

They're both on their feet in a flash.

Mary snaps, "For Christ's sake, get some clothes on!"

The Hatter's almond eyes narrow until they are hooded as he takes in Mary and then Victor and Finn. "Who are these delicious creatures, Your Majesty? Have you finally wised up and got yourself some concubines? And might I say, beautiful ones? Does His Majesty know?"

Mary sucks in an outraged breath when he reaches a beckoning hand out toward her.

I'm about to smack it back when Victor does so. But rather than frustrate the Hatter, it only leaves him even more aroused.

"They," I tell the Hatter, "are of none of your concern. I need you to open up my vault for me."

Behind us, Mary mutters indignantly about concubines and idiots. But the Hatter's attention has now shifted toward Finn, and if a person could undress another with their eyes, that is exactly what this nincompoop would be doing.

I snap my fingers, starling him. "Do not disrespect me, Hatter."

His blinks, his glazed eyes having trouble focusing. "But you told me to never open it for anyone."

I grab his ear and yank him across the room toward a chair bearing cast-off clothes. While I'm quite used to the Hatter's inappropriateness, I'm unnerved by the way he dared to look at Finn just now. "The order was to leave it unopened for anyone other than the Queen of Diamonds."

The Hatter yelps when I let go. He falls to his knees again, prostrating himself before me, and not for the first time, I want to strangle him. "This is maddening. Get up, Hatter. I don't have all day for your ridiculousness."

He crawls over to where I'm standing, and wraps his arms around my legs. "Beautiful Queen, I am, as I always have been, your most loyal servant."

I let out an irritable sigh. Ha! The Hatter is loyal as long as you pay him large sums of gold. "If you are loyal, you will get up, get dressed, and take me to my vault."

"His Majesty will be upset if I open it." The Hatter presses his face against my knees. "Told me just . . ." He peers over at the trembling Hare. "When did we last see His Majesty?"

My heart jumps in my chest.

The Hare briefly glances over at Finn and Victor. "Eleventy, I believe."

The Hatter nods. "Exac-a-tally. He asked if I had ensured your things were untouched. Worried, I think, that perhaps one of the nasties had found it. Told me that if it was opened without his knowledge, bad things could happen. He's always concerned that we're doing as we're told." He drags a finger across his neck before attempting to burrow his head in my skirts and mumbling nonsensically.

I'm surprised when Finn forcibly drags him off my body. "As am I. I believe the Queen told you to do something."

The Hatter stares up at him with stars in his glazed eyes.

"Get him dressed," I tell the Hare. He scrambles over to where the Hatter is still laying, still undeniably aroused to the point he must be in pain.

I let out yet another irritable sigh. The sooner we can get to my vault, the sooner I don't have to deal with these fools and their patented ridiculousness any longer. "Hatter, I am positive His Majesty said what he did when it was believed I would not be present to claim any contents. You are to take me there immediately."

He faceplants as he attempts to put his legs into the pair of pants the Hare is haphazardly holding. "Yesh, Blurgh Memmisee."

"Sober him up," I tell the Hare.

He dashes over to a nearby table and grabs a large pitcher of water. Before the Hatter can get to his feet, the Hare dumps it all over his head. And then, before another word can be said, he hauls his hand back and smacks his boss directly across the face. I discreetly take a step back when the gasping, sopping man shakes droplets out of his hair. He buttons his pants incorrectly but finally stands at full attention. "Follow me, Your Majesty."

Well, he's still slurring, but at least he's vertical.

We exit through a door hidden behind another curtain just behind the bed. Both the Hatter and the Hare grab torches and light them to illuminate the musty darkness.

Behind me, Victor asks, "What's in this vault?"

"Wonderlandian weapons." I then call out to the Hatter, "We will require clothes. Two women's outfits, two men's. Nothing that will have us standing out in a crowd."

The Hare hands the Hatter his torch and veers off into a different corridor. We walk in silence for the next minute until the Hatter stops at a metal door. "Are you sure, Your Majesty?"

"Get on with it already."

He holds out a hand and a key materializes in his palm. The doorknob rouses the moment the key touches its lips. Garbled resistance to the Hatter's efforts ensues until its eyes fall on me. And then the knob opens its mouth wider and closes its gold lips around the key before a click is heard.

The door swings open. The Hatter quickly shuffles in to light several torches lining the walls. As they flare to life, I'm relieved to find everything exactly as I left them. All except . . .

"Where is my sword?"

The Hatter's eyes swing wildly around the room. "Sword? What sword?"

"You know exactly what sword I'm talking about."

He licks his lips. Holds out a finger, as if an idea has freshly struck him. "The vorpal sword, my lady?"

My nod is tight. What sword, indeed.

"It was . . ." He dashes over to the spot on the wall where I hung it last. "It was here! I swear it was here the last time I checked!"

I'm furious. Did he dare sell it on the black market? "And when was that?"

"The day we locked the door together!" He's wild with fear. "I haven't been back yet! I swear it on my life, my lady!"

The doorknob coughs pointedly.

"Do not move," I hiss at the Hatter. I squat down before the doorknob. "Have you been opened since my departure?"

Its eyes briefly touch upon each person in the room before it beckons me closer. Softly, so no one else can hear him, "Yes, Your Majesty. Just once."

Ice fills my veins. Somebody dared to enter my private vault? "By whom?"

When it whispers the answer right up against my ear, I nearly fall flat on my bottom, I'm so shaken.

"Was that the wrong thing to do?" it asks worriedly. "I thought—"

I fight to recover myself quickly, but my heart is beating hard. "No, it's . . . You did the right thing, Doorknob."

It beams as I once more stand up.

Hands wringing, the Hatter descends upon me only to be blocked by Finn. "I swear, Your Majesty, I—"

"Back up," Finn snaps.

"It is fine." I fight for a proper breath. "I will simply make do with what is here."

The Hatter quickly opens a number of trunks to reveal a number of Wonderlandian weapons. Each piece gleams just as brightly as they day they were packed away. And yet, as I stare down at them, I can't help but flash back to the bloody battles they've seen.

And now, my trusted vorpal blade is held by another hand, and sentimentality nearly rolls me under.

"Where is the Caterpillar?"

When the Hatter doesn't answer, I turn to face him and repeat the question more slowly.

He's ashen. "Dead, my lady."

I go still. The air around me stills. Everything stills.

"The Queen of Hearts captured him three months after you left." The Hatter's hurried, slurred words practically trip and slide as they fall out of his mouth. "He refused to concede your royal authority. Got the crowds riled up in your defense. He . . ." The Hatter swallows hard. "She got him during a protest. Crops are failing, Your Majesty. People are going hungry. The Caterpillar voiced his belief that perhaps the wrong monarch left and that Wonderland is making us pay for our sins. Her card soldiers arrested most of the people in the crowd."

My stomach sinks. "How did he die?"

"Public execution, Your Majesty. Every single person she caught at the protest lost their head that day."

Mary gasps, a hand raised to her mouth. "What kind of monster does that?"

"She had the Caterpillar's head cured so it can permanently be displayed at the entrance of the Heart castle." The Hatter's eyes turn glassy.

Fury mixed with agony burns throughout me. "She dared to execute a Grand Advisor? What did the other Courts say about this atrocity?"

"The Red and White Courts immediately and vociferously condemned her actions," the Hatter quickly says. "Once he was captured, there was . . ." He trails off, glancing at the people in the room.

"Whatever you have to say to me can be said in front of them." My voice is hard—yet achingly brittle. "They are trusted companions."

He nods, swallowing again. "A recovery was attempted, but the Queen moved much faster than any of us expected."

"How fast?" I ask. Typical executions go through a trial first, especially in that court. The Queen of Hearts never passes up a chance for a spectacle.

"Less than six hours," he whispers. "No trial was held. Afterward, she gleefully reminded us queens make no bargains."

Good God.

Finn catches my elbow before my knees completely buckle. I ask, my voice embarrassingly soft, "And the head?"

The Hatter scratches his bare stomach so hard that pink streaks rise up. "A plan was brought up to attempt a recovery, but shortly after that, another Grand Advisor went missing. And then council members. Your Majesty, it is with a heavy heart that I be the first to inform you that Wonderland is at war."

"Which advisor?"

Suddenly, the Hare bursts into the room, his arms loaded with clothes.

It hadn't mattered. My leaving hadn't meant a single thing. War still broke out. People are starving.

I ask, praying my voice stays steady, "All of the Courts?"

"All of the Courts are engaged," the Hatter slurs. "Multiple fronts, with each locked in battle against the others."

It takes every last bit of courage to ask, "Are there any other deaths of consequence I need to be informed of?"

But the Hatter knows exactly what I mean. "Hundreds upon hundreds of innocents, but none of the major players have perished."

I want to cry, I'm so relieved.

"There is a war going on," Victor says suddenly, "and you two pricks are hosting parties and orgies? Unbelievable."

Both the Hatter and the Hare startled at the vehemence. The Hare sputters, "We are lovers, good sir, not fighters!"

Finn steps into my line of sight. He wraps his hands around my arms, anchoring me in a sea of desolation. "Does this change our plans?"

"Yes," I whisper to him. "It changes everything."

CAPTURE

WE CHANGE INTO THE Wonderlandian clothes the Hare has brought. He did well—all of the pieces are nondescript and do not bely my royal status one bit. The grays and purples of our linen dresses, pants, and shirts do not tie us to any one Court. While the pieces are far more formal than standard everyday wear of the Twenty-First Century, there is a whimsy to the fabrics and cuts that makes them uniquely Wonderlandian. Hems are uneven, stitches change course, shape, and size, and the textures alter from top to bottom.

I cannot help but think about the Caterpillar.

For years, he served as my most trusted advisor. I had met him as a child, when his disdain for me was at its peak. "Who are you?" he would ask me time and time again, scoffing at my attempts at philosophy and deepness until I could answer him succinctly.

Alice was the answer. The Queen of Diamonds. So simple and yet so meaningful all at once.

I never asked for him to be my Grand Advisor. He simply appeared one day telling me it would be so. From that point on, we would spend hours together as he lectured me on what it took to be a queen. I disappointed him frequently. I frustrated him even more. He begrudgingly loved me and yet found me lacking in every department. Our arguments were legendary, his condemnations even more so.

He died championing me. And I spent months lost, no longer assured of who I was.

"Are you okay?"

Concern reflects in Finn's blue-gray eyes. Concern I've finally accepted has a right to be there. "Yes," I tell him quietly.

"Liar." It's just as quietly voiced.

I am lying. And it's strange, but I'm glad he knows I am.

He touches my face gently, and I'm lost to the sensation. Our mouths drift closer to one another and then—

Sirens sound. Loud, wailing screams that have the Hatter and the Hare terrified.

"What's going on?" Mary demands.

"Card soldiers," they cry in unison. "A raid!"

Both Victor and Finn swear under their breaths as they grab weapons out of my trunks.

"Your Majesty, you must hide," the Hatter nearly wails. "If they catch you—"

I grab a nearby sword. "They will not catch me. Now tell me, and be quick of it. Where is the White King?"

The Hatter's eyes flick back and forth between me and Finn. "His Majesty is on the front lines. You know he would not leave his men and women to fight and risk their lives if he did not offer the same."

The situation just got a thousand, no, a billion times worse. "Which direction?"

The Hatter is horrified. "He will have me thrown in jail if I sent you to the heart of battle!"

"Which. Direction?"

It's the Hare who answers. "He is in the West."

I take a deep breath. "And the White Queen?"

Both the Hatter and the Hare rapidly shake their heads. "She is to the East," the Hatter says. "All of the courts have split."

My eyes widen. "*Split?!*"

"There are six fronts now. His Majesty's army is in the West."

I can barely wrap my mind around any of this. But at least I have this small bit of luck on my side—I will not encounter the White Queen. "I need horses. Now."

"I cannot," the Hatter whispers. "I will not risk your life."

"Four," I tell him firmly. "And fast."

"But, Your Majesty—"

"Now."

His nod is reluctant, but he finally darts toward the door. All the torches are extinguished and the doorknob ensures my lock is once more in place. We hurry through the corridors until we come to a door upon the ceiling. The Hatter pops it open just in time for our worlds to turn upside down.

People are screaming. The Land that Time Forgot is in chaos. Card Soldiers are everywhere, their spears and swords hacking at innocent bodies. Quick glances at their weapons tell me they are Hearts.

My blood boils. My hand is on my sword when Finn grabs me. "We can't fight them all."

"Yes," I say darkly, "we can."

"No, we can't." He grabs my face, forces me to look at him. "I am just as horrified as you about what is happening here. But you need to think long range. There are people after this Timeline's catalyst. War isn't going to mean shit if the catalyst is destroyed, because there will be nobody left to fight."

He's right, I know he's right, but as I take in the blood and tears and fear surrounding us, guilt swarms me. "How can we just walk away from this injustice?"

His answer is lost as the crowd pushes at us, people trying to escapes the dozens of card soldiers flowing in. *I will avenge these people*, I desperately vow to myself. *I will avenge the Caterpillar, too.*

The mass of terrified people in the club grows and surges. New card soldiers appear, ones that are of a different suit. Incredibly, as if on cue, a third suit appears. As swords clash, the terrified screaming crowd becomes casualties in the battle between three armies. The crush becomes catastrophic, with bodies being trampled by revelers desperate to flee. Before I know it, my hand is ripped from Finn's. The crowd engulfs me, carrying me in the opposite direction, and I'm yelling his name but I can no longer see his head in the crowd. Somebody close by shrieks out in agony; a severed head arcs high above me.

Pandemonium is too mild a word for what is going on.

Somehow, I get pushed toward and out a side door. People spill onto the cobblestone street, fleeing in every direction. For a moment, I have no idea what to do. And that, naturally, is when a hand grabs hold of me.

My sword slashes through the space between us only to nearly topple me over when I see who has a grip on me. It's Victor.

"Where is Finn?" I'm frantic as I search the crowded streets. "Mary?"

"I don't know, but I think we need to get the bloody hell out of here. People are dying in there!"

"But—"

"But they can track us. Hurry!" He tugs on my arm once more. "We must get you to safety!"

We're off and running. The entire city is in an uproar. Citizens are shrieking and weeping as they desperately try to lock their doors against the card soldiers. Houses are lit on fire. We keep running until my lungs burn and my feet ache. Victor tries door after door in an attempt to get us off the streets, but all are locked. Finally, he finds a broken-into storefront and shoves me inside. We duck down behind a counter, our hands firmly gripping our weapons.

Terror threatens to consume me. Somewhere, out there right now, are Finn and Mary. If they were to be captured . . .

I cannot even bear to think of the possibility. If the Queens were to discover Finn and Mary's importance to me, what was done to the Caterpillar would be child's play compared to the fate they'd face.

I tug out my phone from my backpack and flip on my GSP—no, GPS. GPS. What in the bloody hell do those letters stand for, anyway? No matter. *Work*, I silently beg the small, glowing machine in my hand. *Find me Finn. Let Finn find me.*

Sweat pours off of me despite the chill in the air. I'm thirsty, painfully so. My breathing is labored, my muscles so tight I fear my limbs might snap off. But just when I think we might be in the clear, glass shatters within the shop.

My breath stills in my chest. Victor's does too, I think.

Footsteps crunch across the littered floor, bringing someone or thing much closer to us. Whoever it is is certain to find us if they cross the counter's threshold—and from here, we have nowhere else to go, as there is just wall in front of us.

I lift up my hand and show Victor three fingers. It is far better to go out swinging than be picked off like apples from a tree. He nods, and I drop one finger. Our grips tighten around our weapons—me with my sword, he with his gun. Another finger drops. He nods once more, determination filling his face. My third finger drops.

We spring up from our location.

I don't recognize the card soldier standing less than a meter way, and he doesn't recognize me, thankfully. He's young, though, and already hardened. His eyes are beady and pink, his hair wild and black. A pike, caked with dried blood and dirt, is jabbed toward us. It takes everything in me to not show weakness and flinch. "Drop your weapons. Put your hands up."

"I have a better idea," Victor says. He cocks the safety of his gun and points the barrel directly at the man's chest. "You drop your weapon, and we'll let you live."

Hints of maniacal laughter overtake the card soldier, but he's good, because he's able to wrestle it under control nearly immediately. But I know better. Whether or not we drop our weapons, we're both good as dead. He's a pike soldier. He's impervious to pain and will fight until his head is cut clean from his body.

But then a miracle occurs. I spy the small emblem carved into the tip of the pike.

Before Victor can do anything stupid, I toss my sword against the counter. "You may collect our weapons on the condition you take us to your commanding encampment immediately."

Small, dark eyes narrow in on me. "And if I don't?"

I simply say, "Gangan."

There is no hesitation. The card soldier shifts his pike until it stands next to him. "As you insist."

Victor is nearly apoplectic. "What in the bloody hell do you think you're doing?"

We don't have the time to argue like he wishes, though. Not when Finn and Mary are still out there in the midst of a Wonderlandian war.

"Give him your guns, Victor."

The good doctor is resolute, though. "I most certainly will not."

"You will," I tell him. "And I promise you, before daybreak, you will get them back."

"What about Mary? Finn?"

Twin twinges of fear and hope course through me. "This is our best shot at finding them. Is your GSP turned on?"

Victor stares at me for what feels like a century before his eyes flick back over to the card soldier, now standing at perfect attention. There are dents covering the youth's armor, there is more blood than either of us would like to see, and his grim face borders on madness.

But then, amazingly, Victor unholsters both guns. "I'm keeping the clips," he mutters. "And it's GPS. Yes, it's turned on."

"Fair enough." I turn back toward the card soldier. "How long until we reach the encampment?"

"If we are unimpeded and can circumnavigate much of the fighting, we can be there within two hours."

A loud blast sounds nearby, rattling the walls around us. Two hours . . . Two hours is a long time to not know where Finn and Mary are. I glance back down at the phone in my hand; no red dots flashes back at me. This may be my only chance at finding them.

The Caterpillar had six hours. I just need to find them within that time period.

I stuff the phone into my backpack. "Then let us depart immediately."

Victor watches in mute fascination as the card solider collects our weapons and stores them in a small, seemingly bottomless satchel. But the fascination soon turns to anger when the card soldier searches the rest of our bags and then claps all-too-familiar thick, silver bracelets around all four of our wrists. "What in the bloody hell are these contraptions?"

"They're called wrist cuffs." I keep my voice calm, lest the card soldier gets spooked. "And if they are removed without the proper card or stray too far from the owner, they will detonate in a rather large, nasty affair."

He's horrified—and justifiably furious. "I don't know what the hell is going on, but you better start talking."

The pikeman snaps, "Follow me."

His pace through the town, keeping to side streets, doesn't falter despite ear-deafening roars of what sounds like cannon fire. When we turn a corner into a dark alley, I lift my arms and brandish my wrists to Victor. "These are used to ensure we keep our word." I lower my voice. "If all goes as planned, they'll be off shortly. Just bear with them a bit more—better wrist cuffs than death."

Fading shouts filter through the smoky trees surrounding the town. I'm impressed that Victor isn't rattled the least by what's going on. "Would he kill us, though?"

"Oh, without a doubt. Pikemen are notorious for being unyielding in the field."

"It was the word you said," Victor murmurs thoughtfully as we jog to keep up with our captor. "That's what changed his mind. What does it mean?"

"Roughly: *safe passage.* Each monarch in Wonderland has a different one that is subconsciously programmed into card soldiers when they join the military." My smile is thin. "Had I issued the wrong word, though, one attached to a different monarch, we would have been killed on the spot."

"I think the two of us could have deflected a single pike. I've been in worse situations."

The card soldier twists his head to look at us. I elbow Victor in the ribs and hush him.

Once the soldier's attention is back on the route before us, I murmur, "Those pikes are undoubtedly like nothing you've ever seen before. Outside of being constructed of a poisonous metal, at the press of a button, the blade open ups, elongates, and whirls like a cross between a whip and a saw. I've seen a single pike take down close to ten soldiers in a matter of minutes. If this one has a pike," I jerk my head in our captor's location, "it means he's terribly strong. Pikes don't go to the weak."

Victor's silent as he digests this.

The farther we push into the silvery woods, the dimmer the screams from terrified citizens become. Soon, nothing but the hum of insects and night flowers and the mournful wail of birds press against us. Our only sights are the colorful red and purple toadstools dancing in between the trees and the riots of dozing pansies and lupine littering the floor There is no chattering to be heard.

At least a quarter of an hour goes by before Victor speaks again. "Do you think they're all right?"

I desperately wish I had that answer. Too many scenarios race around my mind, some abhorrently frightening. If they were captured, if they were to admit knowing me . . .

"They're resourceful." I nearly stumble on the angry brambles below my feet; a nearby violet pulls its head up and warns me to watch where I'm going. "If anybody can survive, it'll be them." And I pray I am right.

I am not ready to lose sight of my north star.

Victor's sigh floats up, echoing through the darkened trees and their velvety gray and blue leaves illuminated only by the sliver of moonlight, but he does not press the issue in the company of the card soldier. But I think about his question the rest of our hushed march, all those insidious scenarios taunting me until the panic in my chest is tight and heated.

If they were captured, if they were brought to one of the ruling encampments, all they would have to do is say my name. Just one word. Just two syllables. And then their heads would be forfeit.

Fear tastes so very bitter upon a tongue.

Stay the course, I insist to myself with each step. This is the best hope to find them. We can track one another. I just need to get us to a safe place and with the supplies to do it.

I think back to those last moments with Finn, of how it felt to know I held his confidence and trust. How he believed in me, and was willing to help me defend a land that banished me. Of how he didn't judge me over the past few months, of how we accepted one another for who we are now rather than who we're seen to be. I think about all of our conversations, and how we gradually gave each other tiny shards of one another but still have many more that need to be passed over. I think about how, as I stumble through these woods toward my past, it felt to have my mouth on his and his body in mine.

I think about how I'm not ready to let that go yet.

I think about Mary, and of her acceptance and her friendship. I think about how much she and Victor truly love one another, and of how this latest hiccup is just that—a hiccup. They deserve the time to make things right between each other.

I think about how these people took me in, of how quickly I was folded into the Collectors' Society. Of how these people are tireless in their efforts to protect those who don't even know of their existences. And of how many lives they've saved with no thought toward their own.

I won't fail them.

I can't.

THE NIGHTRIDER

T HE CARD SOLDIER HAD told us it would take two hours to reach the encampment, but by my estimations of the greenish-golden lights of daybreak filtering through the trees, it's taken much longer than that. So when we finally break through into a large clearing filled with small white tents ringing a larger circle of tents ringing a pavilion, it's all I can do to stay on my feet.

Dirty, tired soldiers both human and animal mill about, sharpening their weapons around campfires. Eyes trail us everywhere we go, as do murmured words I do not try to pick apart. I've got my hood up, but too many have keen eyesight. Let them gossip. It's not as if I'll be able to hide myself much longer.

"Blimey," Victor whispers. "Where are we?"

"This is the current base for the White King."

Both Victor and I jerk our heads up in surprise. These are the first words the soldier has uttered in hours.

"The White King," Victor says thoughtfully. "He was a bit of a bumbling oaf, wasn't he?"

The card soldier whips around, his pike pointed in our direction. I throw myself in between them, my hands held out. "My companion does not know of the White King. His words should not be taken as gospel."

Muscles around the card soldier's eyes and mouth spasm. He does not put his pike away.

I repeat slowly, carefully, "Gangan."

As if he knows his life is suddenly on the line, Victor repeats what he hears from me.

A full five seconds, during which the soldiers surrounding us watch while murmuring furiously, pass before our captor retracts his weapon. "Do not let it happen again. The next time, word or no, I will slay you."

I believe him.

As we weave our way through the camp, the smell of crisped swallows burns my nostrils and sends my salivary glands into overproduction. I can't remember the last time I ate. Drank. It was early in the morning, back at the Institute, and even then, all I could manage was a piece of dried toast. Pikemen are incredibly durable, and he provided no relief or rest the entire walk.

We're led to one of the tents just outside the pavilion. Before the flap is folded back, goose pimples break out up and down alongside my arms. My heart trips over itself; my fingers tremble.

"Wait here," the card soldier tells us before entering the tent.

Victor is uncharacteristically quiet as he takes in his surroundings. I estimate there are at least four or five hundred soldiers in the encampment, which is a surprisingly low and worrisome number. A thought comes to me, one I never remotely entertained before.

What if things are different? The uncertainties plaguing my chest morph into an iron band.

A pair of old, decorated soldiers walk by, deep in discussion, but the moment they catch sight of me, they halt.

I recognize one of them. More importantly, he recognizes me, having been one of my own. "Son of a jabberwocky," he whispers. "Can it be?" He drops to a knee, his head bowed. "Today is the most miraculous of days. Welcome home, Your Majesty. May the bells ring in your honor."

I cut him off immediately. "Thank you, Sir Halwyn. But I must insist you do not announce my arrival."

"Of course, my lady. Please tell this old knight what he can do for you, though. An item? News? Ask it and it's yours."

"I ask that you rise, good sir. I require no prostrations."

Once more upon his feet, his genial concern is torn away by a snarl. "Who dares to place you in wrist cuffs?" The sword from his scabbard is in his hands in the blink of an eye. "Which scoundrel has done this to you?"

Victor pokes at the tent flap. "The chap you're looking for is in there."

"The least I can do is rectify this situation in lieu of the King's absence." The knight knocks the flap aside, but I reach out and grab his arm, alarm coursing through me. The flap closes as he steps closer.

"The King isn't here in the camp?"

He softens at my question. "My lady, he is merely in the field and is expected back shortly. We've had word that this night has been a most successful one for His Majesty."

I ask quietly, "And Her Majesty?" What if the Hatter had been mistaken?

"They have separated across the battlefield in order to utilize the army in the most efficient manner." He points into the distance, toward the East. "Seventy kilometers yonder lies an identical encampment."

I bite my lip and peer in the direction indicated. Seventy kilometers is not far at all, unfortunately. "And the Red Queen and King?"

"They have also separated." He motions first to the North and then to the South. "The Red Queen's encampment is closest; it has edged about twenty kilometers closer to us these last few days."

Bloody hell, this has gotten out of control. "And the Heart Court?"

"My lady, we have yet to successfully locate any of their encampments. They are tricky, deceitful buggers, and have splintered into many small pockets to hide within."

As I process this, he folds the flap of the tent back once more. And then, before I can say anything, the knight bellows, "Who is the bloody imbecile who put wrist cuffs on the Queen of Diamonds?"

I quickly step through the flap, dragging Victor with me. "That's enough, kind sir."

Inside the tent is a handful of men and women I am very familiar with, and when their eyes find me, confusion, elation, and terror fill their brightly colored orbs.

Nightrider Quigley, a tall yet aged and distinguished Unicorn, starts in surprise. The rest of the suit does the same. And then, as if on cue, they all drop to a knee (or the equivalent of a knee for those who are animals) before me—all except the card soldier who brought us here. He's bewildered, his focus flitting quickly back and forth between me and his commanding officers.

The officer next to him yanks him to the ground.

Victor nudges me. "I rather like this. Why couldn't this other fellow have fallen to his knees before you rather than threaten to slay us?"

The tents occupants rise up when Nightrider lurches upright. "SLAY THE QUEEN OF DIAMONDS?!" Spittle flies from his thick lips. "Five of Diamonds! On your feet, private!"

Five of Diamonds, I muse. How deliciously ironic. "This isn't necessary," I say, but a sharp jab from Victor quickly hushes me. He's taking too much pleasure in seeing our captor get dressed down.

The pikeman quickly scrambles to his feet. His lead officer, a burly Griphon whose feathers have begun to gray, barks, "Explain yourself immediately."

"These are the prisoners I was telling you about." The card soldier's lean body goes taut. "The ones I found in the midst of Queen of Heart's assault on Nobbytown. They were carrying weapons, sir. None of the ordinary citizens did so."

The Nightrider's face turns a mottled shade of red and purple beneath his graying, coarse hair. "Do you have any idea who you have insulted, private? Do you know that your life is forfeit now?"

This has gone on long enough. "I must insist that this soldier was only doing his job, and ceased any attempts on our lives once I provided him with the safe word. I beg of you to release him of any accusations of wrongdoing. I am here, in this encampment, which is exactly where I wanted him to bring me."

The Nightrider grunts but concedes to my request. "Get those cuffs off immediately."

I'll give it to him—the card soldier is stoic the entire time he extracts his card. "Yes, sir."

Victor's winsome smile as he thrusts his arms out makes me want to roll my eyes. I bite back a comment about ladies first, and allow him this bit of early freedom. Four quick swipes, though, and the cuffs are off our wrists and back into the soldier's pack.

Victor taps the card soldier's bag. "Our weapons?"

Without a beat, the soldier tugs them out of his bottomless bag and passes them over.

"If I may be so informal," the Nightrider says gruffly, "I'm surprised to find you here today, my lady."

Not as much as I am. "I'm told His Majesty ought to be here shortly?"

"Yes, my lady. I got word via jubjub bird just half of an hour confirming this. May I offer you and your companion some food or drink?"

I smooth my skirts, hating that my hands are once more shaking. "No, thank you. But that reminds me. Gentlemen and gentleladies, I would like to introduce you to a colleague of mine. This is Dr. Victor Frankenstein."

It's then I remember his surname is actually Van Brunt, but Victor takes no offense to my bumbled introduction. While hands are shaken, it's clear the White King's military advisors have taken an interest in his title. One of my former lead Sergeants says, "We have a medical tent set up, but our staff is currently limited as most were recalled to the White Queen's camp a few days prior. There are several soldiers who are in dire condition—perhaps we might have the honor of you taking a look at our patients and facilities?"

For a moment, I worry Victor will refuse them. After all, Mary and Finn are still out there, and we have no idea what shape they're in. But then my friend graciously agrees to do so, even going as far as asking about supplies and conditions.

While he's talking with the Sergeant and a few others, the Nightrider pulls me aside. "My lady, this is no place for you right now. While our encampment is fairly safe, the battles around us are brutal. With the bounties still placed upon your being, I urge you to find safer quarters."

I place my hand on the hard metal covering his chest. It's dinged in far too many places, rusty in others. "I appreciate your concern, but there are things I must discuss with His Majesty before I depart. How bad is it?"

A hoof runs over his face. "May I be frank?"

"Always."

"The situation is most dire, my lady. The contentiousness between the three remaining courts is most egregious. As far as I know, communication has broken down entirely. As a last resort, the White Court sent a pair of diplomats out a month back, only to have their . . ." Bleakness carves lines on his worn, half-painted face. "Well, my lady, both the Queen and the King received identical boxes bearing severed heads. I suppose you have heard about your Chief Advisor by now. I'm terribly sorry about that, my lady. The Caterpillar was a force to be reckoned with."

I cannot help the shudder that overtakes me. Things are bad enough back at ground zero—but to hear that conditions in Wonderland have deteriorated to the point they are? "I am most despondent to hear of such an atrocity. Are the Red and Hearts Courts in collusion?"

The Nightrider is grim when he shrugs. "It is a possibility that cannot be ruled out, but His Majesty does not think this the case."

I glance around the tent, taking in the maps pinned to the canvas walls and the model battlefield and miniature statues that encompass at least half the space. "What does the Cheshire-Cat have to say about all of this?

"The Cheshire has been captured by the Hearts Court." He's uncharacteristically bleak. "His Majesty received an inch of tail a month prior, but there has been no word since. We fear the worst, my lady. Despite our best efforts, we have been unable to find him. First the diplomats, then this?"

"And Her Majesty's Grand Advisor?"

"Also missing."

Good God. The Hearts are systematically taking out the Chief Advisors.

The Nightrider turns toward the old knight who first recognized me, now guarding the flap alongside the card soldier. "Sir Halwyn. A moment, please."

The knight jolts to attention, his armor creaking. "My lord."

"Go to His Majesty's pavilion and tell the page to ready a pair of rooms for our esteemed guests."

Sir Halwyn nods before swiftly exiting.

"Five of Diamonds?"

The card soldier instantly turns toward his commanding officer, his body snapping to attention. "Yes, sir."

"You will be charged with protecting the Queen of Diamonds and Dr. Frankenstein during their stay in the encampment."

Across the room, Victor goes silent, his eyes widening significantly in aggrieved disbelief.

I head him off the pass, as I'm fully aware of why the Nightrider is assigning this soldier to us. "That is most generous of you, but surely you remember I am well-equipped to protect myself. Dr. Frankenstein is also quite skilled in weaponry."

"Your skills are indeed legendary, my lady. But I would be remiss if, in the midst of warfare such as we're seeing, I do not do everything I can to ensure your safety. His Majesty would not wish it any other way."

Words of dissension tickle my tongue, but then it strikes me a native Wonderlander—and a pike wielder, no less—might come in handy. "Very well. We would be grateful for his service."

His chin juts in the direction of the youth. "Despite contrary experiences you may have had with him today, the Five of Diamonds is one of our better pikemen. He isn't much of a talker, though. Chances are, you won't even know he's around."

My eyes follow the Nightrider's over to where the card soldier is standing at attention. "This one is quite young, isn't he?"

"You, of all people, can surely attest that youth has nothing to do with natural talent."

I turn back to find the Nightrider smiling wistfully. "You are incomparably sweet, my lord."

He looks away, voice gruff. "And you have been greatly missed, my lady."

I do not say anything further. There isn't any need to, not when my apologies are best served for another's ears.

THE PAST

A N HOUR LATER, AND after a quick intake of rations from our backpacks, Victor and I are safely ensconced inside the sitting room of the White King's pavilion. Never one for extraneous frivolity like his other half, the walls are bare, the floors covered with simple yet comfortable carpets, and the furniture is functional and practical.

This is not lost on Victor. He glances around as he swallows several pills he's just taken out of an unmarked bottle in his backpack. "This belongs to a monarch?"

My eyes wander over to where the Five of Diamonds is standing, pike at attention as he guards the entrance in. "It does."

"Interesting." His lips curve upward before he takes a swig of water. "Who knew that royalty in Wonderland were so frugal?"

I wonder what type of pills he just took. "Not all."

"But this one is. I suppose I expected extravagance, or at least whimsy." He wanders over to a draft table filled with a model battlefield almost identical to the one in the Nightrider's tent. "Do you know this

White King?"

A twinge plucks within my chest. "I do."

"You're going to ask him for help, aren't you?"

Sometimes I don't think I give Victor enough credit. "I am."

"You think he can help us find the catalyst and Mary and Finn."

I keep my voice steady. "Yes."

Our phones have yet to register either Finn or Mary's movements. Do these blasted machines even work? The waiting is unbearable.

"Can you trust him? I'm sorry to have to ask, but this is my girl-friend and my brother we're talking about. For all we know, this king will blow us off since he's got a multi-front war going on."

A bit of my old madness tickles the back of my throat, because the urge to laugh is strong. I wonder if Mary would be pleased or annoyed to hear him refer to her as such. "I promise you he will assist us."

"You can't promise that."

And yet I can.

I wander over to where he's standing, and for several long minutes, we simply stare at the figures and scenes below us. He picks up a small chess piece of the Red Queen. "Were you frightened when you left?"

I take the piece from him and run my fingers over the crown jutting off the top of the miniature queen's head. "Yes and no. I had hoped a multi-front war could be prevented by my leaving Wonderland, but it appears I was wrong. And that saddens me more than you could possibly know."

He picks up the King of Hearts figurine and stares at it. There's a distance to his eyes, though, one I can't help but guess at.

Even though it's only a hope, I say, "I have faith that your father has found the suspects in our absence."

"I hope so." The figurine is placed back upon the table. "Do you think we will get the catalyst?"

"Oh, most definitely."

"I'm lucky, you know. My original Timeline's catalyst is already safely catalogued into the Museum." And then, more softly, "It's some-times a hard burden to bear in the Society, when so many other Time-lines are not as fortunate."

I think about what Van Brunt told me about his Timeline, and of how Victor and Finn lost Katrina. "You should never feel guilty that your original Timeline thrives."

"I always ask myself, each time we lose one, was there something more I could have done? Or any of us?"

I can only imagine what a terrible feeling that must be for an orphaned child. "Your father told me about your mother."

His smile is fragile, and in this moment, Victor looks more like a young boy than a man of thirty-one. "She was the best. The warmest, sweetest, kindest, loveliest woman to ever walk in any of the Timelines."

He's a good son to think this.

"To lose her was unbearable. We were all helpless and confused, and here was Brom—strong, in control Brom, and his—*our*—family was gone in an instant." He runs a hand through his hair as he stares up at the ceiling. "Katrina and Brom wanted children, but they never could, I suppose. She used to tell me when I was a lad that I made her the luckiest mother in all the Timelines." His chuckle is soft and sad. "She said, 'You chose me to be your mother. I am so lucky, Victor. The luckiest.' And I would argue stupidly, 'I didn't choose you.' She would just laugh and smile and assure me I had. 'You hugged me and kissed me and called me mum. You chose me.'" He lets out a hard breath. "I was the lucky one, you know. I had her since I was just a tot. Finn didn't join our family until he was a teen. He was a hellion in the beginning, used to freedom and no one requiring anything remotely like responsibilities from him." His grin is rueful. "The ironic thing is, Brom was just as bad when he was younger. We always teased Finn that, for being adopted, he sure took after his father. For the first year or so, the NYPD and our parents interacted far too often. But Katrina didn't care about how many times Finn was in trouble with the law. She would tell him, as he raged about, that she loved him exactly as he was. That there was nothing he could ever do that would make her love him less. He was terrified of family, terrified of what it meant because family and the like could be taken away from him. He was quite a nomad in his youth, you know."

I didn't, actually.

"I grew up with the Society. Finn hasn't had as many years as me, as the last published book in his series had him at fifteen. So he couldn't join the Society until after that." He shakes his head. "Even though he came willingly to the Society, he still lashed out a lot back then. It's funny now to think about, considering."

I'm fascinated by all of this. Huckleberry Finn Van Brunt, a hellion? The polite, kind man whose gentle deeds toward others has endeared him to me? "When did you join the Society?"

He scratches the back of his neck as he considers my question. "Honestly, I can't remember. I was young and poor, living on the streets with my biological mum. I remember not wanting to go, but she was sick and knew it was a better life for me, especially as my biological father, who I'd never met, was already dead." A few seconds of pained silence settle between us. "Later on, when I was at University, I had the A.D. track her down for me. She'd died not two weeks after I moved to New York. I think she knew she was dying, so that's why she gave me up so easily."

He'd lost not one, but two mothers. "Oh, Victor," I murmur. "I am so terribly sorry to hear this."

"Katrina insisted that I spend all of my summers in England, as that was where my father was from. This England and my Timeline's England are similar, she reasoned. It would be like me holding onto pieces of my past—or at least learning about them. For most of my childhood, she stayed with me in London. Once Finn arrived . . ." He shrugs. "She stayed in New York to help him out. And I went away to college and medical school in England."

I stare down at my phone, willing it to beep, to show me Finn's signal. "If you two were separated by an ocean, how did you and Finn grow so close?"

"Who says we're close?"

"Me." I nudge his arm. "You two can't hide it."

"It just happened. He needed us," Victor muses, "as much as we needed him."

I'm glad for it.

"It's good to have him on my side. There are those in the Society who worry I'll take up my biological father's causes and start raising the dead and wreaking havoc. Sometimes I wish I could just change my last name. Frankenstein." Another bitter laugh surfaces. "What a bloody joke. But it helps that my brother believes in me."

Uncomfortable memories surface over how, on my first day in the Society, Brom privately expressed to Finn concern over whether or not

Victor's pen truly malfunctioned during editing. "If it's any consolation, they most likely worry whether or not I'll lapse back into madness, too."

"Ah, yes. You and I will find some kind of secret lab in the basement of the Institute, and we'll devolve into madness together." He rubs his hands together before holding them up in the air. "Bwhahaha! Think of the damage we can do! We can play croquet with some corpse limbs down there, drinking tea like we're with the Queen. I'll make us a mad, dead tea party of our own."

Genuine laugher spills out of me at the ludicrous image.

"Do you mind if I ask you something personal?"

"What is it?"

"Is there something going on between you and my brother?"

"My lady?"

I turn away from Victor's unsettling question to find Sir Halwyn at the entrance to the pavilion. "I thought you would like to know that His Majesty has arrived at camp and is headed this way."

All of the frivolity of the moment whispers away. "Does he know I am waiting for him here?"

"I do not think so, my lady. The Nightrider planned on meeting His Majesty on the outskirts of our perimeter to brief him, but a situation arose that has his full attention. Shall I ride out and let His Majesty know?"

"Please, do not bother yourself with such matters. It will all be resolved shortly anyway."

The old knight bows and exits the pavilion. Victor says, "You don't think one of Wonderland's monarchs might like to know ahead of time if an exiled queen and unknown doctor are waiting for him?"

Irrationally, part of me wants to lay the truth at Victor's feet. But nearly a year of holding my tongue has me hesitating. This man is Finn's best friend, his brother—and if Finn is to hear my past, it should come from me and not from hearsay.

So I tell Victor, "You will not lose your head. That is more the Queen of Heart's *modus operandi* than anyone else's. Although, the Red King has taken to favoring it a bit more over the last few years, too."

He doesn't appear reassured. "And what is this White King's *modus operandi*?"

Trumpets blare from beyond the canvas walls, cutting off any explanation I may offer. My heart thumps painfully, my palms begin to sweat. I run through a list of perfectly justifiable and worthy reasons why I did what I've done. He understands—of course he understands.

He was there with me from start to finish.

Murmurs sound nearby, alongside the clanking of armor. At the entrance, the card soldier assigned to us becomes even more statue-like. Clarity, so foreign in these places, batters at me from every side. I made the right choice. I made the only choice I could, the one we both agreed upon. I made the best choice available to me, for us. I do not second guess my choice. I cannot.

I will not. And yet, the muscle in my chest beats in overtime.

"Should I bow?" Victor is asking me. "Is that a thing here? I haven't had to bow to you. Bloody hell, should I be bowing to you?"

The flaps to the entrance fold back. A card soldier I do not recognize stalks into the room, his pike bloody and scratched. For a moment, when his scan of the room ends upon me, his eyes widen, but he snaps to attention quickly. "The White King has arrived."

I think I've forgotten how to breathe properly. Because there the White King is, exactly as I remember him, although perhaps a bit dirtier. Tall, dark hair slightly mussed, his skin pale, his eyes so light, so bright they nearly border on the color of his court. His head is down when he strides into the receiving room, maps in his hands as he confers quietly with a pair of military advisors I know well. But then Ferz Epona, a squat, sharp, but fair woman I've admired for years, looks up and spies me. She halts in her tracks, mouth open.

"My lady," she whispers. She drops to a stubby knee.

The White King's head snaps up. Tracks first back to his advisor and then forward, to where I stand. Disbelief, then shock fills those crystalline eyes of his. The other Ferz, Epona's identical twin brother, drops to a knee, a hand crossing his heart.

Victor murmurs through closed lips, "Should we bow now?"

The room is silent as a vacuum, with not even a single footstep, not a slip of paper rustling registering. So very many words have clamored around my head for months, but now that I'm here, and he's here, none of them want to come out.

"Your Majesty." Ferz Epona's voice is louder now, even though her head is still bowed. "We had no idea you were here."

The map in the White King's hands is shoved toward Ferz Eponi. I open my mouth to attempt any of those practiced words, but the King is already making his way across the room.

"Your Majesty, I want to thank you for receiving us this afternoon," Victor is saying. "Alice has had only kind things to say about this court and—"

And his words die the moment the King's takes my face in his hands.

For a split second, I'm flooded with so many emotions I'm left paralyzed. But then familiarity wins out, and my hands come up to rest against his. Just these smallest slivers of contact send a thousand memories clambering toward the forefront of my mind.

"You're here," he whispers to me. "You're *here.*"

My voice feels sticky. "I am."

His forehead rests against mine for a long minute, and the familiarity of such a small but meaningful interaction is so very, very bittersweet. But eventually he lets go both too soon and after too long. We have an audience, after all, and a curse to consider. "How long have you been back?"

I have to clear my throat. Force myself to think logically—hell, even remind myself that logical thought is now my ally. "I arrived in your camp just a few hours prior."

"Why wasn't I notified immediately?"

"I knew you were busy attending your soldiers. But please, if I may . . . I am here to ask you for two favors."

Those eerily pale eyes of his pin me to where I stand. "You know that anything I can do, anything I have, is always yours to take without question."

I refuse to acknowledge that Victor's mouth has dropped open and that his eyes have narrowed significantly. Or that the oval-shaped Ferzes behind us are shuffling their feet and papers uncomfortably. "I realize that I've come at a most inopportune time—"

"When it concerns you, there is no such thing."

"But I do not know where else to go."

"Then you have come to exactly the right place," the White King says quietly, firmly, "as, no matter what, you always have me to come to."

God, that's so bitterly beautiful to hear. "May we speak in private?" He doesn't hesitate. "Clear the room."

"Me, too?" Victor asks. There's a suspicion to his voice, one that I know he's entitled to as it comes from a genuine place.

The King's attention shifts to my friend, his eyes narrowing. I quickly say, "This is a colleague of mine—Dr. Victor Frankenstein Van Brunt. Victor, this is His Majesty, the White King of Wonderland." I touch the King's arm. "I would like him to stay, as he has much at stake, too."

"You are not a Wonderlander." It's not a question, but it requires an answer all the same.

"No," Victor says, and I can't tell if he's impressed by the monarch so far or annoyed.

The White King waits until the room empties before asking Victor, "Are you also from England? Your accent is much like the Queen's."

Victor scratches the inside of his elbow. "Well, yes, technically . . ."

I hold out a hand. "I will explain it all if you're willing to listen."

"Shite, Alice," Victor murmurs as the King leads us over to a series of couches, "he doesn't look anything like the illustrations in your book, either."

"The Queen has a book?" the White King inquires. And then, a bit slyly, "And it has illustrations of me in it?"

Victor doesn't quite know how to answer that, and I'm not too keen to address it at the moment. "There is much for us to discuss, Your Majesty."

"Much," he agrees softly. "But will you first help me out of my armor? It's been a long night and I'd really rather start a fresh day outside of this metal, if even for a few hours."

It's my turn to blush, even though this is a task pages do without second thoughts. A task I've done countless times in the past. "Of course." I unbuckle the straps holding the arm pieces to the chest plate. "I'm sure you are wondering what I'm doing here."

He holds his arm out for me. "I am wondering many things, actually. For example, I am wondering how, after months of searching for you, you suddenly appear in my tent."

I bite my lip as I gently tug off the first arm piece and pass it over to Victor. He searched for me? But, he knew I went back to England. He was there when the agreements were made. "My reasons are two-fold. But to address one, I must tell the other. Will you hear me out?"

Out of the corner of my eye, I watch Victor wander around with the armor, wondering what to do with it. Finally he sets it down on the floor near the throne occupying the head of the room.

"Why do you even ask when you know I will?"

I slide off the second arm piece and pass it over to the bemused doctor. "After I returned to England, I checked myself into an asylum."

There is weighted silence for the length of time it takes to unbuckle the two halves of chest plates. "Is that a madhouse?"

I nod, and he glowers. While he has always been one of the more logical creatures in Wonderland, he still exhibits hints of madness himself. "Were you mistreated?"

"I promise you I was not." He nods, and then I continue. "After months there, I was contacted by somebody who had a most peculiar job offer." And then, slowly, as I remove his armor down to the padding beneath, I relate the truth of it all. I tell the White King about Timelines, and of catalysts, and of the threat facing Wonderland if I do not find my crown. He listens quietly, taking it all in without interrupting me once. "I arrived with three colleagues," I conclude after many minutes, "but during the raid on the Land that Time Forgot, Victor and I were quickly separated from the others—a woman named Mary Lennox and a man named Finn Van Brunt." I'm embarrassed when Finn's name wavers. "And now, with all the fighting going on . . ."

"You wish to find them before calamity can occur," he concludes for me, a shadow of hurt flashing in his eyes. "Or, before any of the other Courts find them."

"Yes."

"And you wish for me to return your crown to you."

"I do."

Victor's eyebrows shoot up.

The White King says to him, "You are also from a storybook?"

"I'm from a separate Timeline, but I am not a character in a storybook." Victor sits down on the steps leading up to the King's simple throne. "My father was, though. Um, both my fathers, if one wants to be precise."

"And you, my lady?" Faint amusement glimmers in those white-

255

blue eyes. "You are from a storybook?"

I'm positive my cheeks are scarlet. "So I'm told."

"And I'm in it?"

"I haven't read the books," I mutter, "so I cannot verify that."

To Victor, the King says, "But you have."

"I skimmed them," Victor admits. "Before we tracked . . . uh, before Alice came to join the Society."

"You said I was different? As was she?"

Victor's clearly impatient, but he answers the question. "Yes, but the stories took place when she was younger. And you were, well, much older. And more like a chess piece. There might have been a picture where she picked you up. You know, like she would one of your little statues over there?" He motions to the battlefield nearby. "You were about yay high." His thumb and forefinger spread apart. "Or maybe a wee bit bigger." And then, more awkwardly, "But she totally had you in one hand. I'm sorry to say you were a bit of a bumbling fool throughout the entire thing."

For a moment, but the White King and I sit in stunned silence. But then we both burst into peals of laughter.

"A bumbling, old fool," the White King muses. "And a chess piece to boot. I'm afraid I must disappoint, Doctor." He leans back in his chair, his long legs sprawling before him. "And the Queen of Diamonds was nothing more than a child?"

Victor tugs at the collar of his shirt. "Yes. Your story is considered to be one of the most enduring pieces of children's literature."

Those white-blue eyes find me once more. "How curious." And then, more gently, "But as much as I find this talk fascinating, I'm sure you are eager to find your colleagues."

"I am." I want to touch his arm, but I lace my hands together in my lap. "Thank you, by the way."

"I haven't found them yet."

"You believed me," I say. "Without question. You listened and believed."

The White King slowly leans forward. "I have never had reason to not believe you. I doubt I ever will."

For years, this man has been my secret keeper, and I his. We have never lied to one another, and although it aches to be here with him once more, I am grateful to find his faith in me strong as ever, even after hearing what sounds to be fanciful fiction.

Victor is saying, "There are many people in Timelines who resist the truth, unfortunately."

"Some minds are more closed than others," the King says. "They see what they want to see." The corners of his mouth inch upward. "They do not see what I see. Now, come. Let us find your associates. I do not like to think what might happen to them if we are not the first to find them."

STAR-CROSSED

THE FERZES ARE SUMMONED once more, alongside the Nightrider and a handful of card soldiers, of which several served previously under the Diamond banners. The White King, never prone to fanciful speeches in the first place, lays out his wishes in little time. "I want the locations of two non-native Wonderlanders found within the next hour. The Queen of Diamonds has provided pictures for you to study."

The Wonderlanders are taken aback by the images on both my and Victor's phones. For all the wondrous sprinkled throughout their land, it is this that astounds them.

I let Victor explain GSP. As he does, I fiddle with my own phone, wondering why I can't seem to track Finn. Did he turn his on? Does he even still have it on him? Has the phone been destroyed? Panic claws at my chest. I think of his words in the elevator, of how he wouldn't let me go it alone because he'd just found me. And somehow, I'd lost him, lost the man who broke through my impenetrable walls and made me believe that maybe, just maybe, I am not cursed forever.

When the White King makes it crystal clear he will not accept failure, his men and women chorus their determination to do him proud. Jubjub birds and soldiers are sent into all directions. Sir Halwyn personally heads a team, promising me he will do his utmost to find our friends.

When they depart, Victor, claiming he needs something to focus his anxiety upon, asks to be taken to the medical tent to oversee patients. I choose to stay behind, knowing I'd be useless in there. Besides, a talk is in order.

"My soldiers will not fail us," the White King tells me as I wear a path in the floor from all my pacing. "Your colleagues will be found."

They must.

Without turning around, he tells the card soldiers at the entrance, "Resume your post outside."

Pikes sound against the ground before the flap is pushed back. Once they're gone, he steps forward and takes my hands. I watch a long, unsteady breath make his chest rise and fall, and too many memories crash into me from every side. My ear, pressed against his bare skin, his heartbeat strong and steady when everything else was chaotic. His hands, strong and warm, holding me afloat when life was liquid. Words, precious and rare, murmured under moving stars so bright that it hurt to stare at them too long in fear of losing oneself to their mysteries. Fighting side by side, and knowing we had righteousness as our ally. Our bodies joined together, and feeling as if it were the most natural thing in all the world. Making breakfast together, and then eating it in bed.

Planning a shared future and family that will never be.

"Before we say anything else," he murmurs, "promise me you are all right."

That I can easily do.

He lets go of my hands so he can tug a necklace out from beneath his shirt, one I haven't seen in half a year. Once unclasped, he holds it out to me. A golden H dangles from the serpentine chain between his fingers, and just staring at it now makes me feel like a broken thing.

"For all I knew," he says quietly, "you were dead."

I remember when he gifted me the necklace. We were in the tulgey woods, and there were flower songs afloat around us. Wonderland was magic and whimsy personified then. I had already begun the long and steady descent toward love with this man, but was foolish enough to imagine it was a crush on my behalf, but never his. He was the White King, after all, and the White Queen's beauty was lauded throughout the land. But there we were, in the woods, and he held out his hand like he is doing so now, offering me a necklace with an H dangling from it. "Happy," he told me then. "Honest. Humble. Hopeful. Heartfelt. Hopelessly in love with you."

We'd met on a battlefield, when Hs were our first sparring match, a word game that endeared us to one another. I was young then, and so was he (and most certainly not the bumbling old man Victor alluded to), but that was the beginning. From that point on, each time I saw him, I fell down more than just a rabbit hole. I fell deep within Wonderland.

The first kiss we shared, and every single one from that point forward, was far more drugging than anything his world could ever produce.

And now, he's worn my beloved necklace against his heart, just as I'd asked him to.

"You knew I went back to England."

"You wouldn't allow me to the hole, though," he argues bitterly. "Or let me be there when you left. I had no idea if you truly made it through, or if you were captured beforehand."

The wounds between us rip open. "You know why I had to go alone."

"No. I don't." His stubbornness has always been irresistible to me.

I say, my words barely audible, "I couldn't have borne it to have you there when I left. I wouldn't have been able to follow through."

"I searched for the hole. For months." His fingers curl back around the gold. "Sent out parties. Offered rewards on the black market to locate it. Bargained with the Caterpillar to tell me your secrets, and then the White Rabbit. All to no avail."

Practiced words, run through my head like chants or prayers for months, fail me when it comes time to prove their worth. We've been over this, but the last time was so emotional that my memory of our decisions and words is spotty at best. All I can say is, "We had no other choice."

His head tilts to the side as he studies me. I force myself to remember that this is the White King of Wonderland. We are no longer lovers, and that was a choice we both were forced to come to, no matter how painful the execution. But still, the impulse to reach out and hold him rings strong and loud through my bones.

Love, I think, is irrational no matter how hard we try to apply logic to it. And some love, even the kind that is not meant to be, takes root and flourishes anyway.

I should not love this man, and yet I do. I always will.

"We should have given it more time. We—"

"The prophecy was clear." I draw my hand back. Even now, even when I know I've finally found my true north star, one whose light and steadiness have nothing to do with madness or prophecies, touching this piece of me is too painful. "Both of our Grand Advisors were tireless in their quests to find a loophole. There were none." Sadness tears at my chest. "The decks cannot be shuffled. Wonderland will not allow it." Wounds so freshly scabbed over within me rip open. "We cannot ever put our selfishness above the lives of innocents. As it is, the odd number has thrown Wonderland into a tailspin. Do you not remember what the Cheshire-Cat warned us? Of the complete and utter devastation that would occur if we continue on together, with both of us residing in this land?"

He knows I'm right. He was there through it all, after all. When push came to shove, he made the same choice I did. Our lives, our feelings, mean nothing compared to millions of others. Even still, he's hoarse when he tells me, "You leaving changed nothing, though. The only difference is that Wonderland lost one of its strongest champions."

"I am championing it now." I press my hand against my heart. "I am here to collect its catalyst and ensure it is safely hidden away so that no stranger can ever harm you all like they have done to other worlds."

"The people need you here." Fire burns in his nearly colorless eyes. "There is too much corruption and greed within the Courts."

"They have *you.*" I blink back the tears forming. "It was the only reason I knew I could truly go."

He scoffs. "I am one of seven—"

"Six." And then, with the scars upon my heart threatening to rip open once more, "I am not a Wonderlander. I never truly belonged here. You do, though. You are exactly what Wonderland needs."

I've angered him. "I would not hear you disparage yourself in such a way."

"Did you know," I continue, "that the food and drink from Wonderland are actually drugs to my kind?"

Confusion battles with pain. *"What—?"*

"It took me too long to realize it." I shake my head. "No, that's wrong. I learned about it from the Duchess. She was quite keen on letting me know that, even if I wanted to leave, I was a slave to the desires I found here because Wonderland has a way of keeping its non-native inhabitants mad. Several of the Court members knew this—they figured I would be unable to leave, that my head would surely be forfeit. That all of my talk of stepping back would be pointless, because they would have my death to savor."

Dark hair swings about his head as he lets me know what he thinks of that. But we both know they would have never told him, not with such common knowledge of our relationship.

"It's true, though." My smile is brittle. "This place made me a drug addict. The Caterpillar procured a poison which allowed me enough, just enough clarity to exit Wonderland. It took weeks back home before I could get Wonderland's influence out of my system. I thought many a time I was going to die, the pain was so intense. I'd truly gone mad, you see. I was raving, hysterical, especially after I left here under such circumstances. I was committed to an asylum in an effort to fight my demons. That is not the person this land needs. Not somebody who has to be drugged to be effective." Somebody who, I fear, would weaken immediately in this moment if she was still drugged.

It is his turn to swallow hard.

My fingers lace together in effort to remain free of trouble. "I cannot, no matter what I may wish otherwise, ever allow myself to return to such a state of mind. And I do not believe you would ever wish it, either."

"I didn't know." Desperation tints his words. "I had no idea."

"How could you? I'm the first of my kind that you ever met. For all you knew, we were the same."

The space between us is cut in half. "We *are.*"

His unfailing idealism is part of what drew me to him like a moth to a flame. "None of that matters now. I'm—"

"Of course it matters!" His hand juts out once more, the necklace dangling. "It has always mattered!"

Nobody is safe if I don't want them to be, the White Queen told me the day I left, flanked by the Red Queen and the Queen of Hearts in some kind of twisted collusion that lasted just long enough to ensure my ouster. *Not little birds, not grinning cats, not even kings. Not even Diamond Queens and their caterpillars.*

I hated that she took the creatures who decorated my banners and made them sound so weak.

"There is no future for me in Wonderland," I tell him. "None at all. No matter what I may have once wished."

"I love you," he says forcefully. "And I know you love me. Do you think that nearly a year has changed that?"

It hasn't, of course. I love him just as strongly as I always have. I will continue to love him so. But this is no storybook; our ending is not happy. No matter what I feel toward him, or he for me, it simply cannot be. It never will be. There is no loophole, no way to change our fates. He is of the White Court. I am of the Diamond. If we were to shuffle the deck . . .

No. I cannot allow myself to think about this any further. It's too painful. And I'd been so good at putting it behind me. I dig deeper, even though the insides of my veins are collapsing in on themselves. "Nearly a year," I remind him, "hasn't changed the situation, either."

His intake of breath is harsh, painfully audible in the stark quiet of the room.

"Wonderland needs you. You—"

He turns away from me, hands digging into his hair and tugging so hard I fear he might lose chunks.

"The people crave stability. You know as well as I that you are the most stable ruler the land has. You cannot fail them."

He whirls around and grabs my hand. My necklace presses into my palm. "I haven't been, you know. I've been coming out of my skin for months, going mad for want of news of you."

And I the same.

"Nonetheless, you are their hope." My voice cracks. "I cannot stand in the way of that. I won't. You have your destiny, and I have mine. Once upon a time, I thought they might cross paths, but they do not. My destiny, it seems, is elsewhere."

"My heart will not let you go." His forehead falls against mine. "I've tried. I swear, I've tried."

Sobs clamor within my chest and fight their way up through my throat. But I am strong, because they stay within me.

A hand curves around my cheek. His breath shudders against my mouth. And then, before we do something selfish, he pulls back. Eyes closed, his head tilts back, a hand coming to lay across his heart. Red stains bloom from beneath his fingers and spread across the white of his shirt.

This isn't the first time this beautiful man's heart has broken and bled because of me. And yet, each time is just as painful as the last to see.

Sometimes, I wish he could see the pain of mine breaking, too.

"Promise me," he whispers hoarsely, "promise me that, just because we cannot be together, it does not mean that all of this was for nothing."

"It means everything." I'm choking on my words, I want to weep so hard. "It always will." I take the necklace from his hand and gently clasp it around his neck. I tuck it underneath his shirt, so that it once more lays against his bare skin.

He takes a deep breath, centering himself. The White King is one of the strongest people I have ever met. He will, as will I, do the right thing. Even though sometimes, the right thing is the hardest of all.

"I wish," he murmurs, "I could move on like you have."

I wipe away the tears that have dared to escape my eyes. He knows. Of course he knows. He probably knew the moment I asked for his help. This man knows me better than any other person in existence. He heard the tone in my voice when I told him Finn's name. But I cannot apologize to him for the audacity of falling in love with somebody else. Nor would he ever ask me to. He was the one to beg me to consider such a possibility; I was the one to claim I never could.

Love, it seems, can be drawn from a bottomless well, and for many different kinds of thirst.

"I'm—"

"No. Do not dare to apologize to me for opening your heart up. I would not have it any other way."

"I wish—"

"I will find them for you." Our foreheads touch once more. "I will always do everything I can to ensure your happiness. Your happiness is my happiness, even if it means your heart is held in another's hands."

Horns blare; I jerk back and turn away so I can wipe my eyes once more. The tent flaps rustle, and in trundles Ferz Epona followed closely on her heels by Ferz Eponi. The lord hands the White King a sheet of paper. "The Queen of Diamonds' colleagues have been located."

I immediately snatch the sheet. "Where?"

It's Ferz Epona who answers. Her eyes widen at the sight of the blood on the King's chest, but she quickly refocuses on me. "Jubjubs report that two matching the Queen's descriptions have been seen in the company of Heart soldiers roughly two thousand yards away."

Alarm tears through me. *What?*

"Fetch Dr. Frankenstein," the White King says. "He will want to be present to hear this."

Ferz Epona salutes and swiftly leaves the tent.

I grab the King's sleeve. "If she—"

"Last report I got," he says to me, eyes serious, "had the Queen of Hearts edging on the White Queen's encampment. There are been several skirmishes between the two armies, with the latest reported just this past day. She will not be so close to me."

"Why would they take them?" I fight to keep myself from erupting. "What purpose would her soldiers have in such an act?"

"My lady," Ferz Eponi says, "the Queen of Hearts has taken to ransoming hostages of the various Courts. Those who are not paid for are executed or sold into slavery. Chances are, your colleagues were captured alongside a number of other citizens in Nobbytown. The village had recently declared itself sympathetic to His Majesty's causes."

"There is no way Finn would have allowed either him or Mary to be taken. He is a skilled fighter." I'm desperate, curious as I stare down at the crumpled note, but the words jumble on the page before disappearing. The White King has coded his notes. "He—"

"Rumor has it that the Heart army possess a type of spray that incapacitates people," the Ferz says. "They call it SleepMist, and it is believed to work nearly immediately. One whiff and a person slips into a deep slumber that lasts for hours and then fades to partial paralysis for a few more after that. We've been trying to get samples for weeks."

I'm horrified. She dared to go so far?

"The contingency," the Ferz continues, "is supposedly not a very large one. The jubjubs estimate it to be at about fifty soldiers. That said, there are a pair of raths and a half-dozen pikemen present, all surrounding the caged caravans that carry the hostages."

"You're sure that . . . that my colleagues are there?"

"Yes, Your Majesty. One of the jubjubs was able to get close enough to identify." He motions at the paper. "They appear to be asleep, my lady. There is no blood to be seen, at least from the view the bird had."

Victor slips into the tent. "They've found Mary and Finn?"

As I nod, the White King says, "Ready a squadron. We leave in ten minutes."

"Are they okay?" Victor asks me as the King orders his page to come and help him back into his armor.

"I think so." I tell him what the Ferz has said.

"Shite." He runs a hand through his hair. "I don't know how to combat Wonderlandian poisons. Mary, yes, but . . ." He lets out a hard breath. "I'm not going to lie. I saw some bloody terrifying things down in the medical tents." To the White King, he says, "How long will it take for us to get there?"

For a moment, I worry my former lover will insist upon us staying back. Victor, no matter how much I trust him, is still a stranger. But the King says, "Twenty minutes of hard riding. We will come in strong. If there are hostages, I want them all liberated. Your medical assistance may be required, Doctor."

Victor squints. "Is that blood on your shirt? How did I not see it before? Let me have a look at you."

The White King takes a step back. "Is it nothing I have not experienced before. I am fine, Dr. Frankenstein. Let us focus instead on the matters at hand."

Victor doesn't look too sure about this, though. "Fine. What about the catalyst?"

"Once we have your colleagues' safety assured, we will leave at daybreak. It will take us nearly a full day to reach the crown's location."

I ask softly, "You're coming?"

The White King holds my eyes while he says, "Of course I am coming, as will a small amount of guards. The Nightrider will stand in my stead here at camp. You did say this catalyst is of great import to Wonderland's safety, did you not?"

My heart swells. "Yes, I did."

"Then I will be there to ensure your way is clear. Come. Let us find armor to get you through the coming battle."

SLEEPMIST

WHEN WE EXIT THE tent, the soldiers coming with us are already amount. Dozens of blindingly white horses with equally white eyes prance in the morning sunlight, golden rays sparkling through their manes.

"This is bloody uncomfortable." Victor raps on the metal shielding his chest. "How does anybody ever get used to it?"

"You get used to it," Ferz Eponi says from nearby, "when it saves your life, lad."

"Do they talk?"

The Ferz is confused by Victor's question. "Do who talk?"

"The horses!"

"No, Doctor. They're *horses.*"

Finn's brother turns to me. "Am I wrong? There are talking animals who are soldiers in this encampment. The Nightrider is a unicorn after all. *He* talks." He pauses. "Does he ride horses?"

Several of the soldiers around us—both human and animal—glower at Victor's commentary.

I end up hushing him.

We are both wearing armor borrowed from sidelined knights in the medical wing. Thankfully, their fits are close enough that it should pose no problems if either of us is engaged on the field. Still, I can't help but wish I'd thought to change into my own back at my vault in The Land that Time Forgot.

Just before I mount my horse, the White King breaks away from the Nightrider to come to where I am. He kneels down on the ground, my vorpal blade in his outstretched hands. And the sight of him doing this, holding my sword and kneeling before me, tests my strength.

The crowd around us goes quiet. The only sounds are borogrove songs from above and impatient hooves upon muddy ground.

"I beg your forgiveness," he says quietly, "but I could not resist."

"Has it brought you luck?"

His head lifts at my broken words. "Yes, my lady."

"Then my blade is exactly where it belongs. It would be my great honor if you were to carry it from this point on." My blade, in his fist. Wonderland will still have pieces of me through this King.

He takes a deep breath and stands back up. The look in his eyes makes me want to be the one to fall to my knees. "As you wish."

As the King mounts his steed, Victor asks suspiciously, "What was that all about?"

A horn trills. "We must leave now," I tell him. "Do you ride?"

"I grew up in New York and London. No, I do not bloody ride horses."

"Sir Halwyn?"

The elderly knight tugs his horse toward us. "Your Majesty?"

"I would ask that you ensure Dr. Frankenstein does not dismount."

Halwyn's armor clinks as he salutes me. "Yes, my lady."

Victor's cheeks flame red. He hisses my name under my breath, but I am not going to apologize for wishing his safety.

"I need you with us in battle." I settle onto my saddle. "Mary and Finn will need you. And Victor?"

A page shoves Victor up onto his horse. "Yes?"

"Wonderlandian metal is strong. I am not sure if bullets will penetrate it. If you are to use your gun, make sure your shots go for the neck or face."

He grabs his reigns. "You're rather bloodthirsty, aren't you?"

"No." To quote the Librarian: "I'm a realist."

Another horn trills and then blares long and hard. The White King lifts my blade into the air. "I will accept no failures on our behalves today. There are innocents held by the Hearts, and we cannot allow the atrocities plaguing Wonderland to touch their lives for any longer than they already have."

A rousing cheer sends the nesting borogroves screaming from nearby trees.

"Do not fear. Do not falter. Go with the singular purpose that every innocent life deserves our protection."

A song lifts from the clearing, of days of old and in a language lost to many Wonderlanders. And yet understanding sinks meaningfully within every chest that hears the intonations. The knights sing, and as they do, goose pimples break out along my arms. The last time I heard this song, my knights were the one to sing it, and it moves me more than I can say.

A third series of horn trills sound once the song dies. The knights roar, "For Wonderland!"

I keep my horse close to Victor's during the charge. We ride in the middle of the pack, with the King leading our way. His banners have been left behind—this ride is not for glory. This one is purely for justice.

The morning is chilly, and the air stings my face. Cannons boom in the far distance, but no one is worried about them. We have two dozen pikemen with us, including the Five of Diamonds. The White King's forces have always been amongst the best and most loyal in Wonderland, and now that mine have combined with his in my absence, I have no fear whether we will be victorious today. I only fear the effects of SleepMist on non-natives. What if its properties are much like those of the food and water here? What if there are side effects we cannot account for?

I cannot be borne. I will not allow it.

After nearly a half-hour ride through the Orange Fields, the Hearts caravan appears. They must be stupidly optimistic, because from what I can tell as we charge forth, most of the soldiers are enjoying a leisurely breakfast around campfires. At the sound of our approaching hooves, though, they scramble for their weapons and horses, but the element of surprise is definitely on our side.

There are three large caged wagons in the middle of the encampment. I am still at a distance, but I've yet to see any signs of life. There are no hands outstretched from between the bars, no voices calling out for salvation.

The White knights roar their battle cry in unison. And then, much to my surprise, the Diamond battle cry is added. Trees lining nearby groves shudder in their wake, and more mopish, mimsy birds explode frantically into the sky.

I draw my sword, flipping it in my grip. I yell out to Victor, "Get ready! This is no sparring practice!"

I'm gifted a quick, sharp nod. He does not go for his gun, though. A sword is drawn from his side, too. And then I count down from *ten, nine, eight* . . . Hearts horns are sounding. *Six, five* . . . One of the enemy officers is bellowing, but we've given them no time for preparation. *Three, two—*

The two armies crash into one another. The scent of blood is immediate.

Our pikemen quickly dismount; their well-trained horses flee to the edge of the clearing. Blades are activated, and the screaming begins.

I'm viciously pleased by the sounds.

The green raths with their shark-like mouths attack the King, but he and my blade dispatch them as if they were mimsies. The Hearts pikemen abandon their stations by the caravans and join in the fray, but they are quickly overtaken by the Whites. At first, I am stunned, but then it occurs to me that the Queen of Hearts must be so desperate, she's equipping pikemen before they're ready. Most of these, from what I can tell, are mere boys and girls—even younger than the Five of Diamonds.

As for him, he's a demon on the field.

I hack my way through the crowd. To my left, Victor does the same. I'm impressed with the doctor, though. Although it's obvious he's wary upon the horse, he also refuses to give up. Nearby, the sight of the White King fighting dazzles me. I've always thought it appears as if he dances on the battlefield rather than merely fight. My sword in his hand flies, the blade glowing blue as it doles out justice. The battle rages on for many long minutes, but before I know it, another horn sounds.

My relief is immense. It is the sound of a White victory.

The dust settles, and there are three Heart soldiers kneeling before a dismounted White King in the orange grass. All of the rest lay on the ground, blank eyes staring up into the gray morning skies.

"Ferz Eponi?" the King says.

"Yes, Your Majesty."

"Find me the SleepMist. I wish to have every last bit brought back to our encampment."

"Yes, my lord." The Ferz bows and barks out an order for the camp to be searched.

I hand the King the handful of Mindly pills I took from The Land that Time Forgot, ones I remembered to snatch shortly before we mounted. "For our prisoners' ride back to camp." The pills will keep the card soldiers deliriously occupied and honest so that they will not be able to recall the exact route we take. Once he accepts my offering, I am off and running toward the carriages, Victor close on my heels. White knights are already hard at work cutting open the locks, but I'm desperate.

And then I'm horrified. The closer I get to the cages, the more I see that bodies are piled upon other bodies. All asleep, or dead, I cannot tell. The jubjub bird was right, though. No blood is visible, but it does nothing to lessen the chill of mine.

The first padlock is snapped off. I'm up the steps to the caravan, frantic in my search through the bodies. There are children here, teenagers. The elderly, too. Sheep and Rabbits, Toads and Dodos. There are even a handful of Lizards. Victor searches the next caravan, but neither of us can find Mary or Finn in the stacks upon stacks of sleeping bodies.

"Your Majesty!" It's Sir Halwyn. "I believe I have found the Queen's colleagues!"

I'm out of the caravan and barreling toward the third. The old knight is standing in the midst of carefully stacked piles, his feet carefully placed so as to not touch upon any person. On either side of him, just five feet apart, are the people we've been searching for. They are unmoving and appear to be whole.

I have never been so relieved to see a pair of someones in my entire life.

Something between an ugly cry and laugh falls out of me. I'm about to climb in, but Ferz Epona places a hand on my shoulder. "Your Majesty, time is of the essence. Let us lead the caravans back to camp, so that we might begin triaging any possible wounds or medical maladies. There are dozens of bodies here, all in need of assistance."

Behind her, the King is issuing a small portion of the contingency to take care of the dead. Offerings of songs for safe passage to the journeylands begin; even for enemies, this ancient tradition never goes ignored.

"Alice." It's Victor. There is blood streaked across his face. "She's right. Let's get them back to safety. We don't know if anybody is going to be following up on a missing caravan."

"Right." I take a step back. "Of course."

"Doctor," Ferz Eponi is saying, "would you be willing to look at our newly wounded back at camp?"

As Victor confers with the Ferz, I make my way over to the King. "Are there any deaths on our side?"

"No." His smile is tight and sad and yet unsurprised. "But there are many wounded. The Queen of Hearts is outfitting pikemen before they're ready."

"I noticed the same thing." I stare down at one of the pikes in the mud beneath our feet. "Why is she desperate?"

"The people," he says as he also stares at the pike, "are not on her side."

"They never have been. But that's never produced such flagrant desperation before." Wiping my face leaves my hand streaked with sweat and blood. "Has the White Queen said anything of it?"

He leads us back to our horses. "The Queen's Council broke apart not two days after your departure. As far as I'm aware, none have been in contact with the others."

All-too-familiar irritation surfaces. "Are you sure?"

"It is my hope, but I cannot be certain."

"When did you last speak with her?"

He does not look at me when he says, "It has been at least two months since the White Queen and I last spoke in person, and two weeks since our last communique outside of the Ferzes."

I'm stunned, but there is no time for further questions. He calls out to the forces to remount, and within minutes, we are off. Travel back to the camp takes longer than the travel to, as the caravans cannot move as fast as steeds at full speed. Close to two hours pass before we arrive, and by that point, my nerves are a tangled mess.

While the passengers of the caravans are carefully unloaded into already overflowing medical tents, Victor insists that we consume another ration and enough water to, as he claims, "offset the morning's exertions." I'm impatient, but do as he says, especially after he tells me he fears if we get dehydrated, some well-meaning Wonderlander will force upon us water from their wells.

He takes another pill. My curiosity burns once more.

Soon, we get word that Finn and Mary have been unloaded. Rather than being brought to the medical tents, the King orders them into his pavilion. By the time Victor and I enter, our friends are already laid out on cots and are covered with soft blankets.

"They are breathing, my lady," Ferz Epona tells me. "We are positive it is SleepMist. It appears it is longer lasted than reported."

Victor is the first to reach his brother and girlfriend. He peels one of Mary's eyes back and peers in. "You said there would be paralysis following?"

"That's what the rumors claim," the Ferz says. "The paralysis allows potential buyers to assess their purchases or executioners to have docile victims."

Victor swears underneath his breath, disgusted. I am, too. We all are.

"That said, we hear the paralysis lasts a much shorter time than the sleep. It is our hope that, if your colleagues were taken last night around the same time you encountered the Five of Diamonds, that the Sleep-Mist is fading. They should wake soon."

"Did you happen to get any of this SleepMist?" Victor grabs his backpack and rifles through it. A stethoscope is extracted so he can listen to Mary's, and then Finn's, hearts.

"We collected a dozen unlabeled canisters alongside what appear to be large gun-like misters that can be worn on backs," the Ferz says. "The King has ordered a testing of the contents before we can claim otherwise. But it appears that the Hearts can use these contraptions to spray down large quantities of people at once."

"I think I would like a sample," Victor is saying. "I'd like to see what the breakdown is. Would that be possible?"

I'm surprised when the Ferz immediately agrees.

I make my way over to where Finn is sleeping. He looks fine. Peaceful. His eyes are closed, his breathing faint but steady. His hair isn't even dirty—slightly askew, but still in the condition I last saw it in. But his knuckles are raw, as if he'd recently fought.

I cannot help myself. I bend down and gently touch the strands. "Did you find any supplies on my people?"

"No, my lady. All pockets of the hostages were emptied. None carried anything with them. Chances are, the Heart soldiers destroyed everything before they moved out of Nobbytown. Fires were said to rage about the town. It is their way nowadays."

Victor extracts a small penlight from his bag. "That explains why we weren't able to track their signals." He shines it in one of Mary's eyes. "Heart rate is slower than normal, eyes are completely dilated to the point the irises are nearly covered." The doctor rocks back on his heels as he lowers the blanket covering his girlfriend. A sharp rap to the knees produces no movement. "Skin is clammy, indicating no fever. No reflexes visible to stimuli."

Uncomfortable as it is in armor, I squat down next to Finn's cot. None of this sounds good. "You know what this means, of course."

"No sign of REM sleep. Interesting."

I touch Victor's shoulder. "If all their supplies are lost, so are their pens. Their travel books."

Ah. Now he understands my meaning. "Shite. I guess I hadn't even thought of that. Wendy is going to have a fucking conniption over that."

"Can anyone use them?"

He shakes his head. "They're DNA encoded, remember? Only Mary and Finn can use their pens. Everyone else would find them useless. Same with their phones—everything is password protected. I doubt anyone could break into them. It isn't the first time we've lost supplies on an assignment."

"But what if somebody good with gears and mechanics were to take it apart? Would they be able to replicate the pen?"

He considers this. "I don't think so. I remember Wendy once saying she put self-destruct mechanisms in them. Only she and her lab know how to offset it when the pens are opened up. Anybody else?" He holds his hands out and expands his fingers. "Pen goes boom. You and I still have our pens and books, though."

"What about the books?"

He blinks at me.

"The books used for editing. People would have access to the story, and to what the Institute looks like."

He shrugs. "Then they would read a book about themselves or see pictures of a building whose use is not explained within the pages. Life will go on. Now hush and let me examine my brother."

Victor performs the same tests he just completed on Mary on his brother. Once he's done, he sighs heavily. "All we can do now is wait. I need to go to the medical tents to help out. Will you stay with them?"

As if he had to ask.

Once Victor is gone, Ferz Epona implores me to at least allow her to remove my armor. I'm reluctant to leave, but after much nagging, agree to do so. A bath is offered, and at first, I am tempted to say no. But the blood and grime on my skin is too much. I compromise by giving myself a sponge bath.

When I return to the room set aside for Finn and Mary, I find the White King dozing in a nearby chair. His armor is removed, but he has not bathed yet. Seeing him, and Finn, in such proximity nearly does my heart in.

My past and what I hope is my present and future.

The King rouses as soon as I close the flap to the room. "Sorry," I whisper. "I didn't mean to wake you."

"It's fine." He yawns and scrubs at his inky-black hair. "I shouldn't be dozing anyway."

"When was the last time you slept?"

There's that infamously guilty grin that always leaves too many body parts of mine tingling. "Two days ago, I think?"

"You think?"

"Maybe three?"

I sigh. "Why do you continue to do this to yourself? You need sleep."

He makes his way to where I'm standing. "I did not want your friends to be left alone."

The muscle in my chest contracts sharply. His generosity never fails to overwhelm me.

The White King's pale eyes track down to Mary and then to Finn. "Is he a good man?"

I have to fight to swallow back the swarm of emotions flooding my throat. "Yes. Very much so."

"I would hope," the King says, "as a member of this Society you mentioned, he would be. I am glad for that."

He sounds glad. Sad, heartbroken, but glad all the same. Would I be so benevolent in the reverse? I would like to think so—his happiness is my happiness, and has been so for so long. I would like nothing more than to know this man is happy, that his life will reach all the dreams we once set for ourselves. Even if they cannot be with me.

We walk over to the flap and step into the space directly outside. The Five of Diamonds is dismissed to the other end of the tent. "I look forward to meeting him when he wakes."

I say softly, "He does not know."

The King's eyebrows lift up.

"It . . . it was the only way I could deal with what has happened. I can only take a step after another if I compartmentalize it all. They know I am a Queen, and that I could not stay due to the uneven courts, but that is all I've shared."

He doesn't say anything. He just looks at me with all the pain of our history shining in his pale eyes.

I ask, "Was she vicious?"

He knows what I mean. "Why do you think we are on such poor speaking terms?"

My words are barely voiced when I let him know I am sorry.

"No matter what," he tells me quietly, "I do not regret what has happened. And if I could go back and do it all over again, it would be the same. I hope you feel the same way. She and I have always had an understanding since the day our crowns appeared. While we rule the White Court jointly, I never promised her my heart."

I took it instead. *Star-crossed*, the Caterpillar used to mutter frequently. It was not a compliment.

The King reaches out and lays a hand against my heart. I do the same in return. I love his heart. I love the feel of it underneath my fingers and underneath my head when I rest against it. I love the sound, the steady beat I hoped I would fall asleep to every night of my life. I love how his heart is big and beautiful and generous, and that it, when circumstance demanded, allowed itself to break repeatedly rather than allow others' to suffer.

He has the best of hearts. The best of souls.

I would never undo our past; I would never wish our love had not flourished. His presence in my life has shaped me to be who I am now, just as I have shaped him. But while neither of us would undo our shared past, we cannot go back and live in it once more, either.

I take his place on the chair when he finally agrees to go rest, and before long, I'm dozing myself. But when a friendly shout outside rouses me from dreams of bookstores, I find a pair of eyes watching me.

I'm out of the chair is a flash. "Finn?"

Tiny lines form in his forehead; he knows something is wrong. His eyes, no longer dilated black, let me know he can hear and understand me.

"You're fine. You're going to be fine." I touch his face and then peer over to Mary. Her eyes are still closed, but I have no doubt she'll rouse shortly, too. "The Heart soldiers used a drug on you that both puts its victims to sleep and then paralyzes them once they wake."

Alarm flashes in the blue-gray staring up at me.

"Only temporarily." I bend down and press a kiss against his cool lips. His eyes drift shut briefly; the lines of his forehead smooth. "It should wear off shortly. We're at the White King's encampment—your brother is here, too. He's checking in on the wounded right now, but I'll have him sent for. Are you in pain? Blink once for yes, two for no."

Two slow blinks.

Thank God. "Do you remember anything?"

The lines reappear. One blink and then two more follow. Yes and no.

"Are you thirsty? Can you swallow?"

One blink. I dig out my water bottle from my backpack and slowly, slowly tilt it toward his mouth. "We can't find either your or Mary's backpacks. They took your phones and your weapons. All you had on you was the clothes on your back."

When I pull the water back, frustration, anger, and disappointment shine from his eyes. There's no doubt he's understanding what I'm saying. His pen and the books we brought in are gone.

"The good news is that, once you two are up on your feet again, we will head out for the catalyst immediately. The plan is for us to go first thing in the morning."

His mouth twitches, like he's trying to talk. The frustration in him doubles.

Suddenly, Mary's eyes fly open. I say her name, and they swivel toward me. I tell them to hold on, and then I instruct the Five of Diamonds standing just outside my flap to fetch Victor.

Minutes later, the doctor is back. He thoroughly examines them both, but during that time, little pieces of their bodies begin to thaw. Sure enough, within an hour, they are able to talk and move their limbs but cannot yet bear their weights while standing.

My relief is immense.

Whatever anger and resentment held between Mary and Victor disappears. They kiss repeatedly and they both apologize for their stubbornness. It's rather nice to see, although I suppose it would have been nicer had it not come about thanks to poisonous drugs and abductions.

They tell us their story. "After we were separated," Mary rasps, "we got shoved into a locked room filled with card soldiers. People were terrified. They were screaming, there was so much blood . . . We tried to fight our way out, but it was impossible. We couldn't even hold onto our weapons—there was no way to hold onto one in such a crush. It was hard enough to even stay on our feet."

When she swallows, Finn takes over. "They had these weird oversized squirt guns that hosed us all down. I don't remember anything after that. Do you?"

Mary shakes her head, but only a little. Victor takes her hand and kisses her knuckles. "This SleepMist sounds like a handy thing to have. Think about what it would have been like when you guys were in that attic. How quickly they could have subdued Todd and Rosemary had they only had such a weapon. If we could get a sample," Mary says thoughtfully, "I can try to synthesize it back in Victor's lab. It could be quite handy to have on assignments."

"I've already asked, love," Victor says. "I knew you would want some, so one of the Ferzes has promised us a fair amount to take with us. It's already stowed in my bag and awaiting your analysis."

You would have thought he'd given her diamonds by the look on her face. But then it darkens and she asks, "Have you been taking the protocol?"

Victor's face goes blank and then sheepish.

Protocol?

"Dammit, you haven't, have you!" She's livid. "Why not?"

"I was—"

Finn says, just as angrily as Mary, "Jesus, Victor! What were you thinking?"

"I was thinking," his brother snaps, "about you two and how you were abducted. I was thinking about how there are people out there who want Alice's head. I was also thinking about the bloody people in this camp who need my medical help!"

"Tell me you at least took your pills." Livid is too kind a word to describe Mary right now. Incensed is more like it.

Victor's saved when the tent flap pulls back. Ferz Epona peeks her head in. "Your Majesty, the White King is requesting permission to come and verify on his guests' health."

I frown. "He ought to be sleeping."

"An hour's sleep is often all that we get for days, my lady. Today is no different. He is keen to begin preparations for the journey to recover your crown, as he knows that time is limited to your and your colleagues."

Nonetheless, I'm concerned. "Very well. Inform His Majesty that we await his presence."

The Ferz bows and leaves the tent. Two pages appear in his place toting folding chairs alongside two sturdy ones. Once all the chairs have been arranged, the pages help move Mary and Finn into the wooden seats so that they will not need to take the meeting lying down. I'm pleased when Finn attempts to reject their help, because it's obvious his strength is rapidly returning. The cots are pushed to the side just in time for the flap to reopen. Both Ferzes come in clutching maps, as do the Nightrider and Sir Halwyn. On their heels is the White King.

He asks, "Is there anything we can provide you while you are recuperating?"

Mary's eyes go wide in appreciation as she takes him in. I don't blame him—outside of Finn, he is easily the most beautiful man I've laid eyes upon. "Well, well," she murmurs.

"Tequila," Victor mutters in response.

Mary hisses at him to shut up, but the King isn't offended in the least. I make the proper introductions before we get down to business.

"Where is my crown?" I ask.

"In a vault hidden below the house in the tulgey woods."

The muscle in my chest jackrabbits when he tells me this. That was our house, our secret we shared with only a select group of trusted allies, one that we would escape to together.

It was the perfect place to store my crown, even though it will hurt like hell to go there.

"How far are these tulgey woods?" Finn's innocent question has the King's eyes falling away from mine. There's a burning curiosity there as he takes in Finn, one I think only I can see, but it sends my already exacerbated pulse close to exploding my veins wide open.

"If we leave in the morning and are unbothered in our travels, we ought to reach it shortly before the next dawn." Ferz Eponi holds up a map. "The only problem is that the Red King's forces lie in that direction."

I let out a long sigh, which makes the White King crack a small smile.

"He is still just a ridiculous," he tells me. "Possibly even more so. The last I saw of him, he was wearing a bandersnatch hat. Claimed he wrestled it with his own bare hands and skinned it alive. Like that is even possible. When was the last time he even had to lift a fork, let alone strangle a bandersnatch?"

The idea that the Red King could do anything with his own bare hands is ludicrous. He would never dare to get his hands metaphorically or physically dirty. That man always has his minions carrying out his wishes while he sits back, reveling and preening in comfortable non-accountability.

"Is the King's Council still convening?"

"We have had two meetings since your departure, both under the cloak of secrecy. It will come as no surprise that Hearts is still sniveling and terrified of voicing the wrong thing in front of his counterpart, and that Red feels as if he's in charge of all the land."

"Has he directly attacked you, though?"

"He knows better than that. His forces, however, did attack the Red

Queen's a month prior."

I nearly fly out of my seat. *"What?"*

"The Red Court has fully splintered—they have taken to different castles and have separated the army. It is the goal of both to drive the other into submission."

"Why didn't you *tell* me?"

"Because," the King says quietly, "you asked of me two favors, and those took precedence."

Frustration builds so strongly within my chest that my chair clatters to the side when I abruptly stand up. I am livid. Absolutely livid. I was forced to yield my throne and for what? For Wonderland's Courts to become even more divided? The Whites are not speaking. The Reds are at war with one another. Half of the Hearts is weak out of fear. The Diamond is solitary and now abandoned. I gave everything up, and this is how I am repaid? I nearly tear my hair out in rage as I push my way out of the room.

I wish the Caterpillar was here.

I wish—

"Alice, wait."

It's not the White King that says this, though. It's Finn.

He's standing. Walking, albeit slowly, but he's upright, and he's followed me out of the room. "Talk to me."

I do not know if it's in me to do so. I am mute in my desolation.

Finn glances back at the flap behind us. "Let's take a walk." He sees the incredulity on my face, so he clarifies, "I need to stretch my legs. Come with me?"

I slip my arm through his.

Outside of the tent, the sun drifts perilously close to the horizon. Purpled golden clouds float below inky skies, and the trees and toadstools around us erupt in the ancient wailing of hidden nightsingers. Nocturnal flowers awaken, and their chattering carries over the hum of soldiers gathering around fires.

A perimeter of avian bowmen exists in the trees surrounding the furthermost outskirts of the clearing, so I know we're in no danger from straying into the first ring of silver-barked trees. The air is cool, but it does nothing to dampen the bleakness crawling through my veins.

"I imagine it must be really frustrating for you to be back and feel both connected and disconnected all at the same time."

I watch how Finn trails his fingers across the dew decorating a large red and white mushroom cap. "Be careful. Some of those can make you grow or shrink."

"I read the book, remember?"

I nudge a rock from nearby and roll it next to the mushroom so I can climb up and sit. Finn joins me, and for many minutes nothing is said between us. We simply listen to the forest's music.

Eventually, I give in. The pressure of it all is too much. "The Caterpillar favored mushrooms as chairs."

"I can see why," Finn says. "They're squishy and kind of comfortable. Maybe not for hours, let alone the length of a football game, but I can see not minding sitting up on one of these every so often."

A hint of a laugh escapes me before a sob chokes my throat. Finn reaches over and tugs me over against his warm side. Burrowing in his arms feels safe, and that throws me because how can somebody I've only known a few months instill such a sense of peace in me when everything else is chaotic?

I lean my head against his chest. For being asleep and then paralyzed for most of the day, his heartbeat is strong and steady. "We sat upon on these things for hours. I can guarantee you that they cease being comfortable after an hour."

"He seemed like an asshole in your book, to be honest. A know-it-all. Was that different, too?"

"No." Another sob/laugh beats its way out. "He *was* an arsehole. He was the epitome of a know-it-all. But he was always here for me—even when I was the worst of disappointments, he didn't leave." I wipe at my damp cheek. I need to get myself back under control. *"I* left, though. And he died because I left."

One of his hands comes up and twists into the strands of my hair. "From what you told me, it sounds like you didn't have a choice."

I didn't, and that's the problem. My choices were stripped away from me. No, that's unfair. I was given a choice. Stay and be selfish and watch my people suffer. Leave everything I know and love behind, and give them a chance.

"If it had been me, I would have done the same thing. Sometimes, no matter how you may feel differently, things just do not work out.

They are just simply not meant to be."

How ironically, painfully applicable that is.

"You did the right thing. You put," he swings a hand at the vista around us, "the lives of all of the people here before your own. God, I could not be more impressed or proud of you. Do you know how hard that is for most people? They would think of themselves first and others later. I've seen this happen over and over again. But you?" He nudges my cheek with his nose. "You didn't. You walked away from everything that meant anything to you to give them a fighting chance. I know it's hard right now. I know it must be frustrating as all hell. I know every impulse in you, now that you're here and seeing and hearing about all these atrocities, is to pick up that sword of yours and go out there and do your damnedest to make things right. Hell, I feel that way right now, too. But, our best way to help your people is to ensure that Todd and company do not get their hands on this catalyst."

He's right. I know he's right. The Society's goals are not any less noble than those I'd face here. "It's hard to walk away again when so much is in chaos."

A soft kiss is pressed against my forehead. "I know."

He understands me. There is no judgment here, not condemnations of my actions. There is only support and concern.

The ground beneath me turns solid. A fixed point I never thought I'd find steadies me.

My fingers curl into the soft fabric of his shirt. "You must be going crazy, wondering if your father has apprehended Todd."

"It may have crossed my mind a few dozen times in the last hour."

For years, I have been so strong. I rarely faltered in my path, even when I was ousted from Wonderland. But in this moment, with so much uncertainty raging in all directions, on multiple Timelines, I succumb to weakness.

I tell Finn, "I have no idea what to do."

"It's okay to feel like that, you know."

I shake my head.

"It is. Nobody is strong one hundred percent of the time. Nobody."

"Queens are," I whisper.

"Not even queens. Nor kings or emperors or the guy who fixes cars down the street or the person who tears tickets at the movie theatre or presidents or teachers or army generals."

"You're never weak."

His laugh is bitter. "I was weak yesterday."

I pull away. "What?"

"The Hearts soldiers took me down with no effort."

I blink. Blink again. "But—"

"I was sent with you to protect you, and to retrieve the catalyst for this Timeline. And somebody sprayed something in my face before I could even draw my gun, and I was out like a light."

"They drugged you!"

He shrugs, and it hits me. He thinks he's failed me again. And it makes me want to break everything in sight because isn't it obvious? I've failed not only him, but so many others here in Wonderland. "Don't be ridiculous. How could you have known? Prevented it? *I* didn't even know about SleepMist until the Ferzes told me just this morning. Until today, the White Court didn't even have a sample to verify its existence."

"He's coming with us, isn't he? To get the catalyst?"

Something stumbles and trips right in the middle of my chest as his voiced change of subject. "The Ferzes?"

"Them," Finn says carefully. "And the White King."

I haven't the slightest idea what to say. Do.

He scratches at the spongy flesh of the mushroom. "I meant what I said. It doesn't matter to me. Not as long as *this* still means something to you."

It does. Somehow, despite all of the valid feelings still raging about inside of me toward the White King and our shared past, this means more to me than I could put into words. I have no future with the White King, not if we wish Wonderland to thrive. But this man here? This one, who I couldn't help but let in? I tug his face down and slide my lips across his. I whisper, my breath hot against his, "I think you are my north star, Huckleberry Finn Van Brunt."

I feel, rather than see, his forehead scrunch in confusion.

I press a gentle kiss against the side of his mouth. "Wonderland doesn't have one. The stars above move on a nightly basis. One night's sky is always different from the next's. It's hard to anchor yourself when you can't find a north star. Sometimes, you feel like you're floating, lost in space. I was lost, without purpose when I left Wonderland. I feared I would never find my footing again. Never find anything that would help me move past the confusion and desolation and helplessness of my past. But then I came to the Collectors' Society. I met you. My feet found solid ground. A fixed star shines in my sky."

His lips find mine again. I feel the kiss in every cell of my body.

"Maybe," he whispers after many minutes of kissing, "we can be binary stars."

It's enough to make me pull back, even if just by an inch. "What?"

"Binaries are two stars who orbit around one another. They share a gravitational pull."

I lean back another inch. "What?"

He tugs me back. "I took astronomy in college. I'm just saying that—"

I cut him off by pressing my mouth against his once more. I know exactly what he was saying.

Finn Van Brunt just told me he is falling in love with me, too.

THE TULGEY WOODS

DINNER IS MEAGER. VICTOR and I split our rations into two to share with the others. The camp's cook, a burly Walrus who barely fits between the flaps, took great offense at our refusal to eat his food, but after a few quick words from the Nightrider, he went back to the kitchen tent and sulked in silence.

Jubjub birds flew in at regular intervals with updates from the battles raging across Wonderland. Thankfully, it doesn't appear that word has gotten out about my presence yet. The only soldiers outside of the White King's to see me are either dead or in the barracks at this camp, still hopped up on Mindly pills.

"I think," Ferz Eponi says at dinner, "we must leave tonight rather than in the morning."

He is holding a note from one of the White Queen's Ferzes. She has announced a visit in three days' time to discuss a situation that she has apparently discovered concerning the Hearts.

This does not please the White King one bit. He leans back in his chair, the front legs lifting off the ground, and stares up at the canvas ceiling above us for many long seconds. "Send word that preparations will be made to accommodate Her Majesty and her entourage."

"How long has it been since you last saw your wife?" Mary asks with mock innocence.

The King's chair clatters back to the ground in surprise. Mary's obviously digging for information—that, or she's trying to rouse Victor's jealousies despite their recent reconciliation. Either way, I am not pleased.

"Their Royal Highnesses of the White Court are not married." Ferz Epona's voice is strained. "None of the current monarchs in Wonderland are."

This is a surprise to the Society members sitting at the table.

None of this fazes Mary, though. She's not embarrassed by the gaffe one bit. "I suppose I just assumed. Most monarchs are, you know. At least where I come from."

"Wonderlandian politics are complicated," Ferz Eponi explains, "and often contentious. Many of our monarchs do not find it to suit their purposes to join into such a restrictive union, although there are certainly those in the past who have done so. Most of the Courts are built upon alliances and shared goals rather than romantic entanglements. Emotions often muddy decisions." And then his face darkens into a mottled red as his eyes surreptitiously flit between me and the White King. He knows he's taken it a step too far.

Mary will not let the subject go, though. "Do monarchs get to decide who they rule with?"

"No," the White King says flatly. "That is not a choice we are afforded."

It was the most painful of lessons for us to learn.

"It seems as if you and Alice have a decent alliance, though," Mary adds. Her fingers tap against the table as she eases her attention from the King to me and back again. "Clearly, you are allowed to build alliances outside of your Court, as well, correct?"

Both of the Ferzes cough, one right after another. Awkwardness blooms right before our very eyes. Several seconds pass before the White King says, his voice thankfully steady as ever, "It is uncommon, but it does happen."

What he means by uncommon is that we are the first to ever do so—and it has gone horribly, horribly wrong.

The King sets down his napkin. "I believe Ferz Eponi is right. If you are feeling strong enough to ride, we shall begin our travel to the tulgey woods by moonlight. That will give us ample time for you to retrieve your crown and depart Wonderland before the White Queen arrives."

Never one to accept a gentle hint, Mary presses the issue once more. "Wouldn't you want to visit with the White Queen, Alice?"

I nearly choke on the tiny sip of water I've just allowed myself. Finn smacks me on the back. "Easy, tiger. It's a marathon, not a race."

Heat steals up my neck. I tell Mary, whose knowing, small smile tempts unkind words from my tongue, "I think it best I forgo such a visit."

The Ferzes and Nightrider stand up. The commander for the White King's army bows; hilariously, his horn comes within inches of Mary's head. She jerks back, startled. "I shall go prepare for your journey, sire. I expect you will be able to leave within the hour." The Unicorn will stay behind in his liege lord's stead once more.

"Thank you." The King also stands up. "Please excuse me."

When they leave, Mary feigns bewilderment. "What did I say?"

"Sometimes," Victor mutters, "you can be a right bitch, Mary."

She pops a tiny piece of dried meat into her mouth, unbothered. But I'm given an apologetic glance as I finish drinking my water. And then, as we step away from the table, she whispers, "It's important to learn how the game is played, and who all the players are, isn't it?"

It's a lousy apology, but I suppose it will have to do.

An hour later, bundled in warm clothes padded with tove fur to lessen the sting of night air, we leave the camp. I'm exhausted, painfully so, but I refuse to give myself over to sleep. We will be traveling through enemy territory, and while we have Ferz Epona, Sir Halwyn, and a handful of pikemen, including the Five of Diamonds, at our sides, we must remain alert at all times.

Our pacing is brutal. We stop to water the horses every hour and a half along a burbling river whose stream changes direction haphazardly and often depending on the day of the week. The river winds in and out of the path we're taking, but for the most part, our pace does not falter.

Cannon fire pepper the distance, alongside screams and shouts, and it's enough to set everyone's nerves on edge. Battles, Sir Halwyn tells me as we pass a site littered with broken weapons, rusting cannons, and horse skeletons, spring up nowadays like wildfires after a lightning storm. "Can't throw a hedgehog and not hit one, it seems."

Ahead of us, I'm amused to find Victor attempting to make small talk with the Five of Diamonds. The pikeman doesn't know what to do with the attention, though, and spends half his time giggling and the rest trying his best to appear stern. In the end, Victor is insulted enough to move away.

"Where are all the animals?" Finn asks once dawn breaks. "We're in the woods. Doesn't Wonderland have animals—I mean, outside of the ones in the military and all?"

"We do, good sir," Sir Halwyn says. "But many have fled to the outermost boundaries." He sighs as he pans the quiet forest surrounding us. "Our great country has seen better days. That's the honest truth if there ever was one."

"Are they similar to those from home?" Finn asks me.

"You mean, outside of the ones wearing clothes who talk?"

"What do you mean? Those kind are all over New York—or haven't you noticed?" His grin makes my knees tingle. Thank goodness I'm already seated.

I rub my cheek on the tove coat I've borrowed from the Ferz. It's small yet ginormous, as her body is more like an egg than mine, but it's better than nothing. "There are some of those that do not talk which are similar. And then some look like nothing you've ever seen before."

"It's different here than I thought it would be," he admits.

"How so?"

"It mostly looks . . . normal, I guess. There are some things that are crazy, like how the trees don't have green leaves and that the sky changes color throughout the day, but, Alice. I'm kind of disappointed."

My laughter is like a shot in the morning air. "Disappointed!" But that addictive grin of his tells me he's only teasing.

We pause briefly for a mid-morning meal before riding again. An hour or so after our break, the White King raises his hand. All our horses still. Voices, not too far away, drift through the leaves.

Swords are drawn, pikes are readied. The horses dance quietly in place, just as jittery as their riders. Less than a minute later, branches crackle. Somebody yells out, "White knights!"

Less than a dozen Red soldiers charge from the trees. The battle is swift yet ruthless. Their crimson, curved blades are nothing to our pikes.

None of us had to get off our horses during the melee.

There is no time to deal properly with the dead. Bodies are stacked just under the tree line, and the soft songs for safe travels into the journeylands are offered. Less than forty minutes after we'd stopped, we're on our way again.

We push harder come evening. There is no stopping for a meal break, not when a scout sent ahead reports back that there are pockets of Red soldiers littering the way. Luckily, there are no further ambushes, no more chances for any lives to be stolen.

Shortly after midnight, we reach the edge of the tulgey woods. It is dark as we first enter, with precious little light from the moon and stars above, but then, that's always been part of the allure. The tulgey trees are more twisted than others found in Wonderland—their silvery-golden bodies contort into bizarre yet oddly beautiful shapes reaching toward a sky's light that rarely touches them. Dark-purple, velvety mottled leaves that sparkle, sweep against us like gentle hands leading the way. And once we push farther into the woods, lamplight flowers push up through the dead litter of the forest, illuminating our path home.

Our scout reports no Red soldiers have entered the woods. This is unsurprising. There is a lot of fear of the tulgey woods within the villages, of the jabberwocky that resides within, but I've always considered these trees dear. So many happy memories are tied within them. So many dreams, now broken and yet still cherished.

It takes another hour to reach the house. The trees have long guarded our hideaway for us, leaning their branches across the changing, magical wooden slats and blocking them from occasional wanderers. But they recognize us now, because the moment we ride within view of the house, indistinguishable voices whisper through the trees.

Once upon a time, as I laid in his arms in the large bed upstairs, I had told the White King that I believed the forest recognized us, that each time we came, they called out greetings. "They know our names, of that I am sure. They know *us.*"

He'd rolled me over and kissed me senseless before pushing into me once more. As we moved together to the rhythm of tree and flower songs from outside, he murmured, "Of course they do." And now here I am—here *we* are—and it's all so bittersweet. The last time we were here, I broke down in tears in his arms and he cried alongside me. That day, fragile still in my mind, was not happy—passionate, yes, but nothing close to happy.

The pikemen take the horses to a small barn hidden behind the house while the rest of us go inside. Everything is exactly like I remember it, only a bit dustier. My books litter the tables in the main sitting room. A blanket I knitted for him for his birthday lies across the back of a velvet couch we'd had designed just for us. Teacups I picked up at a flea market near my Court sit upon a shelf. A stray shirt of his is draped over one of the dining room chairs. A chess set his father had carved for him sits out, a game partially in progress yet long ignored.

This was our home. This was where we pretended it was all okay, that love conquers all. That we were not the White King nor the Queen of Diamonds, but simply Alice and Jace, and we had a future together and a family to plan no matter what anyone said.

It was a beautiful, beautiful dream. But that's all it was, wasn't it?

"This place is gorgeous," Mary murmurs. To Victor, she says, "Now *this* reminds me a bit of Misselthwaite."

"Because of its gloominess?" Victor is doubtful as he glances around.

"Yes." She lets out a strangely happy sigh as she wanders into the next room.

Ferz Epona lights several candles in the sitting area. "Will we be staying the night, Your Majesty?"

The White King, who has said very little over the day's journey, now turns to me. "That solely depends on whether or not the Queen of Diamonds wishes it so."

Mary peeks in her head from the next room over. "I'm exhausted. We can edit after a good sleep. Nobody knows about this place, do they? Besides, I want to see if there's a garden out back. The view from the windows tells me there might be."

There is a garden, one that both my and his hands cultivated.

So much of me wants to tell them no. Being inside these beloved walls is akin to pouring salt on a wound that will not close properly. But we have all ridden hard and have had little to no sleep over the past few days—most especially the King.

"We'll rest," I say.

After given directions toward the guest rooms littering the second and third stories, Mary and Victor head up the stairs. Ferz Eponi says, "Sir Halwyn, Ferz Epona, and I will keep watch while you sleep."

"Ensure you get some rest, too." The White King clasps his loyal advisor on the shoulder. "And some food. Let the pikemen know they are to rotate their duties. Everyone must have their turn at sleep."

Minutes later, I find myself in the unbearably awkward position of being left alone in the sitting room with both Finn and the White King. They are talking, though—and not spitefully so. The White King has asked about the Collectors' Society, and Finn is more than willing to fill him in on the details. I join them but do not add to the discussion.

I am amazed that there is an ease between the two of them that I would not have guessed at before.

I doze on and off as they talk, doing my best to pretend I'm paying attention. They're discussing politics, I think. Liaisons. The Society. The wars. The Courts. Todd. Rosemary. Catalysts and Timelines. I finally force my eyes to open wide, but it's a rather embarrassingly loud yawn that finally draws their attention. Both men turn a bit sheepish, and perhaps I'm a bit delirious, but I find it adorable.

Past and future all in the present.

"Let us finish this once we're rested," the White King says. And then, carefully, "Perhaps you would be most comfortable in the master bedroom, my lady?"

I know he does not mean it as such, but it is a needle straight into my heart. I do not know if I can go into that room again. So many memories are tied up in there. My clothes still hang alongside his in the wardrobe. My hairbrush lies on a dresser. A painting we had done of the two of us hangs on a wall.

I am still too raw to be amongst such things. I fear I always will be.

"I truly appreciate the thought, but I must insist you take the room. This is, after all, your home." It goes unsaid that my words would have been followed by *now*.

He nods and bids us goodnight.

Once we're upstairs ourselves, Finn gently kisses me on the forehead and then goes into the room down the hallway. I peer in the opposite direction, toward the master bedroom, only to find its door still wide open. The White King has also chosen a different room, and probably for the same reasons as mine. I shut the door of the guest room I've selected behind me and slowly slide down to the floor. And then, as I stare at pictures and objects I hand chose for this beautiful room that hardly anyone else ever used or knew existed but I wished decorated anyway, I finally cry. Not a lot, and certainly not loud enough for anyone to hear, but just enough to relieve a bit of the pressure in my chest.

I'm finally in the only home that I truly felt safe in, only to turn around and abandon it once more.

CATALYSTS AND RABBIT HOLES

MARY IS ALREADY IN the garden.

From a large bay window that curves through the wall facing the back, I watch her wander the small paved paths. Every so often she bends down and intently examines whatever it is she finds. My garden is not large, but its flowers, kept in line by a stern Rose named Begonia, are neat and well groomed. Their morning songs fill the damp air of the morning, pretty ones that highlight floral vanity. A snow-white tree rooted in the middle of the garden sways to their tune, its branches dipping gingerly over her head. They must be thrilled to have an audience now that I have been away for so long.

"She likes gardens."

I turn to find Victor snacking on bits of dried meat as he lounges against a doorframe.

"She grew up with one," he says between bites. "At that gloomy manor house of hers. Found a key or whatnot, and spent all sorts of time bringing it back to life."

"And now she lives in a concrete city," I muse, "and is denied such simple pleasures."

"We all make sacrifices for the Society. This is hers, I suppose."

I ought to mind my business, but my defenses have been weakened over the past few days. The Caterpillar would be utterly horrified. "What is yours?"

"I lost me mum." He pauses as he tears apart one of the bits of jerky. "Both, to be honest." A small smile surfaces. "I imagine you're feeling like you've lost this." He motions in a wide arc.

I turn back toward the window. "I'd already lost it before the Society. I suppose . . ."

He wanders closer as my voice fades.

"I suppose the Society has given me a place of my own now. A new place."

He comes to lean against the wall closest to the window. "It's done that for all of us. It asks a lot, and yet gives in return."

"What are you two doing?"

Finn's come to join us. I'm pleased that there is no hint of his paralysis at all in his gait.

"Watching Mary putt about in Alice's garden." Victor points at the window. "She'd probably be happy to stay ages out there if we had the time. How much do you want to bet she'll find a way to finally create that greenhouse garden on the roof of the Institute she's been prattling on about for years?"

Finn stuffs his hands in his pockets as he ambles over to where we are. "I wish we could allow her this afternoon, especially as she's pissed she hasn't collected everything she needs yet, but I'm afraid we're going to have to leave shortly. I was talking with the King when one of the Ferzes came in with news. Apparently, some kind of birds brought messages early this morning. The Queen of Hearts has gotten wind of Alice's presence in Wonderland. She's threatening to execute some kind of political prisoner she has unless you show your face."

The floor drops out from beneath my feet. *Queens don't make deals*, she always told me. And yet, here she is, throwing one out? "How could she have heard?"

"Their guess," Finn says quietly, "is that somebody in Nobbytown spilled the beans under duress."

I close my eyes and rub my forehead. "The Hatter or the Hare. Or—more likely, both."

Finn reaches out and gently massages my already tensing shoulders. "They were positive it was under duress."

Yet another thing to feel guilty about. "Did they say which political prisoner?"

For a moment, I worry he won't tell me. But then he says, "The King's advisor. The Cheshire-Cat."

Warring feelings of relief and anger pump through me. "I—I need—"

"You need to collect your crown and leave as quickly as possible."

The White King strolls into the room, looking like he got no sleep at all over the last few hours. I know he means well, but I cannot just abandon him to this. "You expect me to leave when the Cheshire-Cat's life is at stake?"

"We have already begun drafting a new plan to rescue him. I failed getting to the Caterpillar in time, failed to find the Cheshire after his initial capture, but I refuse to allow anything other than success this time."

"You went for the Caterpillar?"

So much sadness fills his eyes. "Of course I did. I'm so sorry I wasn't able to save him. But the Cheshire-Cat has a chance now, a chance we didn't know existed. She sent me pieces of his tail several weeks ago, but it was strongly alluded to that he was dead. At the time, I was in the middle of another skirmish with the Red Queen, but I'm resolute in liberating our old friend." And then, gently, "I need you to leave before we go."

"It's me she wants!" I jab a finger against my chest. "If I don't show, she's going to do the same to the Cheshire-Cat as she did the Caterpillar!" My anger and grief nearly blind me. "I cannot let another person who made the mistake of being loyal to me die!"

"Even at the expense of your own head? Because if you stay, that will be her singular goal. She has always hated how the people have championed you. There is nothing more she would love than to have your head decorating the entrance to the Hearts Court!"

"Alice," Finn says. "He's right."

"You're asking me to leave my country, my people, in the middle of a war." I'm furious with the both of them, for this collusion I didn't even know existed. "You're asking me to put my life above others?"

"No. God, no. And I never would ask that of you," Finn says. He tries to grab me, but I sidestep him. "And you know that I get where you're coming from, but we have to get the catalyst back to the Institute. What purpose would your death serve right now? To prove that she was right, that she could have your head if she wants?" He reaches out again, capturing hands that have begun tugging at my hair. "The best revenge is living. Dying for no other reason than stubbornness serves no purpose at all."

"But—"

But I cannot argue with them. They're maddeningly both right. What could I do if I stayed? My army has folded into the White King's. I ceded my land to his rule in my absence, so my citizens rest under his protection. This tiny bit we were allowed, my people with his under one rule—just not a Queen and King united together. My presence would trigger the prophecy to become twice as worse. And if I stayed, I am a realist enough to know that there is no way I could resist the King standing before me. And if that were to happen, our love would turn apocalyptic.

And he knows it, too. The desperate, desolate sheen in his eyes tells me the exact same thing.

"Your purpose is still noble," the White King says. "It is as you said. You are still championing our people and millions of others who do not know you, but deserve your help nonetheless. You may not be doing it on a battlefield, but it is the truth all the same. Do not think that your departure today is a sign of cowardice or weakness. It is not. Our people have held onto the fact that their Queen still lives. You are constantly in their thoughts, in their songs and in their protests. They do not want a martyr. They need you as you are. The strong, selfless Queen who put their lives above her own and paid the ultimate sacrifice." And then, softly, "May I have a moment alone with the Queen?"

Finn doesn't hesitate when he tells me he and Victor will be out in the garden with Mary if I need them.

"Bloody hell, that garden is freaky," Victor is arguing. "Those flowers are talking!"

But his younger brother simply shoves him toward the door anyway, shutting it behind them.

298

When they're gone, the White King takes my hands. It's such a bittersweet sensation, standing here in our house, in our sitting room, holding hands as we overlook our garden. "Alice, please. I need you to go. I will not be able to focus on the matters at hand if I am terrified that those from the Queen's Council will track you down and extract their price at any moment."

"We could fight them together."

"We are." He brings my hands up and presses a long kiss against the pulse of a wrist. Nerves flare to painful life within my body. "Your army is with mine. Our citizens reside together. I bear your blade. I wear your H. When I rule, I think of the wishes we've spoken of for so long. Your dreams for Wonderland are still coming to fruition through me. There is not a day that goes by in which I do not have you in my thoughts or purposes. When I fight, I fight for the two of us. Our soldiers always sing both our songs, so that when they are triumphant, Wonderland knows they have the Queen of Diamonds to thank, too." Another kiss, this time on the other wrist. "You said it yourself. Your destiny is not in Wonderland, not matter how much we may wish differently."

My breath is shaky.

"I also meant what I said. Your destiny, your new purpose, is noble. You will always be a Queen. You will always be doing what is right for others. You just will not be doing it here with me."

Blood stains his shirt once more, and I think, if only he could see how my heart has just broken, too.

His thumbs pull away quiet tears from my cheeks. "Now, let us get your crown."

I follow him down into the basement and then through a sleepy door. From there, we go through a trap door that leads to the vault beneath our home. Inside the loyal double-knobbed door is nothing else but my crown sitting upon a pedestal.

The White King gently places it on my head. A hum fills my ears, a happy hum signaling recognition. My crown, the crown of the Diamonds, feels as it always has since the day it first appeared on my head. It feels right.

I whisper, "If this is the catalyst, and I remove it from Wonderland, it must mean the Diamond line ends with me."

"Then it saved the best for last."

It's my turn to grab his hands. "Promise me you will live. I can't leave unless you do that. *Live* live, Jace. Not some kind of half existence. You deserve more than that."

Our foreheads come together; my eyes close. He whispers softly, "That is my most fervent wish for you as well."

My arms wrap around him, his around me. Every joint in my body trembles as I struggle to hold myself up during this last goodbye. But then, all too soon, we let go.

Upstairs, everyone is already packed and ready to go. We will be heading in two separate directions—The White King to his encampment to collect soldiers for his assault against the Queen of Hearts, and my team to Nobbytown. The Ferzes are beside themselves at the thought of sending me out alone without a team, no matter how strongly Finn and Victor argue otherwise.

But then the Five of Diamonds says, "I will go with them, my lord and lady."

Victor is incensed. "Over my dead body! You were going to bloody kill us before Alice said that safe word!"

"Pardon my rudeness, Doctor, but it very well may be over your dead body if I don't." The Five's eyes stare straight ahead, his pike rigid by his side. "I have been tasked with protecting the Queen of Diamonds, and until I am ordered otherwise by my commanding officer or my liege lord, the White King, I will do so."

The Ferzes looks to the King. The King looks to me.

As painful as it is, the distance between us regrows. How can I live without him? How? Why is Wonderland so cruel to us?

But I say, "Your pike would be much appreciated, soldier."

The Five bows sharply and snaps back to attention.

Victor mutters things under his breath best left unheard as he slides his backpack onto his shoulders. Mary, on the other hand, practically dances up to the poor soldier in an effort to, as she's saying, "Get to know our protector better."

Finn takes me to the side as our horses are saddled. "Is everything okay?"

"Yes." I touch his dear face. "I'm sorry for my outburst earlier."

"That was an outburst?" He shakes his head. "You should have seen my mother. Now she could offer up outbursts that put all others to shame."

"Katrina?"

"Yeah," he says softly. "She was like a firecracker. She burned bright and ended too soon." He looks away, blinking, and this small gesture tugs on my heartstrings. "But we're not talking about her. We're talking about you. Are you still going to come with us?"

It's a serious question, I realize. Even though he just heard me accept the Five's protection to the rabbit hole, even though my crown in now in my backpack, he still asks this of me. And I'm saddened and angry with myself, because in the midst of my past colliding with my present and future, I have not done myself any favors.

"I'm coming home," I tell him. "To New York and the Collectors' Society. I am coming with you."

His eyes briefly close. He whispers, "I want to kiss you so much right now. So. Much." His beautiful blue-gray eyes open and for a moment, I think he just might. But the kiss I'd thought might does not happen. Kissing me here, when my past is so vividly and heartbreakingly before me, would only complicate matters. Finn and I have a shot at a future, one we can build together in New York. A future that is not ruled by prophecies or summits. And he knows this, this smart, wonderful, loving man knows this, because he kisses me on my forehead and then goes over to where the Ferzes and the White King are talking. Soon, Victor joins them. Finn takes several objects out of his brother's backpack and passes them over to the White King. After a minute or so, they shake hands.

What is going on?

I'm just about to go over and ask when Mary sidles up to me. "Well, well," she says, smirking. "Don't think I won't be dragging all of this story out of you when we get back."

I sigh. And then, because I really have no other choice, I laugh ruefully. "What's going on over there?"

"Every Timeline needs liaisons. Just tell me one thing before we go." Her voice drops to a whisper. "Is Finn some kind of second choice to you? Is it like, you're coming back with us because you can't be here? I know he's hot and smart, but I'm not down with anyone putting him second. Nobody puts Finn in a corner."

I'm startled. "A corner?" I stare at the person in question as he and the White King confer. "He's in the open."

She sighs. "It's a metaphor. And you're avoiding."

"No," I tell her honestly. "Finn isn't a second choice or second best or whatever else it is you mean. My feelings for him are completely genuine."

"Aha!" She's triumphant. "So there is something going on between you two!" Her hands rub together. "The A.D. and I had a bet going. He said there was no way you two were going to get involved. Said you were too much an Ice Queen to even think about hooking up." She snorts. "Ha! Queen! Get it?"

I roll my eyes. "I'm from Victorian England, not the Stone Ages, Mary."

"The point is, I'm getting myself a nice, fat pile of money when we get back."

"I'm glad my emotions are profitable for you."

She pats me on the cheek. "For what it's worth, that White King of yours is sexy. Like, way sexy." She fans herself. "Between him and Finn, who—don't tell Victor, or I'll cut you—I've always found to be unbearably yet aloofly gorgeous, you've got yourself a nice little love triangle going there, Alice."

"There is no love triangle." I glance over at the two men she's referencing. The Ferzes now gone, they're left in deep discussion with one another. "There is only my past and there is my present and future. The two cannot collide. I believe physics makes that impossible."

"Editing doesn't." She nudges my arm meaningfully.

But prophecies do.

Another jubjub bird flies in with a note for the King. Word has finally arrived on a possible location for the Cheshire-Cat, which means they need to leave immediately. But before they do, the soldiers with us, Ferz Eponi, and Ferz Epona all drop on their knees before me. Fists and arms cross their chests to touch upon their hearts. The Diamonds song is quietly offered.

I am close to tears.

When they finish, the White King comes before me. We've already said our goodbye, so there will be no production here. Instead, he also drops to his knee and bows his head, his fist and arm crossing his chest to touch upon his heart. I do not have to see the blood beneath his armor to know his heart has just broken again.

Mine has, too. Before I know it, he is riding away on his steed, and the piece of my heart that is his, will always be his, goes with him.

"Goddamn," Mary whistles. "He is *hot*. Victor, love, why is it you never do such things for me?"

"Maybe because we live in the Twenty-First Century?" he throws back. "And I'm not a knight? Or, you know, a king?"

When Finn rolls his eyes, I cannot resist a tiny laugh. I pull him to the side. "What did you give the King?"

He does not play coy. "Brom sent along the necessary equipment to give to a liaison of my choice so we would be able to have contact with this Timeline. I chose the White King."

I'm stunned. "Why?"

"Because you love him," he says simply. "And he loves you."

"But—"

"Last night, neither of us could sleep. We both came back downstairs and ended up talking with one another until I came to find you. I like him, Alice. I respect the hell out of him, too."

Now I'm speechless.

"He told me about you two. Not to rub in your past or relationship or anything—"

"He told you about us?" I cannot believe it. The White King is not one to share his innermost feelings with hardly anyone. Me, yes, but to a virtual stranger? Impossible.

"Well, it's not like he provided details or anything, which was more than fine by me. He told me that the prophecy said you two could never be together without dire consequences. No matter what."

I bring a hand up to my lips. Beg myself not to cry.

"He told me this because, while he knows you to be the strongest person he's ever met, sometimes you put too much responsibility onto your shoulders. He's worried about you, as I'm sure you're worried about him."

I cannot believe this is a conversation we're having right now.

"You two can't be together, but that doesn't mean you have to lose one another entirely. He's agreed to be our liaison. The Society now has a connection to Wonderland. He won't ever lie to you about what's going on here, and this way, you'll still have a say over your Court and people. Your voice will still be heard. You can still make a difference, even if it's from New York. You will be adhering to the prophecy and the summit accords, but . . . This is your loophole."

I take his face in my hands. "Why are you doing this?"

He tells me, he whispers, his heart on his sleeve, "Because you're my north star, too. Better yet, we're binaries, remember?"

It's hard to see, the tears in my eyes are so blurry. The Librarian, blast her, is right. I do so love honorable men. "I want to kiss you, too. So much."

"Soon," he promises, and I'm gifted with one last press of lips against my forehead before Victor calls out that it's time to leave.

Before we mount, I tell the trees surrounding my house goodbye one last time. I beg them to take care of the White King, and to know I have deeply appreciated their devotion and help over the years. Soft whispers dance along the breeze that blows through the woods, and it is my turn to place a fist over my heart.

And then we leave.

BY THE TIME WE reach Nobbytown, just as pale sunlight lifts above the horizon, my bottom is numb. Scratch that—my entire body is numb. It was unnaturally cold as we rode through Wonderland, with breezes turning our noses and cheeks red and the ride brutally uncomfortable.

While we encountered no soldiers on our journey, we did get ambushed by highwaymen twice. The Five of Diamonds gave none of us any time to get off our horses and draw our swords. His pike whirled devilishly fast and had our would-be attackers fleeing in no time.

Nobbytown is quiet, our horses' shoed feet against the cobblestone streets the only sound. Windows that haven't been broken are shut tight, doors are locked. No shops are open, no sellers on corners, no reconstruction for buildings burned or destroyed commencing—it looks like a ghost town. I'm tempted to swing by the Land that Time Forgot to see how the Hatter fares, but dismiss the urge quickly once I take in my companions' faces. Exhaustion colors nearly every move they all make, although I doubt any would admit to such.

When we dismount from our horses several meters away from the rabbit hole, I ask the Five of Diamonds to now switch his protection of me to the White King. "I know I am not your sovereign, but—"

He drops to a knee. "You are, my lady. And I beg your forgiveness for not recognizing you sooner. I will never forgive myself."

Before I can say anything, he presents his pike so that the White King's emblem faces upward. The metal and wood rotate until the opposite side is shown—and there, carved into his weapon, is a bird flying with a diamond.

How had I not noticed this before?

I gently touch his head. "There is nothing to forgive. Your loyalty to both the White and Diamond Courts is commendable."

He stands up and snaps his fist against his heart. "I will stay until you have left Wonderland, my lady. May your journey be safe, may your aim be true. May the steps you take lead you through."

"He's a bloody poet, too," Victor grumbles once we reach the hole.

Mary nudges him. "One might think you are a wee bit jealous of his battlefield prowess, hmm?"

The spiders uncover the hole for us, and then line up at attention, forming a straight path. I tell them the same as I told the pikeman: they are to show the White Knight the same allegiance as they have shown me.

And then without much fanfare, we fall up the rabbit hole and back into Wales, much as I did nearly a year before. Only this time, I am not leaving alone, nor am I adrift in a void.

I have a purpose.

NEW YORK CITY REVISITED

IT'S ABOUT FUCKING TIME you guys show up!"

The door behind us flickers away, leaving nothing but the commanding central office of the Collectors' Society in view. The A.D. is standing in the middle of the room, his eyes wild.

Finn's immediately on the defensive. "What's wrong?"

Wendy barrels through the door, her green hair a right mess. "Finally! Why didn't you tell me they got back, Jack?"

"Because," he says through gritted teeth, "they've *just* arrived."

Wendy waves him off. "Did you get the catalyst?"

I slip my dirty, battered backpack off and zip it open. "Yes." I hold up my golden crown for both her and the A.D. to see.

"Knock that shit off," Finn says suddenly. I'm taken aback, but quick to realize he's talking to a perilously closely lurking A.D.

"Just wanted to have a look, is all." The A.D.'s shoulders slump, but a twinkle of interest in his eyes remains. My grip turns ironclad.

"This is Alice's crown first," Finn says, "and a catalyst second. If I ever find it in your possession, you won't be able to walk straight for at least a week. Is that understood?"

The A.D. kicks a chair and sends it rolling across the room. "You're a right fucking wanker, did you know that, Finn?"

"It's pretty," Wendy says as she peers closer. But then she takes a step backward. "The Librarian has a surprise for you, Alice. She wants to see you in your room."

Talk about a surprise. "Now?"

She nods. "She's already waiting for you. Mary, why don't you go with her? I need to talk to Finn and Victor about something first."

Strange, but okay. I reach out and grab Finn's arm. "Will you come see me when you're done?"

Despite the collective around us, he leans in and kisses me. It's light, a brush really, but meaningful. "Definitely."

Wendy winces and quickly looks away. Mary cackles behind us. "I'll take my sum in hundred dollar bills," she tells the A.D. His eyes are bugging out, and it makes me want to laugh.

"Do I want to know?" Finn asks me.

I'm smiling. I'm finally smiling again. "Later." I rise up on my tip-toes and brush my lips across his. "See you soon?"

Minutes later, both Mary and I are stumbling toward our flats. "Do you mind if I pass on yet another one of the Librarian's fortune teller sessions? I'm dying for a shower—and clean underpants. Remind me next time we go to Wonderland to wear five all at once, just in case some assholes steal my stuff again."

I laugh and then glance over at my door. Is the Librarian truly within?

"Besides," Mary says. "I need to find these two a home and some food. Isn't that right, loves?"

Upon her shoulder, peeking out from beneath her hair, is a pair of spiders. The scuttle forward and drop to their knees when they see me.

"I assured them that they could still help you if they came here and let me synthesize their poison in exchange for room and board."

"Exactly what was your reason for being on the team?" I ask, amused.

"To collect drugs, plants, and medicines from Wonderland." She smiles brightly. "One never knows when the Society can use such things on assignments."

I lean forward and gently pat both the spiders on their heads. "I am glad to have such brave and loyal soldiers here with me in my new home. We will ensure you are well taken care of. Please let us know what you need and it will be given freely."

"Our pleasure, Your Majesty," they cry out in unison.

I glance once more at my door. It's cracked opened. "I suppose I better go in and see what she wants."

Mary leans forward and hugs me in a way that does not jostle the spiders. And then the three bid me goodnight. Once her door is shut, I head into mine. Sitting in my sparsely decorated living room and drinking a glass of wine like she's been there thousands of times before is the Librarian. "You're late."

I drop my backpack down on a chair. "You keep saying this to me. I wasn't aware I was on a timetable."

"May I see the catalyst?"

I'm bereft when I pass over the crown. I haven't worn it in nearly a year, but now that it's once more in my hands, it feels wrong to give it to her to stick into a box deep underground.

"It's beautiful," she murmurs. "Almost exactly as I expected."

If she puts it on her head, I might very well slap her.

"Come. Let us catalogue the catalyst for 1865/71CAR-AWLG." She hands me back the crown.

"Is it possible to wait until I've had a shower and some sleep? I—"

"Now," she says firmly.

So much for being the Queen of Diamonds. I sigh and give a nod of acquiescence. But the Librarian does not lead me out the door and down the elevator. Instead, she leads me to my bedroom.

When she flicks on the light, I find myself looking at a glass case similar to those found in the Library—only the one in my room has its door open and waiting.

"Your crown agreed to come," she says, "on the condition it stays with you."

Surely, I'm too sleep deprived to have heard her right. "Excuse me?"

"Some catalysts are trickier than others. Yours was very particular. If it had to leave Wonderland, it insisted on being with you for the rest of your life. If you are to have heirs, it will stay with them. Your line will remain intact—just not in its native land."

"Crowns," I say slowly, "do not talk."

"This one chose you, did it not?"

I honestly have no idea how to respond to that.

"It will stay here with you, but the keycards for its doors will be stored in the Museum. It's the only way I can provide it the safety we offer for catalysts."

"Wouldn't the safest place for all catalysts be in the museum? And yet there are catalysts scattered throughout the Institute."

"The catalysts choose where they wish to go. Come, let's put it in its new home. There are matters you need to attend to shortly. Your paperwork can wait until the morrow."

"What matters?"

She motions toward the glass display box.

I carefully set the crown down upon a waiting velvet cushion. The Librarian takes over by shutting the door and triggering all the locks with her various key cards. "I know you are exhausted both physically and mentally, but you need to be strong today."

That's it. "Look. I am not fond of these little cryptic messages you like to throw out. I'd appreciate if you—"

"You may not be in Wonderland anymore," she continues on, as if I'm not speaking, "but your guidance and strength will be called upon in the coming weeks and months. Prove her wrong. Make the sacrifices worth it."

I jerk back in annoyance. "Prove *who* wrong?"

The sound of my cell phone ringing drifts out of my backpack. "You need to answer that," the Librarian says mildly.

I let out a long sigh but do as she asks. It's the A.D. "You need to come downstairs to the conference room immediately. There are things to be discussed." And then the little bugger hangs up on me.

The Librarian hooks an arm through mine. "I'll walk with you. Don't worry. Mary will be down soon. She's still in the shower."

And Finn thought I was being overly dramatic about this woman's creepiness.

Shortly before we reach the conference room, the Librarian says, "You're needed in Brom's office first."

I don't even bother responding anymore. We fork in the hallway—her to the conference room, me to Van Brunt's office. But once I open the door, all of my irritability is whisked away, because inside are Finn and Victor, and there are several items that are smashed to pieces on the floor around them.

My eyes widen as I take in the destruction. "What in the bloody hell has happened in here?"

Finn doesn't say anything. It's almost like he can't.

Victor says something, though. He tells me, "They caught Jenkins and Rosemary. They're being held in our detention cells."

Good God, it sounds like Victor is about to turn volcanic. "That's excellent news. What about Todd?"

An ugly jack o'lantern paperweight goes flying from Van Brunt's desk in Finn's fury.

"Escaped," Victor bites out.

I take a step closer to where Finn is standing. "Where is your father?"

Another paperweight is set to fly before I grab Finn's arm. "Talk to me. What's going on?"

For a moment, he doesn't say anything. He won't even look at me. Finally, he says in a low, controlled voice that completely contradicts the wild look in his eyes, "In the hospital."

"What?"

"Todd attacked Brom. He's in the ICU."

I'm stunned. Absolutely stunned. "But—"

Finn yanks out of my grasp. Stalks through the door and slams it so hard behind him, the frame rattles.

I'm torn between running after him and finding out the rest of the story. Victor makes my choice for me, though, when he unspools the tale. "Wendy says that Todd had a catalyst with him, one we had no idea he even had. That he threatened to destroy it in front of the team if they came any closer. They already had Jenkins—Todd didn't give a shite about him, though. They had Rosemary. Knocked her ass out and then they gave her a tranquilizer to subdue her, and . . . Todd took offense."

I stare at the door, eager to go through it. "What happened, Victor?"

"It was a catalyst for 1889TWA-CY."

I wave my hand. "Still learning these designations, Victor. Which

Timeline is that?"

He takes a shaky breath. "One of Mark Twain's."

A sickening dread spreads in my belly. That's the author of Finn's books.

"He was obviously sending Brom a message. He was letting the Society know that he knows who Finn is. First you, now Finn? And then he destroyed the catalyst right in front of them. In the massive explosion that followed, he managed to somehow slash my father's throat."

Oh, sweet heaven. My hand flies to my mouth. I bolt for the room, completely skipping the conference room as I hunt for Finn. It doesn't take long, though. I find him downstairs, nearly out of the door.

"Wait!" I have to run to catch up. "You can't go out like that—Finn, you're still dressed in Wonderlandian clothes!"

"I don't give a fuck," is his response.

"Just—let's go to the hospital. Together. Let's change our clothes and go see your father and then we will sit down and figure out what we need to do to catch Todd. Okay?"

The rage in his eyes is frightening, but he allows the door to swing shut.

"You've got blood on you from fighting. So do I. Don't you think we need to clean up, so that the hospital doesn't worry we are patients, too? Besides. Do you want your father to see you like this? He needs rest, not to worry."

"I'm going to kill him."

I grab his face with my hands. "I will help you."

His voice drops. "They deleted my mother, like she was nothing. And now they try to kill my dad?"

"Todd will be caught," I promise him. "We will find him and justice will be served. But first, please come upstairs and clean up. We'll head to the hospital directly afterward."

He blinks, and the rage fades a bit. "You don't have—"

"Unless you tell me directly otherwise, I am coming with you to the hospital, Finn Van Brunt."

He allows me to take him upstairs. We shower together, but it's brief. All of my kisses are meant to be soothing rather than sexual. While he's changing, I run over to my flat and quickly grab the first dress and pair of boots I can find. When we leave, my hair is still wet.

The cab ride over to the hospital takes forever. I text Wendy to inform her we are heading to see Van Brunt instead of the meeting, and she understands. Victor and Mary are will be on their way shortly, too. Just blocks before our stop, he says quietly, "I feel like an ass."

I take his hand in mine and squeeze. "Why?"

"You just left everything behind again—"

"Not everything," I stress firmly. Thanks to Finn, I have not lost my home entirely.

"And I pressured you to do so. Your advisor, who I get the feeling was like a surrogate father to you, was," he drops his voice so the cab driver can't hear him, "murdered—"

"Finn." I squeeze again. "This isn't necessary."

"And people were out to kill you—"

"Apples and oranges," I throw at him.

"And your people were dying, and you wanted to stay and fight and I told you I thought it was best to come back."

"It *was* best." I lean into him so I can press a kiss against the corner of his mouth. "Don't do this to yourself. What happened in Wonderland and what's happening here are different situations."

He isn't listening to me. "And now, here I am, hearing about my dad—the only dad who actually ever gave a damn about me—and all I can think about is how I'm going to go hunt down the son of a bitch who did this and make him pay."

"He will pay. We will make sure it is so."

"Alice." He's anguished. "They destroyed another Timeline while we were gone."

I kiss him again. Gently stroke his cheek. "Victor told me. We'll find Todd, Finn. But today, let us focus on your father. He will need you and your brother to be strong."

Inside the hospital, we are escorted to an isolated, guarded room. Inside, hooked up to machines and tubes, lies Abraham Van Brunt. His throat is bandaged, his eyes are closed.

"Jesus." Finn's whisper is strangled.

"Please fetch us the doctor immediately," I order the nurse who brought us in.

She doesn't argue before leaving, but then, my tone left her no choice other than to obey.

Finn simply stares at his father, rooted to the spot just to the side of the bed. I hold his hand and wait with him. It isn't until the door flies open, bringing his brother and Mary inside, does he finally move. I let them know I've sent for the doctor, but Victor has his medical bag with him. His examination of his father is immediate.

Mary has tears in her eyes. Victor's are glassy. But Finn's are the ones that scare me the most. His are just blank. I hold his hand in mine the entire time, refusing to let go. I will anchor him like he has anchored me.

A quarter of an hour later, the doctor appears. He says, as he takes us all in, "Hospital policy allows two visitors at a time—"

"Fuck hospital policy," Victor snaps. "Give me my father's chart."

The doctor rears back in surprise.

"Dr. Van Brunt has requested a look at his father's chart," Mary says tightly. "Perhaps while he's perusing it you can fill the rest of us in on what has happened with Brom."

The doctor frowns, but he passes over the chart. "Are you family?"

I'm the one to answer, as Finn and Victor look ready to tear the poor man's head off. "Yes. Now, please, tell us how Mr. Van Brunt is."

It's reluctant, but the doctor does as he's asked. A lengthy, clinical description of the damages to Van Brunt's neck, of how they were nearly fatal, and what was done during surgery to correct the issues. "He's really very lucky." The doctor rocks back on his white rubber shoes before scrubbing a hand across his tired face. "From what the EMT team told me, somebody he was with or found him applied pressure right away. If they hadn't, Mr. Van Brunt might not be here with us right now."

I glance over at the file in Victor's hands. The attack happened last night, shortly before we reached the house in the tulgey woods.

"I expect him to make a full recovery," the doctor is saying. "You'll just have to remind him to take it easy on talking for a while. He'll have a scar, though. A bit like Frankenstein's."

Nobody in the room laughs except for the doctor. And even then, it fades quickly into complete and utter awkwardness as he takes in our reactions.

Mary says flatly, "It's Frankenstein's monster. Frankenstein was the scientist."

The doctor rubs at his head, a flush stealing up his neck. "Yeah, right. Sorry. I always get those two mixed up."

"Get the hell out of my father's room." Victor storms over to the door and practically rips it off his hinges when he yanks it open.

"If you would just give me my file, I'll—"

"My brother said," Finn says in a low, controlled voice, "to get the hell out of the room. We will be finding a specialist to be brought in shortly."

The doctor is horribly confused. "But—"

"Now you're just sounding desperate," Mary says. "Leave already, won't you?"

Victor already has his phone out before the door swings shut.

"What a moron," Mary mutters. And then, with a sly, small smile, she says, "What is he talking about, looking like Frankenstein's monster? Clearly, Brom is going for the Headless Horseman look."

For a moment, neither Victor nor Finn say anything. Their faces are blank as they stare at her. But then, they both laugh—and not in a tiny way, but big, belly laughs that leave tears leaking out of their eyes.

"I'm clearly missing something," I say to no one in particular.

"Brom's story." Mary hooks an arm around my shoulders. "It's about a Headless Horseman who terrorizes an idiotic schoolteacher. Only, there never was Headless Horseman. It was Brom in disguise. He went by the most ridiculous name when he was a teenager. Brom Bones. Can you imagine?"

I stare down at the head of the Collector's Society in shock. This man, this calm, in control man who won't even call people by their given names, terrorized a schoolteacher and went by the name of Brom Bones?

"The jerk was trying to steal his wife," Mary continues. "Well, she was his girlfriend then. So, he and his friends decided to pull a prank. Brom dressed up as this urban legend and scared the guy straight out of town."

He'd told me once, *Not a day goes by in which I don't reflect upon the documented follies of my youth, of how abhorrently irresponsible and petty I was in my actions and behavior."*

Why, that stealthy man.

I find myself smiling along with the rest of them. "When Katrina found out," Mary adds, "Brom got an earful and an ultimatum. It was his first and last time masquerading as something he wasn't. Although, I suppose he'll never live this one down now. Perhaps it's best Katrina isn't here. *She* certainly wouldn't have let him live it down."

"Mary Lennox," Victor says as he pulls her closer, "you're awful."

She lifts up on her toes and kisses him. "I try my best."

We spend the rest of the day there, and are rewarded shortly before dinner. Brom wakes up. Not one to waste time on trivial matters such as slit throats and assassination attempts, he motions for a whiteboard and marker Mary had the A.D. bring over.

He writes: **Did you get the catalyst?**

Truth be told, I am surprisingly unsurprised that this is his first question.

"Yes," Finn tells him.

Debrief

"You just had surgery," Finn says, but his father holds a steady hand up before tapping on the word. Like the good sons they are, they tell him all about our adventures in Wonderland. Well, most of them, anyway.

Once that's finished, he writes: **We need to hit the ground running. We cannot afford a single other Timeline deleted.**

Of that, we are all in agreement.

He erases his message and writes a new one. **Tomorrow, we begin a new hunt.**

And so we will.

GRAVITY

A S MUCH AS FINN and Victor want to stay with Brom all night, the elder Van Brunt begs Mary and me to take his sons back to the Institute. He writes: **They snore**.

I allow him this bit of fun at his sons' expense, even though I know better—at least where it concerns Finn. It takes some cajoling, but his children agree to leave on the condition their father is to expect them in the morning.

Van Brunt gives them a thumb's up just as his eyes drift shut.

I hold Finn's hand the entire cab ride back to the Institute. We don't talk, but there's no need to. I rest my head against his shoulder, and finally, for the first time in days, he allows himself to relax, even if just by a little.

Later, when we reach our flats, he speaks. "I need you."

He's exhausted, yes. So am I. But this is more important. "I need you, too."

His hands drop to my waist. "Can I finally kiss you now? I feel like

I've been waiting forever."

"I believe you kissed me earlier." Even still, I curl my fingers in his wrinkled shirt so I can pull him closer. "Remember? And there were all those times I kissed you in the shower. We've been kissing all evening, to be honest."

He shakes his head. He looks so tired, so vulnerable in this moment that I can practically feel the strings between our hearts knotting themselves into tight braids. All I want to do is make things better for him.

I kiss him then, one he cannot mistake as anything other than what it is. Slowly, hotly, letting my tongue find his. He and I were never very good at waiting for the appropriate moments for whatever it is that is going on between us. Right now, he ought to be focusing on his father, even though there's nothing he can do while Van Brunt is still in the ICU. I ought to be heading downstairs and questioning Rosemary. She and I have many things that need to be said to one another. Together, we ought to be laying out a plan to track Todd down. Sleep should be had, to ready us for the coming days.

But right now . . . right now I think I need to kiss this man more.

We go inside my flat this time, barely ensuring the door is shut and locked behind us. Our clothes form a trail to the bedroom, and soon we become those stars he told me about, orbiting one another. He is a gravitational pull I do not think I can resist. One I do not want to resist any longer. Binary stars, he said. I like that.

"Your crown is in here," he says as soon as we hit my bed. And then, just a second before my mouth finds his once more, he says, "I'm glad."

We kiss. We touch. We relearn one another's bodies. We suck, we lick, we stroke, we tease, we yearn. When he pushes into me, we both gasp on cue. We move in perfect synchronicity, and when we explode, we do it in unison.

Tomorrow, we will head out as the partners we are. We will do our best to find Todd. Assignments will be doled out, missions set into motion. We will be tireless as we work together to ensure the safety of Timelines filled with people who have no idea that this man is my north star, or that I am his, or that there are madmen out there who wish them harm. We will take over for Van Brunt until he is back on his feet again.

Tomorrow is the start of our future.

But tonight—this moment—is our present. And I refuse to waste a single second of it.

A BIBLIOGRAPHY

Curious as to who was featured or mentioned within *The Collectors' Society*?
Here's a list of some of the people and the books they came from.

<u>Abraham Van Brunt (AKA Brom Bones); Katrina Van Tassel</u>
Featured in the short story *The Legend of Sleepy Hollow*, found within *The Sketch Book of Geoffrey Crayon, Gent.* by Washington Irving

<u>Alice Liddel; the White King; the Mad Hatter; the March Hare; the Caterpillar; the Cheshire-Cat; various other Wonderlandian animals and peoples</u>
Alice in Wonderland by Lewis Carroll
Through the Looking-Glass, and What Alice Found There by Lewis Carroll

<u>The Bertram and Price families</u>
Mansfield Park by Jane Austen

<u>Emma Knightley</u>
Emma by Jane Austen

<u>Franklin Blake</u>
The Moonstone by Wilkie Collins

<u>Gwendolyn Peterson (AKA Wendy Darling)</u>
Based loosely upon *Peter and Wendy* by J. M. Barrie

<u>Henry Fleming</u>
Red Badge of Courage by Stephen Crane

Mr. Holgrave
House of the Seven Gables by Nathaniel Hawthorne

Huckleberry Finn
Adventures of Tom Sawyer by Mark Twain
Huckleberry Finn by Mark Twain
Tom Sawyer Abroad by Mark Twain
Tom Sawyer, Detective by Mark Twain

Jack Dawkins (AKA The Artful Dodger)
Oliver Twist by Charles Dickens

Mary Lennox
The Secret Garden by Frances Hodgson Burnett

Sara Crewe
A Little Princess by Frances Hodgson Burnett

S. Todd (AKA Sweeney Todd)
Based loosely upon *A String of Pearls: A Romance,* most likely written by James Malcolm Rymer and Thomas Peckett Prest

Victor Frankenstein Jr.
Based loosely upon *Frankenstein; or, The Modern Prometheus* by Mary Shelley

ACKNOWLEDGEMENTS

BIG THANKS AND HUGS are sent out to my editor Kristina Circelli, my publicist KP Simmon, and my assistant Tricia Santos, all of whom helped make this book the best it could be. Thanks are also sent out to the very talented Victoria Alday for designing the gorgeous cover and logo for *The Collectors' Society*, Stacey Blake for her magical formatting skills, Bridget Donelson for proofreading, and Joanna Ireland for her impeccable Latin.

Jessica Mangicaro, Andrea Johnston, and Tricia, I am so grateful for all the love, time, and feedback you've given these characters and their stories.

To the ladies of my lovely street team, the Lyons Pride, your support of me and my books means the world to me. Vilma, Cristina, Caitlin, Ana, Kathryn, Megan, Jessica, Chelsea, Rebecca, Kiersten, Maria, Tricia, Whitney, Tracy, Sarah, Amy, Leigha, Nicole, Erica, Heather, Cherisse, Autumn, Meredith, JL, LeAnn, Bridget, Lindy, Gina, Amy, Brandi, Rachel, Ciarra, and all the rest . . . you guys are the best. Seriously. I love dishing books with you guys.

No book of mine could ever be finished without the love and support from my family. To my husband and children, thank you for continuing to share me with my characters. I love that my kids will talk about them with me like they're real people. To my dad, thanks for listening to me plot out the book and offer up suggestions. And thanks are sent out to you, too (yes YOU), for coming along on this journey.

ALSO BY HEATHER LYONS

An enthralling mythological romance two thousand years in the making . . .

"Heather Lyons's *The Deep End of the Sea* is a radiant, imaginative romance that breathes new life into popular mythology while successfully tackling the issue of sexual assault. Lyons is a deft storyteller whose engaging prose will surprise readers at every turn. Readers will have no trouble sympathizing with Medusa, who is funny, endearing and courageous all at once. The romance between her and Hermes is passionate, sweet and utterly engrossing. This is a must read!" *–RT Book Reviews*

What if all the legends you've learned were wrong?

Brutally attacked by one god and unfairly cursed by another she faithfully served, Medusa has spent the last two thousand years living out her punishment on an enchanted isle in the Aegean Sea. A far cry from the monster legends depict, she's spent her time educating herself, gardening, and desperately trying to frighten away adventure seekers who occasionally end up, much to her dismay, as statues when they manage to catch her off guard. As time marches on without her, Medusa wishes for nothing more than to be given a second chance at a life stolen away at far too young an age.

But then comes a day when Hermes, one of the few friends she still has and the only deity she trusts, petitions the rest of the gods and goddesses to reverse the curse. Thus begins a journey toward healing and redemption, of reclaiming a life after tragedy, and of just how powerful friendship and love can be—because sometimes, you have to sink in the deep end of the sea before you can rise back up again

Available as an eBook at:
All major ebook retailers

The magical first book of the Fate series . . .

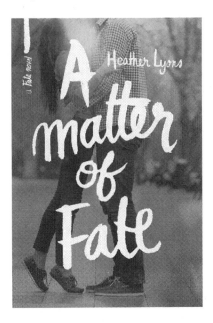

"Love, love, love this book! Such a fun and exciting premise. Full of teenage angst and heartache with a big helping of magic and enchantment. Can't wait to read the rest of this awesome series! Not to mention... TWO hot boys to swoon over." *–Elizabeth Lee, author of Where There's Smoke*

Chloe Lilywhite struggles with all the normal problems of a typical seventeen-year-old high school student. Only, Chloe isn't a normal teenage girl. She's a Magical, part of a secret race of beings who influence the universe. More importantly, she's a Creator, which means Fate mapped out her destiny long ago, from her college choice, to where she will live, to even her job. While her friends and relatives relish their future roles, Chloe resents the lack of say in her life, especially when she learns she's to be guarded against a vengeful group of beings bent on wiping out her kind. Their number one target? Chloe, of course.

That's nothing compared to the boy trouble she's gotten herself into. Because a guy she's literally dreamed of and loved her entire life, one she never knew truly existed, shows up in her math class, and with him comes a twin brother she finds herself inexplicably drawn to.

Chloe's once unyielding path now has a lot more choices than she ever thought possible.

Available as an eBook at:

All major ebook retailers

Follow Chloe's story in the rest of the Fate series books . . .

"Heather Lyons' writing is an addiction…and like all addictions. I. Need. More."
--#1 New York Times Best Selling Author Rachel Van Dyken

"Enthralling fantasy with romance that will leave you breathless, the Fate Series is a must read!" *--Alyssa Rose Ivy, author of the Crescent Chronicles*

ABOUT THE AUTHOR

photo @Regina Wamba of Mae I Design and Photography

Heather Lyons writes epic, heartfelt love stories and has always had a thing for words. In addition to writing, she's also been an archaeologist and a teacher. She and her husband and children live in sunny Southern California and are currently working their way through every cupcakery she can find.

Website: www.heatherlyons.net
Facebook: http://www.facebook.com/heatherlyonsbooks
Twitter: http://www.twitter.com/hymheather
Goodreads: http://www.goodreads.com/author/show/6552446.Heather_Lyons
Sign up for Heather's newsletter to receive updates and exclusive content:
http://hymheather.us8.listmanage.com/subscribe?u=876a2ae066fb2b-cef9954a8ab&id=e6004c27d3

41689058R00191

Made in the USA
Lexington, KY
22 May 2015